Stolen Thoughts

Tim Tigner

ACKNOWLEDGMENTS

I rely heavily on generous fans for guidance while writing my novels. They make my books better and I'm grateful to them all. Many have helped me for years and have become good virtual friends who I "see" at our annual "reunions." David Berkowitz is among them.

Doug went quiet between feedback rounds on Stolen Thoughts and I learned that he passed in late July from liver cancer. I didn't know that he was sick, but I do know that I'll miss him every time I write a book. Rest in peace, my friend.

Editor: Suzanne S. Barnhill **Technical Consultant**: Joe Chasko **Beta Readers**: Errol Adler, Martin Baggs, Dave Berkowitz, Edward Bettigole, Doug Branscombe, Barry Braverman, Kay Brooks, Anna Bruns, Diane Bryant, Pat Carella, John Chaplin, Lars de Kock, Rae Fellenberg, Pamela Goode, Rob Gunn, Emily Hagman, Robert Lawrence, Kerry Lohrman, Margaret Lovett, Debbie Malina, Judy Marksteiner, Michael Martin, Peter Mathon, Joe McKinely, Michael McShane, Michael Picco, John Prince, Lee Proost, Robert Rubinstayn, Ellen Sameth, Chris Seelbach, Martha Smith, Jack Thro, Gwen Tigner, Robert Tigner, Bob Tolich, Wendy Trommer, Alan Vickery, and Mike Wunderli.

"I think it will be technologically possible to invade people's thoughts, but it's our societal obligation to make sure that never happens."

—Professor Marcel Just, Director of the Center for Cognitive Brain Imaging at Carnegie Mellon University, speaking on 60 Minutes (CBS News) September 6, 2020.

This novel is dedicated to Lydia Alexandra Tigner, the Tiniest Tig. She's clearly destined to be the hero of a beautiful story – one I am blessed to help write.

1
The Job

Las Vegas, Nevada

VANCE PANZER was feeling lucky as he stepped from the casino's ornate shopping esplanade into the psychic's stylish studio. Thanks to Cassandra, he'd be leaving Las Vegas six-figures richer than when he'd arrived.

As a guy in possession of all his marbles, Vance had never visited a fortune teller before today. Therefore, Hollywood had framed his expectations for the office. He'd pictured black velvet curtains, astrology symbols, artificial candles, and tarot cards. Perhaps a bit of incense in the air and some mystical music softly setting the mood. What he found looked more like an exclusive resort. Fine furniture, gurgling fountains, tasteful artwork, and warm lighting.

The illusion that this was a five-star spa lasted only a few seconds. It collapsed when the receptionist stepped through an archway to greet him. The man looked like Hagrid from the Harry Potter movies. A super-sized guy in desperate need of a barber. Vance's first thought was that Cassandra had chosen "Hagrid" for security reasons, but a quick appraisal dispelled that notion. Despite his dimensions and wild, reddish-brown hair, the kind, thoughtful look in his eyes made it clear that this guy was more Bambi than bear.

"You must be Walter White," the receptionist said, extending a large hand. "I'm Chewie. Welcome to *Consultations by Cassandra*. Please follow me."

"Like the *Star Wars* character?" Vance couldn't help but ask as they rounded the corner into an intimate lounge.

"My given name is Quinten Bacca, which quickly evolved to Q-Bacca, then Chewbacca, and inevitably Chewie. Would you care for a drink?" He gestured toward a bar boasting top-shelf brands.

Vance was about to request a club soda when a gleaming automatic machine caught his eye. "I'd love an espresso."

"Coming right up. Meanwhile, you can pick a number." Chewie nodded toward an antique table covered with assorted carved hardwood boxes, colorful notepads, and fancy pens. The sign above it read *Your session will be free if Cassandra can't name the three-digit number you pen and place in the box of your choice.*

Given that a twenty-five-minute session with Cassandra went for $1,000, that was quite an offer. Vance noted that the sign and display were positioned near the archway, making them visible from the Bellagio's esplanade. A creative marketing gimmick, to be sure.

"How often does Cassandra guess wrong?" Vance asked while inspecting the small boxes.

"She doesn't *guess*, so *never.*"

"Surely someone has outsmarted her? Perhaps by slipping in a piece of paper they prepared at home?"

Chewie grew a knowing smile. "Believe me, we've seen it all, and nothing matters. She reads your *mind*, not your *paper.*"

Vance knew that was not true. Nobody could genuinely read minds. Victoria Pixler, aka *Cassandra*, probably used advanced imaging technology to scan the box while the client was seated behind her crystal ball. Some system originally designed for airport screenings, he guessed.

Before replying, Vance studied the receptionist's expression. Chewie appeared sincere, but that merely meant he wasn't in on the trick. Cassandra had used her charm and cunning to bamboozle him the same way she did her customers—and Vance's anonymous employer. "Trust me, she really can read your mind," were the last words the man had spoken before slipping an envelope stuffed with money under the hotel suite door.

Vance had gone along, of course. His employer's misguided conviction was undoubtedly what accounted for an offer that was exceedingly generous—given that Cassandra was deaf, a woman, and she accepted private appointments with strangers.

He nodded to Chewie. "I guess we'll find out."

Vance positioned himself in a concealing position, then penciled three light, minuscule parallel lines on a slip of paper such that they were barely visible. He folded the note in quarters and slid it into a rosewood box.

"You look determined," Chewie said, handing over a steaming espresso.

"I play to win."

"Well, you came to the best place in Vegas for that. Cassandra's clients all leave as winners."

As if on cue, the door to the studio swung open, making an ongoing conversation audible. "…can't thank you enough. You've been incredibly helpful."

"Absolutely my pleasure, June."

"I feel like I should give you a hug. Would that be okay?"

"Of course."

A moment later, Vance watched an ebullient woman emerge from the reading room, walk out onto the casino's colorful carpet, and disappear into the passing crowd. The spectacle was so perfect that it had to be an act. A routine performed prior to every initial reading to prime the emotional pump.

Vance turned to Chewie. "That happen often?"

"No."

"It doesn't?"

"Nope. Clients rarely request a hug," Chewie said deadpan before winking. "If there's nothing else I can get you, I'm going to head back out front. Try to look directly at Cassandra when you speak so she can read your lips. She uses a voice-to-text app, but prefers to go old-school during readings. She'll summon you in a minute."

Cassandra emerged almost exactly sixty seconds later wearing a dark reddish-brown evening gown that gave her a simultaneously sexy yet sophisticated appearance. While striking, the formalwear seemed overkill until he remembered that she also did a daily show in one of the Bellagio's theaters.

His focus shifted quickly from her outfit to her face, where it stuck for a second too long. She was a beautiful brunette, with lively hazel eyes framed by large stylish glasses, but it was her lips that drew his gaze. They were so plump and perfect yet innocent that he found himself transfixed.

"Mr. White. Welcome, please come in. Did you pick a number?"

"I did."

"And you're happy with it?"

Bewitched though he might be, Vance wasn't about to fall for that trick and change it now with her watching. "I am."

The reading room was considerably dimmer than the lounge, so the glowing crystal ball on the center of the round table drew his eyes as if they were magnetized. He took the designated seat and, with an inward grin, said, "Please, call me Walter."

"You don't prefer Vance?"

For a second, he froze like arctic ice as a chill shot down his spine. He had used a courier to pay in cash when booking his appointment, and now he was in deep disguise, with a wig, mustache, eyebrows, and makeup.

The explanation struck as he exhaled. A cutting-edge biometric recognition system! Probably one combining facial features with other inputs like skeletal dimensions and gait analysis. All tied to a computer that would rival those at NASA and the NSA. One that had crunched away while he sipped espresso in Cassandra's lounge.

From that data point, Vance leapfrogged to the next obvious conclusion and the explanation for the psychic's reputation. Her entire studio was an illusion. An intelligence hub camouflaged to resemble a five-star spa. A pit bull in poodle's clothing.

"It's okay," Cassandra continued. "A lot of people give me pseudonyms—invented or borrowed. I understand and respect the desire for privacy in these circumstances, given the stigma surrounding my profession. But since my goal is to maximize the benefit you get from your session, I want to encourage honesty and acceptance. The sooner you shed your skepticism, the more time we'll have to explore meaningful issues."

Despite the allure of those lips, there was no chance of any genuine shedding or sharing taking place. Zero. Vance wasn't one to ascribe seemingly unexplainable situations to supernatural causes. He was a science and technology guy—among other things. "I appreciate your understanding. I take my privacy very seriously. Speaking of which, are you recording this consultation?"

Cassandra's reply was swift and sincere. "No. I would never do anything to violate the privacy of my customers or the bond of trust I consider sacred. Besides, reputation is everything in this business, so I'd be torpedoing my career if I did."

"I'm pleased to hear that," he said, studying her, the tablecloth between them, and the small soundproof studio.

"How may I help you, Vance? What brings you here today?" she asked, her gaze going to the crystal ball, as her hands gesticulated an invitation.

For a few seconds, he toyed with the idea of giving her an honest answer. Simply laying it on the line for pure shock value and the thrill of seeing that special look in her eyes and the quiver of those lips. *I've come to slit your throat.*

2
The Tragedy

VICTORIA PIXLER'S LIFE had been shaped, shifted, and defined by tragedies and triumphs. Two tragedies and two triumphs, to be precise.

Until today.

Until a few seconds ago—when the shocking thoughts of the burly client now seated at her consultation table ticked the tragedy score up to three. Vance Panzer had not paid $1,000 to be amazed, advised, and guided. He had come to kill her.

Initially, Vicky harbored hope that *I'm here to slit your throat* was simply the fanciful musing of a sick mind. While her steep fee tended to fend off the mentally ill, it was far from a foolproof filter. But Vance quickly dispelled that idea.

During their introductory discussion, he began rehearsing her murder in his mind like an athlete psyching himself up before an Olympic performance. *...slip the punch-knife from my shoe the first time she looks away, then, when the moment is right, use a left chin sweep to expose her throat to quick jabs from the right...*

Vicky had suffered countless shocks since cracking the mind-reading code nine months earlier in her bioengineering lab at Caltech. Most were depressing. She'd never forget the first day she walked around in public wearing the thick-framed Prada glasses that concealed her invention. While discovering that inner dialogues varied considerably from spoken words came as no surprise, she found the size and frequency of the gaps to be shocking. Concealed sexual urges, self-aggrandizing comparisons, and advantage-seeking deceptions were far more commonplace than she'd anticipated. No prior experience with reading thoughts, however, had stunned Vicky like this one.

Fortunately, she wasn't completely unprepared. To cope with the typical mental transgressions that were integral to her new profession, Vicky had mastered the art of masking her emotions. She'd learned to appear engrossed when repulsed, sympathetic when sickened, and delighted when insulted. Learning of her own imminent execution, however, was both a first and a jolt unlike any other. Staring at the man whose mind was set on her murder, Vicky prayed that the shock had not cracked her mask.

Her life likely depended on it.

Rather than wait for Vance to verbalize a response to her "How may I help you?" session-opening question, Vicky served up a quick distraction. "I sense that you're more skeptical than most of my clients, so rather than wait until the end of our time together, let's begin with your box. Please take it from your pocket." *So I can see your hands.*

Vance complied, but instead of setting the hand-crafted rosewood artifact on the table, he put it on the floor.

Vicky had seen that move before. People got creative when $1,000 was on the line. "You suspect my table of being more than it appears?"

"Am I wrong?"

"You wrote one hundred eleven. One one one."

Vance cocked his head and raised his eyebrows. "Impressive. But, like all illusions, staged. I won't claim to know how you did it. But I do know this: if I asked you or any other trickster to perform a stunt from your show on the street, rather than on your stage, you couldn't do it."

"As a rule, you're probably right, and I admire both your candor and the clarity of your thought. But *my* stunt, as you call it, is an exception, so you're mistaken." Vicky gesticulated with her right hand while her left felt for the pocket beneath the front corner of her chair, and her mind raced ahead.

She had to keep Vance intrigued. Riveted. She needed more time to think.

A recent, rough mugging in Reno aside, she'd never been in a physical fight before. She was a nerd, not a warrior. Chewie, however, had recognized the danger inherent in her private consultation setup. He'd equipped her to fend off assaults of all types—although she was sure he had robbers and rapists rather than assassins in mind. Regardless, thanks to the guilt he felt regarding the Reno incident, she now had pepper spray and a Taser strapped beneath her seat, and she'd studied the instructions for their proper use.

Alas, she had not practiced with those tools any more than she had with the fire extinguisher in her kitchen. Vance, on the other hand, was clearly an experienced professional. He had every advantage—except surprise. Would getting the jump on him be enough? Had he been trained to ignore non-lethal assaults? With his size, strength, speed, and experience, he could probably slash her throat in seconds.

Vicky needed to choreograph her moves in advance. To mentally rehearse. How could she intrigue and distract him while she did so?

With skeptical clients, she'd normally say, "I know why you've come to me today," at which point their thoughts would provide her the answer, just as they revealed their number when asked if they were happy with it. But that would clearly be a bad idea under the present circumstances.

She decided to gamble. "You could have asked for more money."

"What?"

Forcing her eyes to the crystal ball rather than his hands, she said, "You recently got a job. A consulting assignment of sorts. You were offered a lot of money." She spoke softly and slowly, acting as if drawing the information from the ether while literally reading her client's thoughts. "You could have asked for twice as much."

The sensors embedded in her eyeglasses transmitted her clients' streams of thought to her crystal ball and to a screen on the wall, as well as to her phone and watch. The setup mimicked the voice-to-text system she had been using since losing her hearing a decade earlier—except that the thought crawler was invisible to everyone else, thanks to a custom polarizing filter in her eyeglass lenses.

$200,000 for this job? No way. No break-in, no bodyguards. I would have done it for $20,000. Hold on. This is a psychic trick. She said "recently" and "a job" and "twice as much." Those sound specific but are actually vague enough that most people could make some experience fit her story. Still, that's quite a coincidence. "Can you be more specific?"

"Of course. You thought $100,000 was a great deal, but they'd have paid $200,000."

Whoa! How did she guess that? More importantly, did she have any idea what—

Vicky pressed a button under her table.

The door to her reading room swung open.

Vance reflexively turned toward the commotion behind him.

As the assassin shifted his attention, she sprang from her seat, aimed the pepper spray she'd palmed, and squeezed the trigger.

Vance erupted out of his chair, bringing his hands to his face while somehow resisting the urge to scream.

Vicky had harbored hope that he'd punch himself with his own knife, but he was clawing at the chemicals with his palms, so the wicked T-shaped punch-blade protruding between his middle and ring fingers did him no harm. To her horror, she realized that the handy weapon would now allow the professional assassin to quickly dispatch anyone running to her aid. Specifically, Chewie.

She could not let that happen.

Moving fast while thinking faster, Vicky drew the Taser from beneath the right side of her chair, screamed, "Chewie, call security!" then pressed the button beneath her table for a second time—shutting herself inside the studio with her would-be killer.

3

The Surprise

VICKY'S READING ROOM DOOR did not lock, it just latched. She had closed it to create a speed bump. A momentary barrier to both the assassin's exit and Chewie's entrance. She hoped that delay would allow her trembling hands to accurately aim and fire her only Taser shot—before Vance completed his mission.

In the seconds since she'd screamed for help and pepper sprayed Vance's face, Vicky had watched the killer bumble about looking for the door while wiping wildly at his eyes. Although she wanted nothing more than to see the assassin leave, the punch-blade protruding from his right fist made it all too easy to envision a trail of bloody bodies in his wake—beginning with Chewie's.

The big, goofy-looking guy wasn't just her business partner. With her mother now gone, he was the only significant person in her life. She loved him. So before Vance could find the door lever through the fog of tears, she pointed the Taser's twin lasers at his torso and pulled the trigger.

The gun bucked as the air cartridge popped, propelling two thinly wired barbs to the red dots' locations. Vance seized up the second they punctured his flesh. He had essentially been struck by lightning, and that was exactly what it looked like. Her assailant fought to remain on his feet, but the muscular spasms quickly got the better of him.

As he dropped to his knees and then the floor, Chewie burst into the room, smacking Vance with the edge of the door.

"He's got a knife!" she shouted.

While Chewie took in the scene, Vance suddenly stopped writhing and sprang to his feet.

Vicky watched in shock. Was it mind over matter? Had he adapted to the Taser?

Chewie grabbed the assassin's right arm with both hands in a valiant attempt to neutralize the blade, and the two began banging about the room. Vance delivered vicious blows with his free fist and knees as they grappled, but Chewie managed to keep the knife at bay for the second or two it took Vicky to realize her mistake. Taser blasts only lasted for five seconds. They clacked like a robotic rattlesnake while discharging, so the wielder would know when the juice started flowing and when it stopped. But she hadn't heard the signal.

She pulled the trigger a second time and kept it pressed.

Vance immediately seized up and dropped to the carpet.

Chewie delivered a savage kick to the side of his head, then pried the punch-blade from his fist before looking her way. "Let's go!"

She scurried out of the reading room with her finger still squeezing the trigger. Chewie pulled the door shut behind them and then kept hold of the lever, penning Vance in.

"Did you call security?" Vicky asked.

"I hit the panic button," Chewie said, scanning the lounge.

As one of the Bellagio's celebrity performers, the casino provided Vicky with security that included a panic button and an escort to and from her shows. She left the button at reception while the studio was open, since that was where trouble was most likely to present.

"What are you looking for?" she asked, noting Chewie's frantic gaze.

"Something to prop the door lever in place so I don't have to stand here holding it."

"What's going on?" a third voice asked. It was Kyra, Vicky's regular security escort.

"A man pulled a knife on Vicky," Chewie said. "She Maced him and Tased him and now he's locked in her reading room."

"Are you okay?" Kyra asked Vicky.

"I'm shaking and my eyes are burning from some stray pepper spray, but I'm not injured."

Three other people arrived, two security guys and the Bellagio's Retail and Entertainment Manager, Basil Bakhshi. Kyra quickly conferred with them, then asked, "Does he have a gun?"

"I don't think so, but I'm not completely certain. That's his knife." Vicky gestured toward the blade on the floor.

Kyra didn't pick it up. Instead, she nodded to her two colleagues who both drew their sidearms. "Chewie, release the door and step away."

He hastily complied.

Kyra pushed it open.

"I didn't attack her! She attacked me!" Vance yelled. He was sitting cross-legged on the floor with his hands raised and his face a puffy mask of snot and tears. "I came here to ask for insights regarding an antique knife, but before I said word one she sprayed Mace in my face and then Tased me."

"Why did you want to ask her about a knife?" Kyra asked in a calm and steady voice.

"The dealer who sold it to me said it used to belong to Jesse James. I wanted to know if that was true."

Kyra turned to Vicky. "Did he threaten you with the knife?"

Vicky played things forward in her mind. It wasn't difficult. If she was completely honest with her answer, Vance would walk away and she might even be facing a lawsuit. If she fudged the facts to make his mental threat a verbal one, it would become a he-said, she-said situation. She'd lose either way.

As Vicky quickly contemplated that sad state of affairs, a far more distressing thought struck. Someone wanted her dead. Badly enough that he had offered Vance $100,000 to do the deed. Therefore, Vance was no longer her primary concern. The employer was. Until she knew his identity and why he wanted her dead, she would essentially be living beneath a guillotine.

She met Kyra's eye. "I need you to do me a favor."

"What's that?"

Vicky stepped into her reading room. "Wait outside while I talk to him."

4

The Explanation

DESPITE THE DISTRACTING chemical fire raging on his face, Vance had figured out Cassandra's secret. He came to his conclusion a few minutes too late to carry out his assignment but was still in time to avoid whatever trap she had planned as she walked back into the room.

She must have seen him draw the knife from his heel! She must have cameras hidden all over the place. Motion-activated, no doubt. In retrospect, that made perfect sense. While psychics relied heavily on body language for guidance, the draped tables supporting their crystal balls would hide tapping toes, bunching fists, and many other telltale movements. But not from her.

On top of that, Vicky Pixler was undoubtedly able to identify subconscious signals much better than most people could, given that her brain would be compensating for the absence of auditory input by amping up her visual processor. Furthermore, as a professional, she'd know how to interpret every twitch.

Vance had to remain still as a rock during this session to avoid giving anything away. And he needed to stick to his strategy, regardless of the psychological tricks she was sure to employ.

While having the punch blade concealed in his heel was an inconvenient complication, claiming that Jesse James also carried it in his boot would fit his inspired, off the cuff explanation. Meanwhile, going on offense was clearly his best defense. He'd be home for supper as long as he kept the threats coming—and admitted nothing.

"Who sent you?" she asked.

Not a bad opener, Vance thought. Specific and valuable. An

accurate answer would drive almost everything that followed. But he had no idea who'd employed him. He rarely did. Of his thirty-one kills, Vance had only known the man who paid the bill on two occasions. Most of the time, he could venture a good guess, but not today. Who cared if a psychic died? If not an irate ex-lover, it was likely someone who'd bet big on her prediction and lost. But that didn't tell him much. "Nobody sent me. You're going to pay for this assault. I'm going to own you when this is done. So you'd best start treating me with the respect you'd show your boss."

To his surprise, she didn't press. "If you weren't sent, then why were you paid $100,000?"

"I don't know what you're talking about. I'm just a regular guy getting a bit of entertainment in Sin City. One you chose to attack." *Keep going, lady. I can play this all day.*

"The families of your thirty-one victims will surely dispute the assertion that you're just a regular guy."

Whoa! How did she know about them? She couldn't possibly. Unless… Was this a setup? A sting arranged by a victim's family? Had to be. But which victim?

Michael Mancuso maybe? His wife had been a bulldog with the Vegas PD. But she'd moved to Boca Raton.

Sitting still as a statue, Vance began cycling through the list. His curriculum vitae as a killer. *Adkins, Arellano, Baldwin, Ballard, Bullock, Castaneda, Dempsey, Gallegos….* Given their family situations, about half were candidates. None was the obvious suspect.

Cassandra was just sitting there, watching him like a police detective, no doubt hoping he'd find the silence awkward and fill it with a confession as lunkheads often did. *No chance, lady.* "Was there a question hidden in your rambling?"

Cassandra dropped it, just like every other question. *Was she performing? Asking questions so she could then psychically fill in the blanks? Would a jury listen if she did? Earning $1,000 for a twenty-five-minute consultation did buy her credibility.*

"What, exactly, was your plan for me?" the psychic growled.

I was going to pop you like a tire and then vanish like a ghost. "No plan. I simply wanted to know if Jesse James actually owned my knife. I'm just a client. One who's growing wealthier by the minute. You injured my eyes and probably my lungs with that pepper spray. And who knows what damage the multiple Taser blasts and kick to my head did—beyond the obvious pain and suffering."

"I understand why you wouldn't want to talk about your first major failure. Let's talk about your successes instead. Tell me about the Adkins assassination."

Was that who set him up? Seemed unlikely. Jerry Adkins had lost his cock because he couldn't keep his hands off another man's wife. It was probably a lucky guess on Pixler's part. Was she going to list every notorious unsolved Las Vegas murder? "I have no idea what you're talking about."

"Do you remember that day? What you did afterwards?"

Halloween of 2015. Buried the body, delivered the dick. "You know, the longer you keep me from receiving medical attention while engaging in this cruel fishing expedition, the more of your business I'm going to own."

"Well then, let's work on making you rich," Pixler taunted. "Tell me about the Arellano assassination."

5

The Relationship

LIKE MOST PEOPLE, Chewie was familiar with the axiom: You never know how much you love someone until they're gone. What he hadn't known until seconds ago was that attempted murder served the same purpose.

Although he'd only met Vicky half a year earlier, it seemed a lifetime ago. He had been putting his creative writing degree to work by managing a Reno bookstore by day and writing a novel by night when Vicky walked into his shop looking for books on starting a new business.

She'd been coy about the specifics when he first offered to help out, indicating that she would be "working in the field of psychology, attempting to put a new spin on an old business model." Her doctoral degree was in bioengineering, not psychology, but she'd "recently woken up with a gift to see things others couldn't." An ability she "felt compelled to share."

Crazy as it sounded to abandon a prestigious scientific PhD in favor of a psychic studio, it proved to be a brilliant move, because she really did have an incredible gift. An inexplicable and uncanny talent to provide life-altering advice. Chewie was no expert, but according to client comments, Cassandra could accomplish more in half an hour than most therapists could in a year.

Acting as her confidant and advisor over nightly dinner meetings, he watched in wonder while her business rapidly outgrew Reno. Before long, he was helping her move to Vegas to take her shot at the big show.

All as a friend who longed for more.

Chewie made a few savvy marketing moves as her office

manager—including offering free consultations for the Bellagio's dealers and wait staff—and was soon booking consultations at ten times the rate Reno customers were willing to pay. Before long, Basil showed up and offered her a show. A weekend matinee in one of the Bellagio's smaller theaters, which soon expanded to five days a week.

The road ahead appeared to be paved with gold and adorned with roses—until Walter White walked into her reading room.

"You don't believe him, do you?" Chewie asked Basil as they waited for Vicky to finish her private interrogation.

"Of course not. Did you see his face?"

Chewie wasn't sure what the Bellagio executive was referring to. Vance's face was a wreck. A puffy, red, snot-covered mess—thanks to the pepper spray. "What do you mean?"

"His mustache and eyebrows were peeling off. Disguises are considered evidence of deception in Vegas."

That was good news. The big casinos were practically principalities, given their size, income, and local authority. Plus, as the saying goes, they did print money. While Chewie pondered the implications of Vance's disguise, the reading room door opened and Vicky walked out.

Once Kyra closed the door behind her, Vicky said, "He doesn't know who hired him."

"How much was he paid?" Basil asked.

"A hundred thousand dollars."

"Wow! That's well above market rate. You have no idea who would want you dead that badly?"

"No idea," Vicky said, shaking her head.

"Give it some thought. Make a list of possible suspects and I'll have someone look into it. Discreetly of course."

"No need to worry about that, but I do have another list for you."

Basil raised his thick gray eyebrows.

"He admitted to thirty-one prior murders."

"What!?" Basil and Chewie both blurted.

"Give me a few minutes and I'll write down their names. He supplied dates and locations for most."

"That's incredible," Basil said. "I'm speechless."

You wouldn't be, if you'd sat through a consultation, Chewie thought. Basil and Vicky had both avoided mixing business with pleasure. As had Chewie himself, come to think of it.

Vicky pressed on. "One name in particular may be of interest to you. Vincent Castaneda."

"My predecessor? Vance killed Vinny?"

"Used a young prostitute to lure him to a cheap motel, then dumped him in a desert ravine."

"He told you that?"

Vicky pursed her lips. "He'll deny all of it. But he could lead you to the gravesite if properly motivated. He used it more than once."

Basil smiled. "We have a guy who's very good at getting to the truth."

"So you'll deal with this incident in-house?"

"In the family," Basil said, putting an arm around her shoulder.

6
First Mistake

TRENT KELLER CRINGED, then cursed as his twenty-five-year winning streak crashed to a stop—in Las Vegas of all places.

The cold fist of defeat had taken hold of his heart an hour earlier when Cassandra's big receptionist abruptly turned from the desk and ran to the back during Vance's appointment. The squeeze temporarily eased when Bellagio security officers began arriving before anyone left. Not Vance, and more importantly, not Vicky Pixler. The actor-turned-assassin had obviously botched his escape, but had he completed his mission?

With his eyes covertly locked on the archway that separated the public part of the studio from the lounge and reading room in back, Trent waited nearly an hour for that disappointing answer. It came when the psychic walked into sight. She left the studio a few minutes later, flanked by the receptionist and a Bellagio bodyguard.

Trent remained seated on a bench across the esplanade, waiting to see if Vance left on his feet or in a bag. He didn't have to wait long. Within a minute of Pixler's departure, the failed assassin was frogmarched out of *Cassandra* and through a nearby employees-only door.

He was toast.

Casinos were kingdoms that vested their security chiefs with the power of medieval sheriffs. Vance would talk, and then he would disappear. That was a tough break, but Trent felt no pity for the man he'd hired. Vance had been warned, forcefully and repeatedly, to ignore Cassandra's psychic powers at his own peril. He'd also been paid in accordance with that elevated risk. Now, he'd pay the price for ignoring that advice.

As would Trent.

He'd never let his colleagues down before. Not in twenty-five years. Granted, this was their first assassination, but it was far from the first time Trent had clandestinely hired someone for a covert operation. He had no excuse, and he wouldn't try to make one.

He walked outside and headed for one of the Bellagio's uncrowded lakeside terraces to make the mea-culpa call.

"How'd it go?" Colton answered in his trademark silky voice.

Trent replied with a question of his own. "Can you get everyone in the room?"

"I think the guys are here. Scarlett's traveling. Is something wrong?"

"Please call them in." Trent didn't want to have to go through this more than once.

A gurgling noise intruded while he waited on the line, then water jets sprang to life behind him as *Viva Las Vegas* began playing from the lakeside speakers. Bongos, strings, and that unmistakably upbeat sixties sound.

"We're all here," Colton said.

"Are you calling from a bar?" Jim asked. "I hear Elvis."

"The Bellagio fountain show just started. Bad timing. Look, that guy I hired—got caught."

"What happened?" a chorus asked.

"I'm assuming he didn't take my warnings seriously enough. In any case, he's in casino custody and she's secure."

"What does he know? Can he harm us?" Colton asked.

"He knows nothing about who hired him or why. He saw only a door and received only cash."

"You did warn him though?"

"Yes, of course."

"Without specifics, I assume?" Jim asked.

"No specifics. I simply repeatedly stressed that her psychic powers were real, and that he needed to act as if she'd know what he was thinking."

"I'm not surprised that he didn't believe you," Jim said. "Ironically, I don't think we'd want to hire anyone who would."

"Who was he?" Colton asked.

Trent noted Colton's astute use of the past tense. "He was an actor with a computer science degree who tried to make it as a Hollywood tough guy. When he failed, he became a real killer 'to show them.' Something he did thirty-one times before this gig."

"The fact that he failed tells you something about her," Colton noted. "What's your next move?"

"If at first you don't succeed…"

"She's been warned, so the subtle, pissed-off customer approach may not cut it," Walter said, speaking up for the first time. "Instead of one pro, why not see what a gang of thugs can do? Make it a home invasion."

"I agree," Jim said. "Assuming you can figure out how to manage the logistics anonymously."

Trent did not care for the idea of working with outlaws, but striking at home had appeal. "I'll give that some thought."

"Why don't we try talking to her?" Colton suggested, turning the conversation in a different direction.

"We've been through that," Walter said. "What could we say? Sorry you can't use it, only we can?"

"Works for nuclear weapons," Colton said.

"That's because the U.S. has the world's best military standing behind its demand. She, on the other hand, just beat our army."

"I agree with Walter," Jim said. "Pixler chose to become a psychic for chrissakes. That makes her Saddam Hussein with nukes, in my book."

"Trent?" Colton asked, ever the diplomat.

"My vote's with Jim and Walter. Better safe than sorry."

"All right, then. Round two it is. Call us when you have good news."

7

The Revelation

VICKY WOKE UP with a head full of answers, a heart full of hope, and a stomach stuffed with butterflies. She needed to make some major moves, beginning with breaking the last promise she had ever made to her mother. Under the circumstances, however, Vicky knew it was the right thing to do. "Chewie!"

He came running from the next room over. Basil had given her a suite for security reasons, and had thrown in the connecting room for him. "You're awake. How are you feeling?"

"I'm fine. In the mood to talk. Would you make us some coffee?"

She took a seat overlooking the Bellagio's famous fountain, and composed her thoughts while Chewie went to work brewing. It was dark out and the top of the hour, so the fountains were doing their illuminated dance—to Andrea Bocelli's *Con Te Partiro, Time to Say Goodbye*, of all songs.

"Whatcha thinking?" he asked, handing her a steaming mug.

"I need to tell you about my gift."

"What do you mean?"

She took a deep breath. "You know I lost my hearing when I was seventeen?"

"In an explosion at Caltech," Chewie said, nodding somberly.

She nodded. "It killed my father and paralyzed my mother. He was chairman of the Computational and Neural Systems Department, and she was a tenured biology professor. The university was deemed partially liable, since they'd failed to properly secure and maintain the liquid hydrogen tank that exploded. As a result, Caltech agreed to continue paying my parents' salaries for fifty years. They also leased mom and me an on-campus home/laboratory, agreed to provide my mother with full-time in-home nursing, and waived my tuition."

It all sounded so matter of fact, Vicky reflected. So much pain, anguish, and suffering. So many lost opportunities and shattered dreams. Such a complete reversal of circumstance. All neatly presented as a summary of her legal settlement.

Vicky had never shared more than that. She'd never discussed the traumatic shock of going from being the beloved teenage daughter of two prominent professors to being the half-orphaned deaf caretaker for her paralyzed mother, in the blink of an eye. A mother who couldn't hug her. A mother who could only communicate one letter at a time. A mother who, despite all that, had managed to give her daughter both hope and purpose by setting her on the path to inventing a new means of human communication. A mother whose own determination to keep her chin up, her nose down, and her focus on progress rather than pity had motivated Vicky's every move since that fateful day.

"You lived in a lab?" Chewie asked, snapping Vicky back into the moment.

"Legally, I still do," she said with a nod to the absurdity of the revelation. She had kept the discussion of her past to a minimum with Chewie, so he wouldn't have dots to connect. "The idea was to allow my mother to participate in my life and my research as much as possible. Our research is what I need to tell you about."

"Okay," he said, nervously.

"I spent the decade following the explosion studying and experimenting with a single, very-specific goal in mind. I wanted to have a normal conversation with my mother."

"Because you couldn't hear?"

"More because she couldn't write or speak. She could type letters by directing a cursor over a digital keypad using eye movements, but that's as tedious as it sounds. Anyway, long story short, I developed a theory and I dedicated my life to proving it. Last September, I was successful."

"What theory?" Chewie asked, sliding forward in his chair.

Vicky slid back to answer. "The human brain can be compared to an automobile engine. To operate properly, both require myriad components, systems, fluids, chemical levels, electrical charges, and so forth, all of which must be aligned and balanced for proper function. You follow?"

"Sure."

"Most brain-related bioengineering research revolves around attempts to decipher and replicate the 'human engine.' My peers do that by studying the mind's equivalent to starters and carburetors and wiring patterns, etcetera, using imaging, analysis, and experimentation. But I took a very different approach. I conducted no analysis of *what*, *why*, or *how*. Rather, I directed all my research and experimentation in a different direction—not at the engine's components and connections, but at the tailpipe."

"The tailpipe?"

Vicky took a long sip of coffee so Chewie would have a few extra seconds to process. "Thought is not generated at a specific point in the brain. Rather, your mind combines the inputs from multiple regions to produce the output that we experience as a stream of consciousness. That crawler of clear text that pops out of all the biological noise and into our heads.

"I focused on tuning into the signals being sent between the components, and then combining them as the brain does, thereby recreating the same signal."

"Like intercepting letters texted from one part of the brain to another, and then forming those letters into a coherent message?"

"Something like that."

Chewie sprang to his feet. "Wait a minute! You're telling me that you *literally* figured out how to read minds?"

"That's right."

He paced for a minute while trying to swallow that pill, then stopped and twirled to face her. "You, as a scientist, a bioengineering post-doc at the world-renowned California Institute of Technology, developed a system that actually lets you see other people's thoughts?"

"I did."

He raised a finger. "And then, instead of collecting a Nobel Prize and billions of dollars in technology licensing fees, you decided to keep your invention secret and work as a psychic?"

Vicky understood his confusion. She was asking him to accept in an instant a decision she'd struggled with for weeks. "I assure you, that wasn't my plan. Not that I really had one. During my decade of research, I wasn't thinking about fame or fortune. I was focused on making a breakthrough that would compensate for my hearing loss—and allow me to converse with my mother."

"You really did it?" Chewie repeated, at once excited and incredulous.

"I really did. And then, during my very first discussion with my mother, she dropped a bomb. She informed me that I could never tell anyone what I'd done."

"What?"

"My reaction exactly. But ultimately, I came to see the wisdom of her revelation. I'll never forget her words. 'Imagine what will happen when wives can read their husbands' minds. When bosses can read their subordinates' minds. When police officers can intercept everyone's thoughts. When heads of state can't keep secrets, and all passwords and personal data are exposed. If your invention proliferates, it will shred society at every level. And when I say shred, I'm not talking metaphorically. The homicide rate will skyrocket and wars will break out all over the world—because of you.'"

"Wow!" Chewie said, stunned. "That was quite a load she laid on you."

"It was crushing, but it beat the alternative."

"Surely—"

Vicky cut him off. "That's what I said. And mom stopped me in my tracks. 'There are no buts, dear. I've been thinking about this for years, looking for a solution. You know I want you to get credit for your brilliant breakthrough. You know I think you deserve fame and fortune on par with history's most prominent scientists. But there is no way that can ever be allowed to happen. Mind reading is a plague that cannot be contained once it spreads beyond patient zero.'"

Chewie dropped into a chair. "So on the day of your great triumph, the day a decade of blood, sweat, and tears finally paid off, you went from Albert Einstein to Typhoid Mary in the span of a single conversation."

Vicky nodded.

"I can't imagine what that was like. But your mother must have known that her revelation would destroy you. Surely she gave equal thought to helping you move on? Wait!" he said, cutting her off. "Was Cassandra her idea?"

"No. She passed before becoming a psychic even occurred to me as an option. And you're right, she had given my next moves a lot of thought. I'll never forget those words either. 'Listen, dear. Ten years ago, when you lost your hearing, the circle of career opportunities open to you shrank significantly. Certain jobs, certain fields, simply require ears. Today, the circle of opportunities open to you expanded even more significantly. It's now both larger and better. With your invention, you can become the best in the world at any number of professions. But whatever you choose, job one will be ensuring that the secret of your success never gets revealed.'

"When I asked her what specific jobs she had in mind, my mother said: 'I don't know, dear. But imagine the fun we're going to have figuring that out.'"

8

The Confession

CHEWIE'S MIND WAS CHURNING so fast he half expected his hair to catch fire. *Vicky really could read minds!* She had literally cracked the biological code, as a research scientist, and yet she was now choosing to work as a psychic. It was too much to digest in one meal.

As he rose to refill his coffee—for need of movement rather than caffeine—a corollary thought delivered a wallop. "Have you been reading my mind?"

"No," Vicky said with a quick shake of her head. "I don't use my Pradas in personal situations, tempting though it is at times."

"Your *Pradas?*"

"I incorporated my invention into my eyeglasses," she said, tapping the left temple with her index finger.

"*You* built them?"

"Not right away. I did my research on large, sophisticated systems at Caltech. But once I knew exactly what I needed, I ordered custom miniaturized components with the idea of incorporating them into my glasses. There's a directional antenna, a sensor array, and a microprocessor. The battery and Bluetooth are off the shelf."

"And it fits in your glasses?"

"Why does that surprise you? The watch on your wrist can call Japan, take your pulse, play any song you want to hear, and tell you stock prices."

Chewie hadn't considered that. The technology just seemed too big.

"The Pradas collect raw data and send it to my phone, which

converts it to text," Vicky continued. "In that regard it works like my speech-to-text app. I can use any connected device to read the thought stream of the person I'm looking at, including my phone, watch, crystal ball, or other screen.

"But again, I don't have the glasses turned on when I'm talking to you."

"Turn them on. Show me." Chewie was the last person who should be skeptical, given the client success he'd witnessed. But nonetheless, he felt compelled to experience her power directly.

"Okay." Vicky raised her left hand to the temple of her Pradas, as if adjusting them.

What's the range of your glasses? He thought.

"About twelve feet," she replied as if he'd voiced the words. "I have to keep my head angled directly at the skull of the person I'm reading, although my eyes can wander. Given my hearing condition, it's natural for my gaze to stray to my phone, where anyone looking will see my speech-to-text app displaying our verbal discussion."

Vicky used a phone case that had "PARDON MY WANDERING EYES, I'M DEAF" printed on the back, and habitually held her phone so it was visible. The sign saved her time, aggravation, and—Chewie suspected—the depressing impact of having to constantly explain her condition.

But they can't see your thought-to-text?

"No. That text can only be seen through a custom polarized filter on my glasses."

I always knew you were special, but I didn't realize that you were Einstein. I'm blown away.

"I'm not a genius, Chewie. I simply maintained a singular focus for ten years—while surrounded by the brightest minds in the field and benefitting from unlimited access to the best equipment available."

Chewie found himself enjoying this novel means of discussing a sensitive topic. By not actually voicing the words, he felt free to be more direct. More honest. He was just thinking, after all. *Why become a psychic? What other careers did you consider?*

"Lots of them. Among the more interesting were detective, spy, and negotiator."

Yeah! I could see getting excited about those. You could become a real Sherlock Holmes. Or the CIA's greatest asset. Or the person every CEO would want whispering in her ear. But you didn't go that way?

"No, I didn't."

Why not?

"Lots of reasons. I didn't want a boss. Someone who would consider me an asset rather than a person, or who would use me like a tool. Potentially for their own benefit rather than the greater good. I also didn't want my life to revolve around deception. And I didn't want to live in fear of being found out—thereby unleashing the mind-reading plague."

Go on.

"In those jobs and others like them, people would constantly be asking how I knew what I knew—and I'd never have an adequate answer. I also wouldn't have a credential or prior experience to justify my expertise. Given that and my personality, I'd have been living in a state of constant anxiety."

What about psychiatry?

"Practicing psychiatry requires a degree and a license. I'd had enough of school. Plus, psychiatrists have the highest suicide rates of any profession. They're surrounded by mental illness and depression. God bless them, but that's not for me either."

What about becoming a professional poker player? Or chess grand master?

"I considered those, but not for long. I would have been winning by cheating. That would have been wrong, so I'd never have felt right."

Chewie was starting to understand a dilemma he'd never have predicted. The topic was far more complicated than it first appeared. As was the power to read minds. He'd be dwelling on all of this for a long time to come.

Okay, I'm starting to see why you weren't drawn to those jobs, but what drew you toward becoming Cassandra?

"If you ignore the charlatan stigma surrounding the field—which I can do since it genuinely doesn't apply to me—working as a psychic checks all the boxes. I'm using my special skill to help and entertain people. Like psychiatrists or actors. Plus, I'm my own boss. My clients love me. I'm becoming rich and famous. And, most importantly, I don't have to deceive anyone. I'm essentially claiming to be a mind reader, and people simply assume there's trickery involved—because there is with everyone else who calls him or herself a psychic, or mentalist, or magician. So my secret is safe—hidden in plain sight."

Huh. Fancy that.

Chewie was starting to understand her reasoning. He found himself feeling excited by the surprising series of revelations—until a nagging sensation moved from the back to the front of his mind, like a storm front blowing in. *Why are you telling me this today?*

9

The Plan

VICKY REMOVED HER PRADAS before replying to Chewie's big question. It wouldn't be fair to read his mind during the coming discussion. She could have simply hit the power button, but that action would have been invisible, so she set them on the coffee table like courtroom exhibit one.

"I'm telling you today because I figured out who ordered my assassination."

"You did?" Chewie asked, his gaze racing from the glasses to her eyes.

"Not specifically, but generally, and that's enough to drive what I have to do next."

"I don't follow."

Vicky walked to the bed and took a seat. "I just realized that I've been working under a false assumption for years. In that regard, I should be grateful for the assassination attempt. It exposed my arrogance and helped me identify a critical error in my thinking."

"Arrogant? You? Now I'm totally confused."

You and me both, Vicky thought. "I know I've thrown a lot at you. Let me back up. Do you understand why I have to keep my invention secret?"

The question was a warmup, and rhetorical. Chewie had an amazing mind. His grasp of philosophy and technology were both on par with the best professors at Caltech. She'd never enjoyed everyday discussions with anyone so much as she did with him. Add to that his endless enthusiasm and huge heart and Vicky felt privileged to have him as both a business partner and friend. Truth be told, she was hoping for even more.

Chewie settled in on the opposite corner of the bed before answering. "Basically, because the news that mind reading exists would lead to paranoia. Limited distribution would lead to egregious abuses of power. And widespread availability would lead to rampant crime and violence. In other words, mind reading is a scourge that would destroy the fabric of society."

"Wow, well said."

"Thank you."

"So you agree that my conclusions in that regard are relatively obvious?"

"I think everyone who's heard a lover ask, 'Does this make me look fat?' understands and appreciates the importance of having a filter between what he thinks and what he says."

"Nicely put. Now, given that, let's loop back to my foundational mistake. Can you guess what it was?"

"I haven't a clue."

"Thank goodness, because I'd have felt pretty stupid if you got it immediately," Vicky said with a smile, a wink, and complete sincerity. "My mistake was assuming that I was the first to crack the mind-reading code."

Chewie blinked a few times while his processor spun, then began thinking out loud. "Everyone who figures it out will think they're the first, because those who came before kept it secret."

"Right. And?"

"They'll also come to the conclusion that they can't share their discovery."

"Keep going," Vicky prompted.

"He or she or they won't only restrain themselves, they'll also police other researchers, to ensure that nobody else starts the plague, so to speak."

"Exactly."

"Would that be difficult? The policing?"

"No. It's a relatively small field, and the serious players are concentrated at a handful of universities like Caltech and MIT."

"So you would have been easy to identify and monitor."

"Very. When I suddenly abandoned my research, my peers thought I'd given up. But anyone who'd previously succeeded would have suspected the truth—and investigated. I told no one except my mother, and I kept all my notes encrypted, so they would not have been able to confirm my success."

"Okay. Good," Chewie said, nodding along, enjoying the creative meeting of minds.

"Then I opened *Cassandra*."

Chewie froze as the last two dots connected. "Which both confirms your success and appears reckless if you don't really think about it and realize that fortune telling is actually one of the few places where mind reading can be used without raising suspicion."

"Exactly."

"Okay. I buy your logic. How does that conclusion drive what you'll do next?"

Vicky rose and began wandering about the room. "I have no way of knowing if he, she, or they were two months or two decades ahead of me in making the discovery, so identifying them is going to be difficult. And even if I could find them, given that they chose to hire an assassin rather than reach out, attempting to make my case would be an exceedingly risky proposition. Agreed?"

"Agreed."

"Meanwhile, Vance's failure changes nothing. They remain convinced that I'm Typhoid Mary—and therefore will keep sending assassins until one succeeds."

Chewie's face dropped, but he said nothing.

Vicky stopped directly before him. "I've decided to run. To leave Las Vegas, abandon Cassandra, and start a new life in hiding overseas."

She watched Chewie's face as his mind raced the course she'd run a few hours earlier. "I'm sure the Bellagio would offer me security as long as my show's making them money, but I don't want to live that way. A gilded cage is still a cage. And I'd never be able to relax. I know some politicians and executives are content to live that way, but the bodyguard lifestyle wouldn't work for me."

"What are you thinking?" Chewie said, his voice reduced to a whisper.

Vicky took his hands. "I spent the first twenty-seven years of my life in Pasadena, which, like Malibu and Santa Monica and Long Beach, is a suburb of Los Angeles—albeit inland. While I loved my life, I occasionally fantasized about sailing off on one of the beautiful yachts I saw when we went to the beach. Now's my opportunity. I don't have a ton of money, but it's been a really good few months. I have enough to buy a nice used yacht and live a modest life aboard it, exploring distant islands while my trail goes cold and I figure out my next act in life."

"You're leaving?" Chewie said, his voice cracking.

"Vanishing, with a bag full of cash and a burner phone."

Chewie's face grew ever more desperate during a long silence. "I don't know what to say."

"That's okay," Vicky said, taking his hands. "I know what you can say. Tell me you'll go with me."

10
Dark Lord

TRENT KELLER said, "Please!" to the empty hotel suite before logging into the private chat room at the appointed hour. Security wasn't his concern. He had complete confidence in his ability to remain untraceable on the dark web. He was praying for success. For good news.

That news would be in the form of photographs. All of them would have an original 1977 Darth Vader action figure in the bottom left corner. The toy served both as a signature and as proof of authenticity. The rest of the frame would show Victoria Pixler's body in enough detail that there could be no mistaking the fact that she was dead.

Trent appreciated the clever confirmation system designed by *Dark Lord 89109*. Hiring a hitman online was difficult and dangerous. You needed some way of verifying that you weren't actually dealing with a cop or a conman. The action figure photo system adequately addressed that concern.

After his experience with Vance Panzer, however, Trent hadn't taken anything for granted. He'd gone the extra mile. He had used facial recognition software to identify the victims in the Dark Lord's résumé photos, and then match their murders to central Las Vegas zip code 89109. While that corroboration wasn't airtight, it was sufficiently solid to leave Trent feeling optimistic when transferring the cryptocurrency down payment.

The chat room updated while he watched—but not with photos. He got text instead. "She's gone."

Trent sighed with relief. He'd been dreading the possibility of reporting a second screwup. He'd already decided to personally cover the fee for the next guy, if the Dark Lord didn't deliver. That would be far less painful than reporting another failure. He typed an equally brief reply. "Excellent! Photos?"

Three image files appeared. Trent clicked on the first. It showed the action figure outside the door to Pixler's apartment. Trent hadn't been there, but the number was right. Getting addresses was easy when you were wearing the right glasses. All you had to do was ask.

The second Darth Vader photo showed an empty living room. The third an empty bedroom. Only as he began typing an angry reply did Trent understand. "She's gone" meant *moved*, not *dead*.

But moved where? To the Bellagio was his best guess. The casino would want to protect their cash cow, and had the means to do so.

Online, her show and consultations were simply marked "unavailable," just like anything else that wasn't playing on a particular day in Vegas. Taking a break was a normal reaction to a trauma, so Trent hadn't panicked when he saw the notices. But now he was nervous. What if she'd gone into hiding? Run away? In that case, his mistake with Vance would become a catastrophe rather than something soon forgotten.

He had to get to the Bellagio and ask around.

But first, he had to deal with Vader. He needed to keep the ball rolling. Hopefully without renegotiating. A simple reply ought to do it—so long as it was accurate. "I'll get you a new location ASAP."

11
Collateral Damage

St. Croix, the Caribbean

AS DAWN BROKE over the Isle of St. Croix, Zachary Chase and Skylar Fawkes were running—in two senses of the word. Their feet were pounding out a synchronized cadence on the warming pavement of East End Road, and they were running from their past.

While their jogging routes changed as frequently as the islands beneath their feet, sunrise runs had become one of the couple's daily routines. Their ritual for bringing order to what could be considered a chaotic life.

Skylar, once a world-ranked triathlete, was the faster of the two despite being four inches shorter at 5'8". While Chase had always been athletic, their relationship had greatly improved both his strength and stamina. By his count, those were just two of the many ways in which she was making him a better man.

They had been living together aboard their 62-foot yacht for eight months. The *Sea La Vie* had been christened the *C'est La Vie*, but they'd changed it before learning that renaming boats was considered bad luck. Apparently, Poseidon punished people who attempted to fool him. Chase had momentarily considered undoing his handiwork when he heard the folklore, but he was more concerned about the danger of retaining a link to his past life than he was fearful of the Greek god's wrath. And as Skylar noted, *Sea Life* was both more fitting and more deferential than *That's Life*.

The marina where the couple had berthed their floating home was about three miles behind them when they passed their first fellow jogger of the morning, a teenage girl whose determined look made Chase think she had her eye on a track and field scholarship. "Bet she has the soundtrack from some motivational movie blaring from her earbuds," he said.

Skylar glanced over with a knowing smile. "You're probably right."

Chase was in the habit of cataloguing and analyzing people they passed, not just on runs, but everywhere they went. It was a skill he'd picked up during his decade with the CIA and then perfected over the last eight months as a man on the run.

He and Skylar weren't running from anyone in particular. In fact, he didn't believe they were being actively pursued. But making off with sixteen million dollars of a deceased drug dealer's money had made him a cautious man.

Chase gave the determined young jogger a friendly nod as they passed, then shifted his focus to an approaching automobile. It was far from typical for the Caribbean, where cars tended to be older, economy models. The speeding vehicle was a sparkling new sapphire-blue metallic Porsche Macan with matching rims. It appeared as energized as the jogging girl—but a lot less controlled.

Chase used his left hand and a quick "Careful!" to guide Skylar well off the road while his eyes locked on the Porsche's driver. His concern was that the blonde woman's aggressive style might be caused by the adrenaline surge that strikes right before battle, a rush that tends to make amateur operatives reckless. While the odds were long that she was an assassin sent to mow them down, the ounce-of-prevention policy applied.

Taking him and Skylar out with a car accident and then making off with their yacht would be an efficient way to reclaim the purloined loot. Furthermore, a flashy Porsche was the kind of car a drug dealer might choose to use.

The blonde did not return his stare. In fact, she didn't appear to have her attention focused on anything at all, including the road.

Recognizing the situation for what it was, Chase turned and yelled back at the girl. "Look out! Look out! A car!"

She didn't react.

She couldn't hear him.

She was focused on pumping out the miles to the pounding of a soundtrack beat.

Everything was over in a flash. A tick. A blink. The collision, the escape, and the girl's life.

Chase had covered half the distance to the runner before she crash-landed atop the oceanside rocks. Skylar was closer still. But it was obvious before either reached her side that the girl was already gone. Living bodies didn't lie that way. Not still, in any case.

At least it had been quick. Quick as a flash of sapphire-blue metallic paint.

Chase felt for a pulse anyway as Skylar whipped out her phone. "What are you doing?" he asked.

"Calling 911."

"Skylar, we can't," he said with a swallowed sob. "We're lying low, living under false identities. We can't call the police and then run from the scene. And we sure can't stick around to give a statement that will land us under oath on a witness stand."

Skylar's face contorted this way and that as her better angels and bitter demons collided. It didn't take more than a few seconds for the battle to conclude—with the angels victorious. "We also can't let that drunk blonde bimbo get away with murdering this girl. She didn't even look back. We have to call an ambulance, and we have to inform the police. We simply must."

12
Tipped Scales

ZACHARY CHASE was not a fan of courtrooms and courthouses. They usually left him feeling down. While their architecture tended to be grand and the ideals behind them lofty, in his experience they did not showcase the best of civilization. Rather, modern courts frequently demonstrated that civilized life—like Thomas Hobbes' famous uncivilized one—was all too often solitary, poor, nasty, brutish, and short.

Nonetheless, he and Skylar were voluntarily visiting St. Croix's courthouse, hoping to help render justice—without ending up in jail.

Looking across the table, Chase shifted his gaze from prosecutor McKay to the parents of the victim. He'd initially thought it odd that Mr. and Mrs. Mead were present for their update with McKay, but after hearing her news he understood. "You really need us to testify?" he asked. "Affidavits definitely won't be enough?"

Elisa McKay turned slowly to both Glenn and Cora Mead before responding, taking Chase's gaze with her. The couple looked exactly like you'd expect the proud parents of a promising only child to look after her homicide. They were clearly living in purgatory, experiencing endless torment while waiting for the slow wheels of justice to deliver an appropriate verdict.

The trial offered false hope, Chase knew. The Meads would continue to suffer long after *Guilty* rang loud from the jury foreman's lips. But he and Skylar were committed to giving them that moment of satisfaction all the same.

"Your affidavits would likely be enough under normal circumstances if we had more to work with," McKay replied after meeting their eyes. "But the Porters successfully eliminated all the physical evidence, to the extent that there ever was any. You'd be surprised by how little damage cars sometimes sustain when colliding with something as soft as flesh."

Chase risked another glance at the grieving parents. The assumptions he'd made when he first saw their daughter were accurate. Maria had been the star of her high school track team. And she was hoping to receive an athletic scholarship. One that would have made her the first member of the Mead family to attend a mainland university.

She was Glenn and Cora's only child.

Chase and Skylar didn't have children yet, but they planned to someday. Since both were in their early thirties, the biological clock wasn't yet putting the pressure on. Mrs. Mead, however, might well be beyond childbearing years. She and Glenn couldn't start over, even if they found the energy.

"We know it's an imposition for you to remain on the island," her father said. "We hope you'll consider justice to be a sufficiently compelling reason."

"Of course we will," Skylar said.

"What did you mean when you said 'under normal circumstances'?" Chase asked McKay.

The prosecutor shrugged. "The defendant is very wealthy. Court systems, like all others, can be manipulated by people with money. It's safe to anticipate some, shall we say, *distasteful* tricks."

Chase found that a surprisingly candid admission. The prosecutor's honesty increased his desire to help. "I see. Speaking of anticipation, when do you expect that the trial will start?"

"One week from today," McKay replied. "Kitty Porter's counsel, a named partner from a prestigious New York City law firm, has pressed hard for swift justice and we're happy to oblige."

"I see," Chase said. "Do my wife and I need to remain on the island in the meantime, or can we just come back for the trial?"

"I'd prefer that you stay. In any case, Ms. Porter's attorney will need to depose you."

"We won't run out on you," Skylar said, running a nervous hand through her short blonde hair. "When can we expect to be deposed?"

"Three o'clock this afternoon. We'll prep you in the meantime. I've ordered sandwiches."

"Is prep-work really necessary?" Chase asked. "The facts are pretty cut and dried."

The prosecutor squared the stack of papers before her. "The facts won't be considered cut and dried until the defendants rest their case. Bear in mind, there are still millions of people who believe that the Holocaust wasn't real. That the moon landing was faked. That the Earth is flat. All despite the indisputable existence of mass graves, video footage, and circumnavigation."

"No attorney can tell us what we did or did not see," Skylar said.

"Perhaps yes, perhaps no. But a talented attorney can tell the jury how to interpret what you say. She can spin all kinds of narratives."

"What do you mean, perhaps no?" Chase asked.

"The lawyer we're up against, Scarlett Slate, never loses. Her criminal defense record is literally perfect. And she works primarily in New York City, where the prosecutors have considerably more experience with homicide cases than I do, and where the prosecutorial resources dwarf those at my disposal."

"I see," Chase said.

"To be blunt, Mr. and Mrs. Hughes," McKay said, using the phony names they'd supplied, "Given the lack of compelling physical evidence, the only hope we have of getting justice for Maria is you."

13
Off the Record

CHASE HAD SEEN plenty of lawyers on television, both actors in dramatic roles and true attorneys using commercials to chase ambulances. But his personal experience with them had been minimal. A few briefings by CIA in-house counsel was about it. He'd considered that a good thing—until now.

When Scarlett Slate walked into the courthouse conference room to depose him and Skylar, Chase got the distinct sensation that he was out of his league. With her flowing blonde hair, dangerously high heels, haute couture caramel suit, and stylish glasses, Slate was polite, polished, businesslike, and attractive. Only her bright red nails hinted at the blood and fire she supposedly brought to the courtroom.

That and the way she walked. Something about Scarlett's stride made Chase feel like he and Skylar were rabbits in a wolf den. Were she to shout, he'd half expect to see both top and bottom incisors —polished white, of course.

After cursory introductions, Slate set her large designer handbag down on one chair and then took the seat directly across from them. "Thank you for taking the time to meet with me. I believe we'll be able to keep this brief, so you can get back to your fascinating lives."

"You're not going to record the deposition?" Skylar asked across the empty table.

"Not at this time. If that should become necessary, I have the required equipment in my bag. Please tell me about the accident you witnessed."

Skylar's hazel eyes glowed with passion as she related the story, from their habitual sunrise run to their passing a fellow jogger, sighting the conspicuous car with its distinctive driver, and realizing a few seconds too late what was happening. Then came the impact, the battered lifeless body, and the police report.

Slate stopped Skylar there after listening attentively. She then turned to Chase and asked him to retell the story from his unique perspective in greater detail, including what he was thinking about with every tick of the clock.

Chase complied, repeating himself a few times when prompted by the battle-hardened attorney from New York City. They had nothing to hide. The truth would set them free, or more accurately, lock up Mrs. Porter.

"Okay, just a few more questions, and we'll wrap this up," Slate said. "First of all, who are John and Joy Hughes?"

"What do you mean?" Chase asked. "*We're* John and Joy Hughes."

"No, I'm asking about the real John and Joy. You're Chase and she's Skylar," Slate said with nods of her head.

As fast as that—a snapped finger, a door opened, a corner turned—Chase was plunged into a nightmare. His actual, recurring nightmare. Unfortunately, he'd always woken up just after the official caught him red-handed perpetrating a fraud, so he hadn't seen what would come next.

Having sprung her trap, Slate simply sat there staring at him like he was lunch. She practically licked her lips.

The best Chase could do in the face of that blinding surprise was offer a banal generality. "Who we are bears no impact on what we saw."

"Well, you're half right," Slate said, tapping one red fingernail. "You saw what you saw, but who you are is important. If you had, say, murdered the real John and Joy Hughes in order to steal their identities, well, that would matter a great deal."

"We changed our names for personal reasons," Skylar said.

"There's no law against that."

Slate shifted her laserlike focus to Skylar, but didn't speak right away. She sat there as if weighing her words. "So John and Joy Hughes are simply names you decided you wanted?"

"That's right."

"May I ask why?"

It was Skylar's turn to weigh her words. She settled on, "That's none of your business."

This time Slate didn't hesitate. "Fair enough. But for the record, you definitely did not kill them? Didn't stab them in the eye and feed them to the fish, the way you did Tory?"

"Tory who?" Chase blurted, struggling to conceal the panic surging within his chest in the wake of Slate's second shocker. "Where did you hear that nonsense?"

Scarlet smiled. "My source is not something either the judge or the jury will be particularly concerned with, so long as it's true."

Chase was suddenly thrilled by the fact that there was no recording in progress. "That was self-defense. He attacked me."

"So you say. Alas, given their subjective nature, interpersonal conflicts are subject to interpretation. Subtleties matter. What's not so subtle is that you're now living off the millions you stole from him."

Chase could not believe his ears. How could a lawyer from New York City possibly know that? Tory's cash had come from white-collar drug dealers. When Tory tried to kill them and lost his own life in the process, Chase and Skylar inherited his money as the spoils of war.

At the time, Chase had been reasonably confident that he and Skylar could have been awarded all or most of the loot in court—had they taken that route. But the legal battle would have been long and ugly, and by that point they'd already been through more than enough. Furthermore, as with any roll of the legal dice or interaction with violent criminals, there was risk that things could have gone terribly wrong. There were subjective subtleties at play—as Scarlett now noted. So he and Skylar opted to skip the formalities.

They simply took the money and ran. Or rather sailed.

Shortly thereafter, just in case any surviving cartel members came looking for Tory's money, Skylar and Chase changed their names—getting married in the process, on paper at least.

Slate pressed on. "What do you think will happen to you once the court hears your confessions and the transcripts of your testimony are published? Wait, forget I said that," Slate said with a wave of her red nails. "What a bunch of murderous drug dealers learn really doesn't matter to me." She paused there, like an executioner with a raised axe. "Let's focus on how the judge and jury will react to learning that the only witnesses for the prosecution are a couple of murdering thieves living under false identities? I'd call that an interesting question, wouldn't you?"

14

The Yacht

Key West, Florida

CHEWIE COULDN'T REMEMBER the last time he'd been so happy and excited. Certainly not since graduating Berkeley a decade earlier.

Although managing *Cassandra* had been the most rewarding professional experience in his life, closing it down opened the door to a personal experience he'd been craving for months. Freed from fears of ruining their business and released from their employer-employee status, he and Vicky could responsibly pursue a romantic relationship. Something they did about three seconds after she invited him to run away with her.

The idea of escaping to a completely new life was also incredibly appealing. He would literally be exchanging all his worries for sunshine and a sea breeze. Sure, there would be headwinds and storms, but he'd be facing them with the woman he loved by his side.

Back in Las Vegas, Chewie had quickly wrapped things up with Basil and the Bellagio while being careful to leave the door open to *Cassandra's* return should safety permit. Meanwhile, Vicky bought him a ticket to Rio de Janeiro on one airline, and booked herself to Buenos Aires on another. Then they both got off between connecting flights in Miami, where they surprised and delighted a taxi driver with a three-hour ride to Key West—paid in cash.

Confident that they had effectively vanished, they began phase two of their disappearing act: yacht shopping. "You're sure this is the one?" Chewie asked, during their third day in the Florida Keys.

"There's no rush. Back in Miami there's a gazillion more."

"You don't like it?"

"Personally, I think it's perfect. But it's a big commitment, so you should be certain."

The Fairline Phantom 50 was fifteen years old, meaning it would cost only a small fraction of its original price. While its design and systems were a bit dated, the *Vitamin Sea* had been top of the line when new, and it appeared to have been well maintained. The wood was freshly varnished and the leather still soft.

The starter yacht boasted two bedrooms, two bathrooms, a compact kitchen, and a laundry facility below. The main deck and upper deck were both comfortable and luxurious, with captain's stations, dining tables, bench seating, and bar service. The front was perfect for sunbathing and the rear convenient for water sports.

Chewie had expected secondhand yacht shopping to be a stressful experience. Ten times more so than buying a used car. But he'd failed to account for their secret weapon. The stress melted like ice cream on those sun-drenched white decks when Vicky donned her Pradas.

She insisted on walking through each serious prospect with the owner, rather than an agent, reading his mind for the real story while each described his baby in detail. The *Vitamin Sea* had no hidden skeletons, and a genuinely stellar maintenance record. Plus, they both liked the name.

The owner was eager to sell. Although May was a peak boating month, the heat of summer would soon bring hurricane season. He wanted to be free of his floating liability by then.

"He'll go as low as $250,000, which is a bargain and fits our budget," Vicky whispered, as they conferenced off to the side. "And I think he'll agree to spending a few days showing us the ropes as part of the deal."

"Sounds like this is the one," Chewie agreed.

"You really think so?"

He took her hands. "I am one-hundred percent in favor of this decision in particular and your plan in general. I've never been more thrilled in my life."

She popped up on her toes to kiss him, then sealed the deal with the owner.

Four days later, comfortable with their command of maritime regulations and their ability to captain the *Vitamin Sea*, the runaways left Key West heading east toward the Bahamas and the adventure of their lives.

15
The Race

VICKY WAS CHOPPING vegetables for their second dinner at sea when a question popped into her mind. She wondered if Chewie would know the answer. He'd taken to the technical aspects of their new life with childlike enthusiasm. "Do we call this sailing, even though our yacht doesn't have a sail?"

Chewie was facing the stove, cooking a simple fettuccini Alfredo dish. They'd agreed not to get complicated while growing accustomed to the compact appliances with their gimbal leveling systems and guard rails. "Technically, we're motoring, but nobody outside the life talks that way. I think sailing is fine for general discussions. Motoring makes me think of a bus."

"Me too."

Vicky was enjoying the adventure of a novel lifestyle—with a new boyfriend by her side. But despite their luxurious circumstances, the wonderful weather, and a commitment-free calendar, she felt far from carefree. Someone was hunting her with murderous intent. Vicky realized with an inward groan that she wouldn't rest easy until she knew who he was. Or *she*. Or *they*.

Hours before their hasty midnight departure from Las Vegas, Basil had reported that the Bellagio's expert inquisitor had independently confirmed her conclusion that Vance knew nothing about the identity of his employer. For the hit on her, the assassin had been interviewed and hired through a hotel-room door, then paid with cash slipped beneath it. On the bright side, Vance had confessed to all thirty-one prior murders during the second day of interrogation, and had given up the names of the only two employers he knew. Those were among the killer's last words, according to Basil.

Upon hearing that report and absorbing the closure that came with it, Vicky vowed to forever banish Vance from her mind.

After considerable thought, she also resolved not to tell Chewie that she was seriously afraid of a second assassination attempt. Three factors drove that decision. First, there was nothing additional they could do to ensure her safety. They were already hiding in isolation thousands of miles from Vegas, and Chewie was protecting her like a baby bird whenever they left the yacht.

The second driver was Vicky's desire to shield their budding romance from the storm raging in her mind. Their relationship already had more than enough stress to contend with, given that literally everything in their lives was new.

The third factor was the most nuanced. In order to raise the capital required to fund *Cassandra Las Vegas*, Vicky had used her Pradas to win high-stakes poker matches in Reno. She'd accomplished that guilt-free by targeting cheaters. Teams of players who were secretly collaborating to fleece wealthy tourists using sophisticated signaling and betting strategies.

While her plan had proved successful, it hadn't come without cost. One evening, the losers mugged her and Chewie while they were walking home. Although neither of them were seriously hurt during the surprise attack, the blow to Chewie's pride was substantial. In his mind, he had failed to protect her and thus was a failure, both as a companion and as a man. Vicky was certain that the perceived shortcoming remained a festering sore spot to this day, so she absolutely did not want to give him the impression that she felt unsafe in his presence, lest he take it personally.

Fortunately, Chewie was fully absorbed with organizing the yacht while getting to know it from bow to stern. There were lots of moving parts, and he wanted to understand them all. If Chewie was topside with her, she'd brainstorm about how to identify her would-be killers while pretending to read a Kindle. If he was below, fiddling around in the engine room or wherever, she'd search online.

Intuition told Vicky that she was up against a group of people. Maybe large, maybe small, but almost certainly more than one individual. Most serious bioengineering research was done by teams. She'd been a rare exception, thanks to her extraordinary circumstances. Furthermore, the tactic of anonymously employing investigators and assassins also felt more like a committee decision than someone acting alone. What individual would have the time or appetite for so much administrative work on top of all the other delights, demands, and distractions available to the world's only mind-reader?

She figured that identifying the group would prove to be less daunting than it sounded. She wasn't looking for a needle in a haystack so much as a lit match. She hoped.

They had presumably found her as part of a project to covertly identify and track everyone who was conducting serious bioengineering research on mind-reading. Likewise, Vicky figured she could find them by investigating outliers who were working in fields where mind-reading would be maximally advantageous. People with extraordinary records of success.

She began by composing a list of likely career choices. *Detective*, *negotiator*, *psychiatrist* and *spy* came from her own previous considerations, as did *poker player* and *chess champion*. To that initial lineup, a bit of sundeck brainstorming added *venture capitalist, talk show host*, and *news anchor*.

Vicky dismissed her own choice: *psychic*. She'd become familiar with her peers, and nobody was in her league. That gave her six professions to begin scouring for people who, as she had been, were head and shoulders above the competition.

She decided to start with talk-show hosts and news anchors, because that research would be fun and easy. Videos were readily available. Venture capitalists would come next, because she considered that the safest bet, given that the mind readers would have begun as bioengineers. The brightest MDs and PhDs often migrated to venture capital because of the vast fortunes to be made and fun to be had by brilliantly managing money and betting on startups. Personally, Vicky had no interest in either finance or television, but plenty of people did.

Her mind was still racing as she settled in behind her dinner plate and Chewie raised his glass of champagne. The stark, simple reality of her situation struck home as they clinked glasses. While all appeared perfect, it most certainly was not. She had to identify and disable an established group of geniuses—before they found and killed her. She was literally in a race for her life.

16
Stumped

Miami, Florida

TRENT KELLER WAS STUMPED as he speed-dialed Colton Resseque. It was an unusual feeling for him. For virtually his whole life, Trent had been the guy in the room who always knew what to do. As an MIT biological engineering PhD, he understood how things worked. He saw the big picture. The physiology, the physics, the math.

Perhaps that was the problem. The issue here wasn't a thing and therefore not entirely subject to the laws of nature. His problem was a person. Worse, a female.

Trent could lecture on quantum mechanics or carburetors. CRISPR or cloning. But sticking him in a situation where emotions ruled the day was like exposing Superman to kryptonite.

Trent understood why it had to be thus. Evolution required chaos. But he didn't like it. In fact, the older he got, the less he cared to spend time with unpredictable people.

Fortunately, as the firm's behind-the-scenes guy, as their silent partner, he was rarely called upon to interact with outsiders beyond the occasional contractor. It was the perfect setup.

He was very content being the polish that made his partners shine. The dirty rag that kept them clean. The shadowy figure who maintained their equipment and kept their big secret safe. Having a title didn't matter to Trent, so long as he received the respect he deserved—and an equal piece of the partner pie.

Colton answered after a single ring.

"Mission accomplished?" he asked in his silky voice.

"I'm still drawing a blank," Trent confessed. Vicky had indeed left Las Vegas. He'd let her get away, and had taken it on himself to track her down. To redeem himself before the others.

"Tell me about it," his former classmate, old friend, and current partner said. It was a sincere request and a welcome invitation to vent.

"I feel like Edison did when testing hundreds of materials to find a filament. I've ruled out a lot of possibilities, but I haven't moved us closer to the light."

"Why don't you walk me through the details from the beginning. Maybe that will spark an idea," Colton said, his voice sounding as silky as ever.

For once, Trent was happy to talk through his tribulations. "As you know, Pixler didn't fly to Buenos Aires after all. She got off in Miami."

"And you now believe that the Argentina ticket was an intentional misdirection?"

"Yes. It was certainly a time-consuming one. In retrospect, I should have been more alert for deception given that she made no credit card purchases after buying her plane ticket, but I was in a hurry to get to Buenos Aires before the trail got cold, so I flew immediately."

"It was a smart choice for a false destination," Colton said. "Given that Argentina is a classic location for people looking to get lost."

"Agreed. Miami was also a savvy choice. It's America's gateway to the Southern Hemisphere, both by air and by sea. I've been at every airline and cruise line ticket counter in Miami, Fort Lauderdale, and Orlando to see if my 'missing sister,' Victoria Pixler, recently bought a ticket. At some I had to wait for a shift change before finding an agent willing to check their system so I could get a read."

"And you got nothing?"

"Zero. I'm thinking she picked up a fake passport, in which case we're screwed."

"Suppose she intended to continue on to Buenos Aires. Suppose she planned to pick up her new passport in Miami during her layover and got mugged?"

"Huh. That's an interesting idea. People on the run are perfect victims, given that they're carrying lots of cash and attempting to disappear anyway."

"Maybe she's in a landfill? Or a recycling container headed to China? Maybe our problem is solved?"

"Maybe," Trent agreed. "But of course we can't count on that. You see how maddening this is."

"I do. What's your next move?"

"Checking Florida's smaller airports. There's a dozen of them."

Resseque didn't reply for a few beats. "Are you sure she flew alone?"

"She only bought one ticket, and there was nobody significant in her life besides her mother, who died just after her discovery."

"No boyfriend? Or girlfriend?"

"She lived alone."

"That's not definitive. Have you spoken to the guy who resembles a Hollywood monster reject?"

"Her studio manager? No. As I said, I left for Buenos Aires immediately."

"Why don't you do that?"

Colton's idea sounded better to Trent than another dozen laps on the airport circuit. "I will. Any other suggestions?"

"How did you leave things with Dark Lord 89109?"

"He's waiting for me to supply him with a new address. A Nevada address."

"If she was scared enough to fake fleeing to Buenos Aires, I'd put the odds that she returns to the Bellagio at below ten percent."

"I'm not holding my breath either."

"Here's an idea," Colton said in that silky voice you couldn't ignore. "What if we find a contractor who can locate her as part of the package? Someone with both skillsets."

Trent pondered that for a few seconds. "Like a former detective?"

"I was thinking more along the lines of someone who used to track down mob informants or cartel traitors."

Now there was a good idea! Leave it to a lawyer to know how to leverage criminals. Trent had no idea how he'd locate such a person. Former organized crime assassins probably didn't have a Facebook group, and cartel enforcers likely never reached retirement, but he'd think of something.

"Brilliant, Colton. I'm on it."

17
Killer Compromise

St. Croix, the Caribbean

CHASE SQUEEZED SKYLAR'S HAND as prosecutor McKay entered the courthouse conference room wielding a bulky briefcase and the eye of the tiger. "Good morning Joy, John. Are you ready to fight the good fight?"

"We're ready and willing, but unable."

McKay reacted to the last word like a salmon snatched by a bear. She'd been swimming upstream for weeks, only to have the jaws of defeat rip her from the water upon finally entering the spawning pond. "Did you just say *un*able?"

The prosecutor continued with only the slightest pause, after reading their expressions. "As in *un*able to fight? *Un*able to deliver justice to the Meads? Tell me I didn't hear you correctly? Tell me what *un*able even means in this context."

Skylar rose from her chair to release nervous tension. "We've been working around the clock to figure out a way to get our story to the jury, but there just isn't one."

"What on earth are you talking about? You just tell it."

"We can't," Skylar continued. "Not because we don't want to— we desperately do—but because the Porter's attorney has made that impossible."

McKay set down her briefcase with a resolute thud. "Did she threaten you?"

"Yes, but not in an illegal manner," Chase said. "We have a very complicated past. A history that, if exposed, would make us worthless as witnesses."

"And you didn't think to mention that to me? Not at any of our many meetings?"

"We were certain it wasn't relevant because nobody knew," Skylar said.

"We've never been so shocked in our lives as we were when Slate dropped her discovery on us at our deposition," Chase added. "She hit us with bombshell after bombshell. It felt like Pearl Harbor, given the surprise and devastation."

"Why didn't you come to me then? That was a week ago."

"We've been trying to figure out a way to outsmart Slate. To get you what you need without allowing her to shred us on the stand."

"We've spoken to several top attorneys," Skylar added. "None of them came up with anything sufficiently helpful."

McKay stopped pacing and stood facing them with hands on hips. "What does she have on you? Out with it. I promise, I won't use it against you if you come clean."

"We can't," Chase said. "And it wouldn't change anything if we could."

McKay didn't budge. "Justice aside. The grieving parents of Maria Mead aside. This is a political disaster. My boss is going to have a conniption when he hears about this. He's going to order an investigation into you. He's going to shift the blame onto you. He's going to ask me to prosecute you—for whatever it is Slate is blackmailing you with. If it's serious enough to save Porter, it's got to be good enough to prosecute you."

Chase sympathized with her outrage, it mirrored his own. "You won't find it. We've spent these weeks trying to identify and plug the leak, but even with our insider knowledge, considerable resources and extreme enthusiasm still we came up blank."

"Maybe I'll ask Slate."

"We didn't get the impression that she was the type to help prosecutors, but even if she gives you everything she knows, you couldn't prosecute us. There are jurisdictional issues."

"We might just see about that. Nobody is above the law."

"Not even the Porters?" Chase asked, immediately regretting the words.

"We have an alternative proposal," Skylar hastened to add. "One that, while imperfect, we hope will work both for the Meads and for your boss."

McKay stopped pacing. "I'm listening."

"Clearly nothing can bring Maria back. And unfortunately Mrs. Porter's attorney has placed her out of the court's reach."

McKay chuffed.

"But we would like to make an anonymous donation to the Meads or the charity of their choosing," Skylar continued. "A donation your boss can spin however he wants."

"You're trying to wash away your guilt and buy your freedom with money?"

"We're trying to make the best of a terrible situation. We cannot successfully testify. I guarantee that we will lose to Slate at trial. Given that, this is the best we can offer."

McKay deflated. Her shoulders slumped. Her complexion lost its red hue. "You're not looking for credit?"

"Knowing that prosecutors negotiate deals all the time, we're content to allow your office to stage and announce as you see fit," Chase said.

"So even the Meads don't need to know where the money is coming from?"

Chase and Skylar both nodded affirmation.

"How much are we talking about?"

"Seven figures," Skylar said. "An even million dollars."

18
The Firm

AS THEY BEGAN the long, leisurely walk from a beachfront café back to the *Vitamin Sea*, Chewie put his free arm around Vicky's shoulder. He did that so habitually these days that she'd almost taken to calling him Mother Bird. Almost. The nickname had yet to pass her lips and probably never would. Although his protectiveness sometimes seemed a bit much, she appreciated the sentiment behind it, and did not want him to think otherwise.

Once they hit the firm, surf-washed sand and slipped off their shoes, he hit her with a question from out of the blue. "Why aren't you happy?"

"I am happy," she said, reflexively but dishonestly.

Although Chewie didn't push back, the voice in her head did. *Why wasn't she happy?* Her secret fear aside, their life was virtually perfect. The *Vitamin Sea* had proven to be a comfortable home. The weather was idyllic, the islands interesting, the food healthy, cheap, and delicious. Chewie had taken to the captain's life like he'd been born on a sand bar, and she found the setting to be simultaneously invigorating and relaxing.

Vicky did not need to dig for the honest answer. It was top of mind. She'd made no progress in identifying the people she believed were still determined to kill her. Nobody she'd investigated had a years-long record of extraordinary performance that appeared attributable to mind reading. No talk show host, news anchor, poker professional, or chess champion at least. The negotiators and venture capitalists were proving more difficult to investigate, and of course the spies were virtually invisible.

While conducting a fruitless search day after day was frustrating, the toughest part was having to hide the emotional burden from her sole companion. Apparently, she hadn't been as successful with that as she'd hoped.

Vicky squeezed Chewie's hand and expanded on her answer with a shade of the truth. "Despite our wonderful life, I'm having trouble forgetting that someone was so desperate to see me dead that he hired an assassin. It's just something that I have to work through. And I will, I promise. Will you give me time to do that?"

Chewie didn't argue or try to convince her that she was crazy to be living in fear 3,000 miles from the scene of the crime. He simply said, "As much as you need."

With those five words, she was happy. Temporarily, at least.

They walked the rest of the way home in relative silence, but as they climbed back aboard, Chewie held up the shopping bags and said, "I've been thinking about our next destination."

They'd begun their maritime adventure by sailing east from Key West to the Bahamas and had then continued southeast to the Turks and Caicos Islands. While it would have been easy to explore either chain for weeks, they knew it was wise to keep moving in unpredictable ways.

They were technically still north of the Caribbean Sea. It was next on their list, but they had yet to pick the specific port of call. The Caribbean is bordered to the north by Cuba, Haiti, the Dominican Republic, and Puerto Rico. Central America forms its western shore, from Mexico's Yucatan Peninsula to Panama. The southern boundary is formed by Colombia and Venezuela, whereas the famous islands with poetic names like Aruba, Barbados, and Martinique, are scattered throughout the middle and along the sea's eastern edge.

Vicky gestured to Chewie's raised hand. "You have a craving for something you couldn't find at the grocery store."

"No, that's not it. Although now that you mention it, I am missing Peet's Coffee." He set the bags down on the main deck table, then opened the one from a bookstore. Chewie had been going through a lot of paperbacks.

"The Firm?" she said, as he extracted the John Grisham classic.

"Have you read it?"

"I saw the movie. Tom Cruise, right?"

"With Gene Hackman and Jeanne Tripplehorn. Tom joins *The Firm* straight out of Harvard, not knowing it's owned by the mob. Anyway, they spend a lot of time working, playing, and doing illicit deeds on the Cayman Islands, which are renowned for their offshore banking. Ever since hearing Grisham's alluring descriptions, I've wanted to visit Seven Mile Beach."

"You just want to see if you can find the prostitute they used to seduce and blackmail Tom," she said with a nudge and a smile.

"Yes, you caught me."

"She's got to be in her fifties by now."

"You will be someday too, dear. And every bit as desirable as you are today, I'm sure."

"Nice save."

"Thank you. Does that mean we can head for Grand Cayman? Maybe hit Jamaica on the way?"

Vicky was about to answer when she suddenly found herself struck dumb. She'd been a fool. Why hadn't she seen it earlier?

"What is it?" Chewie asked.

She said, "Nothing," even though it was anything but. Chewie had provided the crucial clue. She knew, just knew, who her would-be-killer was. Not specifically, but generally and intuitively. She was up against lawyers. Lawyers! "Go ahead and plot the course to Jamaica. I need to hop online."

19
What If?

THE SKIES WERE DARK GRAY and so was Skylar's mood as St. Croix disappeared over the horizon. She wasn't certain which would clear first, but her money was on the weather.

"Who'd have thought it could be so unpleasant to give a million dollars away," Chase said, handing her a rum punch. "Now I know why McKay's boss didn't want credit. I'll never forget the look on Mrs. Mead's face."

"There was no way to avoid that look. Absolutely nothing we could have done short of testifying. Well, short of shooting Mrs. Porter on the courthouse steps."

"Don't think I didn't consider it."

Skylar knew that the tall, handsome man she called her husband was only half joking. He was a good man. An honest, faithful, hardworking patriot. But he was also a man of passion and action. As he'd once explained to her over another drink on that very yacht, "Once your government decides to solve a problem by commanding you to kill, that method remains stuck in your head as a solution."

Skylar had pushed back at the time, as she tended to do, both to keep their relationship healthy and to sharpen her mind. "A government solution, not a personal solution."

"The orders I received came from individuals, not Congress. And while most were undoubtedly issued with the intent of doing the right thing, I later learned that at times the real goal was benefitting either the guy giving the order or someone further up the chain of command."

Skylar had let it drop then, and she let it drop now. "The Meads' gratitude will come in time. Meanwhile, if it helps them to be angry at us, so be it."

"You're a wise woman, Skylar Fawkes."

Chase dropped onto the sofa beside her. "I'm just so incredibly frustrated by the whole thing. You know I won't be able to relax until I uncover the source of Scarlett Slate's information."

Skylar gestured around the bridge of their yacht. "I know you won't stop, but I think we'll find ways to relax from time-to-time."

"It's not just what she uncovered, but how quickly," Chase continued, ignoring the verbal off-ramp.

"Maybe she didn't uncover it. Maybe she already knew it—and just got a lucky match."

"What do you mean?"

"Suppose she also works for the cartel. Maybe she recognized us."

"Recognized us from where? We never met any cartel members, only Tory."

"She might have seen some security video footage. In fact, that's the only way she could have learned the details of Tory's death. Nobody else was on the tiny island."

Chase shook his head. "That's not the only explanation. A careful autopsy would have revealed Tory's cause of death."

Skylar shrugged. "Either way, my theory holds. Slate had to have seen our faces before she became Porter's lawyer."

"What are the odds of that coincidence? Slate's from New York City, which is thousands of miles from St. Croix."

"And yet she obviously has a reputation in the Caribbean, otherwise the Porters wouldn't have hired her."

"Good point." Chase's face went from expressing excitement for a mystery potentially solved to one showing panic for a fear discovered.

"What is it?" Skylar asked.

"The bigger picture."

"What do you mean?"

"Slate helped Porter by using information she picked up from the cartel. What if the reverse also applies? What if she also decided to help the cartel using information she picked up during the Porter case?"

"You think she told them where to find us?" Skylar asked, certain that her face had also fallen.

"If she wants more cartel business, that's exactly what she'd do."

Skylar agreed with the deduction, but couldn't swallow the ultimate conclusion. "If that's the case, then why are we still alive?"

"Slate would have insisted that the cartel wait for Kitty Porter to be cleared before doing anything, lest our death cast suspicion her way."

Skylar felt her stomach drop another notch. "In which case, they'd wait for us to sail off. Which we've just done." She scanned the horizon for any boats speeding their way. Fortunately, she saw none. "What's our next step?"

Chase set down his glass. "First, we need to give the *Sea La Vie* a thorough inspection. Make sure nothing's been, uh, added or removed."

More butterflies. "You think there might be a bomb on our boat?"

"Better safe than sorry."

"That's an understatement," Skylar said, hoping she'd hit bottom. "What's the second thing on your list?"

"Once we're convinced that the yacht is clean, we set out to confirm your hypothesis."

"We look for a link between Scarlett Slate and a Caribbean drug cartel," Skylar said. "Good idea."

"Thank you."

"Now go check the boat."

20
The Ultimate Blow

VICKY STARED AT THE FACES on the screen and knew that she'd found them. Her fellow mind-readers. Her would-be assassins. The Cains to her Abel.

Competing waves of emotions sloshed over her like the dual wakes of a speeding yacht. Excitement and relief, followed a few seconds later by anxiety and panic.

She longed to share her feelings and her discovery with Chewie, but he'd gone to bed long ago. Should she wake him?

Peeking into their bedroom, Vicky was struck by how peaceful her boyfriend looked. Chewie was a large, strong man with a wild look, but he was fundamentally gentle and kind. An elephant without tusks. What would happen if she told him she knew who was trying to kill her? What would he do? That was an easy question to answer. Her boyfriend would go after them.

Vicky did not yet know much about her fellow mind-readers and would-be killers, but standing there looking at her elephant, the word *hyenas* popped into her mind. Beasts with bone-cracking jaws that attack in packs.

She imagined what they'd do to Chewie—and shut the door. She would not tell him what she'd discovered. Not tonight, and maybe not ever. Her life wasn't perfect, but it could get a whole lot worse. She could be alone and responsible for the death of the only man she'd loved.

Still, she needed to share. The discovery was too big to keep bottled up.

Vicky made her way to the small vanity table in the other stateroom and sat before the mirror at the oblique angle casual conversations often assumed. After spending a decade conversing daily with her paraplegic mother, one arduous letter at a time, Vicky had become an expert at anticipating what Priscilla would say. So much so, that she found it easy to continue their nightly ritual even after her mother had passed.

"Mom, I figured it out. I know who's trying to kill me."

"Congratulations, dear. How'd you do that?"

"I landed on the profession first. An obvious one in hindsight, but one that never occurred to me, probably because there's no connection to science and I have no interest in it. They're lawyers, mom."

"Makes sense, but there are a million of those. How did you identify the individual?"

"I did a search for *most expensive lawyers*. As you'd expect, there's a huge range. Rural and small-town lawyers charge $100 to $200 per hour. In major metropolitan areas, $200 to $400 is more typical. Specialists can charge twice that amount, Manhattan divorce attorneys or Silicon Valley intellectual property experts, for example. The top firms in the biggest cities now charge $1,000 an hour for their senior partners. And then there's Resseque Rogers Sackler & Slate."

"Who are they?"

"RRS&S is a boutique firm in New York City."

"Boutique?"

"Just four partners. Colton Resseque, James Rogers, Walter Sackler, and Scarlett Slate. Three men and a woman."

"What's their rate?" her mother asked with a knowing smile.

"They charge $2,400 per hour. That's $40 a minute, if you can believe it."

"That's an encouraging sign, but it's far from definitive."

"Agreed," Vicky said, smiling in the mirror. "But that's just the start. At RRS&S, they have just one associate per partner. That's very unusual because it's less profitable. Other leading New York firms have up to seven."

"So they're leaving money on the table, but they also have less hectic schedules."

"Right."

"Meanwhile, when a client hires them, he knows that the named partner he's paying for is actually doing the work."

"Exactly."

"A named partner who has the record of a mind-reader."

"A perfect record," Vicky emphasized. "If they accept your case, a win is virtually guaranteed by historical precedent."

"So even at $2,400 an hour, wealthy clients are lining up. That's compelling but not conclusive."

"Agreed. The clincher is their trademark."

"Their trademark? I don't follow."

Vicky pointed to her glasses. "The partners all wear the same eyewear. Classic horn-rimmed glasses."

Mother nodded. "You're right. That seals it. And by the way, your Pradas look much better, dear."

"Thank you. I tend to agree." Vicky laughed at herself. She was feeling giddy. She should join Chewie in bed, but her mind was too wound up to sleep.

And she had lots of work to do.

Identifying her opponent was just the first step in her journey to freedom. The easiest step, she was starting to realize. In fact, once she'd focused on the law as a field where mind-readers could excel, it had taken her only a few hours to lock in on RRS&S for the reasons she'd just recited.

Of course, her opponents would be aware of their discoverability. Therefore, they would assume that after Vance botched his job and tipped their hand, the hunt would be a two-way street. In response, they would likely have raised their defenses and redoubled their offensive efforts.

Her situation was even more precarious than it had previously appeared.

But what was she to do about it?

Offense seemed out of the question. What could one bioengineer do against four high-powered New York City attorneys? That question led to another mystery. How had four lawyers come to possess the technology? Developing it required a highly specific skillset and a very focused effort. A bioengineering effort. But Resseque, Rogers, Sackler and Slate had all gone to Harvard Law School. In fact, the three men had been classmates. Slate had graduated from Harvard Law two years earlier in 1997.

Tasked by that perplexing question, Vicky finally felt the tug of sleep. She yawned and decided to look into the lawyers' backgrounds the next day.

And buttress her defenses. Their disappearance appeared to have been clean. She was still alive. Intuition had served her well in that decision. But as the partners of RRS&S redoubled their efforts to find her, she'd have to triple hers to hide.

While putting her head down beside Chewie's, it struck Vicky that there was one obvious move. The mere thought of it pained her. The injustice was almost overwhelming.

First, an explosion had stolen her status as the daughter of two distinguished Caltech professors. Then, the risk posed by her breakthrough invention had robbed her of glory and her rightful place in history. Now, in the name of safety, her identity would suffer the ultimate blow.

Vicky buried her face in the pillow and screamed.

She needed to change her name.

21
The Guy

VICKY HIT CHEWIE with her big decision as they munched conch fritters at the Royal Jamaica Yacht Club. "You know I've been on edge lately. Not really myself."

"That's completely understandable. If someone had sent a professional assassin after me, I'd be...distracted too."

"I'm so glad you understand, because I've come to a decision in that regard."

Chewie put down his fork. "Okay."

"I've become convinced that we did the right thing by disguising our escape route and then disappearing on a yacht. But the more I think about it, the more I'm worried that's not enough."

"Really?"

Chewie's tone left Vicky sorely tempted to reach for her Pradas. "You sound surprised."

"To be honest, I was thinking about returning to Vegas and reviving *REVELATIONS.*"

"Seriously?"

"Yeah. You were well on your way to becoming a headline act. A legend in your own time. And at a young age. That's a one-in-a-hundred-million opportunity. I understand your security concerns. I really do. But we can work around those. Basil and the Bellagio are clearly willing to help."

"They are?"

"Yes. They put out the word on the street that the assassin sent for you met with his own untimely and most unpleasant demise. You're protected."

"Mob style?" Vicky said, as much a statement as a question.

"A made woman," Chewie said in an upbeat tone.

"So you've been in contact with Basil?"

Chewie reddened. "He emailed me to see how you were. One thing led to another."

"What does he know regarding our location?"

"Nothing, Vic. It didn't even come up."

"If you're going to stay with me, I need you to stop emailing. Close your account. Email can be used to trace people."

"If I'm going to stay with you?"

"Sorry. I didn't mean that the way it came out. Please close your account, for my sake."

Chewie fidgeted with his fork then popped a conch fritter into his mouth. He was buying time to think.

Vicky spent the strained silence regretting her decision not to read his mind.

"What has you so concerned?" he finally asked. "Did you hear something? Remember something?"

Vicky realized she could no longer hide her fear. The best she could do was keep it vague. "There's no reason to think that whoever hired the first guy won't hire a second."

"I can think of a few."

"Can you?"

"Sure. For starters, tempers cool. People move on. Time is the ultimate emotional solvent."

"Okay, I buy that. But what if it was someone or some organization who thinks psychics are satanic? Can the Bellagio protect me from a jihad? Can you?"

Vicky immediately regretted her last quip. It had just slipped out. She had to repress his misplaced feelings of guilt, not feed them. Chewie didn't know what she knew. And he'd been tolerating a lot of behavior that undoubtedly looked irrational if one wasn't in her head. "I'm sorry. That absolutely was not fair. You've been so supportive and I've been so…complicated."

"No need to apologize. I've never been in your shoes, and you make a valid point. Plus I cut you off."

"You did?"

"Back at the beginning, when discussing our disappearance, you said you didn't think what we'd done was enough. Then I interjected my thoughts about reviving REVELATIONS. What else do you want us to do?"

Vicky took a deep breath. "I'm going to become a blonde and assume a false identity."

Chewie struggled to remain impassive, and she loved him for that effort. "To ensure that the next assassin can't track you down?"

"Exactly."

It was Chewie's turn for a deep breath, but he ate another conch fritter instead. "How does one acquire a false identity?"

Vicky wasn't certain. "I assume the same way you buy illegal guns and drugs. You find a dealer."

"Makes sense. How do we do that?"

She liked his choice of pronoun. "We visit cheap owner-operated bars. The kind motorcycle gangs would hang out at if islands had motorcycle gangs, then we ask the bartender."

"Sailors."

"No, the bartender."

"I mean that islands have sailors instead of motorcycle gangs."

"Yes. We ask around in sailor bars."

Chewie rose. "Give me a minute."

"Where you going?"

"To ask the bartender."

"This is a yacht club."

"With a local bartender. Be right back."

Vicky returned to her lunch as Chewie walked off. She didn't want to change her name, become a Brooke, Sienna, or Sasha. But she didn't want to hire assassins either. She wasn't that person, and she couldn't afford it if she were. If $100,000 was the cost of a contract on her life, killing the four big-shot NYC attorneys would probably cost more than half a million. She didn't have nearly that much cash.

If she did, if she returned to Vegas and resumed *REVELATIONS*, she'd use the money for defense. Become a king and hope to build a castle before the marauders arrived, so to speak. But that wasn't a Victoria Pixler tactic. Or a Quinten Bacca tactic. They were a pair of dolphins up against four sharks. Given that she didn't see herself or Chewie transforming into a killer whale anytime soon, their smart move was to maintain a low profile and an ocean of separation.

Chewie returned as she was wiping her mouth before a clean plate. He was wearing a smile.

"Don't tell me you got a name?"

"The marina's maintenance guy says there's a guy you go to for that."

"Great. Where is he?"

"He didn't know."

"Is he here in Jamaica?"

"No, he's pretty sure he's on another island."

"Okay. What's this guy's name?"

"The maintenance man didn't know that either."

Vicky was perplexed. "Why, exactly, are you smiling?"

"Because we've confirmed that he exists."

Vicky remained confused. "I thought we'd already assumed as much."

Chewie rephrased. "What he's saying is that there's a guy. *The* guy. One top guy serving the whole Caribbean whom the natives all know about."

"Except nobody knows who or where he is?"

"Not nobody, just this particular bartender and maintenance man. Anyway, now that we know *the guy* exists, I'm sure we can find him."

22

Information Arsenal

CHASE SLID OUT from behind their dining table and stood to stretch his legs while Skylar continued to study her laptop. He was frustrated and more than a little nervous. His sense of unease had been growing like a tumor since Scarlett Slate first walked into their St. Croix courthouse conference room.

"I'm just not seeing anything connecting Slate to the narcotics trade," he blurted in frustration, half to Skylar, half to the sea.

They'd researched each case referenced on the Resseque Rogers Sackler & Slate website. They'd scoured PACER, the federal government's Public Access to Court Electronic Records system. And they'd been through every RRS&S case on file with the courts in New York City. Nothing revealed a link to the narcotics trade or a cartel kingpin. The closest was work for pharmaceutical companies and medical industry executives, but those were all in the wrong league, starched shirts and glass towers, not side arms and escape tunnels.

Skylar said nothing.

Chase continued venting. "They've represented plenty of cheats and reprobates. Jeffrey Epstein and Bernie Madoff types. But no gang or mafia members. Basically, their clientele are all rich white folk, like the Porters."

Skylar continued to ignore him.

"Are you listening?"

"I think I found it," Skylar mumbled, her eyes remaining riveted to the screen.

Feeling a flash of excitement, Chase stretched to look over her shoulder.

"Clayton Millstone versus Claire Millstone? A divorce case?"

Skylar finally finished scrolling and turned his way. "Claire Millstone used to be Claire Porter. She's Kitty Porter's daughter. Scarlett Slate's partner, Colton Resseque, represented her—last year in New York."

That answered the Porter-Slate connection question, but it didn't add anything helpful beyond. "What business is Clayton Millstone in?"

"He's an investment banker specializing in the energy sector."

No help there.

Chase took a deep breath. Maybe Skylar was seeing something he'd missed. "Where does this leave our search for the source of Slate's information?"

Skylar shrugged. "At a dead end—for now. What do you want to do next?"

Chase stared out across the water. "I was thinking about a swim."

"It's one o'clock in the morning and we're in the middle of the ocean."

As a security precaution, they had stopped docking at marinas overnight, choosing to anchor far offshore instead.

"The moon's out, and I need to burn off some frustration before thinking about sleep."

"How about we motor in for a jog?"

"We?"

"Sure. I'm always up for a run. Then we'll motor back out and sleep in."

They were off Pine Cay, a privately-owned island in the Turks and Caicos that boasted just a few dozen homes and an exclusive resort. They'd found a delightful trail for that morning's sunrise jog.

Twenty minutes later, as they tromped through the forest for which the cay was named, Chase blurted, "Maybe Sargon sold us out." The notorious British thug had supplied the John and Joy

Hughes identities they were using. The identities Scarlett Slate somehow knew were fake. "Why didn't I think of that earlier?"

Skylar kept her eyes on the dimly lit trail. "I'm sure you did— and then dismissed it. He may be the obvious source of the identity leak, but he couldn't have revealed any of the other information Slate knew."

"You're right. I did. My brain is fried. That said, now that we've exhausted our list of possible individuals, we need to consider that Slate may have pieced it together from multiple sources."

"She hardly had time for that."

"I agree. But we're thinking like mere mortals. Who knows what the research department of a powerful New York City law firm can accomplish—given the proper financial incentive."

"You have a point."

"Maybe I should interrogate Sargon."

Skylar didn't immediately respond.

Chase knew she was picturing the back-street British thug with his burly crew of enforcers. One of the big guys had cracked Chase on the back of the head with a sap during his last CIA mission. Knocked him out cold. Then apologized as if it were nothing.

"I think we need to carefully weigh the upsides versus the downsides of doing anything provocative with Sargon," Skylar said.

"Good point."

"It's probably best not to remind a man like that of our existence. Especially to inquire about a sensitive question. He's a shark, and you know what sharks do when they smell blood."

"Another good point."

The couple jogged on. Nights were dark in the coniferous forest, but without clouds, the moon and stars were bright enough to illuminate hazardous branches and roots. Chase found it entrancing, almost dreamlike, silently speeding through blackness with the filtered starlight above and a carpet of needles below.

"You know what we need to do?" Skylar asked as they

completed the circle.

"Get breakfast?"

"We need to change yachts and change names."

Chase had given both ideas some thought. "Scraping the name off the yacht will be sufficient, especially if I add a big blue bow stripe. Boats look so similar that little changes make a big visual impact."

"Works for me. I've grown attached to our first home. What about us? Will a few tweaks do it?"

"You'd make a fetching redhead, and I could grow a stubble beard."

"And our names?"

"We should probably change them—using someone other than Sargon."

"Any idea who we could use?" Skylar asked, jumping a log.

"As a matter of fact, yes. There's one guy who's been *the guy* in the Caribbean for decades."

"And you know where to find him?"

As a veteran of CIA operations, Chase was in the habit of keeping his informational arsenal stocked. "I do. He set up on the island where Caribbean offshore banking began. About six hundred miles southwest of here on Grand Cayman."

23

Subtle Security

CHASE NOTED that their situation was both exactly the same as and yet completely different from what they'd experienced when swapping identities just ten months earlier. That time, he and Skylar had been in London's East End. This time, they were on the West End of Grand Cayman. That time, they'd just knocked. This time, an appointment using their "birth names" was strictly required and current passport photos had to be provided. That time, they'd passed from a dark alley through an unlabeled black sally door into a brick corridor where a sap wielding thug searched them before escorting them to a second armored entrance. This time, a friendly receptionist dressed in colorful island clothes led them up the stairs of a beachfront bungalow.

The Guy was definitely more customer friendly than Sargon. Chase hoped it wasn't to compensate for an inferior product.

A single suite encompassed the building's entire second floor. Large paddle fans slowly stirred the air in the high, wood-raftered ceiling while every window of the open-floor-plan arrangement offered hypnotizing views of lush vegetation and turquoise waters. As offices went, it could not be beat.

A man wearing sunglasses and a palm frond fedora, said, "Good afternoon. Please have a seat, Ms. Fawkes, Mr. Chase." He gestured to an elaborate bar off to the side. "Can I get you caffeine, fructose, alcohol, or mineral water? I have a lovely chilled rosé from Provence."

Chase and Skylar briefly glanced at each other. They definitely preferred The Guy's meeting style over Sargon's. "Some rosé would be lovely," Skylar said.

Their host nodded his approval then sauntered to the bar, where he hit a button on an automated coffee machine. While it went to work grinding beans, he uncorked a bottle of wine, poured two generous glasses, and handed them over polite bow. Before taking a seat with his espresso, The Guy placed the rosé bottle in a chiller and set it down beside them as well. While unstated, the message was clear. This was not going to be a quick in-and-out meeting.

He raised his cup in a toast, took a sip, then said, "Tell me exactly what you're looking for."

That question gave Chase the puzzle piece that made the picture clear. Whereas Sargon used physical security, this forger was using informational security. Beginning with his name.

He was referred to as "The Guy" because that was the name he used. Obfuscation was built in. Chase pictured a frustrated prosecutor trying to generate witness testimony that didn't leave a reasonable doubt. "Which guy?" "The guy." "This guy?" "Can't say. All I heard is the guy."

The Guy had asked for their names and photographs well in advance of the meeting. Plenty of time to do background checks and weed out law enforcement officers. Then, in case anyone slipped through, he forced his customers to state their demands, thereby facilitating an entrapment defense, should things ever go that far.

Given his decades in operation, Chase was certain that The Guy had plenty of powerful friends in the court system and Royal Cayman Islands Police Service. No doubt much of the $2,000 nonrefundable advance consultation fee had been passed along to them as payment for background checks and tipoffs.

After an approving initial sip, Chase set his glass on the table between them. "We're looking to disappear."

"You seem to have disappeared about ten months ago."

"We're concerned that our disappearance was incomplete."

"I see. What's your ideal scenario?"

"We're open to recommendations."

"I really need you to say. I couldn't best direct you to someone who might be able to help without knowing exactly what you need."

Clearly, The Guy wasn't going to implicate himself in any way. "Let's switch topics, if we may," Chase suggested.

"By all means. I'm here to assist in any way I can."

"What would you consider to be the most versatile passport for people living in these parts. People who appreciate their privacy?"

"Versatile in terms of visa-free travel?"

"Exactly."

"Caymanian passports are British Overseas Territory passports, and thus offer largely the same entry privileges as British passports if residency is not your intention. They will get you into about 180 countries, including the United States. Would that suit your needs?"

"I believe it would."

"Excellent. So you're yachters?"

"What makes you say that?" Skylar asked.

"You didn't arrive on a commercial airline or cruise ship. Some of my clients arrive on private planes, but they're generally less tan than you."

Skylar looked at Chase.

He nodded.

"Yes, we're yachters."

The Guy picked up his espresso and gestured toward their wine glasses. "Tell me about it. Where've you been lately? Which islands are your favorites?"

Again, Chase nodded to his wife. He recognized this for what it was. Confirmation that they were who they said they were. The Guy probably wouldn't give any indication if he didn't believe them. He just wouldn't deliver the goods. His security system was far superior to Sargon's, and considerably more pleasant.

The Guy peppered Skylar's narrative with detail-related

questions, and then pulled a laser printed slip of paper from his desk as they finished off the bottle of wine. He slid the paper across the desk, face down. "Thank you for sharing. Come back next Wednesday afternoon and I'll have what you're looking for."

Chase glanced at the paper the way a poker player would his cards. "US$46,000 Cash" was all it said.

"Would Tuesday be possible?" he asked.

"Wednesday afternoon," The Guy said.

"How about Wednesday morning?"

"Wednesday afternoon," The Guy repeated.

"What about next Thursday?"

The guy smiled, acknowledging Chase's clever move. "I only work Wednesday afternoons."

24

The Other Customer

THE LAST BUNGALOW looked like the others on the sparsely populated road, with a cheerful paint job and plenty of porch. As financial services offices went, it beat any Vicky had seen before. Bathed by warm sea breezes and just feet from the sugary sand with no hustle or bustle about, it was the polar opposite of Wall Street.

Or the Los Angeles Financial District for that matter.

Having spent most of her life in a suburb of L.A., Vicky was still shocked by the amount of underdeveloped beachfront property in the Caribbean. To get views half this good in California, people would construct houses on stilts, on the sides of cliffs, in an earthquake zone. This was a different world.

A modest brass sign beside the door before her read:

FINANCIAL SERVICES

By Appointment Only

Despite her lack of an appointment, Vicky knocked a second time because she didn't know what else to do. FINANCIAL SERVICES had no phone number or website. At least none that she'd found.

After much asking around, she had been directed to find the Salt & Battery beachfront café and then go to the last building on the road. "It's a financial services office," the concierge of a resort on Seven Mile Beach had advised them, before adding, "I think he only works Wednesdays."

Well, it was 11:30 Wednesday morning and she was at the financial services office a half mile north of Salt & Battery, but she might as well have been in Jamaica for all the service she was getting.

"How do I make an appointment?" she asked the locked door in frustration.

When the wood didn't answer, she circled the building, looking for signs of life. Finding none, Vicky bicycled back to the landmark café, intent on grabbing lunch and asking around.

This was her first solo adventure since they'd bought a couple of bikes for the purpose of exploring islands. Getting Chewie to agree to let her visit the ID guy alone had taken some convincing. Her boyfriend was clinging to her like a crustacean these days. But Vicky insisted, citing safety reasons.

She didn't want the forger to be able to identify or even readily recall her. Not when the people chasing her could read minds. Although her own appearance was generic enough and relatively easy to disguise, Chewie was distinctive and unforgettable. He marked her like a big hairy beacon.

Salt & Battery was busy with the lunch rush, so Vicky grabbed an empty seat at the bar rather than wait for a solo table. The bartender would likely be her best resource anyway.

"What can I get ya?" he asked, with that relaxed Caribbean cadence she'd come to love.

Vicky fixed her Pradas on him. "I'll take the fish tacos."

"Anything else?"

"Do you happen to know when the financial services office at the end of the street opens?"

"I wouldn't be knowing 'bout that."

"Any idea who would?"

"Financial services? No, not really."

He wasn't lying, but she wasn't done yet. "Do you know anyone who works there? Anyone I could ask? I really need to meet the guy who owns it but he doesn't seem to be around."

"What's his name?"

"I don't know. I'm just told the guy who works there is the best for certain situations."

"If you share with me, I might recommend someone who is around."

"Kind of you, but I need *that* guy. Who might know him, if not you?"

The man rocked his head back and forth. He didn't look optimistic. "My boss comes in 'bout four o'clock. I'll send him your way if you're still here. Or you can come back and ask for Frank. What ya drinkin'?"

"Iced tea."

"Fish tacos and tea comin' up."

Once the bartender turned to a customer at the other end of the bar, the stranger sitting one stool over leaned her way and said something. Vicky had to check her screen to catch it. "He'll be there after lunch."

Vicky whirled to focus on the eavesdropper, grateful that his motion had caught her attention. Her phone knew to wake and vibrate if it detected someone speaking in her direction, but that feature didn't work well in crowded settings. She repositioned her phone so he could read her hearing advisory. "Pardon me?"

"Didn't mean to eavesdrop, but I thought you'd want to know that *the guy* will be in his office after lunch."

The Good Samaritan was a few years older than she and a few inches taller, with intelligent but mischievous gray-blue eyes and an otherwise handsome face put out of balance by a low left ear. He was fortunate not to need glasses, Vicky thought as she directed hers at his forehead. "You know him?"

I have an appointment with him. "You got lucky. He only works Wednesday afternoons," the man said, avoiding her question.

"The guy from the financial services office at the end of the road?" Vicky clarified, using a question to direct his thoughts.

"That's right." *I wonder why she needs a new identity? Jealous ex, I bet. A rich guy.*

"What's his name? I've only heard him referred to as *the guy.*"

"That's intentional. He goes by that name. I think it's a security precaution."

"Smart move," Vicky said. "But how are people supposed to find him?"

Is this a test? Did The Guy send her? Is checking my discretion his last line of defense? A hurdle I need to clear before he'll hand over the goods? "I suspect he relies on referrals. And counts on discretion."

At that moment the bartender showed up with her order and the Good Samaritan turned back to his fish and chips.

Vicky said, "Thank you very much. I'll leave you in peace."

She moved to a table that had opened up about ten feet away. One with a chair facing the bar. She picked up a steaming fish taco, and continued reading the mind of The Guy's other customer.

25
The Invitation

VICKY HAD EXPERIENCED countless surprises since inventing the ability to read minds. In general, people had proved to be less secure and more resentful than she'd anticipated. Less intelligent and more superficial than she'd assumed. Less charitable and more deceitful than she'd hoped. Women were more jealous. Men were more lascivious. All were more prejudiced.

Once she got past the initial shocks and related depression, Vicky turned her magic lens into a mirror. She used it to self-analyze. After much honest introspection, Vicky realized that she wasn't as different as she'd hoped or assumed. She—like everyone else—was just very good at filtering out her own foibles. At using context to excuse her shortfalls, imperfections, and sins.

Her worst shock had not come from an exposed attitude or peccadillo, of course. That distinction went to learning that a client had her homicide on his mind. But that horrific incident aside, Vicky had never been nearly so shocked as she was at that very moment, eating fish tacos at Salt & Battery.

Despite his jovial outward appearance, kindly intervention, and helpful words, the Good Samaritan was fuming inside. While the fact that he hid his rage so well surprised her, the real shocker was the source of his frustration and anger. The man at the bar was being forced to change his identity by a lawyer. A woman Vicky knew but had never met. The female partner at the New York law firm of Resseque Rogers Sackler & Slate.

For a minute, Vicky wondered if this was a setup. If the man was somehow being used to lure her into a trap. After all, what were the chances that she'd run across a fellow casualty of their cruelty? Even if Resseque Rogers Sackler & Slate had hundreds of victims, the odds had to be a million to one given the number of people within direct-flight distance of Grand Cayman.

But not really, she realized after a few minutes of analysis.

Not when Vicky and the four partners of RRS&S were presumably the only five people on the planet who could read minds. Not when the lawyers used their ability to uncover exactly the kind of information that would force people like her and this man into hiding. Not when all the savvy Caribbean islanders used the same guy for false papers—and he only worked Wednesday afternoons. Not when Salt & Battery was the closest restaurant to his office and the only one around.

Heck, after refining the math, Vicky was tempted to read the minds of the restaurant's other diners to see if there were other identity changers hidden in their midst.

But not really.

There was still the coincidence that they'd both chosen the Caribbean for their escape. What were the chances of that? The odds that both she and this guy would choose to vanish on yachts?

Vicky had selected yachting because the nomadic lifestyle was more conducive to hiding than any other. She'd picked the Caribbean because there were thousands of islands in relatively close proximity, where North Americans would fit in, the weather was great, and the attitude famously relaxed.

Come to think of it, yachting in the Caribbean was *the* obvious choice. They were both meeting *the guy* in *the place* for people with *their* needs. In that light, one might say such a coincidence was inevitable—depending on the number of RRS&S victims.

Or destiny.

Then again, maybe she'd just gotten lucky. Very lucky.

In any case, Vicky couldn't let the opportunity to learn more about her would-be assassins slip away. She couldn't let a fellow RRS&S victim turn and walk out of her life without first learning everything he knew.

But how? How could she turn him into an ally without revealing her connection to the unlawful lawyers?

The irony of this particular problem made her smile. They were a woman and a man of similar demographic profile sitting in a bar —and she needed to pick him up. He wore a ring and she was no less committed to her companion, so the obvious answer was out. She'd just have to wing it—with the aid of her Pradas.

Vicky picked up her plate and moved back to the bar. "Excuse me. I've been sitting over there thinking this wasn't the first time I've seen you. Were you at the Yacht Club marina earlier?"

He turned to appraise her before answering. *What do you really want?* "I was."

"My boyfriend and I just docked today as well. I'm Vicky. For now, at least," she said with a wink, extending her hand.

He wiped his hand and shook hers. He was grinning on the outside, but skeptical and moving toward alarmed on the inside. "John. For now, at least."

Normally, Vicky disarmed people by asking them a question about themselves. People loved to talk about themselves. But that was the last thing John wanted to do, so *Have you been yachting long?* was off the table as an icebreaker. "We're new to the yachting scene. Just bought our boat a few weeks back."

Again, he studied her subtly, trying to take her measure. "Where are you from?"

Vicky decided to use openness and sincerity to disarm him. The caliber of his thinking led her to believe they had more than lifestyle choices in common. "Most recently from Las Vegas, but I spent the first twenty-seven years of my life on the campus of Caltech, the California Institute of Technology."

"Are you a test-tube baby?" This time it was his turn to wink.

"My parents were professors, and I went to school there." She went on to give him the basics, beginning with the accident. That led to a bit of back and forth. He lied about everything, but very convincingly. She'd never have detected his deception were it not for her Pradas.

With her glasses and subtle psychic interrogation skills, however, Vicky assembled the stranger's secrets. Zachary Chase was not, as he claimed, a former freelance insurance investigator who made good money keeping a percentage of his recoveries. He was a former CIA operative who'd "inherited" a boatload of drug money when a cartel assassin attempted to kill him and his "wife." He wasn't legally married to Skylar Fawkes, although they'd slipped on rings when assuming their John and Joy Hughes identities.

Vicky was dying to pick his brain on her situation—their situation—with RRS&S, but sensed that she shouldn't push it then and there on the barstool.

"I've got to go," he said as the clock neared 1:00. "It was nice to meet you. Good luck this afternoon."

"Thanks. How about dinner? I'd love to meet Joy and introduce you to Quinten." She strove to ooze humble sincerity. "We haven't met anyone yet. Not in this new life. We're on the *Vitamin Sea*. Say around six o'clock?"

"That would be nice, but we're planning to leave the island this afternoon."

Vicky cringed as he rose. She needed to walk the fine line between enticing him and spooking him. "I know things that could help you."

Chase froze. His first slip. But he quickly recovered with a casually toned, open question. "What kind of things?"

"I'll tell you tonight."

He grinned. "I'll be gone tonight."

Vicky grinned back. "Google 'REVELATIONS by Cassandra'—and bring a bottle of Chardonnay."

26
Good Timing

CHASE DID NOT BELIEVE in psychic ability, but he was intrigued by psychics. More importantly Vicky, aka Cassandra, was clearly not a threat. She was who she said she was, not a cartel assassin.

After reading her online biography and reflecting on her words, "I know things that could help you," he couldn't dismiss the crazy corollary notion that Scarlett Slate had obtained her knowledge through psychic ability rather than secret connections. He didn't believe it. Couldn't believe it. But, in the absence of a more plausible explanation, he hesitated to dismiss it either.

Not without learning more.

Not when it was being offered, gift wrapped.

"It's bound to be a most memorable evening," Skylar said, pulling a Napa Chardonnay from their wine refrigerator as Chase secreted a slim subcompact Glock in the small of his back. Hawaiian shirts were great for concealed carry.

He doubted that the evening would turn violent but preferred to be cautious.

"They're kind of a *beauty and the beast* couple, don't you think?" Skylar asked.

"I honestly don't think he's that beautiful," Chase replied.

After locating the *Vitamin Sea* a mere fifty yards from their own berth, Chase had studied Quinten's features using binoculars and then found him on Facebook among the fans of *REVELATIONS by Cassandra*. Quinten didn't have much of an online presence. He had a master's degree in English Literature from Berkeley and had spent years as the manager of an independent bookstore in Reno.

Friends called him "Chewie," which Chase didn't find the least bit surprising, given the phonetic similarity between Quinten Bacca and the Star Wars character Chewbacca, coupled with his unusual physical appearance.

Vicky was indeed a beauty in the online promotional photographs he'd shown Skylar, but in real life she couldn't compete with his wife, who could even turn heads after a run in the rain.

Chase let Skylar do most of the talking during the introductions, using the time to scan the *Vitamin Sea* for any inconsistencies. Any signs that didn't fit his host's story. The yacht obviously wasn't new, but since it clearly wasn't a rental either, that didn't contradict her story. It merely showed frugality and financial savvy. Boats depreciated very quickly.

Once the Chardonnay was poured and they were seated around lobster salads up top in the open air, Chase dove into the meat. "How did you go from being a bioengineering graduate student at Caltech to a psychic in Las Vegas?"

Vicky was quick with a canned response. "I woke up with a gift and realized that I needed to share it."

"Your online profile says you were born with it."

"For marketing purposes, we're claiming that she's had the ability since birth, even though it didn't present until recently," Chewie said.

Chase kept his eyes on Vicky's, or rather on her sunglasses. "You're saying it's more than just an act you developed? An actual distinguishing ability?"

"I'm blessed," she said.

That's ambiguous. "Does it work all the time, or only in certain situations?"

"Only when I'm in the right frame of mind."

Here we go. "Is that often?"

"You've known Skylar about a year and a half now, is that

right?"

Chase wouldn't have been more surprised if his host had punched him in the nose. Vicky knew his wife's real name, and how long they'd been acquainted.

"That's right," Skylar said.

"And you'd been happily yachting for about a year until a recent run-in?"

"That's also right," Skylar said, clamping her hand on Chase's knee.

"And now everyone and everything is making you nervous. Skeptical. Because you're worried that a buried secret has been revealed?"

"How do you know that?" Skylar practically whispered.

Chase was intrigued, but no longer stunned. Professional cold readers were experts at picking up on cues and using them to make general assertions sound specific. They were also masters at plucking information off the internet and pairing it with related statistical probabilities. Plus, Vicky knew that they were yacht owners who wanted to change their names.

"It's a gift. A sense. I can't explain it any more than most people can explain how they see or hear."

Chase's spy sense told him she wasn't being entirely truthful, but he let it pass. Victoria Pixler was quickly becoming one of the most intriguing people he'd ever met. And despite his skepticism, he liked her. He could tell that Skylar did, too.

Chewie was charming as well. A gentle giant with sophistication and a teenage boy's grooming habits. "Back at Salt & Battery, you said you knew something that could help me."

"I did, and I do. But now's not the time," Vicky said.

That sounded like a stall tactic to Chase. A typical psychic prevarication. But his gut told him she was sincere. Of course, psychics were experts at projecting sincerity along with other forms of manipulation. Still, he had a finely honed lie detector, and it was not buzzing. "I'll just have to trust you to tell me when it is time."

"Please do," Vicky said with a smile.

To Chase's surprise and delight, the two couples ended up spending the next week together. While Vicky waited for The Guy to create her new passport, they sailed sixty miles northeast to Little Cayman and then another five to Cayman Brac—for security reasons. It was a very comfortable way to get acquainted, each couple with their own yacht, both surrounded by the full freedom of the seas.

Vicky and Chewie weren't as athletic as he and Skylar. Well, almost nobody was as athletic as Skylar. But they were both broadly intelligent and very decent people. They also shared his and Skylar's life outlooks, perspectives, and priorities. The foursome's conversations were meaningful and their discussions deep. Psychology, sociology, politics, science, and economics quickly replaced the usual weather, food, celebrities, and sports banter.

Chase had a bottle of Champagne iced and waiting aboard the *Sea La Vie* when Vicky returned from her pickup appointment with The Guy. He popped the cork when she raised her new passport high like a hard-won trophy.

"Congratulations!"

Once they'd toasted and sipped, Chewie and Skylar began discussing dinner options. They were the primary cooks and worked well together.

Vicky leaned his way and whispered, "It's time."

Chase immediately knew what she meant. He also understood that the revelation was to be their secret. He was intrigued, excited, and more than a little apprehensive. What was she going to reveal? Why so much secrecy? He couldn't help but shiver as he flashed back to the last person who'd shocked him with a confidential revelation. Scarlett Slate.

"Am I finally going to get that reading you've been promising?" he asked, speaking loud enough for the others to overhear and putting a playful tone in his voice.

"I suppose you've earned it, if Skylar doesn't mind?"

"You two go right ahead," Skylar said. "We'll be on the *Vitamin Sea*, attempting to perfect our sushi-rolling skills."

27

Adam and Eve

CHASE GRABBED THE CHAMPAGNE BUCKET and followed Vicky to the top deck. She sat facing the stairway and motioned for him to sit directly across from her. "No crystal ball?" he asked, venting a bit of tension.

"Those are actually very useful," she replied to his surprise.

"How so?"

"Odd as it sounds, people often trust sources of information they don't understand more than the ones they do."

"You mean the way wives will turn to passing strangers when attempting to refute their husbands?"

Vicky raised her eyebrows.

"Just a little humor to lighten the mood," Chase said. "Do people actually trust crystal balls?"

She flashed a smile. "Crystal balls, tarot cards, the stars, tea leaves, you name it, some buy it."

"What's the psychological explanation?"

"In a word: desire. Those objects are really just buffers. They serve to take the focus off the psychic herself and transfer the responsibility to something more mystical and thus more powerful than a fellow human."

"I can see the advantage of that."

"Good. However, that's not the main reason I have a crystal ball on my reading table."

This was getting interesting. "What is the main reason?"

Vicky leaned in to answer. "When you worked for the CIA, you were legally required—on pain of imprisonment—to keep secrets. Did you ever betray that trust?"

Chase's sense of shock came roaring back. He was absolutely certain that neither he nor Skylar had so much as implied that he had worked for the CIA. "I've never knowingly betrayed a trust."

She studied him in silence for a few seconds. "Are you certain? Think about it? Did you ever inadvertently reveal a government secret. It's just us. I promise this goes no further."

Chase had no idea where this was headed, but Cassandra was clearly driving at something specific. He'd certainly never betrayed his government. Quite the opposite, he'd been forced out after refusing to break his oath of service. "I'm certain."

"Good, because in order to help you, I need to tell you something that you can never repeat. Not ever. Not to anyone. Skylar included. And let me warn you, it won't be easy. I know that, because I had to keep it from Chewie for a long time."

Whoa. Was she a member of some secret society? Like the Illuminati or Skull and Bones?

"I'm not asking you to join a cult," Vicky continued, as if reading his mind. "Chewie is the only living person who knows what I'm considering telling you."

"Living?"

"My mother knew. She's deceased, but her death is not related. Look, I promise you that this will be very valuable information, but it comes at a cost. The painful price of secrecy."

Chase gave her words the moment of reflection they deserved before replying. "Okay. I will take what you tell me to the grave— so long as disclosing it won't save lives or prevent suffering."

"Actually, disclosing it would almost certainly cost countless lives and inflict great suffering."

Upon hearing those words of warning, spoken with sincerity and conviction, Chase almost buried his head in his hands from shame and disappointment. Of course the psychic lady was crazy. She just hid it very well. He should have followed his head rather than his instinct. What was it going to be, he mused: aliens or ghosts?

"As an accomplished scientist, I understand the source of your skepticism. With that in mind, I'm going to tell you what you need to know, just not how I know it. You can take that information and walk away and live happily ever after if you like, never learning my secret but benefitting from that specific piece of knowledge."

"I'm confused."

"I know. Here goes." Vicky took a deep breath. "You have nothing to fear from Scarlett Slate. She didn't actually uncover your secrets. In fact, I doubt she even remembers them. Furthermore, you did not leave a trail. At least not one that she found."

Chase was speechless. Not because of her prognosis but because he'd never mentioned Scarlett Slate to Vicky, much less the details of her blackmail. As with the CIA, he was certain Skylar wouldn't have breathed a word either.

"I don't understand."

"I know," Vicky said sympathetically. "But you don't need to understand something to make use of it."

She was right about that. People popped aspirin all the time without knowing how it worked, for example. But did he believe her? She clearly had inside knowledge and an exceptional mind. Intuitively, he trusted her, despite her prior occupation and his deeply ingrained skepticism for all things supernatural.

That faith caused him to reconsider his calculations. As he contemplated the situation, Chase experienced a flashback of sorts —all the way to The Beginning. He was in the Garden of Eden, and Vicky was offering him an apple. The original sin. "Given that I know the conclusion, is it accurate to say that you're offering me forbidden knowledge for curiosity's sake alone? Like Eve with Adam"

Vicky cocked her head contemplatively, then paled a bit. "I hadn't thought of it that way, but from your perspective I suppose that's accurate. Well said."

"So why offer it? If what you say is true, why risk those countless lives? What's in it for you?"

She lowered her head a bit. "I desperately need help."

"Why didn't you start with that?"

"Because it's too big an ask."

"Too big how?"

"Look, Chase, we're putting the cart before the horse. I see now that I shouldn't be tempting you."

He reached out for her hand. It was a reflex move, but he didn't immediately retract it. "The Eve reference has you rattled."

Vicky nodded slowly. "Yes, it does."

"To continue the metaphor, you need help with the snake, don't you?"

"Four of them, actually." Vicky removed her sunglasses. As she set them on the table between them, he saw that she was teary eyed.

He squeezed her hand. It was an innocent yet intimate gesture, making him feel at once considerate and guilty. Once again, The Garden of Eden flashed before his eyes.

She didn't pull back.

She shocked him instead.

"You've already been bitten by one of the snakes."

"I have?" Chase asked, releasing her hand.

Vicky donned her sunglasses again. "You have."

Suddenly, he knew. The snake in his vision transformed into an attorney—with flowing blonde hair, dangerously high heels, and bright red nails.

"That's right," Vicky said. "The other three are Colton Resseque, James Rogers, and Walter Sackler."

28
Security Breach

THE GARDEN OF EDEN ANALOGY shook Vicky to her core. She'd never considered herself evil before. Quite the opposite, having forgone fortune and fame for the greater good. But the analogy of tempting Chase with forbidden knowledge held. It was exactly what her mother had warned about.

But what was Vicky to do? Take on four New York City lawyers alone? Ignore the evil they were doing? Let them hunt her down? Did that serve the greater good?

"How do you know Scarlett Slate?" Chase asked, snapping Vicky out of her funk.

"I don't know her. We've never met. I've never met her partners either."

"I don't understand," Chase said, his voice more calming than challenging.

"I know you don't. You couldn't. We're back to the big question. Do you want the knowledge and with it the burden of secrecy? But to be honest with you, I'm questioning the wisdom of asking for your help. I don't want to be Eve."

"Do you need my help?"

"I do."

"Will the world be a better place if I help you?"

"It will."

"Undoubtedly?"

"Undoubtedly."

Chase gave her hand another squeeze, then drew back. "Tell me."

Vicky inhaled deeply. "Think of a number between one and a

thousand."

"What?"

"Pick a three-digit number.... Seven eight nine."

Chase's face went slack. "How did you do that?"

"Pick a four-digit number.... Seven one seven four."

"That's impossible."

"No, it's bioengineering."

"Bioengineering?" As Chase spoke the word, his teeth sliced through the apple. "You're reading my mind?"

"If you think about it, you are too."

"What?"

"Your brain isn't a single cell, Chase. It presents information to you as a simple stream, like the exhaust from an automotive tailpipe. But the processing is done in different parts of different lobes. The pistons and fuel injectors and fan belts of your brain, as it were. All I'm doing is mechanically intercepting their output and duplicating the exhaust stream."

"You are literally reading my mind?" *Purple elephants in pink tennis shoes.*

"Yes. So did Scarlett Slate. She didn't investigate you. She likely knew little about you going into the deposition. She elicited your fears on the spot and then played them against you. She won and then she moved on."

Chase was stunned silent.

Vicky gave him a few seconds, then asked, "Did she take notes?"

"No. No notes, no recording. I was very surprised at the time."

"Good. Given all the other information she's undoubtedly intercepted since then, I doubt Slate remembers the details. Just as I'll soon forget your fetish for purple elephants in pink tennis shoes."

Chase bowed his head in defeat. "But she's out there, with her three partners, selling her secret skill for profit."

"And thwarting justice in the process," Vicky added.

"Did she beat you in court as well?"

"No. The partners of RRS&S sent an assassin to kill me."

"Whoa! Really? Why?"

"This is all speculation requiring confirmation, but after thinking about little else for months, I'm convinced that they developed mind reading technology about twenty years ago. Then they, like me, realized the imperative of keeping their discovery secret. I'm also assuming that they've been monitoring the field ever since in order to prevent other inventors from releasing the plague on the world—and ending their reign."

"So they never reached out to you? Never tried to negotiate?"

"No. What could they say? We're going to practice as attorneys but you can't be a psychic?"

"I see your point," Chase said, rubbing his temples.

She leaned back and let him ponder.

After a minute he asked, "How does the technology work? Physically, I mean. Did you get an implant? Take a pill? Or is that what your crystal ball does?"

Vicky closed her eyes. "I need to stress again how confidential this is. I swore to my mother on her deathbed that I'd never tell anyone. But I am compelled to make an exception for you because I can't stop RRS&S alone."

She paused there, letting the implications sink in. The awkwardness for her. The implications for him. Then she pressed on. "Chewie is fantastic. Lovable, reliable, honest, loyal, and kind. But I haven't told him about the lawyers."

"You're afraid he'd go after them and wind up dead," Chase said with a knowing nod.

"He doesn't have your special skill set. Or mindset for that matter."

"I understand. And I appreciate your faith in me."

"It's not about faith. I know for a fact that you've been keeping highly sensitive national security secrets for years."

"Good point."

"Glad you like it, because you're not going to like it when the other shoe drops."

"What other shoe?"

"I also know those CIA secrets now, Chase. When you thought about them, at my prompting, you gave them to me. Think about that. Think about what it means. If you give Skylar or anyone else this ability, you'll be giving them the secrets you swore never to reveal. You'll be giving them access to every secret out there. Imagine the damage that could be done if the wrong person has dinner with the Director of the CIA."

Chase did as she asked. Vicky watched him do it. His thoughts regarding the national security implications of mind reading ended with a pivot to their present situation. *You didn't answer my question about how your technology works.*

"Think back to your meeting with Scarlett Slate. Picture her in your mind."

"Okay."

Vicky put her cell phone on the table face up.

Chase looked at it. "Voice to text. I know. I've seen others with hearing impairments use those, but Slate wasn't one of them."

She handed him her sunglasses.

"Her glasses?"

Vicky nodded.

Chase donned the Pradas and looked around before focusing on her face. His excited expression turned to one of puzzlement. "I'm not hearing anything."

She pointed to the bottom of her screen. The portion that appeared blank when one wasn't looking through her glasses.

"Oh my god!"

Will you help me stop RRS&S? Will you help me put an end to their evil ways? Will you, Chase?

"Yes. Yes, Victoria Pixler. I will help you."

29
Single Minded Focus

New York City

SCARLETT SLATE quickly glanced at her watch and returned to her research. She still had three minutes to prepare, and she intended to use them all. The news on their prospective new client was breaking hard and fast.

Working with billionaires and tech CEOs was nothing new for RRS&S. In fact, the powerful and wealthy were the norm. Resseque and Rogers were the two most in-demand civil attorneys in America. Just as she and Sackler were the country's most sought-after criminal defenders.

Their case acceptance rate hovered around five percent, making them by far the most selective firm in New York City. Still, as they noted in their rejection letters, the partners at Resseque Rogers Sackler & Slate were five times more accommodating than the justices of the United States Supreme Court.

Market theory indicated that they should raise their hourly rate until supply met demand, but concern over increased scrutiny stifled that reaction. The $2,400 an hour they commanded was already sky high, and frankly, quite acceptable.

Even with their elite status and crowded calendars, rejecting Archibald Pascal's request for a meeting had never been an option. Even though he demanded a "4P," their shorthand for a four-partner meeting. Even when he insisted on gathering in his hotel suite rather than their office. And regardless of his request coming during a tense time.

"It's 4:48, Ms. Slate," her new assistant announced from the doorway. Margaret Gray wore an encouraging smile while holding out Scarlett's slim briefcase.

The four illustrious lawyers with their quartet of beefy bodyguards converged on the open elevator door like subway trains pulling into the same station, silently exuding power and precision.

"What are your bets?" Colton Resseque asked no one in particular as they started to descend. "Why has Pascal called on us now?"

"I bet another witness has come forward," Jim Rogers speculated.

"I think it's a pure power play," Walter Sackler said. "When one of the country's most powerful and influential public figures is looking at serious time behind bars, he's bound to pull out every gun in the arsenal. And why not, when the money doesn't matter?"

"Because it makes him look guilty," Scarlett countered. "One sympathetic client beside one sympathetic attorney standing humbly before a frothing angry mob is the proper way to play this one. He's savvy enough to know that. My money's with Jim's. Some bad news is about to break."

"I think it's habit," Colton said. "He's going with what works. The *Titans of Silicon Valley* documentary stressed that he prefers brainstorming with groups over one-on-one meetings."

The elevator bell ended their discussion, and a moment later the partners of RRS&S emerged onto Central Park West. It was a beautiful summer afternoon in Manhattan. Scarlett wished they could walk to the meeting. Cutting across the southeast corner of Central Park would get them to the Ritz Carlton in ten minutes. But the four of them with their combined bodyguard contingent made for a scene, so they used an armored limo with two accompanying SUVs whenever moving about the city as a group. Fortunately, the partners' apartment building was just a block from the office, so each of them did get a bit of outdoor exercise every day.

Their visit to the tech CEO still ended up creating a spectacle, but did so on the top floor of the Ritz-Carlton rather than on the sidewalks of Central Park. With Pascal's security scanning them while their bodyguards cleared Pascal's Premiere Park View Suite, it was little short of comic. You'd think that normal security procedures would be waived given the location and social status of all involved, but after hearing "exceptions enable assassinations" a few dozen times, Scarlett just rolled with it. As an attorney, she knew all too well the peril that amateurs invited when ignoring professional counsel.

Despite the security arrangements, the four attorneys found themselves seated at the suite's dining table within three minutes of the elevator opening, while all the bodyguards were relegated to standing watch in the hallway. Their host, however, was nowhere in sight.

With all four RRS&S partners present and on the clock, Archibald Pascal's bill was increasing at the rate of $160 per minute. Most people wouldn't waste a single one of those, but the Silicon Valley legend could keep the lot of them on the clock for over ten thousand hours with just one of his many billions of dollars, so Scarlett doubted he was sweating the accounting.

She found that catering to extremely wealthy clients was a double-edged sword. They didn't bicker over the outrageous bills, but they loved the little ego-stroking acts. The kind that put mere millionaires like her in their place. The guys didn't seem to mind. They laughed it off on the way to the bank. But the subtle jabs and slights squirmed beneath her skin.

Archibald Pascal said nothing as he walked into the room already over $1,000 into the red. He didn't even meet their eyes. He just sat down across from them and stared at the table while disciplining himself to think a single thought. He had it on repeat like a catchy advertising jingle. The six most sobering words Scarlett had heard in the past twenty years. *Put your glasses on the table. Put your glasses on the table. Put your glasses on the table…*

30
Dead Certain

The Caribbean

CHASE FOUND HIMSELF appreciating Vicky's warning more with each passing hour. He had not previously kept anything significant from Skylar. They'd maintained a transparent relationship. Now, however, he was not only holding back what had to be the biggest secret on the planet, but was also acting on it. Conspiring around it. Immersed inside it. All behind his wife's back.

With another woman.

He could meet with Vicky inconspicuously while Skylar and Chewie were cooking or grocery shopping, habits they'd fallen into out of mutual interest—thank goodness. The two or so hours a day that yielded were sufficient during the current research and planning phase. Once it came time to implement their clandestine project, however, maintaining the secret would require some serious social engineering.

Meanwhile, Vicky had agreed to work with him the same way she did with Chewie: glasses off.

"Just to be sure we're starting on the same page," he asked, "how do you see this ending?"

Vicky leaned against the top deck railing as she met his eye. "My goal is to stop killers, without becoming one."

Chase groaned inwardly. Skylar had experienced the same initial, naive reaction after her own first close escape. People who'd lived their whole lives on the light side of humanity had no idea how to deal with people who thrived in the dark. "That's a noble sentiment, but it's not a plan," he replied.

Vicky canted her head, exposing the desperation in her eyes. "I was hoping you'd know what to do. You spent a decade working for the world's most acclaimed covert operations organization. Surely you know sophisticated methods?"

Chase turned toward the open water. "The sophisticated methods apply more to gathering information than to coercing action."

"Really?" Vicky pressed. "I thought you guys found pressure points and applied leverage. Spy movies show that stuff all the time."

"Perhaps. But Hollywood makes things look unrealistically fast and easy. Actual operations typically involve lengthy undercover assignments against people with a pre-identified weakness, and tend to require months of preparation. In your case, I believe we're talking about four highly-capable individuals and a condensed timeline?"

"That's right," Vicky said. "Given all that, what would you suggest?"

Chase shrugged. "Four rifle shots from outside mind-reading range. Or maybe a single explosion."

Vicky blanched, but her speech remained steady. "The sniper approach would result in four pairs of blood-spattered glasses being logged into evidence and examined, potentially with catastrophic results. We can't use any tactic that would allow that to happen."

"And the explosion?"

"I know a thing or two about those," she said solemnly. "It would take a powerful one to ensure that all four pairs of glasses were destroyed in the blast. Since we're talking about New York City, innocent bystanders would likely be injured and public property would be destroyed. So that's a no, twice over. As I said at the beginning, I want to resolve this without becoming a killer.

Without fundamentally changing who I am."

"Got it," Chase said with another inward groan. He took a deep breath. "Has your research uncovered anything of tactical value?"

"Nothing leapt out. I didn't find any relationships we could exploit. None of them are married or living with a significant other."

"Really? All four are single?"

"I'm not surprised," Vicky said. "Their firm has risen like a rocket since its founding in 1999, so it's safe to assume that they've had the ability to read minds since their mid-twenties. And given their overtly selfish nature, I'd assume they found the work all-consuming and completely fulfilling. One big winning streak. Why complicate that with traditional family life?"

Chase had read that marriage rates were unusually low among the upwardly mobile in most major cities. And, come to think of it, divorce would be a disastrous complication that the four mind-readers would be determined to avoid.

"For what it's worth," Vicky continued, "I never had a serious boyfriend before Chewie—and I never really wanted one. Between my research and looking after my mother, I was always too busy."

"Okay, so much for gaining access through an unsuspecting spouse. What's their security situation?" Chase asked, virtually certain that he would not like the answer.

"I didn't find any references to that online, but they're rich and aware that I might be coming for them. Plus, they've probably had multiple death threats over the years from the opponents they've bested. Given all that, I'd assume they have quality bodyguards and other proven security procedures in place."

Chase also had little doubt.

For the first time in his life, he felt truly daunted by an operation. Figuring out how to neutralize four wealthy, mind-reading New York City attorneys without killing them or getting killed himself was going to require either a brilliant insight or a stroke of genius. Chase wasn't sure he had either in him.

31
Researchers and Spies

New York City

TWENTY-FOUR YEARS had passed since Scarlett Slate became the first person in human history to have her mind read. She'd been a second-year student at Harvard Law at the time—and Colton Resseque's girlfriend.

Colton was a graduate student at MIT, where he and his three roommates, Jim Rogers, Walter Sackler, and Trent Keller, were PhD candidates.

Scarlett had known what the bioengineers were working on, of course. She'd been their test subject many dozens of times during the year and a half that she and Colton had been dating. She would read her textbooks and cases while they aimed their gadgets and adjusted their dials.

Despite their big brains and the world-famous facilities at their disposal, she'd never expected them to succeed. At most, she'd expected something like a Geiger counter that buzzed louder when her thinking intensified.

They hadn't truly anticipated a home run either. At least not enough to think through the implications. The *what do we do next?*

Once her thoughts began broadcasting into their minds like a radio talk show station, it took them mere minutes to recognize the devastating toll their device would take on society if people could hear each other's unfiltered thoughts.

Being the disciplined scientists that they were, the four immediately swapped champagne flutes for espresso cups and dove into a half-panicked, half-euphoric, entirely surreal brainstorming session on how to exploit their invention without setting the world on fire.

Scarlett had immediately recognized the enormous advantage a lawyer would wield if she could read minds. The five could become the toast of New York, gaining wealth and fame while having a blast. It didn't take her long to get three of the boys to share her vision. The fourth didn't oppose it. Trent was simply wise enough to recognize that he wouldn't make a good litigator, even with their special skill. He didn't have the silver tongue, the people-pleasing personality, or any interest in the spotlight. Fortunately, he loved the idea of being the wizard behind the curtain. The Q to James Bond. The Merlin to King Arthur. For an equal slice of the pie, of course.

While the other three guys left MIT for Harvard Law, Trent set about perfecting a portable system that they could use without fear of detection. He ended up hiding it in plain sight using what became the firm's trademark: horn-rimmed glasses.

Resseque Rogers Sackler & Slate had been formed four years later in 2000, after the guys had chalked up one year of associate experience at a big NYC firm, and Scarlett had three on her résumé.

Their rise had been meteoric and their success had become unrivaled while their secret remained undetected. Until a few seconds ago. Until Archibald Pascal mentally told them to "Put your glasses on the table."

His shocking request wasn't the only recent disturbing development. In September, another bioengineering student, this one from the California Institute of Technology rather than the

Massachusetts Institute of Technology, had successfully replicated their work.

That was a one-off. A single occurrence in a twenty-four-year span. An acceptable level of threat. But Pascal's revelation represented a second recent security breach. Two data points could mark the start of a line. A trend. A wave. Was that what this meeting signified? The beginning of the end? Scarlett didn't know yet. All she knew for certain as she stared across the table at the Silicon Valley legend was that their gig was up.

Put your glasses on the table. Put your glasses on the table. Put your glasses on the table...

Scarlett and her partners glanced at each other—and then, with slack jaws and skipping hearts, they complied. They lined their glasses up on the table like surrendering soldiers.

It was a sad sight.

Looking at the three humbled men beside her, Scarlett couldn't help but picture Lee at Appomattox, Cornwallis at Yorktown, and Napoleon at Waterloo.

"Thank you," Pascal said, using his lips for the first time. "And thank you for coming. I trust it's now clear why I wanted you all here. I hope you can take comfort in the fact that we're alone."

Scarlett said nothing. Her partners said nothing. They were all too shocked. For the first time in twenty years, the lofty lawyers of Resseque Rogers Sackler & Slate were speechless.

"I've got good news, and I've got bad news," Pascal continued. "We'll start with the bad, shall we?"

The four stayed silent but managed nods.

"Obviously, I know your secret. And I must say my hat's off to you—and not just for the invention itself. Concealing something so big for so long is an amazing accomplishment in and of itself. You've had a remarkable run—but it's coming to an end."

Pascal paused there to let them process. "Who wants an espresso?"

Scarlett didn't need any additional stimulant, but she could certainly use the comfort of a warm cup, so she raised her hand along with the others.

While the tech CEO went to work brewing, she reflected on what was happening. Pascal's tactic wasn't unlike the one most prosecutors favored. Shock the subject with a sudden and unexpected threat to their lifestyle. Get them imagining how bad their future might be—then present an offer. A proposition. A preposterous proposal that suddenly looks like a lifeline.

But what could Pascal want from them that he couldn't buy with a small fraction of his billions? Did he simply want to ensure that they took his case? Did he want them to go to work for him, exclusively? Become his in-house counsel? His negotiators? His corporate spies?

And what was the so-called good news?

Pascal dealt the espressos and then began playing his cards. "I've known about your technology for quite some time now. In fact, I've been trying to replicate it for eighteen months—without success."

Pascal left his still-stunned audience hanging while he savored a sip. "Before you ask, I'm the only person who knows your secret. My bioengineering operation is overseas. It is anonymously directed and funded. I'm forced to do most of my research that way—given the gaggle of corporate spies targeting my every move."

"What, exactly, did you tell your researchers?" Colton asked, breaking the RRS&S silence with seven cool, crisp words.

"I gave them the objective of electronically intercepting human thought. I told them that it had to be possible, given the scores of other signals we routinely capture with everything from our phones to our televisions, radios, and garage doors. Why should neural transmissions be any different? It's just a question of sensor type, calibration, and focus, right?"

Nobody replied.

Pascal shifted gears. "It's always only a matter of time before the secret gets out and the crushing competition descends. In my businesses, we embark knowing that our breakthroughs may only enjoy a few months of exclusivity. If we don't grab enough market share to establish dominance during that brief window, if we don't keep our feature set on par with or superior to the rest, we'll end up dazed and confused in history's dustbin, alongside *Myspace* and *Blockbuster*.

"You, by contrast, have enjoyed a market monopoly for twenty years. While secrecy is surely the driver of that remarkable record, the technology also plays a significant role. It's nearly impossible to crack. My guys are the best, and they got nowhere. Nonetheless, the clock is ticking.

"Sooner or later, someone else will figure it out. Or do what I did and decipher how you do what you do. In either case, you'll fall from grace. Hard, fast, and far.

"But don't worry," Pascal continued with a flash of his eyebrows. "I didn't bring you here to blackmail you. I'm not going to interrogate you or attempt to pry secrets from your flesh. That's not the way I operate. I'm a nice guy. Driven, demanding, and intense—but nice."

Resseque spread his hands. "So why are we here, Archie?"

"So glad you asked, Colton. I brought you here to make you an offer. One that will undoubtedly be the best of your lives."

32
Mailbox Money

PASCAL WAS PLEASED with the way his big meeting was progressing. The key had been his creative kickoff. It had simultaneously disarmed and shocked the lawyers. Now that the dominoes were falling as arranged, the sequence should flow smoothly toward his desired result—if he could avoid triggering the diversionary forces of fear, stubbornness, and pride.

He put on a smile and continued with his pitch. "It was a smart move, choosing the law. Given your quick minds and charismatic demeanor, your rise to the top was virtually foreordained. And here you are, working when you want, for the clients you want, and billing out at around $7 million a year—each."

The four attorneys all replied with a single nod as if pulled by the same string. Years of working shoulder to shoulder had synchronized them. They were like a married quartet—who could literally read each other's minds.

With his ducks in a row, Pascal threw his first curveball. "But the law is not the highest and best use of your technology. There's a much more lucrative one."

"Not one that keeps the technology secret," Scarlett said with the authority of a Harvard lawyer who'd spent twenty years contemplating that question. "And it must be kept secret. Society wouldn't survive its widespread release."

"We wouldn't agree to consumerizing mind-reading at any price," Sackler added. "We're doing just fine."

"We're doing just fine *for now*," Resseque said. "Archie has a point. The ride will eventually come to an end. Whether that's a day, a decade, or a century from now remains to be seen." He turned to the tech CEO. "Does your higher and better use keep the technology secret?"

"It does. I wouldn't push it otherwise." Pascal nodded to Scarlett before addressing the group as a whole. "I agree with your assessment. That said, I'm here to propose a partnership. A fifty-fifty ownership deal on a new corporation that leverages your technology's highest and best use."

"What does highest and best equate to, in dollar terms?" Resseque asked.

Pascal let the question hang for a few seconds, filling the air with electricity. "Annual profits in the billions."

"I don't believe it," Rogers said, speaking for the first time. "You can't make billions without exposing the technology."

Pascal didn't flinch. He'd become adept at ignoring skeptical swipes from intellectual inferiors. "I can and I will. There's plenty of precedent. Trade secrets have supported businesses for millennia. Everything from porcelain and silk to Coca-Cola, Kentucky Fried Chicken, and Google's search algorithm."

"The whole point of patents is to get companies to disclose their secrets," Resseque added with a nod.

"It gets better," Pascal said, capitalizing on the positive momentum. "You get your share of the business with that one single act. No further work required. No client meetings. No courtroom appearances. No cranky judges or cantankerous clients. I'm offering you billions in mailbox money."

Scarlett leaned in. "Mailbox money?"

"The checks come in the mail, no work required," Sackler said.

"In exchange for sharing our technology with you?" Resseque asked.

"Exclusively," Pascal clarified.

"Meaning even *we* couldn't use it?" Scarlett asked.

"That's right. It's going to take billions to get the company going. I won't risk that money knowing that it's exposed to a single screw-up on your part. I mean no disrespect, and I recognize that you've kept things completely confidential for decades. But nonetheless, here I am, knowing what I know because you're doing what you do."

"So we have to retire?" Sackler said.

"You get the rare and coveted honor of going out on top—while you're young and healthy. You'll be the envy of the bar."

"Then we just wait by our mailbox for the billions to roll in?"

"At your beachfront estates or mountain chalets," Pascal confirmed with a nod.

The four partners all looked at each other. Pascal was pleased to note that they were clearly excited. What trial attorney wouldn't be? Personally, he wouldn't just walk away, he'd run. These guys lived lives of high stress operating within an extremely slow-moving bureaucratic system on behalf of clients who were largely criminals. Winning cases usually meant inflicting a loss on society. Cheating justice. While incurring the resentment of the law enforcement officers and judicial system employees they'd just outmaneuvered.

Resseque cleared his throat, turning all eyes in his direction. "So, what is the highest and best use of our technology?"

Pascal opened the drawer of the credenza behind him and pulled out four legal folders. He slid one across the table to each partner.

33
MOU

SCARLETT OPENED THE MANILA FOLDER to find a Memorandum of Understanding granting RRS&S LLP 49.9 percent ownership in LEXI, Inc., in exchange for assigning LEXI, Inc., exclusive rights to the Intellectual Property referred to as MRT. It gave RRS&S LLP the option to reclaim their IP in exchange for their ownership stake if LEXI, Inc., did not have revenues exceeding $1 billion within five years of signing the agreement. And LEXI, Inc. agreed to pay RRS&S $4 million each year for consultation services until revenues reached $1 billion.

MOUs were not contracts. The ability to enforce them was very limited. But then, given the extreme secrecy of the subject matter, the courts could not be utilized in any case. This agreement was literally designed to put them on the same page, nothing more.

The 49.9 percent equity was standard enough. It essentially gave them half the profit while preventing 50/50 voting gridlock. That too was all right with Scarlett.

The billion dollars in five years didn't sound as grand as Pascal's promises from a few minutes earlier, but it was still an impressive number, and intended to be a worst-case scenario. She, Colton, Walter, Jim and Trent would each own a ten percent stake in a billion-dollar business. That sounded awfully good to her. So did the annual consultation payment, assuming that the workload was on par with a typical board seat.

Scarlett was more concerned with what was missing. "What does L-E-X-I stand for and what will LEXI, Inc., be selling?" she asked as her partners also looked up.

Pascal tented his fingers. "I will be keeping that confidential until it's clear that the company can be launched."

"And when will that be clear?"

Colton answered for the CEO. "When Pascal knows he's not going to jail."

"The sexual assault charges," Scarlett said. In her excitement, she'd forgotten the presumed reason for the meeting.

"Precisely," Pascal said. "If you get me off, you won't ever have to work again."

"I heard Christine Flack was handling your case," Sackler said. "And that the trial's scheduled to start next month."

"She is and it is. But recent developments have led me to believe that I need to up my game."

Christine Flack was a nationally renowned attorney. They were the only step above her. The fact that Pascal needed that extra bit of lift didn't speak well for his case.

Rather than step in that turd, Sackler shifted gears. "RRS&S actually has five partners. The fifth operates behind the scenes."

"Interesting," Pascal said, drumming his fingertips. "You're referencing the $4 million clause. I'll agree to $5 million and look forward to meeting—?"

"Our silent partner," Sackler said, giving Pascal a taste of his own tactic before turning Scarlett's way with a question in his eyes.

Scarlett nodded slightly.

"As you may know," Sackler continued, "Resseque and Rogers specialize in civil law, whereas Scarlett and I are criminal attorneys. We'll be happy to handle your sexual assault case if there's no smoking gun. As for the partnership, we'll need a few days to come to a decision."

Pascal stood and the others followed suit. "I'm no angel, but I can assure you that there is no smoking gun. It's a he-said-she-said times four, with some circumstantial evidence. Shall we plan to meet Saturday in San Jose? You can give me your decision on the partnership, and present your defense strategy."

Times four. Scarlett was certain that there had been only three witnesses on record as of that morning. The fourth must be the "recent development" Pascal referenced. Her partners' expressions indicated both that they'd picked up on that discrepancy and that it wasn't a deal breaker.

Sackler met her eye, then replied, "That works."

They didn't return to the office, choosing to go home instead. The five partners owned the top three floors of an apartment building just a block from the office. Each floor of the Central Park West building had just two apartments, with Trent and the bodyguards on the tenth, Rogers and Sackler on the eleventh, and Resseque and Slate on the twelfth.

The location was perfect, and since they'd done well as roommates during college, it seemed sensible. Their security consultant had pushed the idea. It allowed for their individual bodyguards to double up in the spacious common areas outside their doors at night, covering for one another during bathroom breaks. Having the top floors with restricted elevator access was also a big plus, improving both privacy and security.

The partners went to Scarlett's terrace, which had a magnificent view of Central Park and a well-stocked bar.

"Thoughts?" Colton asked, kicking things off once the drinks were poured.

Rogers was the first to respond. "If it were anyone else, I'd be skeptical. But if Archibald Pascal's been working on this for a year and a half and he remains ready to dive in with both feet, then I'm not going to second-guess the opportunity." He turned toward Scarlett and Sackler. "I trust you'd have taken his case regardless?"

"Assuming he passed the interview," Scarlett said.

Normally, they employed mind reading during their pre-engagement interviews, so when they took a case, they knew virtually everything relevant that the client had done. It was a defense counselor's dream, walking into a case with complete transparency and no fear of surprises.

"So Pascal didn't need his extraordinary offer as leverage?" Rogers clarified.

"Not unless he lied about the absence of a smoking gun—which would be foolish given the circumstances, and he's no fool."

"Good. How do we feel about retiring?"

All intuitively turned to Colton, who didn't hesitate. "I'd be happy to move on. We've had a fantastic run, but I wouldn't be practicing the law any longer if it weren't for the money."

"I agree," Sackler said. "We have nowhere to go but down if we continue to practice."

"And to Pascal's point," Rogers said, "the clock is ticking. I don't know about you guys, but I have nightmares resembling the first minute of that meeting. Only in my dreams it's a judge who's got our number."

Scarlett wasn't overly concerned in that regard. They kept "clean" pairs of glasses with them at all times in case they were ever challenged. Notes were taken using coded language such as "*What if* X,", to make the harvest from their horn-rims appear like insightful speculation. "I've got no objection to retiring early."

"Excellent," Colton said. "Then we're agreed. We fly out to San Jose Saturday and accept the partnership offer. In the meantime, let's have him sign an engagement letter for the sexual assault case and get copies of everything Christine Flack has. Sound good?"

Rogers and Sackler both concurred, but Scarlett had another idea. "I don't disagree with that, but I think we should focus on two higher priorities before things get hot and heavy with Pascal."

"And what two things are those?" Colton prompted.

"One, we should try to figure out what Pascal has in mind for our technology. At the very least, learning his secret will give us leverage. Who knows, we might even be able to pursue LEXI alone."

"Or negotiate a bigger piece of the ownership pie," Sackler added. "I like it."

"What's the other priority?" Colton asked.

"Now, more than ever, we need to ensure that Cassandra doesn't resurface."

34
Hidden Assets

The Caribbean

CHASE CONSIDERED HIMSELF to be a disciplined guy. A man driven by conviction and guided by principle. He wanted to be a good person. A standup guy. But as he neared the end of a long introspective swim, he was struggling with temptation.

His battle wasn't the one that appeared to concern his wife. He felt no lust for Victoria Pixler. Attractive, intelligent, and vivacious though she might be, Vicky was not for him. Skylar was the love of his life.

That said, Chase was committed to clandestinely helping Vicky, and by extension his country and humanity. In fact, he wasn't just dedicated to it, he was excited by it. He was thrilled to be back in the big game, waging the battle of good versus evil. Unfortunately, the operational situation created a threatening combination. Secrecy and excitement paired with the presence of "another woman." An exotic and attractive woman.

Since Chase couldn't tell his wife why he and Vicky were spending so much time together, he was tempted to cheat. To borrow Vicky's glasses and read Skylar's mind. That was the dream of every man, right? To know the unfiltered thoughts of the woman he loved? To avoid the arguments that arose from male-female disconnects. But of course, that would be wrong. An intrusion. A violation. A betrayal of trust that would almost certainly do more damage than good.

Still, temptation tugged every time he sensed Skylar's pain.

Upon reaching the boat, Chase tossed his swim goggles onto the rear deck and pulled himself from the warm water. The yachting lifestyle was hard to beat.

Skylar was waiting. Watching.

She had been a few strokes ahead of him, as always, but hadn't proceeded to the shower as was their normal routine. She clearly had something on her mind. That wasn't surprising. Swims were great for contemplating.

"What's up?" he asked, meeting her eye.

"I'm thinking it's time to sail on."

"Okay," Chase said, knowing where this was going but hoping to be proven wrong. "What island grabs your fancy?"

"I don't care. I just want our life to return to the way it was."

He needed no clarification and didn't pretend otherwise. It was time to tackle the beast. "Before we met Chewie and Vicky?"

Skylar nodded.

Chase had prepared for this tightrope act. Frankly, he'd expected to be walking it earlier. Skylar was more patient than he would have been. He draped an arm around her shoulder. "If we'd met when I was still with the CIA, I wouldn't have been able to share my work with you."

"Sure, I get that," Skylar said, apprehension apparent in her voice as she followed his pivot to a tangential topic.

"The secrecy wouldn't indicate my lack of trust or a desire to share, just the presence of an overriding principle, and my adherence to an oath."

"Are you telling me you're back in the game? That Vicky the psychic works for the CIA?"

"I'm telling you this is an analogous situation, and I'm asking you to be patient with me. To have faith in me."

Skylar straightened her spine. "But you're not going to tell me what's going on?"

"I can't tell you what's going on."

"Of course you can, Chase. You just open your mouth and the

words come out. Or are you saying that your promise to her means more than your oath to me?"

Chase really wanted those glasses. "Skylar, nobody and nothing is more important to me than you. I'm asking you to believe that, to trust me, and to be patient."

"For how long?" she asked without budging.

"I really don't know. It's very complicated. About a month. Maybe two."

"Two months? Chase, I'm worried what another *week* of this... this situation will do to us."

"I understand. I'll see what I can do. Meanwhile, may I make a suggestion?"

"Okay."

"How about a long soapy shower?"

Skylar didn't crack. She didn't slump or grin. "I have a better idea."

"What's that?" he asked, dreading the answer.

Skylar turned toward the bathroom. "How about you plan on showering alone until this situation is resolved."

"That's another option," he told the waves.

After his solo shower, Chase strolled over to the *Vitamin Sea*. The gaze he got from Chewie as he passed the main deck on the way up top made him feel like a paratrooper in hostile territory. Or maybe that was just his imagination.

The big guy knew that Vicky could read minds, and he knew that she was afraid for her life. But he did not know about the lawyers, or Chase's intent to help neutralize them. He was almost certainly focused on the fact that another man was spending a lot of time with the woman he wanted to make his wife.

Nothing Chase could do about that. It wasn't his call.

He found Vicky reading something on her laptop, researching, no doubt.

"We need to talk."

"We sure do," Vicky said, spinning her screen in his direction. "Look at this headline."

Archibald Pascal hires Resseque Rogers Sackler & Slate to fight sexual assault charges.

"Just think about that," Vicky continued. "Imagine the power they have to pervert justice. For starters, they have full access to the prosecution's playbook. That means no surprises, ever. On top of that, they know the plaintiffs' stories better than their attorneys, including their exaggerations, insecurities, and doubts. They can catch every lie and omission. They also know what the judge is really thinking, every step of the way. And I don't need to tell you what they can do to witnesses."

"No, you sure don't." Chase was interested in exploring the implications, but not until after he set things right with his wife. "Look, I just got an earful from Skylar. She's not comfortable with our arrangement, and it's hard to blame her."

Vicky's face fell. "I don't blame her one bit. I'd be uncomfortable, too."

"I can tell you with absolute certainty that she'd be an asset to our mission. While she didn't have formal training, she does have operations experience."

"And a quick mind. I agree," Vicky said. "But you understand that I can't include Skylar without first including Chewie."

"I do. Fortunately, there's an obvious solution."

35

The Proposal

CHEWIE WAS SURPRISED to see Chase leave the Vitamin Sea only minutes after arriving. Pleasantly surprised. Usually when he and Vicky got to talking, they were at it for a while.

Of course, the same could be said of Chewie's own discussions with Skylar. And when all four of them got together they could easily converse for hours. But that didn't keep jealousy from rearing its ugly green head when Chase and Vicky were alone.

He trusted Vicky. Chase and Skylar too for that matter. But Chewie had been losing out to guys like Chase his whole life. Better looking guys who were more athletic and socially skilled. Guys who might not have failed to protect their girl when she got mugged. So it stung.

"You up for a walk on the beach?" Vicky asked, catching him by surprise.

Truth be told he wasn't. He'd cut his foot on some coral and was trying to keep off of it, but the look in her eyes when he whirled around prompted him to say, "Sure."

There was a lot to love about living in the Caribbean, but Chewie's absolute favorite part was the abundance of new beaches to explore. Beautiful beaches covered with colorful shells and crafty driftwood. Isolated beaches backed by exotic plants and coconut palms. Beaches where you could walk for hours on sand so soft and clean that your footprints looked like history's first.

Since taking up the yachting life and losing his usual modest land-based exercise routine, Chewie routinely used long, lone walks for self-reflection. He loved to crush mountains of sand between his toes while he whispered his worries and dreams to the waves. Both were churning away in his mind when Vicky finally started to speak.

"I figured out who sent the assassin."

"What? Wow! Who? Wait, is that..." Chewie blurted before he could stop himself. Now he needed to finish. "Is that what you've been doing with Chase?"

"No, but that's related. Let me begin with the one question you didn't ask: *When?* In general terms, I figured out who it had to be during our first days aboard the *Vitamin Sea*. I didn't tell you because I didn't want you worried. We had so much else going on. We'd just moved in together. We'd just left everything we'd known behind to try living a completely new lifestyle in a new place. It was great, but it was stressful."

"I remember," Chewie said, desperate to get to the punch line.

Vicky took both of his hands and said, "The most important thing then—as it is now—was making *us* work. I didn't want to pile more stress atop that mountain, so I kept my deduction to myself."

"What deduction?"

"I realized that the assassin was hired by another mind reader. Someone who cracked the bioengineering code before I did. Someone who recognized the need to keep that capability secret from the world." Vicky released one hand then turned and continued walking.

"Sometime later, after a lot of brainstorming and research, I figured out specifically who it was. There's a law firm in New York City that never loses. The four partners charge astronomical fees, and all of them wear thick-framed glasses. It's their trademark."

"Mind-reading lawyers," Chewie mumbled to himself. "Sounds like the plot of a lost Shakespearian tragedy. When did you figure that out?"

"A few weeks ago. That discovery was what prompted me to change my name." Again she stopped and took his hands. "Will you forgive me for my secrecy? I wanted to tell you, but I was afraid of screwing things up while our situation was so fragile and new. We've got a good thing going, Quinten Bacca."

He kissed her, long and hard. "Yes, Victoria Pixler, we do. But I want to hear about Chase before I forgive you," he said with a squeeze and a wink.

"That's the crazy part. When I ran into Chase, he was getting new identities for himself and Skylar because of the very same lawyers."

"No way!"

Vicky went on to explain her first encounter with Chase at Salt & Battery. How it was less coincidental than it appeared. Then how, after investigating him for a week, she'd recruited Chase based on their mutual enemy and his experience with the CIA.

"Chase was CIA?"

"Ten years in operations. Much of it undercover."

"Wow! And Skylar?"

"She really was a triathlete and firefighter."

Vicky continued expounding her fascinating story for miles, a full circuit of the small island. Chewie felt like a new man when they finally stepped back aboard the *Vitamin Sea*. One badly in need of a shower.

"Do me a favor," Vicky said as he peeled off his soaked shirt.

"What's that?"

"Go get Skylar and Chase."

"Now?"

"You can put on a clean shirt first."

He did as requested, without asking why.

When he returned with the spy and his wife in tow, Chewie found that Vicky had thrown on a summer dress and brushed her hair. She'd also set out a bottle of champagne and four flutes. Apparently, she wanted to kick off their partnership in style.

With all eyes on her, Vicky surprised everyone by dropping to one knee and making Chewie the happiest man alive.

36
Threats and Impediments

San Jose, California

GIVEN THAT their already packed schedules had become dangerously overloaded by recent events, the five partners of Resseque Rogers Sackler & Slate decided to use the flight to San Jose for their catch-up and strategizing meeting. They flew private, of course, on a Pascal plane. One which their bodyguards swept for bugs.

That was a hypocritical act, they realized. Four mind-reading attorneys and their covert-operations partner worrying about eavesdropping. But then, as lawyers, their lives were so steeped in technicalities, contradictions, and injustices that the double standard barely registered.

"Is anybody having second thoughts about accepting Pascal's offer?" Colton asked. "About turning over our technology for his exclusive use in exchange for half of his billion-dollar venture?"

Scarlett shook her head along with the others. The more she thought about abandoning the rat race, the more her job felt like a grind.

Prior to Pascal's offer, the thrill of the game and the excitement of the hunt had always exhilarated her. While practicing law had never been pure peaches and cream, the anticipation of victory had always propelled her through the bureaucratic maze in a predatory haze, like a shark smelling blood. Now, however, that same judicial dance struck her as pure drudgery. Even the knowledge that her bank balance was building at $40 a minute ceased to be stimulating. Why work at all when millions in mailbox money was on offer?

"We need to add an exemption for personal use," Rogers said. "I agree to stop wearing our horn-rims for professional purposes, but I want to wear them as a retiree."

"I want to be buried in them," Sackler said.

Scarlett agreed. She hated the idea of giving up her glasses. They protected her against everything from shifty salespeople to snooping reporters to investment scams. At least when meetings took place in person. Alas, none of them ever sat down with Bernie Madoff, the biggest bullshit artist of them all. "Let's meet Pascal halfway."

"Halfway?" Sackler asked.

"Let's concede to being buried without them," she said with a wink.

"All right," Colton said. "If there's nothing else in the second-thoughts category, let's move on to negotiation strategy. Who's figured out what Pascal has planned?"

"I keep getting stuck on the keeping-it-secret part," Scarlett said. "Who makes more than a top New York City lawyer? On a regular basis I mean."

"It can't be routine work, at least not in the predictable, day-to-day sense that we enjoy," Rogers said. "It's got to be deal related and likely commission based."

Colton nodded. "Like investment banking. I agree. Potentates and oil well owners aside, the only professions that earn more than top lawyers are those that make their money taking small percentages off the massive amounts of money moving through their fingers."

"Insurance companies have all the cash," Sackler said. "And don't forget everyone who's getting fat off government contracts."

"Among those options, where would mind reading give one the ability to virtually vanquish the competition?" Scarlett asked.

"Lending and insurance operations would be greatly advantaged by knowing the intentions of their clients. Cutting fraud and default rates would have a huge impact on profitability," Sackler said.

"Yes, but that would require giving all their agents our glasses, and reverting to face-to-face operations. That can't be it."

"All right," Colton said. "We've been pondering this for days and have little more to show for it than general speculation. I move that we hire the best investigator out there to locate and surveil Pascal's secret research operations."

"What about a hacker?" Rogers suggested, turning to Trent.

"If we weren't talking about Archibald Pascal, that would be worth a try. But the nature of his business ensures that he's constantly fending off digital incursions. I have no doubt that his electronic security will be better than his physical security. So let's aim for the weakest link. Even though I'm sure it will be forged from hardened steel."

"Who's the best at that stuff?" Scarlett asked.

They routinely used investigators as a part of their law practice. Both employees and independent contractors. Trent managed them all, and personally performed the lion's share of the most important work, given that he had horn-rims.

"For overseas industrial espionage in the tech field?"

"Yes."

"Are you thinking Asia, Europe, Eastern Europe, or Oceania?"

"Could be anywhere he can keep things quiet," Colton said. "Could be South or Central America. Even Africa or the Middle East."

"Well, then we're going to need more than one investigator. Ideally, we want one guy per country, or even one in every major city."

"We can't create so much noise that Pascal hears the banging. We don't want him walking away out of spite. Billionaires can afford to be irrational."

Trent shrugged. "One per region then."

"No more than half a dozen," Colton said.

"All right," Trent agreed, calculating on the fly. "One each for Central and South America, Western Europe, Eastern Europe, China, India, and Australia.

"You know good guys for all those?"

"I know four. For the other two regions, I know who to ask."

"Good. I think that covers the negotiation. Let's discuss threats and impediments." Colton turned Scarlett's way. As the female member of the criminal defense team, she was the obvious choice for lead counsel in a sexual assault defense. "How strong is the case against Pascal?"

Scarlett turned from the window, where a jet streaking past in the opposite direction had caught her eye. "The strength comes from the number of women and their caliber. The three on record are all well regarded within the industry, but none were friends. There are incriminating emails, but others that could be considered exculpatory. Fortunately, Pascal is not into instant messaging, so the impulse missives that have crucified others don't exist. He is prone to the occasional bout of anger, however, so there will be some unfortunate witness testimony."

"But there's no smoking gun?" Rogers asked.

"None that's been presented. But we don't know who the fourth potential witness is, and we can't be sure of anything before we depose all of them. But barring any surprises, I predict that we'll have this won by the end of jury selection."

People and thus jurors tended to fall into three camps when it came to sexual assault. Those who believed that women were asking for it, those who believed that men were predatory, and those who didn't lean either direction. While everyone claimed to be in the third group, only about forty percent actually were. Stack the jury with people who thought makeup and push-up bras were the equivalent of sexual advances—a trivial task for an accomplished mind reader—and you were virtually home free.

"I'll look forward to learning the results of your depositions but won't be losing any sleep over it." Colton turned back to Trent. "What is keeping me up at night is the fact that as far as we know, Cassandra is still breathing."

"I believe I've identified the perfect guy to cure her of that condition," Trent said with a smile. "Fredo Blanco used to track down traitors for the Sinaloa cartel."

"If he was good, why did they let him go?"

"Word is, El Chapo gave him permission to retire as a reward for a particularly rough job a few years back."

"Sounds promising."

"I think so. We'll know for sure a few hours from now. I've scheduled us an interview with him early tomorrow morning at a hotel in San Jose."

37

The White Elf

Fredo Blanco was pleased and surprised by the face to face meeting request. His clients usually hid on the Dark Web behind encrypted software. He preferred the additional information provided by in-person meetings, and he didn't mind traveling for them. Not when the price of an interview was $50,000.

Fredo could charge fifty grand for a meeting and a million for a case because he held the equivalent of Olympic gold in two highly prized sports: *hunting* and *killing*. His cartel credentials made him the first choice for connected clients who had challenging cases but easy budgets. Clients who required reliability and demanded discretion. Clients with targets other assassins couldn't track or wouldn't touch.

Fredo arrived at the Fairmont San Jose disguised by bronzed skin, a swashbuckler mustache, cheek inserts, thickened eyebrows, and a black beret. The combination made him look more like the love child of Rocky Balboa and Che Guevara than a white elf, a *fredo blanco*—if one linguistically combined Old English with Spanish as his creative yet cruel parents had done. Throw in the boots that boosted his 5'5" height to nearly 5'8", the sunglasses hiding his eyes, and the padded trench coat he wore like a cape to free his arms and disguise his shape, and photographs would be worthless as identification tools.

For offense, he was packing twin .22 caliber pistols and a few concealed stilettos. On the safety side, his beret was lined with Kevlar—a trick he'd learned from the Mayor of Moscow—and he sported a bulletproof vest. His hands were covered, as always.

Having become an extreme germophobe during his last

assignment for El Chapo, Fredo had more gloves than most movie stars had shoes—and a dry cleaning budget that rivaled modest mortgages.

He arrived at the designated suite by exiting the elevator two floors above his destination and walking down. As promised, the door was propped ajar. He hit the *Record* button on his phone, extracted both .22s from the holster in the small of his back, then slipped inside.

Fredo had expected to find a darkened room, but the bathroom light was on and the curtains were open, exposing the dawning California sun. Only the double doors to the bedroom were closed. The armchair positioned to face them from mid-room conveyed the message with the clarity of a neon sign.

Before taking his designated seat, Fredo did three things. He checked the view to ensure that there was no sniper shot through the window. He felt beneath the seat cushion and found nothing more sinister than a manila envelope. And finally, he pulled a small, oldschool detective's notebook from his trench coat. "How many of you are there? Please count off."

After a short pause, he heard "One." "Two." "Three." "Four." "Five." Going right to left from his perspective, like birds on a wire. The fifth was a woman, the other four men, all in that sweet spot between mature and old.

"Did you bring the money?"

"You're sitting on the fifty grand," One said. "The million is also nearby."

"Very good, tell me about the case," Fredo said, putting pen to notepad.

"Use your phone to search for '*REVELATIONS* by Cassandra.'"

He did, and was delighted. Vegas! Fredo loved operating in Las Vegas. It offered tons of cover with all the activity, lights, and noise. Plus great hotels and the desert close at hand. Alas, the website said no shows were scheduled and consultations were not currently available. "Got it."

"She's your target. We don't know where she is. She fled weeks ago after an earlier assassination attempt."

Some slouch couldn't kill a woman? That was a shocker. Fredo loved it when his targets were female. Who didn't like easy money? Maybe they'd made the mistake of sending a woman to kill a woman. "Why did it fail?"

"We don't know for certain since Casino security dealt with the first guy, but we believe it's because he disregarded our warning."

"*He* disregarded," Fredo repeated to himself. So the failed assassin had been a man. "And what warning was that?"

"We warned him not to underestimate Cassandra's psychic powers."

"Are you telling me she sensed him coming?"

"That's exactly what we're saying. Not in general, mind you. In specific. She sensed his murderous intent as he drew near."

Fredo had never heard that warning before. He'd need to ruminate on it. "What restrictions did you place on the job?"

"No collateral damage. And an act that looked like a dissatisfied client rather than a professional hit."

"Is that what you want from me?"

"Yes."

Fredo did not believe in supernatural powers, but he wasn't about to risk his life on something he didn't understand. "Tell me more about these powers of hers."

"She can sense what's on your mind when you're within speaking range," the woman said. "For example, if she were sitting where I am right now, she'd know that you're looking forward to removing your cheek inserts and taking off that heavy hat."

Fredo began searching for the camera. Usually they were too small to spot, but this one had high enough resolution that a substantial lens was indicated.

"There's no camera, Mr. Blanco. I have the same gift. Concentrate on your mother's birthday."

Fredo wasn't going to fall for that old trick. Savvy psychics did research, just like assassins. He wasn't sure how they'd have located his mother, but as a tracker himself he knew such things were possible. He thought about his sister instead.

"Valentine's Day. Your *sister* was born on Valentine's Day."

Wow. This lady did psychology as well as research.

She pressed on, leaving him no time to dwell on her skill. "How do you typically dispatch your targets?"

The question's phrasing put Fredo at ease. His new clients might have special skills, but they weren't killers. Using words like "dispatch" and "target" rather than "kill" and "girl" or "Cassandra" told him they wouldn't bloody their own hands. As for his methods, Fredo avoided anything that exposed him to bare skin or bodily fluids, including blood. Thus stilettos rather than knives and .22 caliber bullets rather than those with the power to create messy through-and-through wounds. Suffocation was good. Blunt force trauma really wasn't his thing—some skulls cracked open easier than others. He was happy to drop people from height, so long as he didn't have to approach the corpse. "I'm not a butcher if that's what you're asking. Like a good deer hunter, I prefer a clean kill."

This time, the woman didn't reply for a while, causing his thoughts to wander. They went back to her psychic tricks. This client had found a lot of information online. He needed to scrub the internet. There were people you could pay to do that.

"What's your favorite movie?" she asked. Quite the non sequitur.

Another psychic trick. Of course he loved The Godfather. *Playing the odds would give her another "miraculous win." What else?* The Day of the Jackal *was also too obvious. Best to throw another curve ball.*

Before he gave it voice, she said "Game of Thrones isn't a movie, but I'll take anything less predictable than *The Godfather* or *The Day of the Jackal.*"

"How are you doing that?"

"As I told you, Cassandra and I share the same gift. I trust you'll take the warning seriously."

Damn right he would. And now he knew his client's motive: eliminating the competition. He could appreciate that. "I will."

"Good. Now that we're clear on that complication, what questions do you have?"

"What's her family situation?"

"None."

"Where does she get her money?"

"Just savings, as far as we know. She's comfortable, but far from rich."

"So there are no family ties or financial links?"

"None that we've discovered. Can you track her down?"

Fredo could track anyone down, given enough time. "I can."

"Can you do it in the next hundred days?"

The hunt was going to be the challenge, not the kill. He could work around her gift. "Estimates are just that, especially at this stage where I know so little about the target. As a policy, I always budget for a year and aim to deliver well ahead of schedule. Usually that hits the hundred-day mark. To answer your question directly: I believe so, but I can't guarantee it."

"Good."

"Will you take the job?"

"I never back away from a challenge, but I refuse to sell myself short either. She's no ordinary target, not by a long shot. And she's been warned by the earlier blunder. Plus you're asking for a rush. Add those up and I'll need twice my usual fee to commit. Today's million becomes the fifty-percent *before*. I get another million *after*, agreed?"

"You'll find the first half in the credenza, along with the burner phone we'll use to communicate. Please keep us posted with weekly updates."

38

Getting Creative

The Caribbean

SKYLAR AWOKE feeling good. She finally understood the nagging sense of unease that had bothered her for weeks. Her head, heart and intuition had been subconsciously at odds.

Now that she knew what was going on between Chase and Vicky, Skylar felt at ease. Everything made sense—and she liked the sense that it made.

Skylar had always been a competitive excitement seeker. An adventure seeker who pushed her limits. She'd been a firefighter and an internationally competitive triathlete. She'd even made the championship podium a time or two, although never the top step.

Because of her split-second shortfalls, sponsorship dollars had remained out of reach. Meanwhile, the runner-up prize money barely covered her travel and training expenses. To pay the bills, Skylar had become a firefighter. That had been a comfortable arrangement, given the good pay and all the free time it afforded for training, until fate forced her to choose between rescuing a child and saving her lungs.

That choice—one she would make again—had dashed her Olympic dreams and put her paid occupation off limits. She'd floundered for a while, but eventually ended up on a yacht with Chase, so nowadays she felt nothing but fortunate. Nonetheless, Skylar missed the competitive thrills that had characterized her life before the fire.

She wasn't alone in that sentiment. Chase also missed his prior life.

Like her, he'd landed on a yacht out of necessity rather than choice.

Now it seemed that fate was evening out the score by selecting them for a special mission. The high-stakes, save-the-planet kind.

Chase had walked her through Vicky's fascinating story and the unforeseen perils of mind reading. He'd also briefed her on the people they would be up against—as members of *Team Vicky*. Despite the stature and means of their opponents, Skylar was walking into their first strategy meeting feeling excited rather than intimidated. Simply put: she craved a noble mission and a novel challenge—regardless of the risk.

"Where should we begin?" Vicky asked, as they gathered around her table.

When no one else jumped in, Skylar voiced a question that had been at the back of her mind. "How do you know it's the lawyers who are trying to kill you, and not some third party?"

Vicky nodded. "Good question. The short answer is that I don't. Not for sure."

Everyone stopped breathing.

"I am certain that they can read minds," Vicky quickly continued. "Your personal experience with Scarlett Slate virtually proves it. When you add to that their trademark glasses and perfect record, all doubt vanishes."

"We also know that they're evil," Chewie added. "Whereas Vicky chose to use her power to counsel and entertain, they chose to pervert justice for financial gain."

"I understand that," Skylar said. "But just because they're evil mind readers doesn't mean they hired the Las Vegas assassin. I'm not trying to be argumentative. I just want to ensure that we address the urgent issue: keeping Vicky alive."

Chewie nodded and turned to Vicky. "How can we confirm that it was the lawyers who sent Vance?"

"That's relatively easy, in theory," Vicky said. "All I have to do is ask—while wearing my glasses."

"Just catch one in an elevator and put the question to him?" Chewie asked.

"It won't be that easy," Chase said, wading in. "They're attorneys who have been at this for decades. I'm sure they've developed thought discipline that normal people don't possess, if for no other reason than to shield awkward thoughts from each other. Getting them to even *think* the truth may require something resembling an interrogation."

"Or finessing," Vicky added. "In my counseling practice, I got people to reveal information all the time without their realizing it. But in any case, I agree we should plan for more than a casual encounter."

"Let's assume for now that we'll find a workable approach and confirm their guilt," Skylar suggested. "What do we do then?"

Chewie put his arm around Vicky. "What's good for the goose is good for the gander."

"Actually, I've been insisting that we be better than the goose," Vicky said, surprising her fiancé before addressing the group. "Surely we can be more creative than club-wielding cavemen."

"You want to negotiate with them?" Chewie asked, his voice more pleading than argumentative. "With the four highest-paid attorneys in the country? With people who have a combined eighty years of experience outwitting other professionals in high-stakes public battles?"

"I want to get creative," Vicky said, slapping her thighs. "What are our options?"

Everyone turned to Chase.

"There are several," he said with a solemn nod. "For starters, you can simply hide and hope to outlive them. You are twenty years younger than they. Alternatively, you could plead for your life, although I would hesitate to expect that group to be either honorable or merciful. You could negotiate, but I agree with

Chewie's assessment and would consider that ill advised. Blackmail is often an option, but that can't involve the obvious because exposing their special skill is the one thing we must avoid. Other than 'the caveman approach' as Vicky put it, that's all I've been able to come up with—so far," he added in a tone that let Skylar know his mind was actively working the problem.

"I agree," Chewie said. "If it can't be blackmail, it's got to be bludgeons or bullets."

Vicky shot to her feet. "Come on, people! There must be other tactics we could use? Something creative. Something twenty-first-century."

Skylar watched her husband working the problem. Vicky had pushed his buttons, deftly making it a matter of pride. Everyone watched his mental struggle while silently sipping their morning coffee.

At last, Chase began to think out loud. "Our goal is twofold. We want them to stop thwarting justice, and to leave Vicky alone. Correct?"

"Correct," Vicky replied.

"The problem exists because they invented the same system you did. And whereas you both quickly realized that the discovery had to be kept secret, they went on to deploy it for evil means, whereas you used it for good. Correct?"

Again, Vicky concurred.

Chase raised both index fingers. "If they lost their ability to read minds, would they cease to be a threat? To you and to justice?"

That was an interesting thought. Skylar wasn't sure it would lead anywhere, but she felt a stab of pride nonetheless.

"It would end the threat to justice," Vicky said. "As for me, well, that's less clear. I suppose I'd still be a threat to the world in their minds, but they'd no longer need to worry about me inadvertently exposing their professional treachery."

"What are you thinking?" Chewie asked.

Chase leaned forward, excitement in his eyes. "Do you know what an EMP is? An electromagnetic pulse?"

"A burst of energy powerful enough to fry electronic circuitry."

"That's right. I'm wondering if that might be the solution we're looking for."

Vicky shook her head before the echo died. "I do appreciate the lateral thinking, but even if we managed to sabotage both the glasses they're wearing and all their spare pairs, I'm sure they'd just build new ones."

"No doubt," Chase agreed. "But I'm not considering using an EMP to fry their equipment. I'm thinking about using one to blast their brains."

39
The Hitch

VICKY QUICKLY DISMISSED Chase's fanciful idea of a mental EMP. A blast that would rob the RRS&S lawyers of their ability to read minds. "I truly appreciate your ingenuity, but the physiology doesn't work that way."

This time, it was Chase who didn't back down. "Not to be insensitive, but wasn't that how you lost your hearing? The explosion overloaded the anatomy of your ears to the point where they could no longer perform an operation as sensitive as distinguishing variations in sound waves?"

"Well, generally speaking, yes. But—" She paused there, remembering.

"What is it?" Chewie asked, after a few seconds of silence.

"The attorneys of RRS&S aren't using brainwave-to-text software like I do. And they don't appear to be using brainwave-to-voice software like I would be if I could hear. I checked every photo I found on high magnification and saw nothing in their ears."

"So, what are they doing?" Chase asked.

"As far as I can tell, their mind reading system works like a bridge." Again, she paused to process.

"A bridge?" Skylar prompted. They were all entranced.

Vicky nodded, as much to herself as to the others. "I briefly considered another approach early in my research. My system collects signals en route to conscious thought and then transforms them into speech, which it displays as speech-to-text. What they're doing, I believe, is transporting that data directly into their own streams of consciousness."

"So there's never a record of what they're doing," Chase said, sounding excited. "That helps explain how they've kept the secret for so long despite using it in court—where all eyes are on them."

"They'd have no record of thoughts they miss or forget," Chewie said, wading in. "But that's probably a wise tradeoff. Would that system be more difficult to invent than yours, or easier?"

"Today, their system would be more difficult, because figuring out how to funnel the data back into a brain is another nut to crack. But back in the late 1990s, which is when they appear to have made the discovery, that may have been easier than thought-to-text or thought-to-voice, because the software and electronics I'm using weren't invented yet. Plus, it's the more intuitive approach. I only sought to go the thought-to-text route because I was already using voice-to-text."

"I don't get it," Chewie said. "Whenever their system is turned on and focused, they have a second voice in their heads?"

"Yes," Vicky said, nodding along. "That would take a bit of getting used to, but it would not be that big a deal. Consider your ability to focus on different voices in a crowded room. Or the way bilingual people can switch languages. Our brains are wired to sort and shift focus between sensory inputs."

"So getting back to my initial question," Chase said. "Do you think the mental-EMP solution is a possibility?"

"It isn't an option if they're doing what I'm doing. But it might be if they're going direct, brain-to-brain rather than brain-to-device."

"Might be?" Chase pressed.

"I'd need to experiment. First to find out if it's possible to selectively destroy the required cells, and then to develop a weapon, if that's what you'd call it."

"That sounds like your next move," Chewie said.

"Wait a minute," Chase said, visibly deflating. "What would be the point if they could just switch to Vicky's system?"

Vicky had already considered that. "They can't switch to it if they don't know about it. Their natural assumption will be that I'm doing what they did. We just need to keep my method concealed."

"But they've surely seen you with your phone," Skylar pressed.

"They've seen a deaf person using voice-to-text—for as long as they've been watching me. Nothing changed when I cracked the mind-reading code, except for adding the glasses, which is what they were looking for."

Chase nodded along. "What we need to worry about is their reading the solution in our minds."

"Good point," Chewie said.

"How long will the experiments take?" Chase asked.

"Knowing what I already know, and given the right biological supplies and equipment and perhaps a bit of luck, I think I could figure it out in a day or two."

"That's fantastic!" Chewie said. "What a great brainstorming session. We figured out how to save your life and the planet without shedding blood."

Skylar also looked pleased, but Chase's expression told Vicky he knew what was coming. She cleared her throat. "There is one hitch."

All eyes turned back to her.

"The only place that has what I need for the experiments is my lab at Caltech. To create an EMP, I need to go home."

40

The Missions

CHEWIE FELT WHIPLASHED from the hard right turn their brainstorming session had taken. One second, Team Vicky was discussing how to outflank the attorneys; the next, his fiancée was talking about walking into the crosshairs of their assassin. "You can't go back to your lab, Vic. That's the one place they're certain to be watching for you."

"No doubt," Skylar said. "Surely you have friends at other universities who would let you use their labs?"

Vicky shook her head. "The equipment I used isn't like a laser printer. You can't just plug it in. It's custom configured and calibrated. To construct my setup, I'd have to tear theirs down."

"Only if it's in use," Chewie pressed. "You could phone around, hope to get lucky."

"Phoning around to colleagues is another easily anticipatable move," Chase said. "If they're watching her lab, they're likely watching her peers too."

"It's not just hardware that I need," Vicky said. "There's software and tissue samples and notebooks. As you might imagine, these are very sophisticated, complex, and precise operations we're talking about. Trust me, my lab is the only option."

Chewie's heart was sinking as his mind snagged on something Chase had just said. "Why did you say '*if* they're watching her lab'? Isn't that guaranteed?"

Chase refilled his coffee before replying. This was quite the breakfast meeting. "Surveillance is a major undertaking. Especially the long-term type that applies here, given that Vicky has been gone for months.

"To provide 24-hour coverage would require a minimum of three people. And where would you put them? That's a long time for a van to be parked across from your lab. Plus, we're talking about a law firm, not the LAPD or the FBI. Lawyers aren't going to be equipped for this. We're likely just up against one guy—given the way bounty hunters and private investigators operate. And remember," Chase added, raising a finger. "They're trying to keep the situation super-secret. Plus there's no real urgency. Cassandra isn't performing, so you're not an active threat."

"You think it's safe?" Vicky asked.

"No, I don't. They'd hire the best guy they could find, which is likely the best guy in the world, given all their wealth and connections. Someone like that would almost certainly put electronic surveillance in place. If I were their guy, I'd covertly enter your lab and install one of those off-the-shelf home security systems that sends an alert with video whenever motion is detected."

"Where would the alert go?" Chewie asked.

"To the assassin's phone."

"And he could be anywhere in the world, right?" Vicky asked. "I mean, they're from New York. I bought a ticket from Las Vegas to Buenos Aires via Miami. What are the odds that the assassin will be in Southern California?"

"Low," Chase concurred. "But not risk-your-life low."

Chewie didn't need mind reading to see his fiancée hatching a plan. That worried him. Her safety wasn't just his concern, it was his responsibility.

He had failed to protect her in Reno, and he would bear the shame of that night till the day he died. And that was before they got engaged. Before they'd even become romantically involved. Now, well, Chewie just couldn't live with himself if he let anything happen to her.

Vicky pressed on. "We could go in the evening and I could work through the night. I'll order the supplies I need in advance. Have them delivered to a nearby hotel. I'll be in and out before he can react—assuming he did as Chase suggested with the security monitor. Not everyone's that savvy. I'd probably have gone to the neighbors under false pretenses and paid them to alert me of any activity—which they'd be unlikely to notice after midnight."

"Sounds too risky," Chase said. "Why risk your life to save theirs, when they put you in this position to begin with? Especially when we don't know if the EMP idea will work."

"I agree," Skylar said. "Bullets are proven. I know that sounds harsh, but take it from someone who's been on the receiving end of an evil plan. It's better to err on the side of caution."

Skylar had hinted that she'd been assaulted during the conspiracy that united her with Chase, but she'd never gone into detail.

Vicky said, "I have been assaulted. They sent an assassin for me."

Skylar shook her head. "I don't mean to diminish that experience. But to use an analogy, narrowly avoiding a car crash isn't the same thing as being in one."

"What happened to you, back then?" Chewie asked.

Skylar turned his way. "I don't want to give you nightmares. Mine are enough for all of us. Trust me when I say that nothing shreds a person's pacifist tendencies like barely surviving a deadly and devious assault."

"I believe you," Vicky said. "But I'm not there and I hope never to be. No offense."

"I understand," Skylar said somberly.

"I just don't want to come out of this scarred beyond recognition," Vicky continued.

"I get it," Skylar said. "I felt exactly the same way. Ask Chase. We discussed it at length back then. But remember, it's not just your life that you're putting at risk. These people wear suits and go to society functions, but they're essentially serial killers. We saw

Scarlett Slate deny justice to a grieving couple who lost their daughter. Just one of a thousand such instances, I'm sure."

Chewie saw that Vicky was stirred but not moved. She said, "We'll take precautions. Don't they make bulletproof clothing for celebrities? We can wear that, just in case."

"When you say *we*, who are you including?" Skylar asked, putting her arm around Chase's shoulders.

"Myself and my fiancée."

Chewie felt a warm and most-welcome jolt surge through his body. Like Skylar, he had been assuming that Vicky was referencing Chase. But she'd picked him. She'd picked him! Trusted him—over Chase—with her life.

A swell of manly pride overtook Chewie and he rode it like a surfer on a perfect wave. He'd never loved anyone more than he loved Vicky at that moment.

"I should go with you to Pasadena," Chase said. "It's a question of experience, not competence. I know what to look for and how to avoid or counteract it."

Vicky crossed her arms. "I won't hear of it. That's not fair to your wife, and there's no need. Chewie's perfectly capable of looking after me."

"I have no doubt that he is—under normal circumstances. But we're talking about evading a professional assassin."

"Which we're doing by going in after dark and getting out before dawn."

"It's not that simple. Why don't we all go?"

"Actually, I was hoping that when Chewie and I go to California, you'd go to New York."

"For what purpose?" Chase asked, although he appeared to know exactly what Vicky had in mind.

"To do the one thing that I, with my familiar face, and Chewie, with his distinctive features, can't do. I'm hoping that you and Skylar will spy on the partners of Resseque Rogers Sackler & Slate.

Identify their weaknesses, learn their habits, and devise a plan we can use to interrogate them."

41
Tripwires

New York City

THE PARTNERS of Resseque Rogers Sackler & Slate all worked similar hours. Similar, but not identical. Each had his or her own morning or evening rituals, be it exercise, caffeination, quiet solitude, or socializing. Therefore, it was unusual for more than two partners to ride the apartment elevator down together in the morning.

Scarlett had been mildly surprised to see Colton exiting his apartment as she opened her door, and more so when the elevator stopped on eleven to allow both Sackler and Rogers to board as well. That made for a tighter ride than the bodyguards would usually allow, with eight passengers total, but her guy and Colton's stepped aside to let the others aboard before closing ranks to create a wall of muscle. An eight-foot phalanx, in sunglasses and black suits.

Sackler glanced around thoughtfully then shot an arm past his bodyguard to hit a button, "Let's stop on ten to get an update from Trent while we're all together."

Walter Sackler, Scarlett's partner in criminal law, was the worrywart of the group. The glass-half-empty, it's-going-to-rain-soon guy. While his pessimism could be bothersome, he'd saved them from numerous blunders over the years, and Scarlett was grateful to have him on the team. Balance was a wonderful thing.

They walked into Trent's apartment to find him sprinting on a treadmill positioned before an open window overlooking Central Park. He was by far the fittest of the five, given that he hadn't spent the last twenty years behind a desk. When they'd formed the partnership, Scarlett had thought Trent was getting the short end of the stick, given that he'd have to remain in the shadows while they garnered fame and glory. In retrospect, she realized that he'd gotten the better deal.

Trent didn't stop or even slow his run as they entered. "Morning. What's up?"

"We happened to be riding down together and decided to stop in for an investigation update," Sackler said.

"That won't take long. I've got nothing to report on either front. Fredo hasn't caught Cassandra's scent yet, and none of my overseas guys have anything definitive on Pascal's secret new venture."

"What do they have that's not definitive?" Colton asked.

"Well, there's the rub. All the big tech firms have secret skunkworks operations, many of which are operating blind. That is, they don't know who's really paying their bills, and they know not to ask. The idea being to further insulate them from exactly this kind of corporate espionage."

"So your guys have found operations, just not ones they can link to Pascal or the name LEXI?"

"Exactly."

"How many, and where?"

"Dozens in China, India, and Southeast Asia. Dozens in Europe, both Eastern and Western. Half a dozen each in the Middle East, Australia, and South America." Trent was speaking normally, despite maintaining a pace beyond Scarlett's reach. She knew that he often multitasked that way, running while talking on the phone, and promised herself to do more of the same.

"So they're going to prioritize and dive deeper?" Colton asked.

"Exactly."

"What's the timeline?"

"Unpredictable. When they find it, they find it. Could be in five minutes or five months."

"And the only way to speed things up is to throw more people at it?"

"Correct."

Colton looked around before answering. "We can't risk it. The operation might backfire."

Everyone nodded. If Pascal discovered that they were looking for leverage to increase their ownership percentage, he might cut it in retaliation. They were hooked and he'd be offended that they'd spurned his generous fifty-fifty split.

"Let's return to the Fredo discussion," Sackler suggested. "What has he discovered?"

"Vicky Pixler drained her bank account and has likely been living off that cash. She's completely off the grid. Given her clean escape and the fact that she's doing nothing electronically traceable, Fredo has been putting tripwires in place."

"Tripwires?" Sackler asked.

"When you can't follow someone, your next best move is to anticipate where they will be going. In this case, rather than stringing wires across jungle paths, Fredo is putting electronic detectors in the virtual and physical locations Pixler is most likely to visit, hoping to discover her whereabouts."

"Virtual and physical?"

"If she visits certain places or uses her passport or a credit card, he'll immediately get an alert with the details."

"That's it?" Sackler said, his tone expressing the disappointment Scarlett also felt. "She's in hiding, living off cash. She knows to avoid all that."

Trent didn't flinch. "Cash runs out and people get lazy, desperate, or bored. Don't underestimate those factors."

"Tripwires trip everyone who doesn't know to step around them," Colton said. "How is he making them specific to Pixler? I assume he doesn't fly to Pasadena every time the mailman visits her house."

"Fredo installed video surveillance systems with sophisticated facial recognition software. They're programmed to look for her. When one goes off, he gets the picture on his phone."

Colton nodded, satisfied. "Where did he install those sophisticated systems of his?"

"He's got one in Pasadena, and another in Las Vegas."

"Makes sense. But there's one more I'd like him to add."

"Where's that?"

"In the lobby of our office building."

Colton's words hit Scarlett like a block of ice. "Won't that tip him off to our identities? I really don't want him learning who we are. I'll get nightmares if he knows my face."

"No worries," Colton said. "Hundreds of people work in our building and thousands come and go every day. There's anonymity in those numbers."

"So the building lobby, but not our office or our apartment building?" Sackler clarified.

"Exactly."

Scarlett wasn't satisfied. "I get the logic, but not the reason. Why risk drawing Fredo's attention to our office building?"

Trent stopped running and wiped his brow. "In case Vicky Pixler gets sick of hiding and comes for us."

42
Oversight

Pasadena, California

THE GLASS CUTTER slipped from his grasp and fell fifteen feet to the ground as Chewie balanced atop the long ladder. Fortunately, he was finished cutting. As he palmed the small mallet that had come from the same Pasadena hardware store, Chewie reflected that he had never broken into a house before. Then again, his time with Vicky was characterized by unique experiences. Bizarre experiences. Mind-bending, eye-opening, horizon-expanding experiences.

He loved it.

He loved her.

The months he'd spent beside Vicky had been the best of his life.

And they were just beginning.

If he didn't screw up.

Chewie had taken Chase's guidance and tutelage very seriously. Deadly seriously. Including the admonition to avoid the front and back doors of her house, and even the ground floor. Fortunately, they could accomplish that by entering on the second floor and taking the elevator directly to the basement laboratory.

Chewie had hoped to find one of the second-floor windows unlocked, but none were. Then he'd hoped to rock one of them off its latch, but all the fittings were too tight. So now he was attempting option three: punching out a hole in the corner that was large enough to fit his arm.

"Here goes," he said, drawing back the mallet.

"Wait! I forgot to disarm the alarm." Vicky whipped out her phone and performed the operation while Chewie's stomach did a cartwheel.

What was he doing? Despite her insistence to the contrary, Chewie was certain that Vicky had brought him rather than Chase to soothe his ego. He should have resisted, but he'd wanted to prove himself. That was selfish and foolish, he now realized. Looking up at the bright Southern California moon, he recalled a line from the movie *Top Gun* about his ego writing a check that his body couldn't cash.

"It's okay," Vicky said, reading his mind without the aid of her glasses. "We got this."

Punching out the glass took more force than Chewie had expected, but once it popped, the rest was a breeze. He reached in, released the lock, and they climbed into the upstairs landing without causing significant damage.

The house smelled of still air with a background layer of floral-scented disinfectant. It made Chewie think of Vicky's quadriplegic mother, and all the effort that must have gone into maintaining her health. He'd heard a few stories while they cruised the Caribbean, but being there really completed the picture.

They avoided both bedrooms and went straight to the basement, which lit up automatically as they walked in. An accommodation for mom, Chewie was certain.

"I'm going to need a few hours here, then we'll head over to campus to use a machine I don't have. Feel free to take a nap," Vicky said.

"Not much chance of that."

He watched with fascination while Vicky went about her magic, consulting encrypted computer files and lab notebooks at first, then moving on to the mice. She'd brought three dozen with them, all pure white and labeled with leg bands. All obtained from a specialty supplier, The Jackson Laboratory in Maine.

To examine the rodents, she was using a small transparent harness positioned at the focal point of multiple sensors. The setup looked like the opening scene of a cartoon where a mouse was about to be transformed into something else. But these mice didn't visibly react to her electronic activities.

An hour or so later, once Vicky had cycled through the first half-dozen test subjects, making adjustments and maintaining focus with robotic precision, she turned Chewie's way. "Time to hit the big lab."

They grabbed the six mice, a special tray, and Vicky's passkeys, then reversed course upstairs, out the window, down the ladder, and across the street onto the central block of the Caltech campus. The labs were long colonnaded buildings that exuded timeless grandeur. Chewie could virtually feel the 130-year accumulation of big brainwaves emanating from their limestone walls.

"What's next?" he asked.

"Functional Magnetic Resonance Imaging, fMRI. I'll be sedating the mice with etomidate to keep them still, and then watching how their brains perform after being exposed to various—" she paused there to smile, "brain EMPs."

"What will you be looking for?"

"Severely reduced activity at a specific point on the spectrum, combined with normal activity on the surrounding ranges."

Sounded to Chewie like she was describing a neurological smart bomb, but he didn't want to get into it at the moment, so he kept the observation to himself. They were tiring, but facing a long road ahead. It was just a quarter past midnight.

She anesthetized the six mice and precisely positioned them in numeric order on the slotted tray they'd brought from her lab. She placed the tray on the bed before the big doughnut of a machine and they retreated to the control room.

"How long will this take?" he asked.

"I already have a program in the machine's memory and their

brains are tiny, so just a few minutes."

"Why just six mice?" he asked, once the machine was humming.

"We'll need multiple iterations as I try to focus in on the most precise settings. If their brain is a country, this will give me the state. Then we'll go for the city, and finally the street we need."

"But aren't mouse brains a lot different from human brains?"

"They're a lot more similar than you'd think. Not as close as primates, but much easier to use in tests for the obvious reasons. Alzheimer's-related experiments, for example, are usually done on mice. And they're a good fit for what I do as well, thank goodness."

"But they're so small."

"Size doesn't matter nearly as much as common sense would make you believe," Vicky said, studying the live image feed. "You can even use fruit flies for some neurological experiments. Where size is an issue, in cardiovascular implant research and training for example, swine models tend to be used. We always try to work as far down the food chain as possible." She stopped there as the machine completed its routine.

"How's it look?"

"I got a clean hit on mouse three, which is a very good sign. Middle of the anticipated range. Time for iteration two."

The campus looked beautiful in the moonlight, with the gently swaying hundred-year-old magnolia trees and the twinkling water features. Chewie was enjoying the connection to Vicky's past. She seemed to be feeling it too, as she reached to take hold of his hand.

It almost felt like a first date as they returned to her house, the only two people out at that hour. Would they ever live there, he wondered? It was a beautiful place. A special place. Majestic at night and no doubt magical when infused with the energy of a thousand of the world's brightest student minds.

He got so caught up in the moment that he didn't realize their mistake until it was almost too late. But something about seeing Vicky reach for her keys flipped a switch and he pulled her back a second before her hand closed on the front doorknob.

Vicky started to voice the obvious question when the answer struck and her face dropped. "Habit," was all she said.

They quickly skirted around to the side of the house where the ladder stood concealed between two cypress trees. They paused there to scan for a reaction while their pulses returned to normal. Nothing appeared to have changed, but then it wouldn't, would it? "I'm going to stand watch on the roof during the next round, if that's all right with you?"

"Better to *lie* watch," Vicky replied. "We don't want anyone calling the police." She kissed him, climbed the ladder, and disappeared inside.

43

Stairway to Heaven

FREDO BLANCO was a homeless millionaire. It made no sense for him to maintain a residence. He was always on the road in pursuit of people in flight. He had no family, and his friendships were of the short-term, superficial variety, primarily with the concierges and bartenders at the four- and five-star hotels where he hung up his weapons at night.

His weapons, Fredo mused.

Theoretically, he owned them, controlled them, but like big dogs with small masters it wasn't entirely clear from the observable activity who was truly in charge.

Fredo had built his arsenal and honed his skills to utilize objects that could pass airport carry-on inspections one hundred percent of the time. Thus his predilection for stilettos that could sever arteries or pass through rib cages with stealth and speed. The thin ceramic blades allowed him to kill silently without spraying blood and then leave the scene before anyone but the victim was even aware of his crime.

As for firearms, Fredo stuck with elegant .22s, which he bought by the case. They were just as deadly as their bigger brothers when wielded by masterful hands, and they created much less mess, staying within the body rather than blasting out the back. He wouldn't want to take them into a gunfight, but Fredo hadn't been in one of those since leaving the cartel. He relied on stealth and surprise rather than superior firepower.

Despite their diminutive size, you still couldn't carry a .22 onto a plane, of course. Therefore, in situations like these, when it was likely that an electronic alert would launch a race against the clock,

Fredo would open a convenient P.O. box during a reconnaissance trip and store a pair there.

Today, the 4:04 a.m. alert that sent him scrambling to catch a 6:00 a.m. flight from Miami to Los Angeles made him very glad he had.

Before tracking his quarry to Miami, Fredo had installed electronic surveillance in the locations to which Victoria Pixler was likely to return. Namely, her home/laboratory in Pasadena and her apartment in Las Vegas.

The facial recognition system hidden in the lamp beside the front door of her home got a hit at 1:04 a.m. local time. The hour indicated either that she'd arrived on a late flight, good, or that she was actively attempting to avoid surveillance, bad.

The video showing that she and Quinten had retreated without opening the door indicated the bad option, avoiding surveillance. The related puzzle, one which had occupied Fredo during his flight, was figuring out what had caused their last-second abort. It was hard to explain without factoring in the psychic powers that his employers insisted she enjoyed, given that his hidden camera was virtually invisible.

In any case, whether Vicky was spooked or not, gone, or not, Fredo considered the sighting to be a big breakthrough. It put him on a hot trail and gave him the cool comfort of knowing that she wasn't camping in Costa Rica or hiking the Himalayas.

Ironically, her wariness also made him hopeful. People on the run didn't return to their homes without a compelling reason. An urgent need. With luck, hers would require no less than nine hours.

A first-class ticket with no bags put him in an Uber at LAX at 9:20 a.m. local time. A forty-four-minute drive dropped him at his Caltech P.O. box just after 10:00. Whether or not he would convert the electronic sighting and subsequent transcontinental dash into an immediate kill or just a hot lead remained to be seen.

The Caltech campus was quiet, as places tended to be on Sunday mornings. Her home showed absolutely no sign of activity. He spent a few minutes studying it from afar with a monocular before circling around the block to appraise it from the back. That vantage also yielded no signs of life. No lights or shadows. No open curtains or stuffed trashcans.

Rather than risk tramping through the backing neighbor's yard, Fredo opted for a much more innocent-looking approach. He waited until the sidewalks on both sides of her road were clear, then went straight up the front walk—triggering his own surveillance system, no doubt, but hopefully attracting no human attention. Just shy of the door he turned right and began circling the house, searching for signs that couldn't be observed from the front or rear.

His heart leapt as he completed three quarters of the circle. Propped between two cypress trees, he spotted a ladder leading to an open window.

44
Soul Concern

AFTER LYING WATCH on the roof through Vicky's second round with the mice, and then again with the third, the light of dawn forced Chewie back inside for the remaining tests. He'd expected a maximum of six iterations, given that she'd started with six mice and had brought thirty-six, but apparently that wasn't how it worked. She was dialing in her settings using three rodents per round, then spending a lot of time studying the fMRI images and perfecting her calculations.

They'd made the last three trips to the Caltech lab without the cover of darkness. Since it was a Sunday morning during summer break, the campus was relatively quiet. Still, climbing in and out of the window was becoming increasingly perilous as the morning dragged on.

At the moment, Chewie was sipping coffee and studying his fiancée. When they first met, he'd been attracted to her beauty and impressed by her charm. Then he got to know her mind and had fallen head over heels. Even after learning her secret, Chewie remained thoroughly impressed. Yes, she had a magical tool, but she also had an incredible gift. She knew how to use it, like Da Vinci did a paintbrush, or Michelangelo a chisel.

Furthermore, Vicky had chosen to use her invention to entertain and counsel. She'd wielded it for good, in stark contrast to her justice-thwarting adversaries.

Now that Chewie was observing a whole new array of Vicky Pixler's skills, his love, already in full bloom, was positively bursting. His admiration was hitting levels he'd never known before.

Watching her press on despite the weariness and stress, he felt deeply honored that she'd selected him, truly perplexed that she'd done so, and profoundly committed to ensuring her safety. Plus, he had to admit as he brewed a fresh pot of coffee on her laboratory machine, he felt a bit frightened that she'd wake up one day and realize that she could probably replace him with a billionaire or luminary.

Instead of dwelling on that uncomfortable thought and allowing doubt to take root, he resolved to work hard to make himself worthy. To earn the coveted spot by that remarkable woman's side.

"Coffee's ready," he called as she shifted her focus from her laptop to a notebook.

"Good. I'm going to need it," she said, stretching. "I'm not getting the results I'd expected and we're running out of mice."

"What's the hitch?" he asked, pouring.

"I'm targeting a minute area on a specific type of receptor, and —." She paused to collect her thoughts and steal a sip. "You've burned things using a magnifying glass and the sun before, right?"

"Sure."

"Well, this is analogous to working with two friends to combine your three magnifying glass beams to brown individual needles on a pine tree without damaging any non-targeted needles or twigs or branches or bugs or bark or sap. You get the picture. Anyway, either the needles aren't getting brown enough or different anatomies are also burning. The challenge is determining which of the lenses needs adjusting and by how much. There are sophisticated models for optimizing experiments like this, but they're not perfect and luck plays a part."

Chewie could only imagine. "How many more rounds do you anticipate?"

"Minimum of one, maximum of five. We should grab breakfast."

"I agree, but if you're thinking five is as likely as one, let's plan to eat at the hotel. We can come back after dark when it's safer and you've got some sleep in you."

Chewie watched her weigh his words, then set down her coffee cup. "Good idea."

As they ascended in the elevator, he asked, "Do you think it's safe to hide the ladder behind a tree, or should we take it with us?"

"To the hotel?"

"We'll leave it in the rental car."

"No, the tree's—" She stopped mid-sentence as the opening elevator door revealed closed curtains. Then Chewie heard a bang and saw a double-flash as a breathtaking blow hit the center of his chest and Vicky toppled backward into the elevator as if struck by an invisible boxer.

His lizard brain grasped the essence of the situation. It drove the focus of his eyes even as his heart screamed and his mind hastened to react. Standing before the big mirror in the corner, as casual as one could be while raising two guns, was an assassin.

This man was much smaller and paler than the one from Las Vegas. Obviously much smarter, as well. He'd waited for them to come to him. He hadn't given Vicky the opportunity to read his mind. He hadn't initiated a brief "say your prayers" or "the lawyers of RRS&S send their regards" conversation. He'd simply pulled two triggers and put two bullets in their chests, center mass.

But Chewie hadn't died.

Two more bullets struck Chewie's chest as he launched himself toward the threat, the small assassin, the evil man determined to end the remarkable life of Victoria Pixler. While he registered the impacts, he paid them no heed. There might be bullet holes in the windshield, but the plane was still flying. He might be a kamikaze, but that hardly mattered. All he cared about, his sole concern, was keeping his size XXL bulletproof vest between the killer and Vicky, long enough for her to escape. He met her eye for the final time in the mirror, and yelled "Run!"

45
Tenacity

FREDO COULD NOT have been happier, although you wouldn't have known it by looking at him. He wasn't one to wear his emotions. In fact, his natural range was pretty narrow.

His creator had cut the tops off his emotional peaks and used them to plug the valleys, benevolently shielding the white elf from the worst of what waited in life. That made it possible for Fredo to survive soul-wrenching experiences without lasting damage. For that saving numbness, he was willing to trade his peak highs—like the euphoria he'd have enjoyed while silently waiting in Vicky's chair, savoring the knowledge that his targets were already as good as dead.

Everybody knows not to use an elevator if there's a fire. Signs warn that they can be deadly traps. What people tend to forget is that there's more than one kind of fire—and more than one type of trap.

Sitting comfortably in the dark as Pixler's elevator began humming, his relaxed hands holding a matched pair of .22s rather than a teacup and box of bonbons, he thought about the second million that was but seconds away.

Case durations were unpredictable, but given his average record, he lived like a guy earning a hundred grand a month. One who might not live to see Christmas. First-class travel, five-star hotels, the finest food, and escorts so hot that all observers assumed he was a rock star.

This job would net him two million in just one month. Time to buy the beachfront bungalow with live-in housekeeper and chef. Or maybe a hilltop estate. While waiting for the next just-right job to come along, he'd spend his time talking to real estate agents.

But first...

Fredo stood and raised both .22s as the elevator drew closer. The angles at which he held his arms were quite different. His left pointed straight out, given that Victoria's height matched his own. His right angled upward toward her mammoth companion's center of mass.

The elevator door slid open.

The oblivious couple emerged.

Fredo fired. Two simultaneous trigger squeezes.

The woman toppled backward.

The man remained standing.

That was predictable, given the size of the slug that had hit him.

While there were many reasons that Fredo favored .22 caliber handguns, the drawback to his selection was bullet mass. Stopping power. The F in $F = ma$. Even though he used a heavy 55-grain .22 caliber bullet, that only gave him about half the mass of a .38, a third the mass of a 9mm, and a quarter the mass of a .45.

There was, however, a simple fix to the shortcoming presented by Newton's Second Law. To increase the force delivered by his bullets, Fredo simply had to fire multiple times. Fortunately, that was not a difficult task when two handguns were in play.

Bringing his left arm up parallel with his right, Fredo gave both triggers a second squeeze.

The ogre kept coming.

Fredo squeezed both again.

The ogre barely flinched. It was almost as if his target's mammoth companion was bulletproof. Dammit! Fredo realized he'd failed to predict the obvious. His mark and her makeshift bodyguard were discreetly wearing bulletproof clothing.

Fredo hated the unpredictability of headshots. Heads turned, bowed, ducked, and canted. They had thick bones running at irregular angles. But most of all, he hated the mess. The head was more vascularized than any other part of the body. And shots to the head differed from shots to the chest in that the blood had no place to go but out.

Therefore, he always aimed center mass.

But at that very moment, in that very room, with that tenacious target, he had no choice. By the time he'd fired the third set of rounds, the charging beast was nearly on him. He was so close as he shouted "Run!" that Fredo couldn't even hold his arms straight as he pointed one barrel at each unflinching eye and squeezed.

46
The Loss

THE EXPLOSION that had taken her father, her hearing, and her mother's mobility had changed Vicky's life in the blink of an eye. It had cleaved her existence into two sections so varied, so different, that they seemed unrelated but for the common thread of Caltech.

Unfortunate as that life-altering incident had been, the explosion had bestowed one blessing. It had rendered her unconscious.

The concussive blow that had thoroughly fried her auditory canal had knocked her out for hours. By the time Vicky had come to her senses, she was already in a hospital bed. She'd been spared the sights, sounds, and smells of the carnage. She hadn't seen her father's corpse or her mother's mangled body. Her memory skipped straight from an afternoon stroll with her family to awakening in an unfamiliar bed. Disconcerting, yes. Nightmare-inducing, no.

This time, the cleaver was not so kind.

This time, the question wasn't whether nightmares would come, but whether they would ever stop.

This time, the sights and smells of the carnage were recorded. Because of the mirror, she'd seen Chewie take two bullets to the face as he used his last breath to send her running from the scene.

Her body had obeyed his command as her mind struggled to process his sudden, violent death. She'd run down the stairs and out the door. Across the street and up the block to their rental car. She'd pushed the button then punched the gas and rocketed around the corner without looking back.

Vicky zigged and zagged through turns that took her ever farther away, refusing to drag the little assassin into this freshly severed section of her life. This inconceivably sad, tragically predictable new beginning.

Before she knew it, Vicky found herself back in their hotel room.

She could not believe that Chewie was dead.

The incident simply couldn't be real.

But it was. The bloodshed had been unmistakable.

She wanted to sit in the shower and attempt to soak the grief away. She wanted to send her sorrows down the drain while wailing and mourning beneath a soothing torrent of cleansing water. But she resisted the urge because it wouldn't be safe. Chewie had been carrying a hotel key. A branded piece of plastic that could lead his killer to her location.

So she grabbed the few items they'd brought from the yacht and bolted. She headed north, toward Burbank, and then randomly stopped at an independent hotel. The kind of establishment that, like the one she'd just abandoned, appeared amenable to cash.

Five minutes later, she was in a tub under a shower. Wailing and grieving and letting it out. Fifty minutes after that, she still hadn't moved, but her thoughts were thawing. As the ice receded, inch by inch, she found the power to push her grief aside, if only temporarily. Her thoughts expanded accordingly. From the immediate need to follow that most basic instinct and Chewie's final instruction, to the steps that followed. Those that would begin her new journey.

Where should she go?

Someplace safe and serene was the obvious answer. The compelling, consoling, calming answer. A few months at a remote meditation retreat sounded perfect. Safe for both her body and her mind. She could use that time to reflect, reprioritize, and plan. To thoroughly think through her future moves when the haze of battle and fog of loss weren't hanging so heavy.

California had plenty of such places.

So did Tibet.

The friction of the destination decision melted a few more neurons. Enough to encompass emotions and impulses beyond those driving basic safety. Enough to include feelings more sophisticated than sorrow and fear. But she still felt rudderless. She needed guidance. A push in the right direction. The nudge of a trusted hand.

During her adult life, Vicky had essentially relied on just two people for advice. Her mother and Chewie. Both were now gone. Vicky fought the impulse to go to her mother's grave. To hug the tombstone and let it all out. That was perhaps the single most predictable move she could make, and hence the most foolhardy. Even riskier than visiting one of Southern California's major commercial airports.

One idea leapt forth as she pondered that sad fact. It hit her like a delayed reaction. As if a train of thought dispatched long ago had been delayed by ice on the tracks. Chase and Skylar. She needed to tell them what had happened—and let them know that her plans had changed.

She turned off the water, toweled dry, and trudged out to the pile of clothes she'd abandoned at the base of the bed. Her phone was not there! She searched the small suitcases. It wasn't there either. Vicky was about to check the car when the chilling memory struck. She'd dropped her cell when the assassin's bullet had knocked her off her feet. It was in her house, but it might as well have been on the moon, given the odds of her going to retrieve it.

Before she became a mind reader, losing her cell phone would not have been a big deal. But since she used highly sensitive software to read minds, Vicky no longer synched to the cloud. She kept her phone backed up to flash drives instead. One copy was at her house, the other was on her boat.

Bottom line, Vicky wouldn't be replacing her phone until she returned to the Caribbean, and that was a problem. Without her phone, she was cut off from Skylar and Chase. She had failed to memorize their phone numbers.

In her moment of greatest need, she was all alone.

47
Charles

New York City

CHASE WAS ENJOYING the easiest reconnaissance job of his life. The partners of Resseque Rogers Sackler & Slate not only worked together in one building, they also lived together in another building that was just a block away. Furthermore, given their top-floor locations on Central Park West, both home and office had park views. Therefore, given the nature of optics, people in the park also had views of them.

"I'm concerned that Vicky hasn't called," Skylar said, setting down her birdwatching binoculars.

"They'd planned to work through the night. I bet it took longer than they anticipated, as complicated things tend to do. They likely pushed through and then collapsed in contented exhaustion. She'll call when they wake up."

"It's four o'clock."

"In California, it's only one."

"Yeah, but their body clocks are on Caribbean time."

"Body clocks often don't apply after an all-nighter," Chase said, speaking from experience. "Did you try calling her?"

"I didn't want to wake her."

"But it's four o'clock."

Skylar elbowed him, then hit the second speed dial on her phone. "Hi, it's me. Just checking in. Please call back," Skylar said.

Chase was pleased to hear her keep the voicemail anonymous. They were using burner phones for a reason.

"Let's inspect the residence, shall we?" he said, rising.

Skylar took his proffered hand.

Chase stuffed the blanket and picnic remnants into his backpack, along with the binoculars.

Normally, in a situation like this, he'd have visited the law offices in the guise of a client pitching a case. But the normal rules of reconnaissance didn't apply when one's opposition could read minds. For that matter, as a basic operation security protocol, he and Skylar had agreed to steer clear of anyone who was wearing thick-framed glasses.

Hopefully the doorman at the RRS&S apartment building had perfect vision.

"What do you figure apartments like theirs cost?" Skylar asked, looking up toward the target of their attention as they waited to cross the street.

"I don't know. They're probably north of ten million dollars."

During their first evening in New York City, Chase and Skylar had investigated the RRS&S office building. They'd begun with a quick question in the lobby, then continued with binoculars in the park. Once they knew which floor to study, locating the four partner offices had been easy. The building had only four corners.

Chase had anticipated a tougher time finding their residences. He'd hired four bicycle messengers to follow them home, offering $100 an hour payable if and only if the messenger delivered a photo of their target entering a residence, with a $100 bonus for identifying the floor they went to and another $100 for the specific apartment number. Three had proceeded to walk directly home and the fourth had stopped along the way at a members-only club, before following an hour later, still wearing his necktie. The messengers had made out nicely, and Chase too had been pleased —with everything but the bodyguards. Each partner had one, and all appeared top notch.

"Do you think the partners rotate offices?" Skylar asked.

"What do you mean?"

"Two have park views, two don't."

Chase rode that train of thought to the next stop. "Can you imagine the interpersonal dynamics required for four people to live and work together in the pressure cooker of a New York City law firm for twenty years—when each can read the others' minds. They should write a relationship book."

Skylar gave him a knowing smile. "I think you can explain their success with three common characteristics."

"Oh, yeah? What are those?" he asked with a reciprocal grin.

"A unique ability. A shared secret. And greed."

"I'll defer to your superior intuition on that. Meanwhile, let's focus on giving them a common future." He opened the door and guided his wife toward the prestigious apartment building's concierge.

They made a handsome couple, both being muscular, lean, and tanned as byproducts of their earlier professions, present circumstances, and lifelong habits. And they were richly dressed in European designer clothes that expressed both learned sophistication and a leisurely lifestyle. In other words, inherited wealth.

In Chase's experience, the concierges at elite establishments tended to tack their egos just below the lofty level of the people they served, thereby positioning themselves to look down on everyone else. He figured this affectation was an attempt to balance things out, to subconsciously offset the extreme obsequiousness their pampered employers required. Chase and Skylar had dressed with that in mind.

"Good afternoon. Lovely residence you have here," Chase said in a British accent.

"Thank you. It is a jewel on America's crown. How may I help you, sir, madam?"

"I'm Charles and this is Kitty," he said, extending his hand. "And you are?"

"Also Charles."

"Fancy that. Well, Charles, Kitty and I are looking to spend some time in New York and we want to do it right. This is one of the few buildings that caught our eye. We were hoping for a quick tour."

"A tour? I'm afraid we don't offer those, this being a residential building."

"No, I'm sure you don't. Not typically. But a ten-minute walk through of the common areas and landings could surely be arranged as a courtesy."

"Ah, yes. Realtors typically do as you suggest on the rare occasion when a unit becomes available. Alas, none are listed for sale at the moment."

Chase keyed in on the word *listed*, but didn't pounce. Staying true to his assumed character, he played the ball obliquely. "If I might ask, how many units are there, in total?"

"Twenty-four. Two on each floor."

"All with the same floor plan?"

"Except the ground level," Charles said, gesturing around.

"Excellent. I don't suppose you could recommend an exceptional estate agent? Someone who learns of listings at prestigious properties like these before they become publicly available?"

"As a matter of fact, I can recommend a person fitting that exact description." Charles reached for his desk drawer.

Chase accepted the card of Cynthia Jacobs, Real Estate Agent. While pocketing it, he produced two $100 bills. "We'll be sure to tell Ms. Jacobs who referred us when we call. Meanwhile, how about that walk-through? Perhaps on your bathroom break?"

48
Grave Conversation

Pasadena, California

DESPITE HER BETTER JUDGMENT, regardless of the risk, and against all her impulses but one, Vicky decided to visit her mother's grave. Time had exhausted her willpower and frustration had overridden her restraints. She could no longer resist the urge to unburden her heavy heart.

After many hours of sobbing, she had managed to sleep most of the day away—with the assistance of a few pills and in the absence of any rest the night before. After waking and staring at the ceiling for most of the evening, she'd gone to the self-service shop in the lobby where a pint of coffee toffee ice cream spotted during check-in had caught her eye. As it vanished, the sugar, caffeine, and a noisy neighbor had prompted her into action outside the hotel room.

She'd gone for a drive and been drawn toward the cemetery despite the danger. Pulled toward a mother's comfort by the most primitive of instincts. Once she was close, a bit closer seemed acceptable. It was night after all. Dark and quiet. The next moves followed the same rationale that had taken her to the bottom of the pint container. Just a little bit more.

Before she knew it, Vicky was hugging her mother's tombstone. Her tears resumed flowing at a rate that threatened dehydration, but she immediately felt better. "I lost him, Mom. I found the right man. A smart, kind, and caring man. A man who shared my hopes and values. He said yes, and then I got him killed."

"You blame yourself?"

"Of course. There's no question. If we'd never met, he'd still be alive."

"So you're God now?"

"No."

"Then he was a puppet?"

"No, Mom. Nothing like that."

"Like what, then?"

"He died saving my life."

"From an assassin."

"An assassin sent to kill *me*."

"Sent by who?"

"The lawyers who figured it out first. How to read minds, I mean. Now they want me dead."

"To keep their secret safe."

"Exactly."

"So your fiancé is dead and some selfish lawyers are attempting to kill you."

"That sums it up."

"And what's your solution to this problem?"

"It's not a problem, it's a situation."

"Same difference, dear."

"I'm distraught, depressed, and for the first time in my life I have no clue what to do."

"So you're feeling sorry for yourself."

"No. Well, yes. That's not the point."

"What is the point?"

"The point is that I don't know what to do."

"Well, the first step is obvious. You need to get your facts straight."

"What do you mean?"

"You didn't kill Chewie. He was assassinated by the same people who are attempting to stifle you. Which brings us to the second step."

"Which is?"

"You need to decide which is more important to you: his life or his death."

"What do you mean?"

"Which is going to direct your actions? Are you going to keep doing what you'd be doing with him, or are you going to give it all up because he's not there to do it with you? Which would he want?"

"It's not that easy."

"I think it is. You have to decide. Are you going to honor his sacrifice, by continuing on? Or are you going to let his death kill the fight that's within you? You've always been a lion, Vicky. A fearless, determined go-getter. Don't let Chewie's death transform you into a lamb. That would turn his death from heroic to tragic."

"It's hard, mom."

"Of course it is. And it will be for a long time. But you have to force yourself to move on, for Chewie's sake."

"I'm not sure how."

"Do you remember what I used to tell you whenever you were feeling sorry for yourself?"

Vicky would never forget that broken record. "You quoted from *The Power of Positive Thinking.* You said, 'The best way to forget your own problems is to help someone else solve theirs.'"

She hugged the stone tighter. "Who is that someone else?"

"The same someone you were helping by forgoing your accolades in the first place. Everyone. The greater good. There's a knife pressed to Lady Liberty's throat, and the people holding it are the same ones who shot Chewie."

"And I alone can stop the bleeding. I love you, Mother. You're so wise."

"It's all you, dear. Now go get some sleep, then get back to work."

49
Recovery

IN WHAT BECAME his final mission for the Sinaloa Cartel, Fredo Blanco had tracked down a gang of traitors known today as the Gritando Cinco, the Screaming Five. A greedy group of regional managers who had created a sophisticated cash skimming scheme that had netted them tens of millions of dollars over the course of several years—without ever being detected.

After sufficiently stuffing their mattresses, the five had faked their own deaths by blowing up a fishing boat they were all known to be aboard. Meticulous planning placed the blame on the rival Jalisco New Generation Cartel, and flawless execution left little doubt. The ruse worked and would never have been detected had it not been for a single oversight and the suspicious mind of the man at the top.

El Chapo noted that with the five gone, the revenues coming from their territories actually increased. Rather than fly into a public rage and put the traitors on alert, he kept his conclusion confidential and quietly put Fredo on the case.

Despite the fact that the five had stuck together, lowering their profile to a single spot on the globe, it had taken just four months for Fredo to find them on the Caribbean island of Margarita, off the coast of Venezuela. At that point, he informed El Chapo, got the small army he needed, and turned their retirement castle into a torture chamber.

For five weeks, Fredo broadcast a daily thirty-minute show where he worked the five traitors with tools designed to produce increasingly graphic displays. A show that El Chapo required his organization to watch. While this gave the drug lord his desired result, it led to an unforeseen consequence for his hit man.

The repeated exposure to the spraying and splashing bodily fluids of five debaucherous drug and sex addicts eventually gave Fredo a nearly fatal cocktail of contagious conditions. After the five expired during the season finale, he spent three agonizing touch-and-go months in a hospital recovering. When he finally emerged, he was free of the cartel—a rare thank-you from El Chapo—but saddled with mysophobia and hematophobia, the fears of germs and blood.

While suboptimal for sure, Fredo now considered it a good trade, given the millions he was making from freelancing, thanks to his cartel credentials.

At least he had until today.

Until he found himself pinned to an armchair by a two-hundred-fifty-pound fountain of blood.

Until the horrors of his hospital months came crashing back in a single wave so unexpected and powerful that it snapped a mental circuit breaker and sent his mind scrambling for the serenity of unconsciousness.

Of course, the blown fuse was a reprieve rather than an escape. When his eyes snapped open—some seconds, minutes, or hours later—he was still drenched in blood and pinned to a chair.

Oddly, Fredo did not go berserk.

Perhaps it was the stillness of the situation that made it tolerable.

Perhaps his sensors were still numb from overexposure.

Maybe the extreme overdose had rendered him immune.

In any case, he remained calm. He remained calm while wriggling out from under the crusting corpse. He remained calm while stepping into the shower and standing beneath the torrent until the water going down the drain was no longer pink. And he remained calm while exiting the house, hiding the ladder, and driving away.

He had been unconscious for nearly two hours and in the shower for twenty minutes more. Plenty of time for the police to respond to a 911. Clearly, the neighbors had not been alarmed and Vicky herself had not called. While he was thrilled to have caught that break, Fredo was disappointed that she'd been so savvy.

Women weren't usually smart about such matters.

Had Vicky gone to the police, they'd have interrogated her for hours. He'd have known where to find her. Once Fredo knew a target's location, completing his contract was just a matter of time.

On that note, Fredo realized that despite the loss, he wasn't depressed. If the incident had cured his phobias, if his temporary immunity turned permanent, the net result would be a blessing. In any case, he'd be back on her now-hot trail soon enough.

First, however, he had two unpleasant tasks to complete. The first was calling his clients with an update. He wouldn't actually be using the burner phone they supplied, although the number displayed would match. Out of an abundance of caution, he kept their phone turned off and thus not easily tracked, with its calls forwarding seamlessly through a scrambling relay to his cell where they could be recorded in case a client tried to renege or he was arrested and a deal needed to be made.

This particular call would likely include lots of screaming, but as they say, sticks and stones...

His second pending task was a bit of recruiting. Fredo had to find a few outlaws willing to immediately exchange a few hours of dirty work for a few thousand dollars in cash. Fortunately, he knew of a nearby biker bar that attracted exactly that type of man. All evidence of the crime and Quinten Bacca's corpse would soon exist only in Victoria Pixler's memory.

50
Not Focused Enough

The Caribbean

VICKY WAS THRILLED to find the *Sea La Vie* still berthed next to the *Vitamin Sea*. With its lights on.

She didn't know what she'd have done if her friends' slip had been empty. She had travelled that far by harnessing the winds of grief and converting emotion into motion. But if momentum stalled because her partners had vanished, if she truly found herself alone, Vicky feared her sails would go slack and she'd sink beneath her burden of sorrow.

"Skylar! Chase!" she said, stepping aboard.

The couple emerged from the main room, beaming with relief. "Oh, thank goodness," Skylar said, moving in for a hug. "We were so worried. Sit down, tell us all about it. Where's Chewie?"

The last question hit Vicky like a sledgehammer. She'd known it would be coming, but that didn't keep her chest from cracking. She collapsed in Skylar's arms.

It was daylight when Vicky awoke in the guest cabin of the *Sea La Vie*. Fortunately, she recognized the room, even though she had no recollection of going there. Most of the previous evening was a blur of teary sobs and supportive hugs.

"Good morning," Skylar said, setting down a paperback while rising from a bedside chair. "How are you feeling?"

Vicky took the question seriously. She sat up and did a self-appraisal as her mother whispered a reminder to *Be the lion*. "I feel like a new person. How long did I sleep?"

"About eleven hours," Skylar said, then added, "You took a couple of pills."

That made sense. "Is Chase aboard? I'd like to talk about next steps."

Skylar didn't resist or question. She appeared to intuitively understand Vicky's need to stay afloat by generating forward momentum. "Sure. He's been looking forward to that. We can talk over breakfast."

Vicky did her best to ignore the empty fourth place at the familiar table. A table which, now that she thought about it, was emblematic of the most socially active period of her adult life. The only period during which she not only was part of a twosome, but also enjoyed a relationship with a couple of a similar stripe.

"How much did I tell you last night?" Vicky asked after her first swallow of coffee.

"You walked us through the attack and your escape, but not much else," Skylar said.

"Was I clear? I really don't remember. I was in pretty bad shape."

"You didn't mention the police," Chase said. "Were they involved?"

"You know, I never even considered calling them. At first, all I could think about was fleeing from the killer. After that, it was all about remaining sane, if that makes sense. Reliving the events through hours of police interrogation, while exposing myself to a second, no, a third attempt on my life..." She shook her head, picturing herself locked in a police interview room. "After the discreet and efficient way Bellagio security handled things in Las Vegas, and given that I've been in hiding ever since, calling 911 never struck me as an option. I suppose that puts me in a tough place now, though."

"We'll want to get your story to the detective in charge. I'll take care of that, using an attorney." Chase opened the Notes app on his phone. "I'll emphasize that it was the second professional assassination attempt on you, a celebrity entertainer, and that you have once again fled the country for safety's sake. We'll want to refer him to someone in Las Vegas to corroborate your story. What name should I give him?"

"Basil Bakhshi at the Bellagio. Thank you." She paused there, her train of thought derailed by images of police interrogations.

Skylar took her hand. "Do you need a break?"

"No, I want to press on."

"I understand. Earlier, you mentioned wanting to talk about next steps?"

"Yes. What did you learn in New York?"

"We learned a lot," Skylar said with an encouraging smile. "They all live in the same building, which is just a block from their office. They occupy the top two floors, which require a key to reach by elevator but are also accessible using the stairs. There's a 24-hour concierge desk in the lobby, beneath which are three security monitors, one showing the outside view from the front door, one showing the lobby from the front door, and one split screen showing the inside of both elevators. In short, it's got good security for a residence, but it's no Fort Knox.

"The four RRS&S partners each travel with a bodyguard. As near as I could tell, the bodyguards rotate every eight hours to maintain protection 24/7. Again, very good but it's not the Secret Service.

"Their single biggest security attribute is, of course, their ability to read minds. For that reason, we did not venture inside their offices. We only entered the building's lobby."

"Excellent. Thank you. So to summarize, you think we can get to them but it won't be easy?" Vicky asked.

"Get to them for what?" Chase replied, his voice eager with anticipation.

"How far did you get with your experiments?" Skylar added.

Vicky thought about using her pine needle analogy, but decided to keep it even simpler. "Far enough to make me believe that I can fry the receptor cells required for mind-reading, but short of the focus required to be confident that I won't inflict additional brain damage."

Skylar looked away.

Chase asked, "Where does that leave our operation?"

Vicky felt a warm rush from his choice of pronoun. *She was not alone!* "After what they did to Chewie, I'm no longer concerned with their well-being. Frankly, I couldn't care less about causing additional damage to their brains—assuming they are the ones who sent the assassin."

"Which we'll find out by interrogating them before zapping them."

"Exactly."

"You know, I've been thinking about how we might pull that off," Chase said. "The Pascal trial provides us with perfect cover."

"How so?" Vicky asked.

"If we focus our questioning around Pascal's defense, the lawyers will assume we were sent by either one of the state's witnesses or their lawyers or a woman still in the woodwork. There are plenty of people out there eager to collect millions from the subsequent civil suits."

"In other words, they won't suspect that you sent us," Skylar added, squeezing Vicky's hand.

"I like the sound of that."

"So it's settled," Chase continued. "We're headed to New York."

51
The Third Way

New York City

VICKY SMILED at the real estate agent, happy to be wearing her Pradas with purpose again. Granted, she was using them as a weapon rather than a tool, but ridding the world of those four lawyers was for the greater good, like weeding God's garden. "Cynthia, could you give us a minute alone?"

"Certainly. I'd say take your time but I have another couple coming for a viewing in twenty minutes."

"Thank you. We'll be quick."

Vicky, posing as the British couple's assistant, turned to Skylar and Chase while the listing agent excused herself to the third-floor foyer. "She's not lying about the next appointment, but she's been showing it for a week without takers. Her claim that it just became available refers to the owner moving out, rather than the traditional definition."

"What about the price?" Skylar asked.

"She's expecting to get the full asking price, but isn't certain she'll get it for the full half-year. Hard to find people with both that much cash and the same calendar requirement."

The owner of apartment 3B, a successful romance writer, was going to be spending the next six months in Paris, researching the novels she hoped would put her on the charts in the lucrative French marketplace.

Meanwhile, she hoped to rent out her four-bedroom, five-bathroom Central Park West apartment for a staggering $50,000 per month.

"Do you think she'd take $250,000 if we offered the cash up front?"

Vicky did the math. "That gives Cynthia $15,000 in commission rather than $18,000. I think if you agreed to take care of Charles directly, she'd go for it. He makes ten percent of her six percent, so he's expecting $1,800."

"That sounds like a plan," Chase said.

"Are you sure?" Vicky asked. "That's a lot of money. And I don't know when or even if I'll be able to pay you back." Saying her future was uncertain was like calling Vladimir Putin powerful, or Jeff Bezos rich, or Archibald Pascal inventive.

"There's no need to pay us back. We're in this together as fellow victims of their atrocities," Skylar said.

"And there's no more appropriate use for that money anyway," Chase added.

He opened his wallet and extracted a blank check from a corporate account. After filling it out for $250,000 he handed it to Vicky and said, "Go close the deal and get the keys."

She did.

"Thank you both again," Vicky said, handing over two heavy sterling silver key rings. "Cynthia will swing by tomorrow with the completed paperwork and will answer any questions you might have about the apartment at that time."

Chase nodded. "Getting into the lawyers' building was a stroke of luck to be sure."

"You're really not worried about Slate recognizing you?"

"We'll be careful to avoid her, but between Skylar's new hair color, my stubble beard, and the fact that we'll be wearing wool suits rather than cotton shorts, I'm confident that we'll be safe so long as we don't end up face to face."

Skylar glanced up from her exploration of their new kitchen. "Slate's not looking for us and would probably second-guess herself if she thought she did, given that she only knows us from a short meeting in St. Croix."

While Vicky processed their logic, Skylar motioned to the fancy, fully automated coffee maker before her. "Shall we grab a drink and sit down to discuss our next steps?"

Once each had made a custom beverage and they were seated around the antique oak breakfast table, Chase opened by saying, "I need to better understand how your EMP device will work. Will it be like a ray gun we can shoot them with from across a room? Or more like a bomb we can blast them with in the lobby?"

Vicky waggled her hand. "I have some flexibility, in that I haven't built it yet. Theoretically, I could design a device that used either the ray or the bomb approach. That's largely a question of how much power it employs."

"Theoretically?" Skylar asked.

"Right. While I won't lose any sleep worrying about doing unnecessary damage to their brains, I don't want to be reckless, and I refuse to allow anyone else to be injured in the process."

"We don't want that either," Skylar said.

"How long will the treatment take if the power setting isn't reckless?" Chase asked.

"I'd want to zap them for a full minute."

"Well, that rules out the equivalent of a sniper shot, but it's still manageable."

"What would be the best-case scenario?" Skylar asked, adding, "Let's aim high."

Vicky knew exactly what she wanted to do. "I'd like to use a closed system rather than an open one, to eliminate the possibility of collateral damage. That means placing the device in contact with their heads, like a pair of headphones, rather than employing it from a distance like a gun."

"So we swap out their earbuds for ones that will also shoot the ray?" Skylar clarified.

"That's the right idea, although the system will be much too big and bulky for earbuds."

"But your glasses are so small?"

"Apples and oranges. My glasses are receivers coupled with a tiny Bluetooth transmitter. This is more like a radio station."

"How big are we talking?" Chase asked.

"Like a set of noise-cancelling headphones or a virtual reality headset," Vicky said. "Assuming it will be placed on their heads. It would need to be more like a large toaster or a microwave oven otherwise."

"We could spy on them to see if any or all of them happen to use either device," Skylar suggested.

"That won't work," Chase said. "I'm sure the weight change will be too significant not to notice. We'll need to trick them into putting on our device."

"Or do it at gunpoint in the elevator," Vicky suggested. "Now that we're in the building that shouldn't be too difficult to orchestrate."

"Maybe for the first one, but not for the next three. And don't forget the bodyguards. Or underestimate them."

"Rats. I did forget. And you're right, we'd need to get them all at once that way."

"There is a third option," Skylar said, rising from the table as if hoping the movement would power her thought into flight. "One that doesn't rely on deception, luck, or force."

"Go on," Chase said.

"We could zap the lawyers in their sleep."

52
The Mix-up

VICKY WAS PLEASED with the plan they'd pulled together over the past few days, and thrilled to be actively engaging her enemy. Creative offense fit her personality much better than cowering defense.

And it helped keep her mind off Chewie.

She'd been so swept up in the brainstorming and reconnaissance sessions of the preceding forty-eight hours that the gaping hole in her heart had failed in its efforts to suck her into darkness and swallow her soul. Skylar and Chase deserved most of the credit for that. They had worked hard to keep her occupied, body and mind.

Vicky's affection for the couple was increasing with every step of their shared journey. So was her admiration for their attitudes and skills.

For his latest trick, Chase had picked the stairwell lock to get them into the eleventh-floor foyer, while Skylar was standing watch in the lobby.

"Excuse me," Vicky said, as the housekeeper closed the door on Jim Rogers' apartment. "Are you Laura? The office just sent me over. Would you mind putting this on his desk?" She held out a white legal-size envelope with the RRS&S logo in the corner.

The weary lady managed an "Of course," but paused as she took the envelope. "Can't we just slide it under the door?"

"Better to put it on his desk, don't you think? We wouldn't want it missed or stepped on."

"You'll wait here? I can't let you in."

"Of course. Thank you very much."

As the maid keyed back into the apartment, Vicky scanned the walls for the alarm pad. Their plan depended on Vicky being locked on Laura's mind while she keyed the code, which required the pad to be within a dozen feet of the front door. That was a good bet, but not guaranteed.

She spotted the panel as the door was closing, and locked in on the maid's mind. *4-1-3-1-2-1-9-1 disarm.* The instant she heard the confirming beep, Vicky ran across the foyer to Sackler's door and slid a straightened piece of paperclip into his lock. She then ran back, refocused her Pradas on the same spot, and said, "I really appreciate your help."

No reply.

"I really appreciate your help," she repeated, a few seconds later.

This time she heard, "It's not a problem."

That was enough to get her system refocused in time for *4-1-3-1-2-1-9-1 arm* to crawl across her phone.

After Laura exited and locked the door, Vicky held up a second envelope and gestured toward Sackler's apartment. "This one too, if you don't mind."

The kind housekeeper again said, "No problem," but she spoke too soon. Her key wouldn't fit Sackler's lock. After a few seconds of fruitless fumbling, Vicky said, "Let me try. I worked my way through paralegal school doing janitorial work. Tons of keys. Walking around with all of them I felt like a goat wearing a bell, but it paid the bills."

Laura handed her the small keyring, held from above by Sackler's key.

As Vicky tried the lock to no avail, she said, "Do you have any lip balm in your purse?"

"I think so. How would that help?"

"I'll show you."

While Laura searched her purse, Vicky surreptitiously clamped Sackler's key in a clay sandwich prepared by Chase. A tiny "book" with clay pages adhered inside the covers, which she had clipped behind the hem of her suit coat. It instantly made a mold of Sackler's key. She quickly repeated the procedure on Rogers' key, using a second book.

While Laura dug deeper, Vicky brought her suit coat pocket into contact with the keyhole, prompting the powerful magnet therein to grab the impeding paperclip and extract it from the brass cylinder as she pulled back.

"Will lipstick work?"

"A chapstick would be better. Ooh, I got it," Vicky said, sliding the key home.

"What was wrong?" Laura asked, opening the door and triggering a *beep beep beep* from the adjacent alarm panel.

"I'm not sure. Usually it's collected bits of pocket lint that jam up the works. Sometimes locks just get dirty. The wax from lip balm works as a lubricant in a pinch." While that was true, according to Chase it was bad for the lock. The wax would attract dirt and gunk up the mechanism over time.

"Anyway, now you can put the envelope on Ms. Slate's desk."

"Ms. Slate's desk?" Laura asked, her tone inquisitive.

"Please."

"But this is Mr. Sackler's apartment. Ms. Slate is up on twelve."

Vicky brought her hand to her mouth as Laura, shielding the panel with her body, disarmed and then rearmed the alarm. "Oh, my. I got mixed up. Which means we put the first envelope on the wrong desk too. It's for Mr. Resseque."

"That's Mr. Rogers' apartment," Laura said, gesturing over her shoulder with apparent dismay.

"I'm so sorry. I'll need to ask you to retrieve it. If you'll be so kind. I don't want them upset with me."

"It's not a problem."

Vicky cocked her head in question. "Is Resseque's housekeeper also named Laura?"

"She's Lara. I'm Laura."

Vicky nodded at the coincidence that was truly to blame. "Well, I'm so sorry to be inconveniencing you, Laura. Please, allow me to pay for your taxi ride home." She pulled three twenties from her wallet.

53
Rodents

DESPITE THE HORRENDOUS twists of fate that had put her there, Vicky was happy to be back in a home laboratory. This one was on the east coast rather than the west, and she was on the third floor rather than in a basement, but at the end of the day, a lab table was a lab table and a soldering iron was a soldering iron.

This being New York City, America's biggest market, and with all the technology and medical corporations nearby, she had no problem obtaining premium equipment quickly. Not with the bottomless debit cards of her kind benefactors at her disposal.

To create her zapper, Vicky began with a set of earphones. The kind used by jackhammer operators and airport runway technicians. To these, she added technology drawn from ultrasonic surgical scalpels and microwave ovens, creating a device designed to disrupt the membranes of the target cell type, but no others. In other words, precision, precision, precision.

Based on incomplete data.

From tests on mice.

As Vicky silently laughed at the absurdity of her situation, Skylar walked into the bedroom-turned-laboratory carrying a teapot and two small cups. They liked experimenting with different styles and blends of tea—when circumstances didn't require the kick of coffee.

"What do you have?" Vicky asked, setting down her forceps and screwdriver.

"Green tea. A loose leaf Japanese sencha. This one is a Toku Jô Sencha, which the shop owner said is *extra superior*. I'm not sure we'll notice the difference in taste, but the price was definitely extra superior. In any case, I prepared it at seventy degrees Celsius, as he insisted."

Skylar poured two cups. "How's your work coming?"

"I'm almost done."

"Will it fit in the headphones as you hoped?"

"Yep. And I've set it up to use the on/off switch they came with, so it will appear ordinary."

"I didn't know they had an on/off switch. I thought noise-cancelling headphones were just insulation."

"They used to be, and the passive ones still are. But nowadays the good ones are active. They detect ambient noise using a microphone and then create what is essentially an equal and opposite sound wave, cancelling it out."

"That doesn't seem possible. One plus one equaling zero rather than two."

"It's one minus one, actually. Picture the drawing of a wave going above and below a horizontal line, then add a second wave which crosses the line at the same points, but going in the opposite direction. The two "smash," resulting in a flat line. Sound cancelled.

"They're putting the technology into high-end cars now, and it's moving into rooms. Probably starting with five-star hotels and apartments like this one," Vicky said, gesturing to their $50,000 a month residence.

"Interesting," Skylar said, sampling the tea, then raising her cup in approval. "Nice."

"Yes, I like it too," Vicky agreed, after sipping. "Just don't tell me what it cost." She'd thought California prices were high, but those in New York City were positively bonkers.

Skylar motioned to the headphones, which still lay open. "What are all the internal dials for, if there's just an on/off switch?"

"The smaller ones allow me to modify the transmission wave, which is actually very sophisticated. The term *wave* doesn't conjure up an adequate picture. The larger one controls the power level—the dose. But don't worry, they'll all be hidden inside."

"Why do you need them? Is there a way to test your device?"

Vicky grew a stern smile. "Just one person at a time."

"Can you try it on mice, like you did in California?"

"I could if I had access to a functional magnetic resonance imager. But I'm not going back to my lab before this situation is resolved, and I can't risk using a friend's either."

"Could we buy one?"

"That's not an option. They're enormous, require extensive setup, and cost more than a million bucks."

Skylar drained her teacup while swallowing the implications. "You wouldn't need additional testing if the assassin hadn't disrupted your research at Caltech, right?"

Vicky nodded, knowing where this was going. "That's probably accurate."

"So, in essence, it was the lawyers who forced you to use them as guinea pigs."

"That's true too."

"Well, all right then," Skylar said, setting down her cup. "If the calibration is off, it's not on you. It's on them."

54
Moore Drinks

CHASE HAD WORN countless disguises during his decade with CIA Operations. Enhancements designed to alter his appearance, either to avoid recognition or to resemble a character type, be that a bum, a biker, or a banker. But this was only his second attempt at impersonation, at wearing a disguise designed to make him look like someone specific. Today, that person was hedge fund manager Jeffrey Buster.

Jeff had earned the honor with two qualifications. One, he looked a lot like Chase might if he were ten years older. And two, he was a member of Club 3E.

Although the venerable Central Park West establishment with its symmetrical pillar-esque logo was actually named for founder Ethan Elijah Evans, Chase's research indicated that most members and wannabes thought the name was shorthand for *elite, exclusive,* and *expensive.*

As he and Skylar quickly discovered, one need only examine a membership application to understand why. The paperwork was no less personal and probing than a proctology exam, while the wait for people who passed the reputation, recommendation, and financial hurdles was estimated to be between six and seven years.

Chase and Skylar had passed through the large, hand-carved double doors with the apparent intent of introducing themselves as new arrivals to the neighborhood, and inquiring about club membership—with Charles' and Kitty's British accents on full display. While Skylar charmed the receptionist and peppered him with questions, Chase slowly wandered about the antique-festooned lobby, surreptitiously planting two tiny cameras, one with a full view of the front door, the second directed at the membership-card reader.

They repeated the performance that evening just before closing to retrieve the cameras while a different receptionist was on duty. Back at the apartment, Chase then used the first stored video to select the member he most resembled, and the second to copy a picture of that man's membership details and barcode.

Tonight, he was flashing his fake Jeffrey Buster card from his phone.

The card reader's light beeped red.

Chase flashed it again.

Another red.

The evening receptionist said, "May I help you?"

"I'm getting red, would you buzz me in?"

"May I see your phone?"

"Of course."

"That's the problem. You're using a screenshot rather than the live app. It should work fine if you open your card in the app."

"My nephew uninstalled the program. I reinstalled it, but forgot my login info."

The receptionist consulted her computer, then turned the screen toward Chase.

Below Jeffrey Buster's picture, he read:

User ID: JBuster

Password: Big$4me

Member Since: 14/06/2006

Locker: 141

Chase entered the information, flashed the card screen at the reader, and got green. "Thank you very much."

"Enjoy your evening."

Chase continued on to the locker room. He hadn't expected to learn Jeff's locker number and wasn't about to use his phone to open it now, lest he be spotted by one of Jeff's friends and be unmasked, but it was good to know.

With the checkpoint behind him, Chase hid "Jeff's" glasses in the trash, then stepped into the shower, where he went to work reverting to his natural appearance. While the shampoo washed away the combed-in gray, he scrubbed the artificial wrinkle lines from his forehead and around his eyes, then removed the jawline fading lightener and artificial beauty mark.

Ten minutes later, Chase was scanning the dining room while walking toward the corner bar. The layout had clearly been designed with three functions in mind. The perimeter was lined with high-backed mahogany-paneled booths. Clearly, that was where the business was done. Further in was a ring of two-top tables, no doubt used primarily by single diners, members busy with their newspapers or laptops as well as their Scotch. In the middle, burgundy leather couches and armchairs in varied configurations circled coffee tables designed for drinks and hors d'oeuvres. The social section.

Chase settled onto a stool at the bar.

A bartender who looked like he might remember the Second World War approached.

Chase gestured toward one of the overhead muted televisions. "Where does Jim Rogers usually sit?"

The old guy glanced up at the screen showing coverage of the Pascal trial. Rogers wasn't personally working the case, but Chase figured the bartender would know that one of his regular clients was a named partner at the firm handling the hottest court case in the country. "You're new here." It was a statement, not a question.

"I'm Jeff Buster's brother. Just visiting from London," Chase said, extending a hand.

"Paul Moore," the bartender replied. "Most people call me Moore. I'll let you guess why."

Chase smiled at the joke.

"You'll find Jim at the two-top near the far corner, 'bout twenty minutes from now."

Chase followed the gesture with his eyes. "What is his drink?"

"He tends to wander across my top shelf in the Whisky section, but he usually comes back to Macallan 24. Takes it neat. That's before dinner. After a small Caesar salad with no croutons and extra anchovies he leans toward cognac. A 1914 Pierre Ferrand has been his favorite of late."

A man of discipline and habit. Most of the successful ones were.

Chase didn't know what a 24-year-old Scotch would cost at a place like this, but he did know that food and beverage purchases would normally be automatically charged to the member—Jeff Buster's account in his case—so Chase pulled three $100 bills from his pocket while asking, "I'll take Jim his drink, if you'll kindly pour me two. Plus a club soda for while I wait?"

Moore made the money vanish and the drinks appear with the smooth efficiency of a veteran dance instructor, then moved on to other imbibers with an acknowledging nod.

"What do you think of the trial?" Chase asked a few minutes later, when Moore had all his other customers happy.

The bartender studied Chase's face for a few seconds before answering. "I think the women agreed to make a trade, one job for another, and now they're reneging on the deal because society suddenly decided to change a system that's been working since before Moses came down from Mount Sinai."

"You've given this some thought," Chase said, actively suppressing his anger.

"It's been a hot topic for a while now. Lot of members are nervous. I think it's going to backfire on women. In the short term anyway. Executives won't want to risk having them around."

"And in the long term?"

"Things will snap back to the natural order. Jim's firm will help with that, by getting Pascal off."

"You think they'll win?"

Moore harrumphed. "No doubt about it. They always win. Excuse me, one of my regular orders just walked in."

Chase watched the bartender prepare a Manhattan with the precision usually reserved for science experiments and cancer medications. Moore put the cocktail glass on a silver tray and took it to a bow tied gentleman who had just seated himself before a copy of the current *New Yorker*. Chase used the opportunity to put a tablet of Rohypnol into one of the whisky tumblers, then took a sip from the other to help ensure that he'd keep them straight.

Moore returned with his empty tray and went about preparing drinks for the waiters as Jim Rogers walked in—with a bodyguard.

The bodyguard approached Chase, but then sat at the two-top nearest his corner, side-by-side with another bodyguard who was also watching the room. That could be a good or a bad development. Putting two bodyguards together would either make them both more vigilant, as they tried to impress each other, or more careless, as they shared the responsibility of scanning for threats. Chase hoped for the latter as he loudly thanked Moore for the drinks and walked toward Rogers' table.

55
Two Faces

JIM ROGERS WAS WEARY but upbeat as he headed for his usual seat at 3E. Weary because it had been a long week, upbeat because the Pascal case was going well for the defense, according to both his partners and the news coverage. That was no surprise, of course.

People tended to think of justice as black and white. Right and wrong. Guilty or innocent. What virtually everyone outside the profession failed to realize was that jury trials had little to do with absolutes and much to do with the predispositions of the jurors. Jury members were every bit as diverse, opinionated, and irrational as the public at large. Therefore, getting the "justice" you wanted essentially amounted to performing two tasks better than the competition. The first task was selecting jurors whose predispositions slanted them in your direction. The second was providing them with information that fit their natural view of the world.

The first was a difficult task under normal circumstances. People tended to hide their biases. They wanted to appear reasonable and fair—both to outsiders and to themselves. But their honest inclinations rang louder than church bells when one could listen in on their counteracting internal monologues and sympathetic, rationalizing explanations.

Sackler and Slate had dismissed over a dozen potential jurors for cause after drilling down during voir dire with a direction and precision that mystified the candidates and infuriated the prosecution.

Later in the week, Sackler had methodically stripped the state's first witness of all credibility by forcing her to clarify exaggerations and white lies. With that on the record, Slate was able to compel her to confess to prior career-enhancing acts that could be considered sexual in nature.

It was almost too easy.

Human nature was responsible. People tended to think about the things that worried them. The stuff that might go wrong. All Rogers and his partners had to do was ring the anxiety bell and then listen in as the self-incriminating thoughts poured forth.

As he settled into his chair, Rogers actually felt bad for the women testifying against Pascal. He'd felt bad for many of RRS&S's opponents. But justice was not the lawyer's job. Their mandate was to win—without breaking the law—which was exactly what he and his partners did. There was no law against mind reading. Just ask a jury consultant. They all claimed to be masters at it.

Rogers' Scotch appeared, right on cue, but it wasn't served by a staff member. "I wanted to thank you and your partners for what you're doing."

"And what's that?" Jim asked.

"Sticking up for men. Moore and I were watching the news coverage earlier. He tells me you never lose."

"We do our homework, and juries tend to reward us for it."

The man raised his tumbler. "Here's to a rewarding jury."

"To a rewarding jury," Jim repeated, before savoring that first sweet sip. "Thank you. I hope you enjoy your evening."

"Likewise," the man said, taking the hint.

Jim didn't mean to be antisocial. He was at a social club after all. But he came for the atmosphere, not company. He never had to wait, always got exactly what he wanted, and was rarely disturbed. The club was a buffer between office and home. If he lived across the park rather than just down the street from the office, he might not need the club.

Of course, then he'd need a cook. And a trainer to burn off the extra calories from her tempting meals. No, this was simpler.

As he wound down with his whisky and homework, Rogers found himself reading the same paragraph time and again. He was really dragging. No need for cognac tonight. Must be the subconscious stress of the whole Pascal affair. Not the trial, but the lifestyle change that looked likely to follow.

He'd enjoyed his job until the option to walk away as a future billionaire arose. Then, all of a sudden, the work was a chore and the idea of making only a few million a year was lackluster. *How much was enough? The best you could imagine.*

Jim accepted a few more congratulatory remarks and supportive nods as he headed for the door. Not one of Pascal's supporters would dare to show an ounce of support in public. In fact, most would be loudly voicing their support for the women allied against him if someone put a camera in their face. But here, in private, well, men were honest. In that sense, 3E was like another elite club: the United States Congress.

Normally, Jim would put on some classical music when he got home. Then sit by the fire and think about his legal docket for the next day or coming week. Do a bit of strategic planning while his mind was at ease and the creative juices were flowing free. But tonight, he was whipped. He might go straight to bed.

56
In the Closet

SKYLAR WAS HAVING all kinds of fun for all kinds of reasons. She was helping the women's movement, which was always worthwhile. She was helping her new best friend, another perennial winner. She was hindering corrupt lawyers, a time-honored calling. And she was doing it all on a covert mission, her favorite place to be, now that Ironman championships were out of reach.

Technically, her actions were criminal. Sufficiently felonious to land her behind bars for years—if she screwed up. Morally, however, Skylar knew that her moves were entirely laudable. Praiseworthy enough to merit the hero role in a big budget movie.

Chase had told her long ago that there was nothing like dancing the line between hero and felon to spike the adrenaline and focus one's attention. She could now confirm from personal experience that his pronouncement was accurate.

The mission had kicked off some thirty hours earlier, when Chase gave them a crash course on home incursions and then took them on a three-minute reconnaissance run—into Jim Rogers' apartment.

With a raised finger and twinkling eye, Chase said, "There's one telltale clue that even the pros tend to leave behind after thoroughly searching a car or home. Can you guess what it is?"

"Footprints on the carpet?" "Smudges in the dust?" They'd guessed.

"No. They might well leave those behind, but people aren't likely to notice. The answer is *smell*.

"Spies and thieves wear shoe covers and take pictures to ensure that everything looks the same after planting bugs or searching for safes, but—"

"They leave their stink behind," Vicky said.

"Be it booze or smoke or sweat," Skylar added, picturing the stereotypical gangster.

"Exactly."

"How do we avoid that, given that we'll be there for hours?" Skylar asked while resisting the urge to sniff herself.

"When we go in to identify your hiding place, we'll snag samples of Rogers' toiletries for you to shower with before returning for the overnighter."

Chase went on to explain that, "The first thing the bodyguard will do when bringing his boy home is search the residence. He'll know the potential hiding places, the closets, crawl spaces, and gaps beneath beds. He'll check them all, every time. It will be quick and cursory, but complete."

"And the goal of our 'reconnaissance run' is to figure out how to avoid detection during that sweep?" Vicky asked.

"Right again."

"And you have a preliminary plan for that, assuming Roger's apartment has the same layout as ours?" Skylar asked.

"Correct. There are a couple of good places for a duck blind."

Chase didn't clarify his use of the hunting term until they were upstairs, looking at the long, narrow guest room closet that Rogers used to store winter coats. "This is where you'll construct it." He'd taken pictures, confirmed the measurements, and used a knife to carve out a paint sample before adding. "Better safe than sorry."

Skylar and Vicky were anticipating entering the closet 'duck blind' any minute now. It had been two hours since Chase left them in the eleventh-floor foyer to drug Rogers' drink at Club 3E. They'd spent the time waiting in the lawyer's kitchen, that being the place least likely to absorb and reflect telltale signs, given the constant use and confounding sensory barrage that came from cooking and storing food.

Skylar's phone buzzed as they were watching news coverage of the Pascal trial on her phone. She put it on speaker so Vicky's voice-to-text app would work.

"Yes."

"He's on his way."

"Did he drink it all?"

"Every drop, and it's working. He skipped his after-dinner drink."

"Good job."

"Keep me updated with texts. Love you."

Skylar turned to Vicky. "I'll double-check things here while you set the alarm. Meet you in the closet."

They'd used a stretchy fabric to create the duck blind, but since its depth was just eighteen inches, it still required quite an acrobatic act for them to secure it tautly in place from the inside.

Skylar entered first and suspended herself at the top beside the clothes bar by pressing her back against one wall and her knees and feet against the other. This allowed Vicky to crawl in backwards while eyeballing the scene, ensuring that the hanging coats appeared natural before she pinned the painted fabric to the baseboard. Vicky then straightened up while Skylar straightened down. By the time they heard the door opening and the alarm deactivating, they were nose to nose and holding their breath.

Vicky stood facing the room with her mind-reading glasses directed toward the door. That would give them advance warning if discovery was imminent—for all the good that would do.

For her part, Skylar felt like Anne Frank avoiding Nazis as she glanced sideways toward the closet doors, which folded outward from the middle on both sides.

About twenty seconds after the alarm emitted its deactivation chime, Skylar heard the bodyguard's footfalls on the hardwood floor, followed by the opening of their closet doors. Light filtered in, but only for a second or two before the doors closed and the footfalls receded.

Just like that, the initial danger was over.

Shortly thereafter, she heard the front door close, indicating that the bodyguard had left the apartment to assume the night watch with Sackler's guy in the foyer.

"What was he thinking?" Skylar whispered—not toward Vicky's ear but into her phone.

"All I got was *Nothing there, and nothing there, and*—" Vicky whispered back.

Skylar strained her ears in the dark, hoping to decipher activity as their breathing returned to normal. An opening refrigerator door. A running shower. A creaking bed. She heard nothing. After half an hour of silence, with the cramped standing becoming increasingly uncomfortable, the two infiltrators slowly and silently slipped out of the duck blind, working carefully so as not to pull it from the wall in any place but one bottom corner.

They weren't done with it yet.

After their interrogation session, which the Rohypnol should cause Rogers to forget, they would slip back into the closet and wait for him and his bodyguard to leave in the morning.

But that wouldn't be for hours.

For now, feeling confident that their presence had not been detected, the two lay down in the closet, hoping to catch a few winks before beginning the inquisition that would span the wee hours of the night.

57
Nightmare Scenario

AMONG THE MANY surprising things that Jim Rogers had learned during twenty years of mind reading, perhaps paramount among them was the extent to which brains worked differently. Like everyone, he'd grown up aware that his sense of sight, smell, hearing, touch, and taste worked pretty much the same as his peers' senses. Therefore, he'd subconsciously assumed that brains were also very similar.

He'd been wrong.

As a mind-reading lawyer, Jim had come to realize that unlike our senses, our brains were as nuanced and varied as the instruments in an orchestra, with some sounding as if played by school kids and others as if wielded by pros. It made him all the more grateful to be living his adult years as a conductor.

Despite the wide-ranging intellectual dissimilarities, Jim still assumed that some dreams were universal among humans. Nightmares in particular. Prominent among those was waking to find oneself in mortal danger. Therefore, he was confident that everyone would immediately understand the utter terror he experienced when opening his eyes to find his mouth gagged and his head in a bag.

He started to struggle as the shock set in—only to find that his wrists and ankles were bound.

While the initial experience already topped his list of life's worst moments, it quickly got worse.

"If you make any noise, I'll take out your eyes." The voice was a whisper, emanating just inches from his ear. Something sharp then dragged across his forehead, stopping in the socket beneath his right eyebrow. "Are we clear?"

Jim wasn't about to nod his head, and he couldn't speak with the sock or whatever it was in his mouth, so he just grunted, trying to sound agreeable.

The rope holding his gag in place was released, then a hand slipped beneath the bag and pulled the sock out. There were at least two people in his bedroom, judging by the number of hands at work. At least one was a woman. She asked, "What's your strategy for discrediting Beth Barrymore?"

It took Jim a moment to process the question. Despite the shock, his mind was still slow with the fog of sleep. *Beth Barrymore? The Pascal trial!*

With tens of millions of dollars at stake in forthcoming civil suits, and the case against the billionaire CEO collapsing live on national television, the opposition was getting aggressive. Even so, threatening murder and committing it were entirely different matters. They were likely bluffing. As a lawyer, Rogers was well acquainted with that tactic. "I'm not a member of Pascal's defense team. I do civil law. That's criminal. You need to ask Sackler or Slate. Not that I'm suggesting you do."

The reply was fast and forceful. "We know you're in the loop. We wouldn't have picked you otherwise. Best of all, since you're not assigned to the case, your mutilation or death won't impact the trial. Now, tell me the strategy for discrediting Beth Barrymore!"

There was no predeveloped strategy. Not a detailed one. His colleagues' quick minds didn't require those. The only prep they needed were the starter questions that would lead Beth's thoughts toward her vulnerabilities. "We do a lot of background research, then work by intuition. That's the strategy. If you study transcripts of our trials, you'll see that's true."

The voice kept probing trial tactics without lowering the knife. Rogers remained oddly calm throughout. Perhaps decades of doing battle in court had hardened his nerves, he thought with pride.

Eventually, miraculously, they moved on to Louise O'Brian, another of the state's primary witnesses. Surviving round one gave him hope. And a bit of bravado. "Can I have some water?"

In answer, a bottle worked its way under the bag. It tilted upward once he locked his lips around it. Either they had it on standby for him, or they were sharing their own supply. "Thank you."

The whispering woman drilled down on Louise for a while, then hit him with a non sequitur from out of the blue. "How many people have you killed?"

Blackmail! They were going to get a confession and then coerce him into sabotaging the trial. "Nobody," he blurted. "I'm not a murderer." *I hire assassins for that.*

"But you give the orders."

"No, I don't." *Trent handles that.*

"Don't get cute. We know about Trent."

An easy deduction. Keller's name wasn't on the letterhead, but he was listed in the partnership documents and tax filings. "We're lawyers, not killers."

"You lawyers may not pull the trigger, but you hire people who do."

You can bet I'll be sending Fredo Blanco for you when he's done with Cassandra. "Nonsense! We've never paid to have anyone killed." Technically, that was true. While Cassandra's partner had died, his death wasn't part of the contract.

"Really? Do you swear—on your eyes?"

58
The Trap

SKYLAR HAD NEVER been so fascinated in all her life. Before that evening with Jim Rogers, her experience with Vicky's mind reading appliance had been limited to a brief courtesy trial on the *Vitamin Sea*. But tonight, wearing her own pair of specially polarized lenses, Skylar was enjoying the full mind-reading experience alongside her friend.

It wasn't just watching the disconnect between the wily, drugged lawyer's thoughts and words that she found fascinating, but the skill with which Vicky coaxed them from him. Skylar didn't know if that was a natural gift or something Vicky had picked up as a psychic, but her subtle nudges and subliminal provocations were spellbinding to observe.

Vicky repeated her last question while Rogers' mind raced and his panic surged. "Do you swear on your eyes?"

Jim took a deep breath. *Please, Lord, don't let them take my eyes.* "I do."

Skylar wobbled the pencil tip she had poised like a dagger against his right eye.

"Noted," Vicky said ambiguously before hitting him with another mental punch while he was still off balance. "How much is Pascal paying you?"

Billions—if his idea pans out. I'll use my share to track you down and pry your eyes from your skulls with a rusty spoon. "He's paying our standard rates, which we draw from a five-million-dollar retainer."

"I'm not talking about the contract. I'm referring to the kicker."

Surely they didn't know about that? Pascal claimed that he hadn't told anyone how he planned to use the mind-reading technology. No, they didn't know. Couldn't know. This had to be a fishing expedition. A hunt based on extensive research into the man and his methods. Or— That was it! They'd found an inside source who knew that Pascal had lots of secret deals and collaborations with bonus payments or "kickers" as she called them. Someone had sold the CEO out. Or betrayed him out of spite. A secretary who'd baked his potato, perhaps. Or a programmer he'd passed over for promotion. "There is no kicker." *Just a promise.*

"You don't have another deal with Pascal?"

"No. Absolutely not." *We only have an understanding.*

"Don't lie to me," the voice hissed. "Lying makes me twitch."

"I'm not lying." *We won't learn the details of his billion-dollar idea until after we win.*

Skylar gave the pencil another twirl.

"Tell me about Scarlett Slate," Vicky whispered. "Her strengths and especially her weaknesses."

Vicky continued to barrage the drugged lawyer with questions that gave them valuable intel without disclosing her identity. As the clock neared 4:00 a.m., Rogers voiced the words he'd been thinking with increasing frequency. "I need to pee."

"Hold it in. We're not releasing your bonds until you've answered all our questions."

Vicky kept pressing. Their captive's answers became ever less guarded as he found it increasingly difficult to think about anything but relieving himself. He was using images of prison cells and monstrous bunkmates to steel his will, but his bladder was relentless.

Only when he was close to giving into the indignity of soiling himself did they loosen his bonds enough to work a wide-necked bottle into position.

Once his business was completed, Rogers asked, "Are we done?"

Skylar looked at the lengthy scroll of incriminating thought and nodded the affirmative. They didn't have everything, but they had more than enough.

Rather than responding directly to the crooked lawyer's question, Vicky slipped her new device over his ears and reinserted his gag. She didn't know if the emissions from her zapper would be noticeable, much less painful, but with the bodyguards standing by, she wanted to play it safe.

Once the socks were stuffed back in, Skylar cupped a hand over Rogers' mouth and Vicky hit the switch.

The lawyer tensed for a few seconds, then went limp.

Vicky's face reflected surprise and then concern, but she kept the current flowing for the full minute she believed was required to denature all the target cells. Meanwhile, Skylar couldn't help but picture an egg exploding in a microwave.

Once the complete dose was administered and the zapper withdrawn, Skylar slowly removed her hand from over Jim's mouth.

He didn't react.

She checked his carotid pulse, then put her ear to his chest. She felt nothing. Heard nothing. "He's dead."

Vicky nodded slowly as panic contorted her face. "My calculations were off."

The news sent Skylar's thoughts in a very different direction. "He won't be going to work. We're trapped in his apartment—with his corpse."

59
The Morning After

VICKY STARED at the corpse of the man she'd killed. *She'd killed.*

"He murdered Chewie," Skylar said, as if reading *her* mind. "And he tried to kill you, twice. His death is essentially the ricochet of a bullet he fired."

"Thank you."

"I've been there. I got through it, tougher and wiser. You will, too."

Vicky stared at the body. "What do we do now? We can't leave, but we can't be caught here with the corpse either."

"The bodyguards!" Skylar said.

Shoeless, they ran to the front door where Vicky put her eye to the peephole. Both guards were lounging in chairs, awake but with their eyes on their phones. She flashed Skylar a thumbs up, then stepped aside and pulled out her phone to see what they were thinking. The screen stayed blank.

"What's on their minds?" Skylar whispered after glancing through the peephole herself.

"Nothing. They're watching TV. No thinking is involved."

Skylar cocked her head at the profound revelation, then tucked it away for later analysis. "Let's call Chase."

They retreated to the bedroom, where the lawyer appeared to be sleeping. "Rogers is dead," she told Chase with the phone on speaker.

"How did he die?"

Skylar looked at Vicky. "A massive hemorrhagic stroke. It's probably going to look weird in the autopsy, since he likely bled from multiple points rather than the typical one, but nobody is going to guess what really happened."

"So the coroner will have a clear and common cause of death?" Chase asked, his voice crisp and operational.

"Right."

"They'll find the Rohypnol in his bloodstream, so you need to leave the box in his nightstand. It's sold overseas as a sleep aid, so it will look normal enough there, given his international profile. But first, wipe it clean of your fingerprints, inside and out, and then apply his. Can you do that?"

"I'm on it," Skylar said.

"You'll want to make the room look normal. Including the body. The picture should say 'he died in his sleep.' Got it?"

"We got it," Vicky said, happy to have clear marching orders. "But what then?"

"Then we let things happen exactly as they would if he'd actually died in the night from a stroke. He won't come out at 7:50 as he usually does, so around 8:15 or so his bodyguard will likely knock or call. When he doesn't answer, the bodyguard will go in and find him. He'll call 911. The police, an ambulance, and eventually a coroner will appear. Then they'll carry out the body."

"And we're supposed to be hiding in the closet through all that activity? The police and paramedics?" Vicky asked with strained voice.

"No, you're going to slip out when the bodyguard goes into the bedroom."

"What if he sees us? Or hears us?"

"Assuming the scene looks natural and nonthreatening, his eyes are going to be locked on the body. As for him hearing you, Rogers' alarm clock should take care of that. Find what he uses and make sure it's on at a good volume."

"What about Sackler's bodyguard? Won't he see us leave?"

"Sackler is the early bird. He'll be in the office on his second cup of coffee by then."

"Right, I forgot," Vicky said.

"This probably goes without saying, but use the stairs to avoid the elevator video. I'll be waiting in the stairwell, and I'll have something with me to block the door after you in case you're being pursued."

"You mean a door jam?"

"Something like that. I still have to figure it out. Good luck."

They spent the next hour returning the apartment to normal. They began with Rogers himself and worked their way to the bed and the greater bedroom until eventually they were back at the closet where they'd literally lain in wait. There they removed the duck blind, returned the relocated clothes, and packed all their supplies, including Vicky's deadly earphone zapper, into the backpacks they'd used to tote it all in.

"Had you heard about their fifth partner before?" Skylar asked once the waiting game began.

"Trent Keller? Yes and no. His name rang a bell and I finally figured out where. I think it was on the building's list of tenants. I haven't seen the partnership papers Rogers referenced," Vicky added.

"I'll text Chase to look into him. He'll be happy to have something to research while we're waiting."

"Have him research Fredo Blanco too."

"That was creepy," Skylar said, putting her hand on Vicky's shoulder. "Hearing the name of the assassin attempting to kill you."

Vicky had seen Fredo's face, so he was plenty real to her already. "In hindsight, I wish I'd asked Rogers about him. It might be useful to know his background. Terrifying, but useful."

"Whoever Fredo is, he'll stop coming when Trent tells him to. We just have to figure out how to make that happen."

Once satisfied that the dead man's apartment looked normal, the two infiltrators slipped into their new hiding place near the entrance. As Vicky closed the coat closet door to a peep-able crack, she realized that what lay behind them was the easy part. The tough part would be waiting for the call or knock that would signal the start of their escape—or capture.

It came five minutes earlier than Chase predicted, at 8:11 a.m. Vicky wondered if the bodyguard had called at 8:10. From the closet, Skylar might have missed the ringing phone over Rogers' alarm, which she said was playing a collection of Bach violin sonatas at an invigorating volume.

Skylar signaled when she heard the front door open, and Vicky caught the verbal probe. "Mr. Rogers? Mr. Rogers?"

A second later, the bodyguard walked past their hiding place toward the bedroom.

Barefoot and barely breathing, they slipped out of the closet and through the front door as quietly as possible, hoping that the guard would not silence Bach before the lock clicked closed behind them.

He didn't.

Before Vicky knew it, they were running down the stairs with Chase. Toward what, she had no idea.

60
One of Us

WHILE THE JUDGE, jury, and courtroom full of reporters all watched with rapt attention, Scarlett glanced at her co-counsel before taking the witness questioning in a new direction.

The jury is intrigued, Sackler thought for her benefit. *Maintain the same tone.*

Scarlett refocused on Beth Barrymore, the second of the now four witnesses accusing Archibald Pascal of sexual assault. "Ms. Barrymore, you've been working in the tech sector for the past fifteen years, correct? Ever since graduating college?"

"Yes."

"And how many companies have you worked for during those fifteen years?"

"Let me see," the plump, thirty-eight-year-old redhead said. "Eight."

"Eight companies, in fifteen years. Is that a lot?"

"Tech is a volatile industry. People move around all the time."

"Was it stressful, changing companies every other year?"

"I found it refreshing."

"But why so many changes?"

The prosecuting attorney, Oliver Branch, shot out of his seat. "Objection, your honor. Relevance."

"Goes to mindset," Scarlett said, knowing that Judge Whitcomb wasn't buying "refreshing" any more than the jury.

"Overruled. The witness will answer the question."

Barrymore momentarily bowed her head. "Better opportunities came along."

"More money? More responsibility? A better title?" Scarlett

asked.

"That's right."

"But you started as a marketing associate out of college, and you were a marketing manager at Mr. Pascal's company. Isn't that just one promotion in fifteen years? At eight companies?"

"Two promotions. I was a senior associate as well."

"How many times did you lodge complaints with the Human Resources departments at those eight companies during those fifteen years?"

Branch rose again. "Objection, your honor. Relevance."

"We're establishing a pattern, your honor."

"Overruled. The witness will answer the question."

"I don't recall," Barrymore said.

"How many times at your first employer, Lutech?" Scarlett asked.

One, two, three. "I don't recall."

"Does three sound right?"

Barrymore looked at Branch.

Branch nodded.

"Something like that."

"Something like that, or exactly that?"

"Yes, three."

"Were all three complaints for unwanted attention?"

Again Barrymore turned to Branch. Again he nodded.

And so it went until Scarlett got Barrymore's twenty-two prior grievances on the record and Judge Whitcomb tabled court proceedings until the following morning.

Scarlett's relief from a day well played turned to concern when she spotted Colton Resseque and Trent Keller waiting for them in the back hallway by the restroom door. The partners of RRS&S had learned early on of the importance of freshening up before going out front to talk to the press. They always made a pit stop before exiting to flashing cameras.

Colton's expression did not reflect the contentment or relief she was feeling after a triumphant day of courtroom combat. In fact, he appeared downright grim. Keller's expression, as usual, reflected nothing.

"What is it?" Sackler asked.

"Not here. Judge Holstein has given us the use of his chambers."

That wasn't a good sign. Scarlett wanted to slip on her glasses and get a preview of coming attractions as they followed their partner upstairs and down the hall, but she resisted the temptation to break Rule One.

Colton ushered them into the judge's office, closed the door and gestured to the small conference table.

The four sat.

"Jim suffered a stroke last night. He didn't survive."

Scarlett couldn't believe her ears. "What?"

"A stroke?" Sackler said.

Trent nodded. "They rushed the autopsy for me. It's not complete yet, but the cause of death, as confirmed by a CT scan, was a massive hemorrhagic stroke."

"A stroke," Sackler repeated. "Dead from a stroke at fifty-one. I can't believe it."

"Was it due to natural causes?" Scarlett asked.

"His bloodwork was clean of amphetamines and cocaine, which apparently are leading causes in people our age. The only odd finding was Flunitrazepam, more commonly known as Rohypnol."

"The date rape drug?" Scarlett asked.

"Apparently it's a common sleep aid outside the United States. He had an Ambien prescription for sleep, but it wasn't in his bloodstream."

I use Lunesta, Scarlett thought.

Sackler nodded.

"They found a box of it in his nightstand, beside the Ambien bottle," Trent said.

Scarlett put her head in her hands. "I can't believe he's dead. One of us."

"A massive hemorrhagic stroke at fifty-one," Colton said, his voice strained rather than silky. "I can't stop thinking about that. The odds of a healthy white male our age dying from hemorrhagic stroke are less than one in a thousand. I asked."

"It is tragic. But as we well know from our work, tragedies happen all the time."

"I know, I know. It's just, well, an unexpected death, coming at a time when we're doing what we're doing. I can't help but be suspicious."

"Stalin died of a hemorrhagic stroke," Trent said in his typical monotone. "There's speculation that he was killed with rat poison."

"Rat poison causes strokes?" Colton asked.

"That's right," Sackler said, still in a daze. "It's an anticoagulant. The rats bleed out. Or rather bleed in."

Trent grew an ironic smile. "Wouldn't be the first time someone inflicted a rat's death on a lawyer."

The three all turned to glare at him.

He held up his hands. "But we know that's not what happened to Jim. As I said, his bloodwork was clean."

61
Rising Up, Powering Down

CHASE WAS SCROLLING through the thought and voice transcripts on Vicky's phone for the second time when she walked into the room. He immediately set the special glasses aside, rose and returned them to her. It wasn't unusual for people to experience anxiety when separated from their connected devices, and that had to apply tenfold in Vicky's case, since her phone literally functioned as her ears. "Thank you. Do you feel better after your nap?"

"Much. Skylar still sleeping?"

"She is."

After returning to their apartment from Rogers', the women had collapsed. Chase caught a few winks as well, but curiosity soon roused him.

"Did you finish?" Vicky asked, waggling her phone.

"Read most of it twice. It's concerning to say the least."

"What's concerning?" Skylar asked, walking into the kitchen. "Or rather, which concerning thing are you discussing?"

Good point. Their list of concerns was growing, not shrinking. "No discussion yet. We're just getting started." Chase kissed his wife and continued making coffee. "I was referring to Pascal's plan to monetize the lawyers' mind-reading technology. The transcripts indicate that Rogers didn't know how Pascal plans to use it, just that his idea's worth billions." Chase turned to Vicky. "Did you learn or sense anything more?"

"No. We wanted to probe, of course, but as you know we couldn't ask about it, even tangentially, in case he ended up remembering the encounter despite the Rohypnol."

Chase nodded. "I understand."

"With hindsight, I wish I'd pressed harder. But I don't think he knew much more than what we intercepted."

"If they don't know what Pascal's plan is, then clearly they didn't go to him with the idea. Which means Pascal came to them. But how did Pascal learn about their technology?" Chase asked.

"I don't know, but I can speculate," Vicky said. "Archibald Pascal is a genius and an innovator. His core strength is studying the big picture and identifying ways to improve it. As a fellow scientist, I can tell you that one of the tactics used is studying exceptional performers with the aim of figuring out what they're doing differently. For example, what allows lizards to climb walls? Or seals to survive arctic waters? Or hummingbirds to hover?"

"Or lawyers to never lose," Skylar said.

"Exactly. When a guy like Pascal reads an article about America's most expensive lawyers, he doesn't simply assume that someone has to be the best, the top 0.001 percent. He studies them to determine what they do differently."

"And he studies them with the eye of a technology guru." Chase said, rising to stretch. "So he figures it out, but doesn't stop there. He takes it further than even they ever did. He doesn't ponder the best way to use the technology today, he contemplates what it could be tomorrow."

"Right," Vicky said, nodding along. "When it became clear that I couldn't continue as a scientist, because that would require disclosure, I looked at careers where I could use my invention in secret. It never occurred to me to create a whole new profession."

Skylar set her cup down. "I don't know. Pascal is obviously a creep and probably criminal in his treatment of women. But do we really think he'd unleash mind reading on humanity in order to make a few more bucks? Surely, he came to the same conclusion that you and the lawyers of RRS&S reached about what it would do to the world. And even if he didn't, it's hard to imagine the lawyers going along with a plan that inflicts that plague on society."

"I tend to agree," Vicky said. "Although one should never underestimate the powerful hold that greed can have on the rich— or overestimate the scruples of lawyers. Nonetheless, I assume that Pascal's come up with a blockbuster idea that doesn't require disclosure."

"What could that possibly be?" Skylar asked.

"That's literally the billion-dollar question," Chase said. "We should try to figure it out, but plan our next moves assuming that we won't."

"Speaking of our next moves. Has there been anything in the news about Rogers? Specifically, if there's an investigation into his death?" Vicky asked.

"Probably not. It's too early for that. A rich lawyer dying in New York City is a daily occurrence."

"But are we safe?" Skylar added.

"A fifty-one-year-old man with a very stressful job dies in his bed from a massive hemorrhagic stroke. That probably happens somewhere every day. This one had a bodyguard outside his door and there were no signs of foul play. He has no immediate family and his partners are swamped with other work, as are the police— who won't be shedding any tears over losing a lawyer like him. Unless there was a screw-up we're not aware of, I think we're safe," Chase said.

Vicky blew out a long breath. "That's a relief."

"So what do we do next?" Skylar asked. "Last night was a tactical setback, given the, um, medical outcome. But at the same time the urgency of what we're attempting to do just increased a thousand-fold. It's not just Vicky's life and the continued violation of the justice system that's on the line. Now we know that one of the most powerful people in tech is about to unleash mind reading on the world, in one way or another. That simply can't be anything but bad."

"Only if Pascal wins at trial," Vicky clarified. "If he loses, there should be at least a temporary reprieve from that threat."

"True, but we can't count on him losing," Skylar said.

They considered their situation in silence for a while, sipping coffee and staring at the granite countertop.

Chase eventually broke the calm by asking Vicky, "Do you know what went wrong with your device? Or rather, how to fix it?"

Vicky frowned. "I definitely had the power set too high, meaning the device delivered too much energy to his brain. Remember, my laboratory work was based on rodent models. Mouse brains. Human brains are about two thousand times more massive, so I had to scale up the power. Clearly, I went too far. The next move is dialing the power back. The big question is: *How much?*"

"It's tough territory for trial and error," Chase said, standing to burn nervous energy. "But we really don't have a choice. Suppose we start low and see if it works. If it doesn't, we up the dose and have another go. And then another, until we get it right."

"Where *right* means we've robbed them of their ability to read minds without ending their lives?" Skylar asked.

"Exactly."

"I agree," Vicky said. "A Sackler interrogation should fill in some blanks on the billion-dollar project. If we're fast and lucky, it will also diminish Pascal's chances of winning in court."

Chase leaned forward with both fists on the table. "So we're agreed. We interrogate and zap Sackler tonight."

62
How Bad?

VICKY WAS THRILLED to see Chase smiling as he walked through the apartment's front door. She and Skylar immediately set down their teacups. "Success?"

"Nothing to it. Not when you have a key and the alarm code. I've been thinking about that, about how mind reading makes alarm codes and other passwords virtually worthless. The ripple effects are mind boggling."

Vicky had logged hundreds of mental hours exploring those ripples in her head. It was fascinating. Depressing yet exhilarating at the same time. She literally had the power to profoundly change the world. Perhaps she should have been Pandora instead of Cassandra. "A world without secrets would bear little resemblance to the one we know today."

"It wouldn't all be bad," Skylar said with a mischievous smile. "Politicians would have to be honest. Imagine what that world would be like."

"Yeah. Too bad we wouldn't get to pick and choose what's disclosed," Chase said, before turning to Vicky. "Maybe that's your next project. Your next brilliant invention. Figuring out how to selectively deploy your technology."

"Oh, how I wish that were possible. But back to reality—and your brilliant idea. No issues upstairs?"

Walter Sackler wasn't in the routine of stopping for a drink on the way home from work, so slipping a sedative into said beverage was not an option. However, given the aggressive questioning they had planned for him, the memory-blocking effects of Rohypnol were crucial. To remedy that, Chase concocted the idea of using their access to his apartment to slip the sedative into his nightly healthcare routine.

"No issues. I put it in his toothpaste. Coated his toothbrush and the cup by his sink. I also replaced a little white pill in the Friday section of his weekly pill box with a filed-down Rohypnol tablet. And—" Chase pulled out his phone and pointed to a picture. "I hid a nanny cam in the light fixture over his sink so you'll be able to see how much he ingests. If he skips his pills and doesn't brush his teeth, you shouldn't risk zapping him."

"Got it," Vicky said, hoping they wouldn't be spending the night in his closet for nothing—and praying they wouldn't miss this opportunity to prevent the rotten lawyers from ruining the world.

"I also put a nanny cam in his bedroom, so you'll know when he's sleeping. The Wi-Fi range on the cameras is limited," Chase continued. "So you'll need to link to them once you're in the apartment. I'll add the app to your phones and text you the linking instructions."

"Fantastic. Great idea."

"Yeah, I'm kicking myself for not thinking laterally with Rogers too. I went straight for the traditional in-his-drink move."

"Don't kick too hard, it worked."

As Chase acknowledged Vicky's point with a nod, Skylar said, "Rogers' obituary published while you were upstairs. It says he died of natural causes. Funeral is Sunday."

"That's a relief. And quick on the funeral."

"His partners didn't have much choice regarding timing, given that the Pascal trial must go on."

Satisfied that they were all up to date and on the same page, the three went about preparing for the evening and night to come, then watched the daily news coverage of Pascal's trial. It included video of Sackler and Slate descending the courthouse steps wearing smiles but offering "no comment."

Before Vicky knew it, game time had arrived. They doubted that

Sackler would come straight home, but couldn't risk being wrong. By 5:15, Vicky and Skylar were upstairs.

Sackler's apartment was a mirror image of Rogers', and identical to their own, eight floors below. The two lawyers had different palettes and style preferences, with Sackler opting for vibrant colors and a modern feel whereas Rogers had selected earthy tones and classical furnishings, but both had left the walls white, turned their second bedrooms into studies, and were using the guest bedroom closets for additional storage. So once again, she and Skylar quickly built and sealed themselves inside a duck blind.

"I wish we also had a view of the entryway and kitchen," Skylar whispered, looking at the nanny cam feeds.

"We can bring those tomorrow, if we need to come back."

Skylar grimaced. "I hope that's not necessary. What did you end up doing with the power setting?"

"After a literature review, I dropped it by two-thirds."

"You think that will do it?"

"I don't know," Vicky said, attempting to hide her frustration. "I'll also be pausing the procedure after every six seconds to see if he loses consciousness or complains of a headache."

"What if he does?"

"Depends on how bad it is."

"If it's really bad?" Skylar pressed.

Vicky shrugged. "Then we'll likely have another dead lawyer on our hands—and all the scrutiny that comes with it."

63
In the Dark

HIDING IN A DARK CLOSET, focused on the only bright object, Vicky flashed back to her youth. To clandestinely reading Harry Potter after mom sang "Silent Night" and turned out the lights. The memory sparked a thought that made her smile big and broad. The movement felt good, like stretching a stiff muscle.

Skylar reached out and squeezed her arm.

Vicky looked up at her friend. They were standing practically toe-to-toe, facing each other in the closet, although Skylar was a couple of inches taller.

"What is it?" Skylar mouthed.

"Just a memory," Vicky whispered.

"Care to share?"

She did, actually. Despite the somewhat rocky start to their relationship, Skylar was now her best friend. "I used to dream of growing up to be Hermione Granger, from the Harry Potter books."

"Sure. What girl didn't?"

"Yes, well, it just occurred to me that—I did. In a manner of speaking. Is that a horribly arrogant thing to say?"

To her relief, Skylar smiled back. "It's an entirely accurate thing to say. What you've done is magical. Miraculous. Only you're not Hermione. You're Cassandra."

Vicky enjoyed another muscle stretch. "Maybe that was my mistake. I picked an ill-fated name."

"It might be your mistake, but it was clearly the world's gain."

"What do you mean?"

"If you hadn't done your magic, then the sexual predator and his lawyers would be poised to ruin the world."

Vicky looked down to hide a third smile as her face flushed.

"What do you think?" Skylar asked after a few seconds of silence. "Is it time?" She gestured toward the screen showing Walter Sackler sleeping.

They'd heard him come home late and had partially seen him change out of his suit into a T-shirt and shorts before turning on *Breaking Bad* in the living room. The television camouflaged his other movements, which were already hard for Skylar to hear from the closet, so they lost track of him for the span of two nerve-racking episodes. Vicky spent that time irrationally worried that the closet doors might open at any second as Sackler sought to calm his mind by cleaning his closet, or looking through the boxes of old photographs stored over their heads.

Fortunately, once the second episode concluded he began the predicted bathroom routine, which included taking his Friday pills and brushing his teeth. Then bed with Walter Isaacson's latest book, which he set aside almost immediately. That had been an hour ago.

"I think it's time," Vicky replied, hoping she didn't sound as nervous as she felt.

"It's justice, not experimentation," Skylar said, reading her expression. "These guys dispatched assassins without giving you a second thought. You, in stark contrast, have gone to great lengths to save their lives."

"We don't know that they didn't give me a second thought. We couldn't ask Rogers."

"You can ask Sackler. We're already betting big on the Rohypnol's memory-erasing ability. It's your call. In any case, we know that when the first assassin failed, they sent a second."

"Okay, let's do it!"

The wrist and ankle binding procedure went as smoothly as it had with Rogers. A sign that the drug was working. This time,

234234

234234

234234

234234

234234

234234

234

however, the question that followed "If you make any noise, I'll take out your eyes," was much more shocking to the recipient. "What is Pascal's plan for your mind-reading technology?"

Who are these women? How do they know we can read minds? What a disaster. How did they learn? Same way as Pascal, watching and deducing? What's their connection to him? They must be his competitors. Can I bluff them? Can they read minds? Ask them, like Pascal did. Can you read minds? Can you read minds? Can you—

"Answer the question and answer it honestly or lose an eye."

"I don't know Pascal's plan. He wouldn't tell us, and we couldn't figure it out. He's an inventive genius. A modern Thomas Edison."

"Did you try to figure it out?"

I'm so dizzy. Did they drug me? Was it truth serum? Will it damage my brain?

"Did you try to figure it out?" Vicky repeated.

"Yes, of course."

"How?"

Was this a bluff? Was Pascal testing their loyalty? Would he be mad if he found out? Or would he secretly admire their spunk? "We employed spies."

"What have they learned?"

"Nothing. We can't find his operation."

"Are you still looking?"

Pascal must have a spy on his team. Someone close. "Yes."

"Who else can read minds?"

"Nobody. It's a huge secret."

The dagger twitched at the corner of his eye. "Don't lie."

"There's one other woman. A researcher from Caltech."

"Where is she now?"

"We don't know."

"Is she a threat?"

"She's being dealt with."

"How."

"Professionally."

"Who's the professional?"

Oh, God. Did they work for Fredo? Had he deduced their identities? Was he testing them? Was he investigating them, looking for an even bigger payout? Had the $2 million fee simply whetted his appetite? Were they—

"This is not going to end well for you if I have to keep repeating myself. Now, who's the professional?"

"A guy who used to hunt down cartel deserters."

"Where is he now?"

"I don't know. Here or Pasadena probably. My partner manages him."

"Which partner?"

"Trent Keller."

"When are you going to give Pascal the technology?"

Back to that. Was this lady a litigator too? Or a cop? "After we win his assault case."

"And what is he giving you in exchange?"

"Half the company that will be using it."

"To do what?"

"I told you, I don't know."

"But you believe his claims that it's worth billions?"

I did until now. This is making me wonder what's really going on. "It's Archibald Pascal. Technology is his domain. He knows what he's doing and he has no reason to lie."

"Aren't you worried what will happen to the world when mind reading becomes widely available?"

"It won't. He's keeping it secret. Pascal isn't going to tell anyone. We would never agree otherwise. Not at any price."

"How is he going to make billions without telling anyone? That doesn't seem possible."

"I know. But it's Archibald Pascal. And he's going to tell us his big secret before we reveal ours. That's the deal."

Satisfied that they had almost everything important that Sackler could tell them, Vicky slipped her zapper over his ears and hit the switch. She let it run for six seconds, then killed the power. "Are you going to keep practicing law after you make the exchange with Pascal?"

"No. We're retiring."

"All of you?"

"No choice, really. The deal gives him exclusive use of the technology."

"How are you feeling?"

"Tired. Dizzy. What did you give me?"

She gave him another six-second dose. "How long ago did you learn to read minds?"

"About twenty years."

"Who discovered it?"

"I did, with Colton, Jim, and Trent."

Another six seconds. "At MIT?"

"That's right."

"What about Scarlett?"

"She was our test subject."

Third zap. "Why her?"

"She was Colton's girlfriend. They were living together. We all shared a house."

Fourth zap. "Whose idea was it to become lawyers?"

"Scarlett's. She was the law student."

"You've been monitoring mind-reading research ever since your discovery?"

"Yes. That's Trent's job."

Fifth zap. "How many other people have made the discovery?"

"Just the girl at Caltech."

"In twenty years, just one? Don't lie to me."

"It's an extremely sophisticated and precise process. During the early years we were worried, but after two decades without competition we were surprised when Trent reported that she'd done it."

"Then you decided to kill her."

"She was being reckless. She went to work in Las Vegas as a psychic. Even got a show at the Bellagio. It was only a matter of time before her secret leaked."

"You practiced law for twenty years. Why is that different?"

"You're asking me how a lawyer differs from a psychic?"

"You were both using your skills in public."

"We're very careful."

"And she wasn't?"

"We couldn't risk it."

"Do you want some water?"

"Yes, please." *Give me a minute to collect my thoughts.*

Vicky slid a small bottle under the pillowcase, found his lips then elevated it until empty. They'd laced the water with twice as much Rohypnol as they'd used on Rogers, given the increased need to keep any current memories from imprinting.

As Sackler fought back sleep, Vicky administered the final zap, then stuffed the gag back in. He tensed, but didn't have the energy to fight it.

"We're done. Sweet dreams." She backed away from the bed to wait for him to nod off. There was no need to worry about him faking. She could read his mind.

As a scientist, Vicky found it fascinating, watching a person's mind go to sleep. Watching thoughts slow and flicker before disappearing. She'd been disappointed to learn that her Pradas did not pick up dreams, but perhaps that was just as well. She did not need another can of worms—for the moment, at least.

Once Sackler was sawing logs, they removed his bonds and returned everything else to normal. Then they retreated to the closet where they would stay until he left the apartment—or died.

64
Headaches and Worries

WALTER SACKLER considered himself to be a simple yet sophisticated man. Simple in that he knew what he liked and he limited his life to those few things. Sophisticated in that he was highly discerning about them. He liked eating out, but only at excellent establishments. They didn't need to be five-star—street carts and pizza parlors could be excellent—but they had to be special. He liked socializing over his meals, but only with people whose minds and means were in the same rarefied stratosphere as his own. Fortunately, New York City was the perfect place to find both.

Given the unpredictability of weekdays and evenings, Sackler had just two standing social events on his calendar. Both were on weekends, and both were with fellow elite members of the legal community. First Fridays were poker nights at the Harvard Club with fellow law school alums. He kept his glasses powered off during those. Well, except when Arnie Levitz showed up. Arnie had won the class trophy their year, and Walter had vowed he'd never be bested by that little prick again.

Saturdays kicked off with a 9 a.m. attorneys' brunch at Tavern On The Green, the legendary Central Park eatery. A two-hour, Mimosa- and Bloody-Mary-soaked palate-cleansing session used to share frustrations of the past week so they wouldn't fester during the week ahead.

At least, that was the stated idea. The founding principle.

Sackler gained additional advantages at both, of course, but especially at the brunch where he could read his colleagues' minds. While the legal elites were all in the stew together, fighting the same temperamental judges, tangled bureaucracies, and twisted rules, they were also, of course, competitors. Both for clients and for ego points. It served Sackler well to know what his peers truly thought as they smiled over shared meals and pretended to be friends.

Except that today, he was not being served.

As Lowell Matthews chimed in on the masterful managing of the witnesses in the Pascal case, Sackler could not read his mind. Just as he wasn't able to read the other four minds around their table. Or the server's for that matter. It was their usual table, so the odds of some atmospheric interference were small, but it felt that way. He could catch an occasional word, but not much more. His glasses had to be on the fritz.

Except maybe they weren't.

He'd woken with a terrible headache and an uneasy feeling. Neither was like anything he'd previously experienced. His first thought was food poisoning. He'd joined a few friends for dinner at a trendy Japanese restaurant, where they'd drowned the week's stress with sake and sushi. No one had opted for the potentially deadly Fugu, the puffer fish, but it was in the kitchen along with who knew what else. The Japanese were well known for eating anything you could pull out of the ocean.

Another thought that struck him as he exited his steamy shower was a forgotten concussion. Physical trauma. An impact that had smashed his brain against his skull. He didn't play football, and he hadn't been in a car crash, but he had the vague recollection of something bad happening. Had he slipped? Hit his head and gone to bed? Or maybe fallen out of bed at night? The polished marble floors were beautiful but, well, hard as a rock. A cursory feel hadn't revealed a bump, but maybe he should get his head looked at.

If it wasn't simply an eyeglasses malfunction. He had a spare pair at home and another in the office. Under biometric and combination lock, of course. But better to go straight to Trent. Keller assembled and serviced their eyewear. He could try his glasses there and then and— No, that might be a bad idea. What if it was him and not the glasses? What if it was permanent? Without mind reading, he'd no longer be on par with his partners. He'd be putting himself at a significant disadvantage. No lawyer worthy of his membership to the bar ever did that. Then again, he couldn't effectively hide it either. Not during a trial. He'd be handicapped. You might as well take away his eyes, given the extent to which he relied on his sixth sense.

"Are you all right?" Lowell asked.

Sackler refocused and saw that everyone was looking at him. He took a deep breath. "Actually, I have a killer headache. Woke up with it, and the coffee didn't chase it away."

"That's a Bloody Mary in your hand, Walter," Gavin Gates said, trying to coax a smile.

"Good point." He raised his hand and quickly caught the server's eye. A benefit to being a regular customer and big tipper. "I'll take a double espresso, please."

He was eager to leave, to swap out his glasses, but couldn't show any weakness to this crowd. He would finish his brunch—without another sip of booze—then swap out his glasses at home. If that didn't solve his mind-reading problem, he'd head to the hospital for a checkup. If they didn't find anything, he'd take it easy and hope to wake up healthy tomorrow. If that didn't happen, well, then things were going to get interesting when court resumed on Monday morning.

65
Creative Cooking

CHASE HANDED his server $100 before following Sackler and his bodyguard from the famous restaurant. As predicted, the attorney headed northwest, toward home and the office, rather than deeper into Central Park.

Keeping pace about fifty feet behind, Chase popped in an earbud and speed-dialed Skylar. He expected the call to go straight to voicemail, given that she'd been up for most of the night, but she picked up immediately.

"How's it going?" she asked.

Skylar had kept him apprised of developments in Sackler's bedroom and bathroom by texting from the closet, so Chase was ready and waiting when Walter walked out the lobby door at 8:50, heading for his 9:00 brunch.

"We just left Tavern On The Green, where he met five guys for lunch. Looked like a lawyers' club, but I'm guessing. I couldn't get near enough to overhear anything or smell the brimstone."

Skylar chuckled. "What's the verdict?"

"I think it worked. He seemed distracted and irritated. He ended up breaking with the bottomless Bloody Marys in favor of espresso during the middle of his meal."

"Vicky will be thrilled to hear that."

"She asleep?"

"Yep. What's next?"

"Looks like he's heading either home or to the office. I'll keep you posted."

Chase kept his promise by walking through their front door five minutes later. "I'm back," he called while heading toward the big window in the living room.

"What are you doing?"

"I stuck a camera on the lobby wall, just inside the front door. I can grab the signal from the window seat."

"You're just going to sit there and watch it until he leaves again?"

"Well, I'm hoping you'll relieve me for a bathroom break or two if necessary, but I don't think it will be. I think he's going to be heading out soon."

"Why's that?"

"What would you do if you discovered that your ability to read minds had vanished?"

"I'd check my equipment."

"Right. I assume he's putting on a spare pair now. But we know the glasses aren't the problem. So what's next?"

"Next I'd go to my doctor. Complain of a severe headache or something similar in order to get tested."

"Exactly. And there he is now, talking to Charles. Gotta go."

Chase switched his polo shirt from black to white and his sunglasses from black framed to gold aviators on his way out the door. He ran down the stairs and entered the lobby only to find Sackler still chatting up Charles and not looking happy while his bodyguard blended into the woodwork.

Chase walked past them and out the front door without observably paying anyone the slightest attention. He headed for the nearest crosswalk, hoping to follow them to a hospital from in front. Mount Sinai, Lenox Hill, and Presbyterian Hospital were all across the park. Given the weather, he was hoping Sackler would walk rather than ride.

Two minutes later, that was exactly what the lawyer did.

Chase didn't enter the hospital elevator with the ailing attorney and his bodyguard. He didn't need to know the office or floor. The very fact that Sackler was seeking medical attention was all Chase needed to know.

He returned to the apartment to find Vicky brunching with Skylar. Both looked his way expectantly. "What did you learn?" Skylar asked.

Chase looked at Vicky. "He went to a concierge medical practice over by Mount Sinai. You did it!"

Vicky exhaled, long and slow, then asked, "Did you hear Sackler speak?"

"Not really. He only talked at the table, where he was too far away to distinguish. I'd have tried to listen in if not for the bodyguard."

"Did you get the impression that his speech was normal?"

"I did. Nobody was looking at him funny. He seemed anxious and preoccupied during the meal and after, but otherwise normal."

"And he looked healthy? His face in particular."

"No sign of stroke, if that's what you're thinking."

"It is."

"So your opinion is that the procedure was a success?" Vicky pressed.

"It is. Sackler seemed normal enough until—my assumption—he realized that he wasn't reading minds. That tells me he didn't have other significant symptoms."

"What do you think they'll find at the hospital?" Skylar asked.

"I don't know. His bloodwork will probably still show the Rohypnol, if they look for it. A CT scan might reveal signs of stroke, but it might not. Depends on whether the low-power zap caused bleeding while denaturing the target cells. Given what you've reported, I'm hopeful that it didn't."

"Won't the scan show the cell damage your device did inflict?"

"It would show up if anyone were looking for it, but they won't be. Medical screenings follow protocols based on percentages and they're analyzed by people trained to look for specific anomalies."

"In other words, they're not Sherlock Holmes investigations,"

Chase clarified.

"Exactly. Who's got time for that?"

After a moment of silent digestion, Skylar asked, "So now what?"

"Now we zap the other three," Chase said.

"The other two."

"Three. Don't forget Trent." Chase had confirmed that RRS&S's silent fifth partner did indeed live in the same building. He owned an apartment on the tenth floor. Vicky had inquired with Charles, Pradas on, and learned that Trent occupied 10A and the bodyguards 10B.

"Ah, yes. How could I forget the psychopath? I should be drinking coffee rather than tea." Vicky rose and walked toward the coffee maker. "Actually, it's four. Don't forget Pascal."

Chase felt like he'd been punched in the gut. Pascal! Of course. The tech exec was the biggest threat of all. And a whole new level of challenge. Simply zapping him wasn't going to do it. They had to interrogate him first. They couldn't defend the world from his billion-dollar idea if they didn't know what it was.

"Let's worry about Pascal and his plans once we've sorted out the lawyers," Vicky continued, after pressing the brew button. "Resseque, Slate, and Keller aren't going to be as easy as the first two. I can't see us breaking into Trent's apartment. Not with the off-duty bodyguards right there on the other side of the peephole. And we don't have keys to the twelfth-floor apartments either."

Chase's mind was still reeling, but he managed to push the mess aside. He'd made a mental breakthrough on another front and was eager to share it. "I'm hoping we won't have to worry about any of that. Tell me, does the zapper need to be in contact with the head to work? Or could it be, say, three feet away?"

Vicky canted her head and took a sip of coffee before replying. "The technology could work at three feet, using increased power, from a modified system. But as you know, I don't have a way to calibrate it, so it would be risky. What are you picturing?"

"I'm picturing a microwave oven."

"A microwave oven?" Skylar blurted. "As in—a big one we invite them into?"

"Exactly," Chase said with a smile before turning to Vicky. "Only there's no invitation required. Could you design a zapper that I could attach to the elevator roof?"

66
Stressful Circumstances

COLTON RESSEQUE was not prone to panic. Given that his naturally high-powered analytical mind was augmented by a unique mind-reading ability, and he'd been working the same job with the same partners in the same system for twenty years, he found life predictable. When you could predict what would happen, panic was rarely warranted. One simply accepted that there would be rough spots and then pressed on, past the lumps and bumps that were part of life.

But the predictability of his routine had virtually vanished overnight. His partner of twenty years and friend of thirty had been lowered into the ground that very morning, and now the venerable business they'd built was crumbling before his eyes.

"Say that again?" Colton asked.

Sackler cleared his throat. "I appear to have lost the ability to read minds."

The four surviving partners were seated around the coffee table on Scarlett's terrace. This was supposed to be a day of remembrance and mourning. They'd just lost a man who'd played a role on par with a parent or child in all of their lives. But Walter had insisted on an emergency meeting, and now it was clear why.

"What do you mean, appear to have lost?" Scarlett asked.

"It's become like trying to listen to a radio station after driving out of range. I still catch a word here and there, but there's no music, so to speak."

"That's not you, that's your glasses," Trent said, pulling a pair from his breast pocket. "Here, try mine. Read my mind."

Colton noted that Walter did not look relieved by the news or offer. No doubt he had already checked his spare pairs.

"Nothing," Walter said.

Trent took the glasses back, put them on and focused on Walter. "You already tried both the spare pair at home and the ones in your office," Trent said, reading Sackler's mind before removing the glasses.

"When did this start?" Scarlett asked.

"I noticed yesterday morning at brunch. I'd woken up feeling woozy with a headache, but assumed it was from too much sake or some bad sushi the night before. I didn't think I'd drunk that much, although I felt totally wiped out when going to bed. At the time, I'd figured it was the stress of the week culminating on a Friday night, you know?"

Everyone nodded. They knew.

"We'd lost Jim," Walter continued. "And then there was the circus of the Pascal trial, in which so much is at stake. I was thinking maybe the stress got to me more than I realized."

"Maybe it has," Trent said.

"Maybe. Hopefully. I went to see Dr. Kahn. He ran toxicology and oncology tests, and he took CT scans of my head and chest. He called me with the results just before the funeral."

"And?" Trent prompted.

"Everything was clean."

"So what's going on?" Colton asked.

"I have no idea. Frankly, I'm scared. But of course I need to push that fear aside because Pascal's trial resumes tomorrow."

"The final week," Scarlett said. "And we all know how important it is to end on a high note. To have a grand finale before the jurors head off to deliberate."

"Which is why I called this meeting," Walter said. "Under less stressful circumstances, I might have taken another day to see if things improved."

"We'll all be hoping for that, but we can't count on it," Colton said.

Scarlett was a bit less diplomatic. "This is a disaster for us all. The most important case of our lives, and we're crippled."

Colton clunked his heavy tumbler on the table. "Normally I'd offer to step in, but I'm slammed. I'm doing double duty with Jim gone."

"You can't postpone for a week?" Sackler asked.

"Not on these cases, and not with my judges. I couldn't lie about why, given that I'll then be on TV defending Pascal. There's no way they'd let me screw up their dockets to 'go grandstand for the cameras.'"

The three attorneys all turned to Trent, who reddened.

"I've never worked in a courtroom. You know that."

"Desperate times call for desperate measures," Scarlett said. "You could sit in the audience and take notes. Slip us anything important."

"No way I could get away with texting?" he asked hopefully. "Couldn't you slip a phone around security and pass it to me?"

"Not a chance. The courtroom is packed and Judge Whitcomb will sanction me before the jury in a second," Sackler said.

Trent spread his hands in surrender. "Okay. I'll do it."

"So we're agreed?" Scarlett asked. "Trent and Walter will work together until we win the case or Walter gets better?"

The lawyers all nodded, then reached for their drinks but stopped short. The alcohol would have to wait. They turned back to Trent, who was staring into space with a look of shocked contemplation. Their attention snapped him out of it. "Right. Time to get to work."

67

Balance Beam

SCARLETT COULDN'T REMEMBER the last time she'd been so relieved to hear a judge say the words, "Court adjourned." She couldn't recall a time when one of their mid-trial analysis and planning sessions had been so contentious. And she was certain she'd never anticipated her next day in court with such dread.

As they walked home, she asked, "Are we agreed, strategy session over breakfast at six?"

They all nodded.

She sent a text to her assistant, then held Colton back as Trent and Sackler walked ahead. Just the few steps required to gain a bit of privacy so she could vent. "I'm struggling without special assistance from Walter. I knew it would be a challenge, but even expending twice the energy, I'm only half as effective. Obviously, mind-reading isn't required to practice law, but—"

"We've always relied on it," Resseque said, completing her thought.

"Exactly! All our courtroom prep and practices are built around both of us having use of our glasses. We're a team with a finely tuned and highly effective routine."

Resseque nodded. "I get it. Your cart has lost a wheel. After two decades of effortlessly rolling along, you're suddenly wobbling around beneath the weight of an unwieldy load. I'm going through the same thing. Fortunately, my cases aren't such a circus."

Scarlett had been so focused on her own situation that she'd forgotten what Colton was going through having lost Jim. Well, forgotten wasn't the right word. It just hadn't been front of mind. She had no mental bandwidth for anything but the sexual assault case and its implications. "It was a brilliant move on Pascal's part."

"Linking our lives to his verdict?"

"It's every client's dream. We feel for them all—to a greater or lesser degree—but I've never been nearly as vested in an outcome before."

Colton put an arm around her shoulder. "I know. Me too, and it's not even my case."

"Pascal's not very pleased with us."

"That's understandable. You had an off day, and then you refused to include him in the strategy session."

Scarlett threw up her hands. "It was for his own good. He can't be allowed to know what's going on with us, and we needed to discuss our situation to serve him, so he couldn't be there. It's so frustrating!"

"I get it. I'd be frustrated too." He gave her shoulder a squeeze. "You're doing it right. You did the post-game analysis and set your team up to play better tomorrow than you did today. Now you need to get a good night's sleep and pray that Walter and Trent do too so you all bring your A game to court in the morning."

"Good point."

"With luck, this time tomorrow we'll be sitting around a table with Pascal, toasting your stellar performance. Take that image to bed with you. Dream it and make it so."

"I'll do that. Thank you, Colton."

The apartment lobby was empty when they walked in. Walter and Trent had already gone up to bed. Scarlett hoped they had psyched each other into a positive state of mind the way Colton had her, but she doubted it. Trent didn't work that way.

She and Resseque didn't speak during the elevator ride up. She didn't want to risk stepping off the mental balance beam, and he seemed to sense that. As she exhaled to relax, to breathe out the day's stress while literally transitioning from work to home, from plugged to unplugged, on to off, she felt a killer headache coming on. One of those deep-brain pains she associated with the lack of vascular pressure coming from caffeine withdrawal. In this case, however, it was as if the cessation of stress had opened up her mind to the toxins floating around.

Scarlett knew what to do. She'd drink a big glass of water, take a hot bath, then do some stretching before bed, all with soothing spa music playing in the background and images of a victory celebration dancing in her head. With luck, she'd wake to a much brighter world.

68
Hardware and Software

THE PARTNERS of RRS&S had a strict policy against reading each other's minds, and that generally extended to the personnel dedicated to supporting their peers. It did not, however, apply to their own staffs.

It could be argued that their trademark horn-rims were the world's single best personnel management tool. What could be better than knowing exactly what your employees were thinking? When they were unsure or insecure or feeling overworked or undervalued? When they were hiding disagreement or hoping for praise? In the hands of a professional—someone who had learned to disregard the noise, the stray thoughts, foibles, and fetishes that invaded everyone's thoughts from time to time—it was extremely powerful.

Scarlett also used her precious tool to get honest feedback during tense times. "Thanks for coming in early, Margaret."

"Whatever I can do, Ms. Slate," her assistant said, arranging the breakfast delivery. Everyone had their favorite foods, and Margaret knew them all. Each of the assistants did.

"How are people doing after the funeral?" Scarlett asked.

"We're all sad. Chloe and Mr. Anderson are a bit anxious. They want to know what's next for them."

"It was very unexpected, so we haven't figured everything out yet, but Chloe and Mr. Anderson will be fine. With Jim Rogers gone, they're more important than ever."

"I'll let them know, if that's okay."

"Sure."

Margaret began turning to leave, but hesitated. "Is everything okay, Ms. Slate?"

"Why do you ask?"

"I feel that I've upset you. Did I say something I shouldn't have?"

"No, no, Margaret. Thank you."

Scarlett checked her watch as her assistant walked away. Five minutes to six. Under the circumstances, five minutes would feel like forever.

"Good morning," Colton said, walking into the partners' conference room early, as if in answer to her silent prayer.

"I'm not sure it is," Scarlett replied, her voice cracking

"What is it?" he asked, riveting his full attention on her.

She stared at him.

"You're wearing your glasses," he said.

"Have you put yours on today?"

"No. Why, is there a problem?"

"Mine aren't working."

Colton whipped his horn-rims from his breast pocket and put them on in a single fluid motion. He stared at her as his face paled. "Mine either."

"What's going on?" Sackler asked, as he and Trent entered the room.

"We— We appear to have lost it too," Colton said, his voice off by an octave.

Trent shifted his gaze back and forth between them a couple of times before donning his own glasses. "Oh, my God. How could this happen?"

"That's the *million*-dollar question," Colton said. "The *billion*-dollar question is: can we fix it in time to save Pascal?"

"Is there a chance that it's the glasses? That some component exceeded its shelf life and they're all failing at the same time?" Sackler asked. "I tried all my pairs over the weekend, but I didn't test anyone else's."

Everyone turned to Trent, who assembled and maintained their devices.

"It's possible. I was just reading a story about how our Stealth aircraft suddenly became visible to radar one day. Turned out that DuPont changed an ingredient in the paint without informing the Air Force. Off the top of my head I can't think of what our faulty component could be, but it's worth checking."

"You keep our old pairs locked up in the shop, right? Let's try them first," Colton suggested.

Trent had converted the panic room in his apartment into a workshop that was easy to secure. "Do you want to come with me, or shall I run for them?" Trent looked at his watch. "We need to be in court in three hours."

Colton said, "Run. We need to leave from here." He turned to his fellow attorneys as Trent made his exit. "If it's not the glasses, what else could it be?"

"It's either hardware or software, right? There's no third option," Sackler said.

"The software being our brains," Colton clarified.

"I can think of a third option," Scarlett said. "There could be interference, like a jamming signal."

Colton turned to her, visibly impressed and pleased. "Right! The Wall Street guys are constantly doing outlandish things to increase their transaction speed by a few billionths of a second so they can arbitrage the system and scoop the next guy. Who knows what secret new technology they might have installed nearby."

"I hope that's it, but I seriously doubt it," Sackler said. "It's affected me everywhere I've been, including Tavern On The Green."

Colton waggled his hand. "Maybe it's a satellite thing. Or some new cell phone technology that's everywhere the carrier's phones are." He held up his Samsung. "This could be the problem. You know how precise our system has to be. How accurate the calibration."

"Good points. I pray you're right."

"I do too," Scarlett said. "But I have to say the thought that it might be a *software* problem scares the skin off me. What if this is the early stage of whatever killed Jim?"

"A disease that we and only we are getting?" Colton asked with a skeptic's intonation.

"It could be environmental. When the Russians poisoned that guy in London by putting polonium in his tea, he wasn't the only one who got sick. The whole bar became radioactive. People were coming and going for weeks getting radiation poisoning before Scotland Yard figured out what happened."

"What are you saying?" Sackler asked.

"I'm saying we have a crazy, deadly situation and in the interest of saving our lives we should consider every angle."

"Including *the Russians did it?*"

"That was just an example. Point is, if it's our brains and not our glasses that are malfunctioning, we need to look for environmental factors and enemies."

"What kind of environmental factors?" Colton asked.

"Well, the glasses themselves, for starters," Scarlett said. "We've been beaming other people's thoughts into our brains for twenty years. Maybe there are side effects."

"I don't see how."

"I don't either. And unlike you, I was never a scientist. You guys invented the technology, not me. Can't you run some experiments? Figure it out using ferrets or whatever?"

Sackler removed his worthless glasses. "None of us have been in a biology lab for decades. I'll speak for myself, but I very much doubt the other guys feel differently. I'm way too rusty to work on something so sophisticated. Seriously, how much of your college calculus classes do you remember?"

Scarlett set her glasses aside as well. "If you can't do laboratory experiments, then at the very least we need to get ourselves laboratory tested. Let's use our wealth and connections to have our heads thoroughly examined without disclosing why we're concerned. If this is a side-effect of our technology, we need to know."

"I already did some tests," Sackler said. "But now that you mention it, I was looking for specific things based off recent events: food poisoning and stroke. It makes sense to go broad and deep. The question is *when?*"

"Colton can call in sick and go now. We can go tonight. Colton, will you make arrangements with Dr. Kahn?"

Resseque nodded. "I'll head over there as soon as Trent confirms that reverting to old eyewear doesn't fix the problem. Meanwhile, I think we need to consider the other environmental option."

"What other environmental option?" Sackler asked.

"The non–side effect one," Scarlett said as her stomach shrank another size. "The one where this was intentionally inflicted through some devious means, like the Russian polonium thing."

Sackler nodded. He understood. "Cassandra."

Colton surprised Scarlett by smiling. "What is it?" she asked.

"If it's Victoria Pixler and not Mother Nature who's causing our problem, we're well equipped to fight back. All we need to do is let Fredo know that she's here."

"How do we get him to New York without revealing our identities?" Sackler asked.

"That's easy. We tell him she's after Archibald Pascal."

While Scarlett nodded along with her peers, another idea struck. "We should modify Fredo's instructions. Change the order from *kill* to *capture*. That way we can learn what she's done, and how to fix it."

Her partners all nodded. They were also more nervous about the medical threat than they'd been letting on.

"Okay," Trent said. "I can call him right now."

"Put him on speaker," Colton said. "I want to hear his reaction."

69
From Daydream to Nightmare

ARCHIBALD PASCAL wasn't sure how much more courtroom drama he could take. The prosecution's asinine arguments were absolutely unfair and positively maddening. Yet he had to sit there with a smile.

To force the required facial expression, Pascal retreated to the solace of his own mind. He was a living legend for good reason. While he hadn't dropped out of Harvard like Zuckerberg and Gates—he'd earned a degree from Wharton—Pascal had dropped out of a PhD program at Stanford after just a few days. And now he was ranked alongside them on *Forbes'* most coveted lists: the World's Richest people and the World's Most Influential.

Racking up that record had not been easy. Or abrasion free. While millions now admired him, *still* admired him, nobody had ever called him a saint. Power and wealth did not come without costs. Costs to earn them and costs to keep them.

He would not have been there, in that courtroom chair, if he had not been a wealthy or powerful man. That was the real injustice here. He was being prosecuted for a commonplace occurrence solely because he was powerful and rich.

And the whole world was watching, because he was powerful and rich.

Although Pascal had endured plenty of unpleasant situations

while building his fortune and name, nothing from his history compared in size or scale to the shitstorm he was suffering now. The humiliation didn't bother him, not really. Not yet, anyway. No, what chewed his cherries was the requirement to sit there for days on end, sympathetically meeting the gaze of women who were attempting to disgrace and then rob him—while the world watched and cheered.

It had been bearable when his lawyers were winning. The satisfaction of squarely landed counterpunches had offset the occasional painful jab. But for the past two days, he was taking the hard hits and the bitches were the ones struggling to suppress smug smiles.

Worst of all, for the first time in years, he was looking at the real possibility of losing something meaningful. Something more valuable than money or even power. Something he couldn't recapture or buy back. Instead of thanking him for advancing their careers with highly paid jobs, the vengeful cows were trying to steal his time.

And for what?

They'd all had sexual encounters a hundred times before and a hundred times since. Why was their experience with him any different? What distinguished that particular tryst from their scores of others? What separated it from the countless other times they'd used tits, winks, and smiles to get what they wanted? Just one thing, and everyone knew it. Pascal had money.

Unwanted attention? Please. If attention was unwanted, why were they wearing high heels and pushup bras? Why the makeup and painted nails? You want to be treated like a guy? Dress like a guy. But don't wave a red cape, then blame the bull.

A knee nudge under the table snapped Pascal back into the moment. He looked over at Sackler, who was pointing to two words scrawled small on his notepad. *You're glowering.*

Just then Wanda Willet, the she-devil who wanted to use his

carcass as a stepping stone to the DA's office, said, "Your honor, the prosecution calls Diane Maestretti."

Pascal felt his stomach drop as Slate shot to her feet. "Objection, your honor. Ms. Maestretti is not on the witness list."

"Rebuttal witness, your honor. Ms. Maestretti has firsthand knowledge that the relationship between Mr. Pascal and Ms. Barrymore was not always cordial, as the defense just claimed."

"Overruled," Judge Whitcomb said.

Again Slate rose. "Your honor, we'd like to request a short recess to discuss the new witness with our client prior to her testimony."

Whitcomb looked ready to deny their motion but then his expression changed. Perhaps he needed a bathroom break. "Granted. Court will reconvene in fifteen minutes at three-thirty." He tapped his gavel.

Pascal's attorneys ushered him to a quiet corner of the courthouse while their bodyguards coordinated to form a human barricade some twenty feet back.

"Who is Diane Maestretti and why am I hearing her name for the first time?" Slate said, sounding neither calm nor cool and collected.

"A woman I briefly dated. I'd honestly completely forgotten about her."

"Well, now that you do remember, perhaps you can tell us what she's going to say, so we can attempt to keep you out of prison."

"We went out once. That was it. Nothing special."

"One time?"

"One time."

"When was that?"

"About six years ago."

"Six years ago is when you had the contentious encounter with Beth Barrymore."

"I know."

"Did you discuss Ms. Barrymore with Ms. Maestretti?"

"I vaguely recall crossing paths with Beth while I was out with Diane."

Slate turned red.

Sackler asked. "What will her testimony be? Come on, we have no time to spare here."

"I really don't recall, but after some very expensive cognac, I might have said something to the effect that she was an employee with benefits."

"An employee with benefits?" Slate asked. "As in a friend with benefits?"

Pascal shrugged.

"Is that it?" Sackler asked. "Tell me that's it? Tell me nothing else has slipped your mind."

"Actually, now that I'm thinking about it, about her, I'm remembering why we never had a second date."

"And why was that?" Sackler pressed.

"The morning after our first date, while we were out at breakfast, mind you—meaning after she'd spent the night—she asked me why I hadn't stopped when she said *no*."

70
Greed

SCARLETT HUGGED COLTON HARD as he walked through her front door. They'd been in an exclusive relationship for years, since back before becoming wed to their careers, and they still enjoyed the occasional roll. Usually that took the form of a midnight walk across the connecting foyer, when one was feeling the need for release without courtship or complications and the other was willing.

The same had been true on the eleventh floor.

The four were eminently compatible in more ways than one. Their intellects, preferences, and personalities were all on par.

Trent was a bit of a misfit. While his IQ equaled theirs, his instincts and inclinations were a tad mismatched. Nonetheless, the shared history and parallel goals made the five of them an effective unit. A team that had not seriously struggled in twenty-five years.

Scarlett released her partner and gazed into his eyes.

"I know," he said. "I know."

At least that form of mind reading still worked. "This is absolutely the lowest point of my life."

"Mine, too."

"But I'm fearful that I have yet to hit bottom," she said, leading him to the living room seating area she'd set up for their meeting.

"Me, too," he repeated, taking his usual seat. "It's particularly painful because just one week ago, we were at the high point of our lives and living with the expectation of rising even higher."

"Exactly, Colton. That's exactly it. How could this happen so fast?

"I've been thinking about that. Our situation is not so

uncommon."

"What?"

"Happens all the time. Successful people like us, cruising along, enjoying life while optimistic about the future. Then *Wham!* the doctor says 'Cancer.'"

Scarlett hadn't thought about it like that before. She didn't think that doing so now would help.

"And we're going to do exactly the same thing those people do," Colton continued. "The smart ones anyway. We're going to fight it and we're going to beat it. Mind over matter—plus the right kind of medicine."

"And what medicine is that?" she asked, hopeful that he had news.

"Well, answering that question is why we're meeting."

"What question?" Sackler asked, as he and Trent walked in.

"How to cure our cancer," Scarlett said, deflating.

"Nice analogy. Feels like testicular cancer to me," Trent said.

Scarlett changed the subject. "Any word from Fredo?"

"Nothing."

"But he is in New York, attempting to capture Cassandra, correct?"

"Right on both counts."

"Good."

"Have we completely ruled out hardware?" Colton asked, also turning to Trent. "I know that even the old glasses don't work, but that's not definitive, is it? There could still be some common component that expired, right? It's possible?"

Trent took Jim Rogers' usual seat. "The only way to completely rule out this being a hardware issue is to put a pair on someone else and then ask them what they're hearing."

They all nodded solemnly, knowing that could never happen.

"So I did."

"What?!" everyone said at once.

Trent raised both palms. "Relax. I did it with a random guy I'll never see again. A dishwasher taking a smoke break out behind a restaurant on Staten Island."

"Still, now someone knows. He's going to talk," Resseque said, his voice an arctic blast. "*Anyone* who learns that mind reading is possible is going to talk."

"Come on, Colton. Where's your lateral thinking? Did you lose that, too?"

"You killed him?" Scarlett asked.

"You guys. Seriously. Has fear frozen your brains?"

"None of us are ourselves at the moment, Trent. Please, tell us, why won't he be talking? And more importantly, what did you learn?" Sackler asked.

Trent calmly opened a bottle of water and took a sip before replying. "I memorized a few lines of dialogue from *The Bold and the Beautiful* and repeated them in my head while holding the glasses on his temples. Then I took them off him and asked if he'd heard the soap opera. He thinks it's a new style of wireless headset."

That was smart, Scarlett thought.

"So it worked? They work? The glasses are fine?" Sackler asked.

"It's definitely a software issue," Trent said, continuing with the euphemism.

"Crap," Colton said, expressing what they all felt.

Scarlett rose and stared out the window, buying a peaceful moment to think before returning her attention to the group. "We're not going to fix a software issue before court tomorrow. And it's highly unlikely that we'll figure it out before Pascal's case goes to the jury. Agreed?"

Everyone nodded.

"So rather than waste time on that, we need to pour all our efforts into two things. One," she threw a finger. "We need to win. A week ago, the Pascal contract was a nice-to-have. Now, with our legal careers essentially over, it's a must-have—which we won't get if Pascal is in prison. Agreed?"

Colton and Trent said, "Agreed," but Sackler asked, "Why do you say our legal careers are over? We can still practice without mind reading. It's what literally every other lawyer does. Our perfect reputation will take its first hit if Pascal gets convicted, and that will be a big hit, but we won't have any trouble finding clients willing to pay astronomical fees."

Scarlett recognized the emotion behind her partner's reasoning: greed. She wasn't immune to it herself. They'd earned tens of millions as attorneys, but they'd also spent accordingly. Society life in New York City was exceedingly expensive, and they'd availed themselves of all of it. You only live once, right?

Even so, they'd have been fine if they hadn't invested almost everything with Bernie Madoff. When his firm collapsed in scandal, their life savings were among the $17.5 billion that vanished.

Fortunately, they had one huge investment that had gone untouched. Their apartments. The block of six apartments had appreciated very nicely, and as of last month, the mortgage was paid off. Each of them owned tens of millions of dollars in real estate, plenty to fund a luxurious retirement—outside New York. She'd be happy to move, as would Colton. Trent was an unknown. But Walter definitely wanted to remain in the Big Apple. To do that, he had to keep the paychecks coming.

Scarlett sensed a major clash brewing. The first since the founding of their firm.

71

Unintended Consequences

SCARLETT EXPERIENCED a chill of foreboding as Walter's words sank in. Practicing law without mind reading? She wanted to kill that idea in the crib.

Colton beat her to the punch. "We all agreed that we were tired of practicing law, and that was with our superpower. Working without it, for the first time, at this stage in our careers—" He shook his head. "That would be about as pleasant as a car crash.

"Imagine what life would be like if every day were as disastrous as today. We knew Ms. Maestretti was mixing half-truths and lies into her story, but we couldn't string her up with her own words because we couldn't read her mind. We had to sit there and take it on the chin while smiling for the circus. It was humiliating."

Colton waved his arms. "And now— Now we're hiding from both the media and our own client for chrissakes. Phones off, office closed. Scared and shy as kicked cats. It's disgraceful, Walter. Last week, we were lions. No, sir. I will be retiring. No question about that."

Colton shook his head while everyone stared at him in silence, then he turned to glare at Sackler. "Theoretically, you could continue practicing law if you wanted, but you'd be smart to put yourself on suicide watch first."

"Why did you say theoretically?" Sackler asked, ignoring the emotion and focusing on the details, as a good attorney should.

Colton dropped his bomb. "I, for one, will be voting to dissolve the firm after the Pascal case. That way, we either retire on a high note with a perfect record, or we retire after our first loss—which would also be the stuff of legends. *They went undefeated for twenty years and then dissolved the firm after their first and only loss. Can you believe it?* Those are both legacies I can live with. A slow spiral into disgrace is not."

"I agree," Scarlett said, jumping in forcefully with both feet. "No matter what, this is the last case for Resseque Rogers Sackler & Slate."

Sackler couldn't hide his disappointment. "What about our other cases? Colton, you aren't even on Pascal's team."

"I've already handed off my existing case load. I gave them to friends, citing 'personal reasons.'"

"What personal reasons?"

"I'm not saying, and they're not asking. But with Jim's recent sudden demise, it's not shocking anyone."

Trent rapped his knuckles on the coffee table. "Can we get back to urgent business? How are we going to ensure a not-guilty verdict for Pascal? I ask because we've had two disastrous days in a row, and are now huddled here hiding from the most important client in firm history?"

Instead of answering Trent, Sackler turned to Scarlett and picked up on their prior thread. "What's the second thing we need to be pouring our efforts into?"

"Glad you asked," Scarlett said. "But let me answer Trent first. Regarding getting to *not guilty*, all we can do is focus on strategy tonight, and then on flawless execution tomorrow. All four of us. Agreed?"

"Agreed," all replied.

"Good. Our second essential task is to absolutely, positively ensure that Pascal does not learn that we've lost the ability to read minds. Certainly not before we sign the contract, if we sign the contract."

"What do you mean, *if we sign the contract?*" Sackler asked. "Is there any question?"

All three partners turned their laser like stares on her, but

Scarlett ignored the heat. "Yes, there is a question. We can't sign the contract until we know what Pascal is going to do with the technology."

"Right. That's been our plan all along," Sackler said. "We weren't going to give him exclusivity on our technology if we didn't believe his business plan was viable. But we never really questioned that it would be. At least not in my mind or in any group discussions. This is Archibald Pascal, after all. The top investment managers bet on him all the time."

Scarlett took a deep breath. "Right. That's all true. But the reason we might not want to sign has nothing to do with Pascal's business sense—"

"But you just said: 'We can't sign the contract until we know what Pascal is going to do with the technology,'" Sackler interjected.

Tensions were high all around, Scarlett noted. And rightly so. "I did. Look, if Pascal is going to use it to personally make billions by running some super hedge fund or whatever, fine. We've had a good twenty-year run and he will too."

Everyone nodded.

"But if Pascal has some other use in mind. Something that will expose large numbers of people to whatever medical condition we have. Whatever killed Jim. Assuming it was a side effect of wearing the glasses and not Vicky Pixler. Well, then by signing the contract with Pascal, we'd become mass murderers."

72

The Transformation

SKYLAR COMPARED Vicky's face to the one on the photographs for the hundredth time, then said, "I think it's time to show Chase your transformation."

"I agree," Vicky said, rising from the vanity stool and slipping on her new pair of glasses.

They walked out to the main room, where Chase was busy on a laptop.

"What do you think?" Vicky asked.

He gave her a quick study, then made a few mouse clicks, no doubt pulling up the same surveillance pictures of Scarlett Slate's assistant that Skylar had been using. His eyes went back and forth a few times as Vicky slowly rotated her head. "You don't know what I think?"

Vicky glanced at her phone screen, but Skylar didn't need to read it to know what was on her husband's mind. They'd nailed the match, achieving a look that was at once sexy and sophisticated.

Vicky blushed before removing the horn-rims. "Thank you."

The three of them had spent Sunday brainstorming ways to locate and then interrogate Pascal. Finding him was not easy—at least by conventional means. Half the New York press and paparazzi were searching for the tech CEO while he was in the city for his trial. Fortunately, it was nearly impossible to hide information like that from a woman who could read minds. When asked, even Pascal's stone-faced driver couldn't help but recollect the name of the Cathcart, a midsize luxury hotel a few miles from the courthouse.

The real trick, of course, was creating an opportunity to

interview Pascal in private, again at a time when half the New York media was angling for exactly that honor, and Pascal had ordered his bodyguards to prevent it.

Chase discovered the first piece of the interview puzzle when he noted that one employee at RRS&S looked a lot like Vicky would if she were blonde, busty, and presented with the right clothes, hairstyle, and makeup. That employee, he then learned, was none other than Scarlett Slate's assistant. Meaning that Pascal was likely to have seen Margaret Gray, but probably had little if any direct interaction with her.

"You really do look just like her," Chase added.

"At least the part that matters most to a guy like Pascal," Vicky said with a smile and a downward glance.

The padding in her bra was not the usual foam. Chase had employed a CIA trick that he said was devised in Moscow during the Cold War. He'd used feminine hygiene products rather than foam to provide the alluring lift, thereby creating a diaper into which drinks could be poured when one wanted to get an adversary drunk. "Works great with vodka shots," he'd said. "And presumably with Pascal's favorite vodka martinis. But he's also a fan of red wine, which would be wise to avoid."

Skylar had helped Vicky practice covertly emptying various types of glasses into her boosted cleavage, to get the drainage just right. She seemed to have the technique down, but was wearing a burgundy dress just in case. One with all the right cuts and contours, of course.

The second piece of the get-to-Pascal puzzle revealed itself to Skylar on Monday—in court. While Vicky and Chase were busy in her workshop creating eyewear that matched the RRS&S trademark style, and concealing a second device in a pair of hair barrettes, Skylar was watching the train wreck performance of an attorney unaccustomed to working without mind reading. Although that was a satisfying confirmation that Sackler had been zapped, it wasn't the breakthrough.

The key insight came after court as a direct result. It struck during a hushed and huddled conversation, which left Pascal furious and frustrated while watching his attorneys walk away. A gap was growing between client and attorney. An opportunity gap.

The acrimony worsened on Tuesday when the remaining RRS&S partners were also forced to work without cheating. The stress and strain created an opening which Vicky was about to exploit. Or rather "Margaret Gray" was.

Chase offered Vicky two items after she set her new glasses aside. The first was a fake RRS&S building security card key, created to resemble Margaret Gray's actual ID. It wouldn't unlock anything, but it would perfect her disguise. The second item was a tube of lipstick. "Please take this with you," he said, holding it up.

"I've already got one in my bag, but I don't expect to need it since we won't be eating."

"It's a gun."

"What?"

"It's only good for one shot, but it should slip past the bodyguards. It's a last-resort option. Think of it as a security blanket." He went on to demonstrate while she warmed to the idea. "You need to prime it before firing. Do that by rotating the bottom two full turns after removing the cover. You'll feel it click when it's ready.

"To fire, you hold it between your middle and ring fingers with the base firmly against your palm, like this, and you punch your attacker as hard as you can. Preferably in the head, back, or chest." He demonstrated different strikes a few times, emphasizing grip and arm movement. "Got it?"

"I think so."

"Repeat it back while you show me."

She did, then asked, "Where did you get this?"

"Made it in your lab. I've made them before. It's a simple

construction. Keep it in your jacket pocket, rather than your purse. That way it will always be handy. Put a tampon next to it as a camouflaging deterrent."

"A camouflaging deterrent?"

"The guy searching you will be that much less tempted to take a close look if the lipstick's not alone. Trust me."

Skylar produced one, on cue.

"I will," Vicky said, pocketing both before adding, "Armed and dangerous."

The lipstick wasn't the only weapon she'd be taking into the most important battle of her life. In her handbag, she had the zapping headphones and a second cell phone that was linked to her barrettes. It had been modified to self-wake ten minutes after being powered off. Finally, Chase had form-fitted Rohypnol tablets under her long acrylic pinkie and ring fingernails, where they'd be easy to access without anybody noticing.

"Skylar and I will be in the lobby, sitting as close to Pascal's bodyguard as inconspicuously possible, tracking your phone. If I spot trouble, I'll pull the fire alarm. If you hear it, run like the building's burning."

"Got it."

"Wait!" Skylar said. "She can't hear fire alarms."

Vicky flashed an appreciative smile. "My phone recognizes alarms for what they are and will vibrate until silenced. It's a safety feature."

"The hotel will also have strobe lights in hallways and stairwells," Chase added.

"Glad to see you're both way ahead of me," Skylar said before turning to hold Vicky's eye. "You sure you're okay with this plan? It might not be necessary. Pascal might lose. Sackler and Slate are floundering without their secret skill."

"I'd love to believe that, but I know better. He won't lose. The evidence may be shifting against him, but Pascal will still benefit from the jury Sackler and Slate picked when they were empowered."

"You think that's enough?" Skylar pressed.

"I do. One thing you learn while reading minds is that people aren't easily swayed by logic on emotional issues. Even if that weren't true, I'd still have to do this. We absolutely, positively have to learn what Pascal has planned—and then we have to stop him."

Skylar recognized the look in her friend's eye. It was a blaze the lawyers had ignited when they killed Chewie.

"You sound so determined," Chase commented.

"I've been thinking about it. About his plan to make billions without revealing the technology."

"And you figured it out?" Chase asked, moving closer.

"Not specifically, but generally—based on world history."

"I don't follow," Skylar said.

"If someone is making billions doing something in secret, there's one thing about which you can be absolutely certain."

"What's that?" Skylar asked.

Vicky glanced down at the lipstick gun. She'd been nervously rolling it between her thumb and fingers. She looked back up and met Skylar's eye. "It's evil."

WITH HER HEELS clacking out determination on polished travertine, Vicky walked across the Cathcart Hotel's lobby toward the man Chase had told her was likely a member of Pascal's security team. He was sitting in the corner pretending to wait for a colleague to show.

She stopped directly before him and flashed the key card she had clipped to her purse. "Please tell Mr. Pascal that he has a visitor from Resseque Rogers Sackler & Slate."

The bodyguard wasn't supposed to acknowledge that Pascal was there, but his thoughts betrayed him. "You recognize me, right?"

Those tits are familiar, and she has a badge. He read the name off her ID card. "Margaret Gray."

"He'll recognize me," Vicky added.

"Hold on." The bodyguard snapped her photo and sent it off with a text.

Vicky walked around the lobby to hide her anxiety, but stayed clear of the front desk so the staff wouldn't get a good look at her face. Chase was convinced that if she came and went without drawing attention to herself, the bodyguards would not mention her to the police. Why invite an investigation? Why make themselves look bad? Why risk lawsuits while ruining careers? Implicating the winningest law firm in the world was the exact opposite of a smart strategy, especially when Mother Nature could take the blame. Vicky found the logic solid, and desperately hoped it proved predictive.

One minute passed. Two minutes. Four. Then the bodyguard signaled.

"He'll see you. Follow me." The large man led her to an elevator, then waved a hotel keycard over the control panel. The button for Floor 20 illuminated. The penthouse floor. She glanced at the bodyguard long enough to grab two nuggets from his mind. He wasn't suspicious, and Pascal had reserved the entire floor.

She was met at the penthouse elevator by another burly bodyguard. This one held a metal-detecting wand. "Ms. Gray, may I please see your bag?"

Vicky handed it over but retained her cell phone.

He pulled out the headphones, spare phone, and massage oil, then ran the wand over her bag, inspecting every buzz. Once satisfied, he powered off the cell and raised the wand in her direction. "Your turn."

She pulled the lipstick and tampon from her dress's concealed accessory pocket, flashed them to him with an open palm, then assumed the raised hands pose used inside airport scanners.

After the wanding, he held open her purse. "Please turn off your cell phone and watch, then put them inside."

"I need the phone." She showed him the printing on the back of the case. PARDON MY WANDERING EYES, I'M DEAF. "My phone and watch have voice-to-text. It's how I hear."

"I have to follow protocol. You can ask Mr. Pascal for them back. Meanwhile, you seem to do just fine reading lips."

Chase had predicted as much. Vicky nodded acquiescence as she slipped her toiletries back into her pocket.

He walked her to room 2001, where a second bodyguard opened the door without knocking. He remained in the hallway while she was escorted inside by the man with her purse in his hand.

"So you're the brave one," Pascal said. "Is your boss still huddled in hiding with her partners?"

"They are fully focused on preparing for tomorrow. I'm here to show you something special."

"And what's that?"

"It's a private matter, having to do with our other business arrangement."

Pascal's focus went to her glasses.

"You know about that?"

"I'm a very dedicated employee. Ms. Slate trusts me with everything, and I never let her down."

"Well then you'll understand if I ask you to please remove your glasses."

She did.

Pascal turned to the bodyguard. "What's in her bag?"

"Her watch, two phones, plus a big pair of headphones and a bottle of massage oil. No wallet."

"No wallet?" Pascal asked.

"I was mugged once. Now I use my watch to pay for things."

Pascal nodded then turned to his bodyguard. "Put the bag in the bedroom and leave us."

The tech exec studied her until they were alone, then said, "Back to that *something special.*"

"Not so fast," she said, gesturing toward the bar. "Let's have a drink first."

Archibald Pascal had no trouble getting women, but doing so during his sexual assault trial would be extremely ill advised. Meeting with his attorney, however, was entirely acceptable. Plus, Ms. Gray promised to be more than just an hour's entertainment. There was a sparkle to her eyes, a sultry something in her gaze, and of course the temptation of forbidden fruit.

Scarlett Slate had sent her, of course. Perhaps against her will, perhaps not. Clearly she was there for a bit of quid pro quo. The usual female quid for his extraordinary quo. His billion-dollar idea.

The lawyers of RRS&S were hedging their bets.

That was not a good sign in regard to his assault case, but it was understandable. He'd have been disappointed if they hadn't shown the spunk to try. And this offer was both a bit creative and insightful. This was conceivably one of his last free nights for a long time to come. Scarlett had shown a savvy bit of psychological insight there, although she'd underestimated his ability to keep secrets. Perhaps the story of his long-ago lapse with Ms. Maestretti had inspired her. In any case, he wouldn't be tricked or seduced into revealing his big secret to their Mata Hari. But he most assuredly would enjoy the game. The cat and mouse. The tit for tat. "Sounds delightful. Can you make a good martini?"

74
Sidewalk Slip

FREDO BLANCO FIGURED that he owed much of his success to two distinct personality traits. The first was a naturally calm disposition. He could operate normally in extremely abnormal situations. Stressful, dangerous, and dreary situations. As long as he wasn't worried about infectious pathogens, he could perform pretty much anywhere with the same insouciance that prevailed at ballgames and brunches.

The second secret of Fredo's success was his relentlessness. That characteristic resulted from his loving the hunt every bit as much as the kill. The process of detecting clues and anticipating moves energized him. While his targets grew weary from endless fear and perpetual motion, he grew stronger. He built up while they wore down until success became inevitable.

The incident in Pasadena had been disappointing and most unpleasant. While he was mad at himself for not anticipating the bulletproof clothing, he was pleased with his success at walling off the bloody memory.

Best of all, Fredo was now getting his second shot at that mark sooner than expected thanks to his anonymous employers supplying additional information. Crucial information. They'd let him know that Victoria Pixler might be hunting Archibald Pascal during his trial in New York City. His clients also happened to know what half the local press wanted to uncover: the location where the legendary entrepreneur was staying during the last week of his trial.

The Cathcart Hotel was a nineteenth-century twenty-story French Renaissance–inspired château-style building that dripped wealth and oozed tradition. The elegance of the lobby and fastidious nature of the employees did nothing to deter the white elf, however. He immediately placed facial recognition cameras covering both front and back entrances.

While such an installation might sound tricky, especially in a location as busy and sophisticated as New York City, there was actually nothing to it—if one was bold and invisible. Dressed in his usual hide-in-plain-sight disguise, a janitor's uniform, Fredo had simply "serviced" the emergency exit signs. He did so while the lobby staff were swamped checking guests in and out, and the maintenance staff were occupied resolving issues he'd created.

Fredo always used the best equipment and the most sophisticated software, but this time he'd also been able to feed the facial recognition system plenty of high-resolution imagery, thanks to his target's prior public persona. As a result, very few false positive alerts appeared on his phone. Nonetheless, he'd almost dismissed the one from the Cathcart's front lobby.

The face in the photo was right, but the woman pictured was blonde, busty, and dressed in a provocative burgundy dress. People disguising their appearances usually went for inconspicuous options, whereas this woman was sure to attract amorous eyes. Having learned to trust his software, however, Fredo took a closer look and decided that the identification had likely been accurate.

He smiled as the implications registered. Victoria Pixler wasn't stalking Archibald Pascal from the high grass. A lioness eying a lone hyena. She was hunting him undercover.

Fredo could fall for a woman like that. A woman with the balls and brains of a man. Too bad this one wouldn't be "available."

His employers had attempted to modify their order from *kill* to *kidnap*. They'd pushed hard for that. All five of them had gotten on the phone to put the pressure on. Fredo had pushed back. "If you told me she was hiding out in a mountain retreat, I'd say 'no problem.' But you just gave me the name of a luxury hotel in New

York City. That means lots of eyes, lots of cameras, and no convenient place to park a car. I can't be hauling unconscious bodies around in that environment. I'll do what I can, but I offer no guarantees."

"We need her alive," the silky voiced one had insisted. When Fredo again pushed back, the others again chimed in. They were nervous. An emotional state the assassin had not detected in them before.

After their second round of pleas, Fredo forced them to decide. "I'll do my best, but if kidnapping is not possible, do I let Pixler go, or kill her?"

The phone muted for a minute, then the chorus of voices came back on. "Kill her."

That predictable reply had sealed the psychic's fate. He wasn't going to risk his freedom to improve client satisfaction. Of course, he could have asked for more money in exchange for the guarantee requested, but that would have been an amateur mistake. Getting greedy and overextending was what landed guys like him in prison.

Given the way Pixler had entered the hotel, Fredo figured she would likely exit the same way. Out the front door, chin high, heels tapping. An assassin who would vanish before anyone became aware of her crime. He knew the tactic well, and admired her for using it. Stealth was a good choice, given Pascal's contingent of bodyguards. Three by Fredo's count.

He would need to account for them too.

Eliminating the tech CEO's protectors wouldn't be problematic in and of itself. Fredo was highly effective because even the professionals never saw him coming. Three seconds, three shots, and the guards would be gone. Pop pop pop. But that would create a conspicuous and messy scene. He hated those. Best to wait for her outside. Maybe she'd screw up and the bodyguards would do the dirty work for him.

If Pixler did survive her mission and emerge alive, Fredo would simply brush by on the sidewalk and stab her heart with his stiletto.

75
Détente

VICKY IGNORED Pascal's pat-the-couch invitation as she handed him a drugged martini. "We have something in common, you and I," she said, taking a seat across the coffee table.

"And what's that?" he asked, his tone telegraphing both that he was up for the game, and that he planned to win.

"We are the only two people who have figured out how the partners of RRS&S do what they do."

"Really? You figured it out? They didn't tell you?"

"I did. It was a lucrative discovery, I assure you." She raised her glass.

"Well played," he said, taking a sip. "And well made," he added, raising the glass again before a second swallow. "So now Scarlett's hoping you'll put your intelligence and intuition to work on me?"

"A sensible move, given that you're guilty of the charges—and many more. Wouldn't you agree?" It was a risky play, calling him guilty to his face. But Vicky needed to know, given what was to come.

He studied her sideways for a second, as if trying to read her mind.

She winked.

"You weren't repelled by the challenge?" he asked.

"Fascinated is more like it. What a mind you must possess, what spectacular genes, to have conceived and executed so many brilliant business plans." As Vicky spoke, she thought she could see the Rohypnol going to work behind his eyes. Then again, perhaps that was wishful thinking.

"I work very hard. The press makes it look like my businesses were overnight successes, but they were all years in the making. Trust me, I've had my share of failures and sleepless nights."

"Speaking of big brains and sleepless nights, my colleagues have been burning the candle at both ends trying to figure out your latest billion-dollar idea."

"And?"

"They've gotten nowhere. Despite the knowledge that it's possible. Even with the clue of knowing who figured it out. They've got nothing. They're worried you're bluffing. Are you bluffing, Archie?"

"To what end? To get them to work harder on my defense?"

She ran a fingertip around the rim of her martini glass. "That would make sense."

"Not really. There's no evidence they need to work harder. They've literally never lost," Pascal said, his eye on her finger.

"But why risk it? Tell me, just between us, is it real?"

"It's real."

She continued toying with the glass. "If it truly is, then answer one question. Hypothetically speaking, how would it be possible to generate billions in revenue without exposing the technology that makes it possible?"

Pascal held her eyes. "What happens if I play along with your hypothetical game?"

"Well, then we can take it to the next level."

"And what level is that?"

Vicky rose and collected Pascal's glass for a quick refill, adding sway to her stride during her round trip to the bar. She wouldn't use the second tablet yet. Her plan was to playfully stir it into his drink when the time was right. For now, another martini should provide sufficient lubrication. "Depending on your answer, it might be the level that involves my toys."

"I would love to play with your toys."

Vicky smiled but said nothing.

"Okay. I'll give you an example. Google makes billions off its search engine, right?"

"Right—" *She was doing it. He was talking! More importantly, he was thinking.*

"And everyone knows that, right?"

"Sure—"

"But how does Google do it? Why do they win the search engine battle?"

"Their algorithm is the best."

"Exactly. Their algorithm is the best. But what's in their algorithm?"

Vicky struggled to fight back her excitement. "Nobody knows. That's the big secret."

"There you have it."

One can only hope. "So you're going to make a better search engine?"

"No. That was just the hypothetical example you asked for. Now, fair's fair. Tell me about your toys. The massage oil I can guess. What about the headphones?"

"They cancel noise, helping you focus and heightening the pleasure."

"That's it?"

"Oh, no. That's not it at all, Archie. That's just a chocolate sprinkle. There's a whole cupcake underneath."

"I like the sound of that."

"I thought you would," Vicky said, playfully bringing a finger to her lips.

"Tell me about the frosting."

"First, you tell me what's not hypothetical."

"I will be delighted to. But only after your partners win my freedom."

"So it's not a better search engine?"

"No."

"Is it similar?"

"How about the cake? Tell me about the cake?"

"Finish your drink, and I'll think about it."

Pascal did.

Vicky made another. This time, she sat beside him on the couch when she brought it back. "Can you imagine … what sex is like … when your partner is eager to please you … and she can read your mind?"

Pascal blinked a few times, then grew a broad smile.

Vicky dipped her nail in his drink and began stirring suggestively. "If not the next Google, then what?"

"If you're really nice, I may tell you in the morning."

"Really?"

"Honest."

"What, exactly will you tell me?"

"What it's like."

"Not some abstract reference? Something specific and concise?"

"Yes."

"A two- or three-word summary?"

"I'll give you a whole sentence," Pascal said with a wink.

"You'd really do that—for me?"

"I might. But it's definitely not going to happen if your act falls short of spectacular."

"I believe that's what they call détente," Vicky said, putting verve in her voice to camouflage the nervous tension. "Finish your drink, then come join me in the bedroom."

76
One Word

THE FIRST THING Vicky did in Pascal's bedroom was confirm that her second cellphone had been capturing the output from her mind-reading barrettes. If it had not, all that good thought she'd coaxed would be lost like the sound of a tree that fell when no one was around. And given that this would be the last opportunity to learn the details of his devious business, she'd have to go further than planned in the bedroom.

The thought repulsed her. The idea of being with any man other than Chewie brought tears to her eyes. She wouldn't be ready for that for a long time to come. But tonight, she would bite the bullet for king and country if absolutely required.

Vicky tried to psych herself up as she scanned the text on her phone, knowing that her next act needed to be completely convincing. Pascal was exceptionally intelligent, powerful, and intriguing. She forced herself to focus on that, while walling off his arrogant attitude toward others and utter lack of respect for women.

The transcript was there! She scrolled through it to the point where she'd said, "A sensible move, given that you're guilty of the charges—and many more. Wouldn't you agree?" His mental response followed. Three magic words, and a window to his soul: *That I am. Does that bother you? Or turn you on?*

Knowing that time was tight but needing to confirm that she'd obtained the main mission objective, Vicky skimmed on. An odd, repeated word caught her eye. *Lexi.* The code name for his billion-dollar idea was Lexi. Or LEXI. Or Lecksi. Vicky's software converted the mental voice to text, so the spelling of unfamiliar words was just a guess.

She wanted to read more, but couldn't risk being caught with the phone and eyeglasses. Even in his sedated, inebriated state, that sight would likely raise a big red flag. One that might result in his yelling for a bodyguard. So she tucked her mind-reading tools away and turned to her toys. She set the headphones and massage oil on the nightstand, then shot over to his closet, in search of accessories.

A minute later, Vicky was sitting seductively on the puffy white duvet. Four of Pascal's silk ties were draped around her neck, and her burgundy dress lay like an invitation on the floor. She wore a come-hither look and lingerie designed with alluring optical illusions in mind.

But Pascal didn't come.

She found him on the couch with an open mouth and an empty vodka glass still in his hand. The second tablet had been too much.

Tempting though it was, Vicky couldn't leave him there. Not only did she need Pascal to look like he'd made it to bed, but now she wanted to ask him about Lexi.

One tug made the task appear Herculean. His arm was like a heavy rope, and his body an anchor that had sunk into the couch. That image made her remember the first rule of holes: when you find yourself in one, stop digging.

She called Chase.

"Yes, I'm here. Are you okay?"

"I'm fine. He passed out on the couch."

"Well done. We read the transcript. It's good, but insufficient. He has amazing mental discipline. Do you think you could wake him up and ask a few more questions?"

It took Vicky a second to orient. She'd forgotten that Chase had made himself a clone of the second phone, which synced with hers in real time.

"About Lexi?"

"Exactly."

"That's what I was thinking, but I need to get him into bed before beginning the next phase, right?"

"Definitely. It won't look right if he's found clothed on the couch. Oh," Chase said, catching on. "*That's* why you called."

"Yeah. He must outweigh me by fifty percent. I figure I can probably haul him to the bedroom if I focus my rage, but even picturing Chewie I don't think I can lift him onto the bed."

Chase responded with a speed that told her he'd been down that road before. "Use the ironing board as a ramp. Pull him up it by bracing your feet and using your legs."

Vicky pictured the process. She should have thought of that. "Okay. Hold on."

It was still a struggle, given that she didn't have firm footing during the critical parts. Halfway through she started laughing at the irony of how tough it was for her to get Pascal into bed. The giggles gave her the boost she needed to get him there. Two minutes later, Vicky had his clothes off. She considered hanging them up, but decided it would look more natural if they were left discarded on the floor.

"Done," she said, while returning the ironing board to the closet. "Should I tie him up as if for sex games, as planned?"

"Better safe than sorry. Just make sure you can untie him when you're done."

Vicky bound the billionaire to the bedframe with his own silk ties, then gave him a few face slaps and a vigorous shake. "He's not waking up."

"Clamp his nose between two fingers while pulling his mouth shut with your thumb. Hold it until his eyes pop open. Call me back if it doesn't work."

Vicky returned the phone to her bag, then did as instructed. It didn't take long to achieve the desired reaction.

"What happened?" Pascal asked, his voice at once rattled and groggy.

"Looks like I was just too much for you, big boy. But to be fair, you were nearly too much for me too." She stroked his face while he struggled to remember her body and his performance. "Now fair's fair. Tell me more about Lexi."

"Ask Lexi," he said, closing his eyes with a smile. "Just ask Lexi," he repeated, drifting off.

Was Lexi a person? His Cassandra? Was Pascal's big idea repeating what she'd already done, but bigger? Not just a live show, but a phenomenon? Like the Oracle at Delphi? A brand? That would be ironic. And a relief. Vicky slipped on her glasses and pulled out her phone, knowing that he was too zonked to recognize them for what they were. "How does Lexi make money?"

He didn't reply.

She gave him a shake.

Nothing.

She clamped his nose and mouth again.

He reacted, but slower and groggier than before.

"Hey, Archie. How does Lexi make billions?"

The corners of his mouth moved, more like the start of a smile than speech. He said nothing, but his mind managed a one-word answer. *Advertising.*

77

The Show

FREDO WAS NOT the kind of guy who'd daydream or listen to baseball during a surveillance op. For him, it wasn't a waiting game. He'd use the time for reflection, analysis, and planning. He'd plot contingencies and prepare countermeasures. Since he'd studied the Cathcart Hotel's architecture prior to placing his cameras, Fredo was already familiar with its entrances, exits, service areas, stairwells, and security systems. Therefore, his first move while waiting for Victoria Pixler to emerge was to identify which room she had entered.

Ironically, Pascal made that easy, particularly for a Latino dressed in a generic gray janitorial uniform. Fredo simply took the stairs to the top floor, confirmed the presence of a bodyguard by the elevator, then noted the number of the room where the second dark suit was posted.

With that information in hand, the white elf set about figuring out how long he was willing to wait, and what he would do if and when that time expired. He ran those calculations from a curtained perch on a scaffolded building across the street.

The *how-long* question was one of assumptions. In this case, Fredo assumed that if Vicky didn't emerge within two hours of entering—looking like the kind of woman with whom most guys would love to spend an intimate hour—then she was likely staying the night. In that case, she'd either be planning to make her escape in the wee hours while her mark was supposedly still sleeping, or first thing in the morning, while he was assumed to be showering. If her assassination attempt failed for whatever reason, then she'd likely leave with him in the morning.

That last scenario was unacceptable. Departing with Pascal meant exiting via a secure route in the presence of bodyguards.

Fredo decided that he'd wait until 1:00 a.m., then take action.

The *what-then* question was answered during his second hour on watch by a combination of location, luck, and personal experience. Fredo had found that the easiest way to force a stranger from a crowded building was to create an evacuation event. Luck and location lent a hand when the fire station down the street noisily dispatched a hook-and-ladder along with a smaller engine and command vehicle.

Dressed in his anonymous gray coveralls, Fredo simply slipped into the nearly empty station and stuffed his go-bag with a few items that the firehouse had arranged for fast access, namely a uniform, helmet, and boots. All were a bit big, but the smallest among them would do. He ignored the implication of the residual floral scent on its fabric.

Before returning to his perch to watchfully wait out the clock, Fredo bought a few additional supplies at an all-night pharmacy. When the clock hit 1:00 without a sighting or electronic alert, he launched Plan B.

He toted his heavy bag around back to the Cathcart's service entrance, where his bump key quickly defeated the mechanical lock. Once inside, he took the service elevator to the eleventh floor, then hit the stairwell, where he donned the firefighting garb atop his janitorial uniform.

Fredo liked being a firefighter much more than a cop. In his experience, people had mixed reactions to police uniforms. While most were deferential and a bit fearful, a decent percentage were less than respectful to a lone officer of Fredo's size. They attempted to feed their frail egos with lame displays of pseudo-bravery. Usually the assault was verbal, but occasionally it presented physically, with the rebel blocking his path or some other quasi-passive move.

Firefighters, by contrast, got nothing but respect. Going that route made operations more efficient and led to less collateral damage.

Fredo found the maid's closet, which was conveniently located next to the stairwell. He tested the door. Locked. He then listened at the doors of five surrounding rooms. All quiet. As was the hall.

He pulled a 32-oz bottle of 91% isopropyl alcohol from his bag, and tipped it so that the contents ran under the closet door. He did that five more times with the surrounding guest rooms, then walked the circle again to collect the empty bottles.

Once they were all back in his bag, Fredo again listened for signs of life by cupping an ear to each door.

He again heard nothing. No snoring, no television, nobody asking, "What's that smell?" It was the middle of the night, after all.

Satisfied that circumstances were ideal, Fredo pulled a wedge from his bag and propped open the stairwell door. He dumped everything he didn't need down a trash chute, then extracted the first of six matchbooks from one of the uniform's big pockets. "Let the show begin."

78

A Million to One

RATHER THAN ATTEMPT to wake Pascal again in hopes of learning more, Vicky decided to leave well enough alone. She didn't want him calling out or creating abrasions by pulling on his bonds. Hopefully his one-word clue would allow them to decipher the Lexi question.

She removed the neckties binding Pascal's ankles and wrists, then returned them to his closet. She tucked him in, arranged the bed, and pulled her dress back on. Once she'd zipped up, Vicky walked to the main room and, using a tissue, took Pascal's martini glass to the sink where she thoroughly rinsed the inside before adding a few drops of vodka and setting it beside hers on the counter, with his fingerprints still intact.

Returning to the bedroom, she adjusted the duvet and pillows to improve the post-coital vibe, then slipped the headphones over Pascal's ears. At that point, Vicky froze. Should she do this? Could she do this? She'd killed Rogers, but that had been an accident. The direct result of one of his attempts on her life.

This would be intentional. Premeditated murder. And Pascal had not tried to kill her. He had assaulted multiple women. He did deserve life in prison and he would get it if justice was served. But this was the death penalty, and it was for a crime he had yet to commit. Preemptive punishment.

She considered calling Skylar and Chase, but that wouldn't be fair. It would add to their guilt without lessening her own. Instead, she thought back to their earlier conversation. "Do we zap Pascal too?" She'd asked.

"Not good enough," Chase had said. "The man's an

entrepreneur. If he loses the ability to use the glasses, he'll surely sell the technology and idea to someone else for a percentage of the take."

"That's even worse," Skylar had concurred.

"So, what? We kill him?" Vicky had asked.

"Aside from rendering him an idiot, literally frying his brain, there's no other way."

"I don't know if I can do that."

"I understand," Chase had said. "But consider this. Governments train their citizens to kill all the time. It's been the way of the world since the dawn of humankind. And it's accepted, because it's for a cause. It's for the greater good. For the innocent."

"But I'm not a head of state. Nobody elected me."

"No, you're not, but as the world's leading expert on the issue at hand, there is no better judge. What happens to human civilization if Pascal unleashes mind reading upon it?"

Vicky knew that answer by heart. "Disaster. Social unrest. Wars. Likely the temporary breakdown of civilization itself."

"So lives will be lost?"

"Of course."

"Thousands?"

"For sure.

"Millions?"

Before answering that one, Vicky had reflected on the thoughts she'd heard while wearing her Pradas. The insults, slander, and lascivious musings. The inadvertent confessions of crimes, slights, and infidelities. Then she had imagined what might happen when an inadequate ruler with an army or a nuclear button experienced the unfiltered truth. "Yes, probably millions."

"And all just to make one rich man even richer. There's no doubt about it. Serving justice means stopping Pascal—by any means necessary."

"But what if his plan really would keep it secret?"

"What are the odds of that? One in ten? One in two? What if there's only a ten percent chance that he'll blow it? What if it was your life? Would you sacrifice your life for a ten percent chance of saving millions?"

Standing there in Pascal's hotel room, Vicky reflected on her answer. "I would if I could find the courage."

She hit the power button.

Vicky had returned the headphones to the setting she'd used with Rogers. The lethal setting. Pascal jolted as they powered on, a bit less dramatically than the lawyer had, but he too went limp.

This time, she knew what was going on inside the skull. The capillaries in Pascal's prefrontal cortex were rupturing, leaking blood into his brain while depriving it of oxygen. She didn't want to watch, but couldn't help it. This was a car crash. A train wreck. An unnatural disaster.

While Vicky stared at her victim, a cellphone began vibrating wildly, causing her to jump. She checked her smartphone screen. FIRE FIRE FIRE FIRE. The hotel's fire alarm was sounding. A signal from Chase. She needed to flee like the building really was ablaze.

She pulled the headphones from Pascal's ears and shoved them into her bag. She gave the room one last glance, then ran for the door. It burst open before she got there and both bodyguards filed in. She said, "He's passed out in the bedroom," as they brushed past like she wasn't there.

Vicky ran for the elevator. At least she started to. A fireman blocking the hallway directed her toward the stairs. She wanted to reply, "No worries, it's a false alarm." She needed to make her escape before the bodyguards behind her determined that their charge was dead rather than drunk or sleeping. Before they could detain and accurately identify her. Before they could arrest her for murder.

How fast could she run down twenty flights of stairs in high heels? Should she get off on some random floor and wait for Chase, hoping the bodyguards would run past?

She nodded to the fireman, who was now holding the stairwell door open. "Thank you."

While the words passed her lips, a question crossed her mind. How had he gotten there so quickly? Chase had pulled the alarm only seconds earlier. She met the fireman's gaze and her blood went cold. She knew the eyes concealed by the shadow of that yellow hat. She would never forget the face of the man who had killed Chewie.

Conclusions came quickly. Chase had not pulled the fire alarm. Fredo Blanco had.

The man before her was not there to fight the fire.

He was there to kill her.

79

Defied Expectations

FREDO THOUGHT he caught a flash of panic crossing Pixler's face, but she didn't scream. She didn't reverse course and retreat into Pascal's suite. She didn't call for his bodyguards. Instead she did as he asked and hustled toward the stairs. The sight of his uniform must have sparked her fear of fire.

"The bodyguards will take care of Pascal. My job is clearing the top floor and getting you to safety," he said, pushing open the stairwell door. It was a quasi-preposterous proposition. A concierge-style escort for penthouse guests, brought to you by your local firehouse. But who was going to resist assistance from a fireman during a fire?

All Fredo needed to complete his job and get away clean was a few seconds alone with her. The top of a stairwell was the perfect place—as long as he could act before the bodyguards evacuated Pascal.

Pixler paused as he held the door, then stooped to slip off her shoes.

Frustrating though the delay was, all he could do was wait. Hard to argue that it would be faster or safer to keep her heels on during twenty flights of stairs. She followed the sensible move with something odd. Rather than holding onto her shoes or stuffing them into her large handbag, she tossed them into the hallway behind her. Then, as his eyes instinctively followed, she bolted past him and began running down the stairs.

Fredo charged after her. Or at least he tried. The damn firefighting boots had him at a disadvantage. They were designed for insulation and protection, for safety and stability, not for speed.

Was she onto him? Had her psychic ability alerted her despite his disguise and the disconcerting situation? Or was there another factor in play?

Perhaps she'd just killed Pascal! Was that why he'd seen panic in her eyes? Were the bodyguards about to give chase? Would they shout, "Halt!" and "Murderer!"?

She was getting away. He couldn't keep up in those damn boots. Should he do what she'd done and ditch them? That would spoil his disguise.

Fredo tried another tactic. Rather than taking stairs one or two at a time, he began bounding down them, guiding and controlling his descent by lightly running his right hand along the rail.

It worked.

Judging by the lack of other people in the stairwell, almost everyone was ignoring the alarm. That was hard to believe despite it being the middle of the night, given the noise and flashing strobe lights. They must have been conditioned by annoying tests and false alarms. This one wasn't false, but it wasn't a threat either. The heat from his isopropyl alcohol fires would have set off the sprinkler systems in six rooms, automatically triggering the building alarm and alerting the very fire station from which he'd stolen his clothes.

Although the sprinklers had probably already extinguished his handiwork, rendering everyone safe, the guests might start second-guessing themselves when they heard sirens and saw flashing lights outside. Then again, lazy might continue to win the battle if they didn't smell smoke. In any case, Fredo had to act fast. He needed to dispatch Pixler before the stairwell got busy.

As he gained on her, the smell of smoke drifting up through the open eleventh floor door gave him an idea. He shouted, "We need to use the fire escape."

She didn't reply. Didn't slow.

"I just got word on my earpiece that the fire has spread to this stairwell. We need to use the fire escape," he shouted.

The Cathcart Hotel had no fire escape, but Pixler wouldn't know that. Plenty of New York's older buildings had them. He just needed to keep her confused for another moment. A single second by her side would do it. That was all his hands required for an in-and-out stiletto strike. Countless hours of practice during stakeouts had made his jabs quick as a chameleon's tongue.

His slim five-inch blade didn't look like much. Certainly not when compared to the broadswords of old. But it could bring a person down just as quickly when used with precision.

A quarter-inch puncture on a finger or foot isn't a big deal. The flesh can cope. The wound can coagulate before the body bleeds out. But place that same incision between the ribs and make it deep... Well, then you've got an entirely different story. A very short story. Slice through the wall of an artery or a beating heart and there's simply no recovery. Certainly not during combat, when all five quarts of blood are pumping at four times the normal speed. Under pressure like that, a properly placed pinprick can be as deadly as a guillotine.

Again Pixler didn't reply. Didn't slow. Then he remembered. She was deaf! She hadn't heard him.

With one last long leap, Fredo landed at his victim's side. He practically heard the cha-ching of the second million hitting his account as his boots clomped onto the landing and his hand clamped onto her shoulder. To his surprise, she didn't pull back as he surreptitiously reached for his blade. She didn't attempt to escape or scream. Such was the power of the fireman's uniform, he realized. Women would trust it to the end.

As he used a smile to distract her eyes, to keep them from spotting the stiletto blade springing from its scabbard and locking into place, she again defied expectations. She punched him, square in the chest. She punched him hard, like she meant it. He caught a flash of gold and heard a familiar noise; then Fredo Blanco, the white elf, learned what it was like to be on the receiving end of a fatal blow.

How many times had he stared into the eyes of men he'd just shoved off life's cliff? Men whose minds were reeling from the shock and certainty that they were mere seconds from slamming into a grave? Fredo had lost count.

How many times had he wondered what was going through their minds? Were they thinking of the loved ones they were leaving behind? A wailing widow? Their orphaned children? Or were they focused on those who had already passed, the parents and friends they now might meet again?

Were his victims enduring anything beyond grief or anticipation: fear of the unknown; regret for the undone; pain from their wound; the panic of uncertainty?

Fredo experienced none of those foreseeable scenarios. His mind snagged on a thick, nasty thorn and never ripped free. As the land of the living forever faded to black, Fredo had just one thought. A painful, poignant, irrepressible thought. He'd been bested by a woman.

80
No Coincidence

CHASE JOLTED INTO ACTION as the fire alarm blared to life. That was supposed to be his signal, not Vicky's, but it worked both ways, of course. He pulled up the SLAM-based app he had running in the background to check her whereabouts within the building. The Simultaneous Localization And Mapping software did exactly that, displaying Vicky's interior position on a three-dimensional map it generated while being toted around in her pocket.

"This doesn't make sense," he said. "It shows that she's still in Pascal's suite. No wait, she's moving."

"Why doesn't that make sense?" Skylar asked, now also on her feet and studying the screen.

"You can't manually trigger a fire alarm from a hotel room. The pull boxes are only in hallways."

"Are you saying Vicky didn't pull it?"

"Either she didn't pull it, or she's not with her phone."

"But if she's not with it, how will you find her?"

"I'll have to wing it. Wait for her here while I look upstairs."

A hotel employee held up a hand as Chase ran toward the elevator. "Sir, you need to evacuate the building."

Chase was about to blow him off completely but thought better of it. "Where's the fire?"

"Eleventh floor. Firefighters are on the way."

Chase nodded and diverted toward the stairs, ignoring the shouted objections. There was smoke in the stairwell, but not a lot. People were evacuating, but not many. Was this a coincidence? Had someone burned the toast, so to speak? Had a smoker said "To hell with it" and lit up in bed? Perhaps after emptying the minibar?

Normally Chase would dismiss any such explanation, as it required a coincidence and those were rare during operations. But given that the fire was on eleven and not twenty, the other apparent explanation also involved coincidence. The coincidence of timing.

While Chase had no doubt that plenty of people wanted to see Archibald Pascal dead, given the sexual assault case playing out on the nightly news, what were the odds that someone else would be making a play for him at the same time they were?

The smoke got thicker as he climbed higher, but as Chase passed the fifth floor it still wasn't bad. It didn't feel like an active fire. Despite the noise, people weren't flooding out either. The alarm had probably only been sounding for a minute or so. Sixty seconds, give or take—but it felt a lot longer.

What if the diversion wasn't designed to facilitate an attack on Pascal? What if Vicky was the target? Was Fredo Blanco upstairs now? Had he linked Vicky to the tech CEO?

Chase's mind raced as his legs leapt and his heart pumped. If the killer had perfect knowledge, that made perfect sense. But did he? Had his employers included "around Pascal" in the list of places she was likely to show up? Of course they had. Chase felt like a fool for not thinking of it earlier. If Fredo succeeded because Chase had failed, he'd be burdened with guilt for the rest of his life.

As Chase passed the seventh floor, a single burst of discordant noise disrupted the otherwise rhythmic blaring of the fire alarm. The horn instantly swallowed the sound, but it had been so portentous and familiar that another drop of adrenaline released into his bloodstream. A gunshot! Up above.

While Chase's legs attacked the stairs, his mind absorbed the implications and spit out questions. Had the shot come from the lipstick tube, or a gun? Was Vicky the shooter, or the victim? Would the next bullet be aimed at him? Would he hear it, or just go black? Would Skylar be next?

Chase pulled out his gun as he pumped past nine. He attempted to land each footfall with quiet precision, to keep his approach a secret, but fatigue was swiftly turning that task from difficult to impossible, and adding to the danger.

There's a reason for pairing shooting with cross country skiing as an Olympic sport. It's difficult to shoot straight when your chest is heaving from heavy exercise. Chase was familiar with the techniques that Olympians used to compensate, and he was in decent shape, but he hadn't practiced enough to achieve bullseye precision when his heart was hammering away.

He slowed. There had been no second shot. Thus there was no need to rush. Not recklessly, anyway. What was done was done. If Vicky was the shooter, she was fine. If the assassin had pulled the trigger, Chase needed to prioritize his own health.

Suddenly, she was there. Vicky came around the corner as he passed the open hallway door on eleven. She was barefoot and breathing heavy, but appeared unharmed. He hugged her hard and was about to scoop her up and start carrying her down, when he thought of something and guided her onto the steps instead. "Sit down for a second, I'll be back before you can count to ten."

Vicky said nothing. She was in shock.

Chase helped her take a seat and then took off running. He didn't need to go far. The assassin's body was just three turns away on the thirteenth landing. Fredo was dressed in a firefighting uniform. Chase instantly understood the scenario for what it was. He also spotted the item he'd ascended to retrieve. The lipstick case, with its incriminating fingerprints. He scooped it up and was about to reverse course when instinct prompted another move.

A quick search of the assassin's corpse yielded assorted weapons, which Chase left in place, and two other items, which he took. The first was a rental car key, the second a smart phone.

Although nervous about the clock and Vicky's mental health, Chase knew he'd be wise to spend a few more seconds with the body. He used the dead man's face to unlock the phone and assign a new password before running back to Vicky's side.

She still looked shocked but hadn't lost control. Chase checked her bag. It held the headphones and her glasses, but not her shoes. "Vicky, where are your shoes?"

She blinked at him a few times before speaking softly. "Upstairs. I threw them into the hall as a distraction when I made my break."

"Up on twenty?"

"Yes."

He had a more sensitive question to ask, and no time to go at it obliquely. "Is Pascal dead?"

She nodded.

That settled it. He couldn't risk going after the shoes. "Great job, Vicky. You're amazing. Nobody will ever know it, but you just saved the planet. Let's get you home. Can you walk? Or would you like me to carry you?"

"I can walk."

Chase caught commotion coming from above as they passed the ninth floor. The fire alarm stopped as they neared seven. Over the ringing in his ears, Chase heard firemen talking on radios. Obviously, they'd taken the elevator.

Was it safe to enter the lobby? Yes, for the moment at least. That would change once someone discovered Fredo's body, or the bodyguards reported Pascal's.

Chase took Vicky's hand and descended faster. Soon they were on the ground floor, walking with Skylar toward the street. He flashed his wife the assassin's rental car key. "I'll meet you back at the apartment."

81
Evil

VICKY WAS RELIEVED to find Skylar and Chase in the kitchen, despite the early hour. Perhaps the smell of their coffee had subconsciously drawn her into the cold day from her warm bed.

The night before, after determining that she was physically fine and in no immediate danger, the couple had given her a pill and put her to bed like a sick child. She hadn't resisted. A bit of mothering had been most welcome after what had turned out to be the second most momentous evening of her life.

"Good morning. How are you feeling?" Skylar asked with cheer.

Vicky had half a mind to give Skylar her Pradas. Mind reading would be disastrous for relationships in general, but it might do wonders for therapy sessions, and her lazy side welcomed the efficiency at that moment. "Actually, I think I'm all right. Intellectually, I know I did good. I mean, *we've* made the world a safer place by virtually ensuring that the technology won't spread. For now, at least." The "virtually" qualifier was necessary, and that bothered her. But she'd set that concern aside for now. She had no doubt that the three would soon be discussing how to silence the surviving partners of RRS&S.

"That's great. You should be extremely proud. A difficult and dangerous job needed to be done, and you selflessly rose to the occasion."

"Is it in the news?" Vicky asked.

"It's all over the news. The police are still investigating and the autopsy results have yet to be finalized, but unnamed sources say they're leaning toward natural causes rather than foul play."

"That's a relief. What about the other thing?"

"The other thing," Skylar said, repeating her euphemism, "is getting plenty of coverage as well, given that it happened in the same building at roughly the same time. The bodyguards insist that the arsonist—that's what they're calling him—never stepped foot on the same floor as Pascal. Given the weapons found on him, however, there's speculation that he was attempting to lure Pascal into an ambush."

"But Fredo was the one who was killed," Vicky pressed.

"They're speculating that he argued with a coconspirator. The fact that the gun barrel was pressed to his chest when fired indicates that he knew who shot him."

"Huh," Vicky said, liking the sound of that.

"How do you feel about Fredo's death?" Skylar asked.

"He shot Chewie and I shot him. That feels like justice to me."

"Good. It should," Chase said.

Vicky knew the emotional echoes would prove to be considerably more complicated. She was certain she would frequently return to that scene. In nightmares. In daydreams. Every time she entered a stairwell. But for now, she wanted to shelve the discussion and freeze her emotions on the high note of justice served. "Did you find anything in his rental car?"

"You saw me wave the key?" Chase said, sounding surprised. "As a matter of fact, between Fredo's phone and his car, I found everything."

"Everything?"

"Well, everything we need to give us leverage over the lawyers. Meticulous notes which I've translated from Spanish, and recordings of phone conversations in English."

"Fredo carried around incriminating evidence?"

"Nothing historical. Just his current case. I'm sure he's in the habit of destroying everything the minute he's done the deed and gotten paid."

"Before which it's not evidence because there's no crime," Skylar added.

"So why did you say you have everything we need to deal with the lawyers?"

"Because this time there was a murder *before* he completed the contract."

"Chewie," Vicky said as her heart skipped a beat.

Chase nodded. "There's also an extraordinary conversation where the lawyers ask Fredo to capture you rather than kill you. No names are used, other than yours, but I make out four distinct client voices, including Scarlett Slate's."

"I can't believe the lawyers let themselves be recorded."

"I'm sure they didn't know. Fredo had a second phone in his car. A simple burner that made and received calls only to and from another burner from the same series. A phone used by the lawyers. I'm assuming they gave it to him as a security precaution, and he secretly forwarded it to his smart phone, which has a recording app."

Skylar chimed in again. "The attorneys are obviously distraught during that incriminating call. It was after Rogers' death and Sackler's zapping. People don't think clearly when they're under stress and afraid for their lives."

"Wow. How are we going to use that?" Vicky asked, at once excited and nervous. "I don't want to do anything that risks exposing the technology."

Chase canted his head. "I'm not sure yet, but it will probably involve bluffing. Pretending to have more than we actually do."

As a former psychic, Vicky understood the art of deception. She also recognized that they needed to get a grasp of the big picture before developing what would no doubt be an audacious plan. "Have you analyzed the transcript from my talks with Pascal?"

"As a matter of fact, we have," Chase said.

"And?"

"I know what Pascal was planning."

Skylar snapped her head in his direction. "You do? Why didn't you tell me?"

"It's a recent development. I'm still processing it."

Vicky had been doing the same, and she was more excited about her conclusion than Chase appeared. Perhaps she was further along. "He's going to do what I did, but much bigger, right? Lexi won't just be a Vegas show, she'll be televised. *Ask Lexi* will become true must-see TV, with all the draw of professional sports plus reality TV combined with a talk show. Michael Jordan plus Survivor plus Oprah. With celebrity guests and big questions, televised globally with translations, all on its own channel. Right?"

"That's an interesting idea, but that's not it," Chase said, sounding solemn.

"Really? Are you sure?" Vicky was virtually certain she'd figured it out.

"Don't leave us hanging," Skylar said, glancing at Vicky to express solidarity. "Fill us in."

"I'm not sure I should."

Skylar's tone lowered. "What are you talking about? Of course you should."

They both turned toward Vicky.

Intuitively, she understood. "He's worried about temptation."

"Temptation?"

Vicky smiled at Skylar before turning to Chase. "Pascal really did it, didn't he? He figured out how to generate billions—without divulging the technology?"

"You're right on all accounts."

Skylar glanced back and forth between them. "I don't see the problem."

Chase said, "Pascal's plan is exactly what Vicky said she feared it would be, back when we were talking about making billions doing something in secret. It's evil."

82

Protégés

SCARLETT PUT DOWN the phone and looked at her partners with relief-filled eyes. "Given all the attention, the coroner's office rushed the autopsy. They're calling Pascal's death the result of natural causes. He had a stroke, end of story. The medical examiner did note the unusual presentation, but also the extreme amount of stress in Pascal's life at the moment."

"Is he linking it to Jim's stroke?" Colton asked.

"No. But then Jim had a different M.E."

"Are *we* linking it to Jim's stroke?" Sackler asked.

Colton rubbed the bridge of his nose. "I don't see how they could be connected. Pascal wasn't wearing glasses."

"It's just quite a coincidence," Sackler pressed.

"I don't trust coincidences any more than you, but they do happen. Did you know that shortly before John Wilkes Booth killed Abraham Lincoln, Booth's brother saved the life of Lincoln's son?"

Scarlett didn't want to waste time running down rabbit holes. "What if Pascal was secretly wearing glasses? He confessed to trying to replicate our work. Said he worked hard at it for eighteen months before coming to us. Maybe it was really eighteen years."

"What are you suggesting?" Colton asked.

"Pascal may never have stopped his own project. What if his promise of billions was just a ploy to get close enough to steal our secrets?"

The three men all stared in silence as the implications sank in. Trent was the first to speak, and he nodded as he did so. "The man was a master negotiator and tactician. In high-tech, you have to be. Think about how Zuckerberg played the Winklevoss twins at

Harvard, using deception to delay their website's launch while building Facebook."

Scarlett wasn't a tech expert like Trent, but she'd seen the movie *The Social Network*, so she knew the story—and it clicked.

"The bastard," Sackler said, drawing out the first 'a' as he shook his head.

"He's dead, Walter," Colton said.

"Sorry. The *dead* bastard."

"So the billion-dollar idea was all a hoax?" Scarlett said, as much a statement as a question. "He identified the one thing that could excite us, people who had it all. People who were making millions living celebrity lives full of accolades and peer admiration."

Colton completed her thought. "Billions instead of millions, and all without lifting a finger. We should have known better. We fell for the oldest trick in the book."

"The offer of something too good to be true," Scarlett added, completing his thought this time.

They sat in silence for a while, swimming in a shared pool of shame and sorrow.

"Where does this leave us?" Sackler eventually asked.

Everyone turned to Colton.

"On the downside, we're crippled."

Trent chuffed. "That's a bit more than a downside." He looked around and saw nothing but disapproving frowns. "Sorry. Go ahead."

"On the upside, we remain wealthy and have retained our perfect record."

"So we can milk it," Trent said, again butting in. Again getting glares. "What?"

"So we can go out on top, like quarterbacks who quit while wearing the latest Super Bowl ring. Fans will be screaming for more, and our legacies will remain forever unblemished. Our names will sit atop the record books for all time."

Scarlett liked that picture.

"Your scenario certainly has its merits," Sackler said. "But since it doesn't keep the money flowing, there is an alternative we ought to at least consider."

Trent perked up.

Scarlett was curious, but at that moment would prefer not to hear it.

"We could pass along our *talent* to four protégés. 'Hand-picked successors, trained in our ways,'" he added, sounding like a press release.

"In exchange for a significant share of the profits," Trent said. "How much are you thinking?"

"Generally speaking, we could take lawyers who are already skilled enough to earn $1,000 per hour and give them the ability to double that—in exchange for half their earnings."

"But they'd just break even," Trent said, obviously wanting it to work but not convinced that it would.

"They wouldn't just break even. They'd get prestige, their pick of cases, and the joy of knowing they would never lose."

"Right," Trent said with a smile. "That gets my vote."

Colton raised both palms. "Hold on. Setting the risks versus rewards aside for now, even though they too will require much contemplation and discussion, we have to factor in the recent changes to our health."

"I've thought of that," Sackler said. "While we still haven't definitively linked our condition to the glasses, let's assume that the cause-and-effect relationship exists. We've been reading minds for twenty years, and are only now seeing the side effects. Suppose we write the protégé contracts so as to effectively limit the use of the glasses to ten or fifteen years? We could, for example, select fifty-year-olds and require retirement at age sixty-five."

Trent leaned forward. "Meanwhile I'll be supplying and servicing their glasses, so we maintain complete control while we each rake in about $3 million a year. I like it."

Keller and Sackler turned toward Scarlett and Colton, like tank turrets aiming at the Maginot Line.

83

Virtual Assistance

SKYLAR LOVED HER HUSBAND because of who he was and what he did and the way he made her feel, but moments like these were why she felt so fortunate to be with him. She'd never met another man with so much genius and compassion.

"I'll go pick up some pastries for breakfast," Vicky said, after Chase suggested that she might be better off without the knowledge of Pascal's evil plan. Without his placing that shiny apple of temptation forever within her reach. "That will give you two a chance to talk it through. Then we'll sit down, or not, when I'm back."

"Thank you for understanding," Chase said. "You're amazing."

Skylar was glad the temptation didn't apply to people without Pradas, because the curiosity was killing her. She had seen the same transcript of Pascal's words and thoughts as Chase, but still had no idea how the tech exec was going to secretly turn mind reading into billions. In fact, she thought Vicky's TV show idea was an excellent one. By far the best they'd come up with. But Chase thought he had something better. Or worse, as it were. And he was clearly confident in his conclusion.

"So what's his big idea?" she asked, grabbing the clone of Vicky's phone and finding a key section of text. "Is LEXI an acronym you've heard before? I tried figuring it out, but couldn't get further than Something-Something-Something-Intelligence."

"Lexi's not an acronym. It's a name. And Pascal revealed exactly what Lexi is."

Skylar scanned the transcript. Pascal hadn't said much, or, more importantly, thought much. Between the vodka and the double dose of Rohypnol, he'd had one foot squarely in la-la land and the other on the brink.

"I don't see it."

"Ask Lexi," he prompted, making air quotes. "Just ask Lexi."

"A search engine? Pascal was going to use mind reading to beat Google? Like in his secret-algorithm example?"

"Not a search engine. A virtual assistant. Like Amazon's *Alexa* or Apple's *Siri* or *Google Assistant*."

Skylar thought out loud as she considered that proposition. "A virtual assistant that can read your mind. In some ways, their suggestions make it feel like they already can. *Did you want to reorder this?* Or, *Is it time to go to that?* But those are based on patterns. I can definitely see how true mind reading would be useful, and how such a system would quickly come to dominate the virtual assistant market, but I don't see how to keep it secret. Or cash in on it. Alexa and Siri are free."

"Pascal gave us the crucial clue."

"He did?"

"It was the last coherent thing he thought as he drifted off."

Skylar checked the transcript. "Advertising? I see how that makes money, but how does advertising keep things secret? Isn't advertising the exact opposite of discretion?"

Chase smiled. "How does Google make its money?"

Skylar caught his smile. "Advertising."

"I did a bit of research. Took two minutes. The global market for digital ads is around half a trillion dollars. Google alone brings in over a hundred billion from it. Facebook is closing in on that figure. Alibaba, Amazon, Twitter, and others are also raking in billions from ad placements."

"Okay. But what's the connection? Pascal can't replace Google and Facebook and Twitter, can he?"

"No, he can't. But he doesn't need to."

Skylar reached for her coffee. "I don't get it."

"That's because you're forgetting the intermediary."

"What intermediary?"

"The half-trillion doesn't come from the consumers, the people using Amazon, Google, Facebook, and Twitter. It comes from the companies placing the ads on those platforms. They're Pascal's real customers."

"Okay. Keep talking."

"In short, if Lexi can truly 'figure out' what consumers are and are not interested in, by using a 'secret formula' to predict buying behavior, then companies will only spend their advertising dollars on platforms where Lexi is consulted."

"Because the ads will be so much more cost effective?"

"Exactly."

"But how would Pascal implement it? How could he make Lexi a part of Google and Facebook and Twitter without giving the technology to those companies, which essentially amounts to making it public?"

"Simple. He follows the lead of the world's richest man and puts his smart speaker in every affluent person's home."

"The world's richest man," Skylar repeated, thinking out loud. "Jeff Bezos and the Amazon Echo!"

"Just ask Alexa," Chase said with an affirming nod.

Skylar's head was spinning. "I'm starting to grasp the economic model, but I still don't get the secrecy part. How does he keep people from figuring out what's going on?"

"Pascal told us that earlier on."

Skylar frowned. "I missed that too."

"He'll do it the same way the other big tech companies do. Their algorithms are secret, remember. Granted, Pascal has to be careful how he markets Lexi's capabilities, but I'm sure he figured that out. Something like: 'Lexi predicts human behavior by synthesizing body language and other verbal and nonverbal clues, delivering users a more satisfying experience.'"

"Clever. Sounds like that could work externally, with users and advertisers. But what about internally, with programmers and manufacturing technicians?"

"That's accomplished through compartmentalization. I once read that the recipe for Kentucky Fried Chicken is kept secret by having half of the herbs and spices manufactured in one plant and half in another, with neither knowing what they're making. Then, at the restaurants, the minimum-wage workers combine Bag A with Bag B before frying the chicken. Or think about Coca-Cola, which bottles its secret formula all over the world. There are plenty of examples of successful trade secrets—including the algorithms used by Amazon, Google, and Facebook."

"Well, you were right. This was exactly up Pascal's alley. And it is evil."

"Evil and legal. There's no law against reading minds. And all the tech companies shield themselves from invasion-of-privacy and other lawsuits with the Terms of Use Agreements we all *Accept* without reading."

"Some people read them. Competitors' lawyers, for instance," Skylar said, pushing back.

"Right, but that won't matter. They'll use the same innocuous phraseology we just discussed, about permitting the collection and use of verbal and nonverbal information, including body language and other whatever."

Now Skylar's head was really spinning. "Wow! The more you look at this, the bigger it gets. This is huge. Pascal would ultimately have had the ability to read everyone's mind. Think of the power he'd have possessed."

"I try not to."

"I definitely understand why you hesitated to tell Vicky. At the moment, the situation is kind of like the chicken recipe. She has half with the mind-reading technology, we have half with the billion-dollar idea, but neither of us could cash in if we were suddenly struck by greed."

"Or coerced by blackmail or legal pressure."

Skylar took her husband's hands. "Will you tell her if she asks?"

"I don't know," Chase said, giving her a squeeze. "I'm hoping you can convince her not to."

84
The Reversal

BEFORE HER ASSISTANT KNOCKED on her office door, Scarlett would not have thought that her day could possibly get worse. Her extremely high-profile client had died of a stroke, an affliction that looked equally likely to strike her at any second. Her hope of becoming a billionaire on Easy Street now appeared to be based on an elaborate con, perpetrated by said dead client. And two of her three remaining partners were currently gunning for her to exchange peaceful retirement for fifteen years of stress and risk. *Please, by the grace of God, let this be good news.* "What is it, Margaret?"

"A mister Fredo Blanco is here to see you. All four of you," Margaret said. "I've alerted the others."

"How did Mr. Blanco get past security? We left clear instructions: no visitors."

"I believe he called up from the lobby and Mr. Keller approved the meeting."

Trent had no choice, Scarlett realized. They could hardly turn away their assassin. Fredo had failed to find Pixler, but clearly he'd succeeded in identifying them. Great. Let the blackmail begin.

As she walked to the partners' conference room, Scarlett tried to convince herself that it could be good news. Perhaps Blanco had located Pixler. Captured her even. Maybe the psychic was locked in his trunk and they were about to learn whether the strokes and their condition were natural or electronically induced. Maybe an hour from now they'd have the cure and could put their glasses back on. Maybe she wouldn't have to spend the rest of her life worrying about a deadly or debilitating stroke. What a relief that would be. Like waking up from a long, cruel nightmare.

But that was an unlikely scenario. In all probability, Blanco was about to blackmail them, and, even worse, their condition was the natural result of long-term exposure to their unnatural tool.

She said a short prayer before opening the door.

It wasn't answered.

The fourth man in the conference room wasn't Fredo Blanco. He was tall, handsome, white, and vaguely familiar. Where had she seen him before? Regardless, the other partners obviously knew that he wasn't their assassin and they had chosen to sit with him anyway. In silence.

Once she'd also taken a seat, the Fredo imposter opened the backpack at his side, withdrew a laptop, and set it on the table so that it faced their direction. He proceeded to open it like he was presenting the first course at a Michelin-starred restaurant. Voila!

The computer had clearly been set to remain awake while closed, because the screen showed a videoconference already in progress. The sight gave Scarlett a jolt of electricity. Vicky Pixler!

Catching sight of the other mind reader drew Scarlett's attention to the glasses the imposter was wearing, and those her partners were not. Her heart seemed to seize up as the implication struck home. They were being read!

Right on cue, the imposter said, "Remove your glasses."

While Scarlett complied, her stomach shrank to walnut size.

Although they could no longer read minds, the partners of RRS&S continued to wear their glasses for the trademark image and the corrective lenses. However, they didn't have them powered on. No sense risking the radiation without the benefit. But of course, the psychic and her companion didn't know that. Or at least they hadn't before this meeting began.

Pixler moved on. "Before you ask, *yes*, my colleague is wearing my glasses, but *no*, he can't read your minds. They're interfacing with the computer to transmit your thoughts to me instead. I have not and will not share my technology with anyone."

The man turned toward each of them in turn, a move Scarlett knew well but one which made her feel violated. At least his robotic execution reinforced the assertion that he didn't regularly wear the glasses.

"I will start by noting that I'm extending you a courtesy that you did not show me. You should be grateful to be breathing. Grateful that I did not dispatch my assistant to kill you, as you did yours. Twice." Pixler added with bite. "Frankly, that was a difficult decision, given that Fredo murdered my fiancé before my eyes. Thus far, with the help of friends, I have managed to let my angels prevail. Whether they keep my demons at bay will depend entirely on your future behavior. Are we clear?"

Again the man spent a few seconds studying each of them. Again Scarlett felt as if she were being violated with her clothes on. She was not enjoying her first experience negotiating as a non-mind-reader. A deep sense of dread sank in as she realized that this was what the rest of her life would be like—if her condition had no cure.

"Now, I'm going to point out that I have bested the four of you, along with two of your assassins. I can beat you again, if need be. But I'm hoping we can come to an arrangement." Pixler paused there, allowing her words to register.

The imposter seized the opportunity to speak for the first time in her presence. "Before Ms. Pixler offers you anything, I'm going to have to insist that you apologize, and you better sound like you mean it. Quinten Bacca was my friend."

His voice did the trick. St. Croix! The witness from the Porter case. The killer hiding out under a false name. Hughes or Hayes. How had he connected with Pixler?

This was too much information for Scarlett to digest at once. She turned to Colton. He'd had a bit more time to process their sudden reversal of fate. She could see him calculating, a master negotiator's mind at work, albeit without the aid of his trusty tool.

"What are you offering?" Resseque asked.

With clenched jaw, the imposter pulled a phone from his pocket. When Trent tensed at the sight, the man turned to Keller. "You recognize it. The burner phone you supplied Fredo. He didn't actually use it, you know. He had it forward calls to his cell. The man nodded to the laptop where Pixler momentarily held up an iPhone before pressing a button. "I'll do my best, but if kidnapping is not possible, do I let Pixler go, or kill her?"

Scarlett recognized Fredo's voice, and she remembered the conversation. She'd also never forget the two words that had ended their last call with him. Words that she and her partners had all spoken. "Kill her."

The man she'd met on St. Croix gave them a few seconds to adapt to the gravity of their situation, then said, "Fredo gave us everything before he passed. His recordings. His notebook. The man was meticulous when it came to record keeping, did you know that?"

"What do you want?" Scarlett asked. She wasn't going to play games with a killer who had them cold. And she wasn't going to further antagonize the one person on the planet who might be able to save her from stroking out.

The man turned her way. "I told you, I want a sincere apology. I want you to look in Ms. Pixler's eyes and beg her forgiveness for sending Vance Panzer and Fredo Blanco to kill her. Then I want you to get down on your knees and tell her how sorry you are that your assassin killed her fiancé."

Scarlett could hear Colton's thoughts, even if she couldn't read his mind. He was asking: "Or what?" She didn't need to ask. The answers were obvious. The meeting would end before they learned the cure. And then Pixler would take the recordings and the notes to the FBI. Soon, the psychic would somehow arrange to depose them as part of an attempted murder investigation—with her glasses on.

"I'm sorry," Scarlett said. "I'm sorry we sent Panzer and I'm sorry we sent Blanco and I'm mortified that your fiancé was killed."

"Because of you," the man said. "Quinten Bacca is dead because you sent an assassin to Pasadena."

"Because of us. Because of me," she said, dropping to her knees. "I apologize, wholeheartedly. Please, forgive me."

85
The Revenge

COLTON RESSEQUE ROSE to his feet with the taste of bile in his mouth, having swallowed his pride for a shot at the cure, and groveled to avoid going to prison. Lawyers negotiated plea deals all the time, but he'd never expected to be making one for himself. Certainly not for contracting murder.

Convicting him and his partners would be tricky, even with all their voices on tape and the meticulous notes Fredo had allegedly made. But Colton knew better than to go up against an adversary who could read minds. That was the mistake many of the country's top attorneys had made when facing him and his partners. He wasn't foolish enough to follow their footsteps over a cliff, now that he was on the other side of the lenses.

His colleagues had clearly come to the same conclusion. And they were undoubtedly also anxious to learn if the Caltech grad knew anything about their neurological condition. Particularly, how to cure it.

"Thank you," Pixler said when Colton was back in his seat beside the other three. "Here's the deal. In order to avoid incarceration, the four of you must immediately retire. Not just hang up your glasses, but destroy them. Do that, and the FBI will never learn of your attempts to kill me. Do that, and you won't have to experience a humiliating fall from grace or endure the indignities of life behind bars.

"You've had a great run, but it's over. I'm sure you were considering retirement anyway, given the brain damage you've been accruing these past twenty years."

So she did know about the condition. Had she just learned of it by reading their minds, or did she discover it during her own research? Colton was dying to know and atypically helpless to find out. Life on the other side of the lenses was rough!

"How is it that you didn't know about the neurological degradation?" Pixler asked. Then a second later, "Oh, wow. You've been hit. But you didn't connect the dots? Well, I guess that settles the MIT versus Caltech debate. I'd say *Go Beavers*, but I know that's your mascot, too."

"Tell us about the neurological degradation," Colton said. "If you please."

"I'll please once we're agreed on your retirement. Are we? Will you hang up your glasses, forever? Will you close RRS&S—tonight?"

The robotic Fredo imposter studied each of them in turn.

Colton, like the others, agreed.

"Say it out loud," Pixler said.

"We agree to retire," they said. "We agree to close the firm."

"Good. Now, before we discuss neurology, there's just the matter of restitution."

"Restitution!" Colton blurted along with his partners.

Pixler said nothing in response. Instead, her steely eyed messenger pulled copies of a contract from his backpack.

Colton scanned the document with the speed of a pro and felt his blood run cold. "You want us to sign over the ownership of our apartments to the Innocence Project?"

Between Bernie Madoff and Colton's assumption that the music would never end, he had very little in the way of liquid assets. That apartment represented about ninety percent of his net worth.

"As a block, they're worth hundreds of millions of dollars," Sackler said, practically choking. Colton knew that Walter shared his financial position. They all did. They'd all been living like people who'd be making $2,400 an hour until they chose to retire.

"The majority of our net worth is tied up in that real estate,"

Scarlett added, her voice also dry.

"Are you looking for pity? For mercy?" Pixler growled. "For yourselves rather than for people who've been wrongly imprisoned?"

Nobody replied.

"After spending decades living decadent lives financed by thwarting justice, helping to fund that charitable effort is the least you could do. The least!" Pixler practically shouted, daring them to say otherwise. "Now sign and notarize the contracts! Then we'll discuss your medical condition."

The document was expertly written, Colton noted. No wiggle room. The apartments would essentially cease to be theirs the minute the ink was dry. This would make him a much less wealthy man. Given what he knew after decades of practicing law, however, he'd gladly go bankrupt to avoid even a single year in most prisons. In any case, at that moment, he was more concerned with health than wealth.

He met his partners' doleful gazes, then signed.

Once her messenger had collected the executed contracts, Pixler said, "Thank you. I'm pleased that we could keep this civilized. You have until the end of the month to be out of your apartments, but I expect the Innocence Project gift to be announced tonight along with the firm's closure and your retirements."

Normally, at this point in a negotiation, Colton would be calculating the steps required to turn the tables. Today, however, he stopped short. He'd spent twenty years winning literally every negotiation based on one simple fact: he could read minds, and his opponents could not. Today, and every day he dealt with Vicky Pixler, she would have that advantage. She would win. He knew that the smart move, bitter though it might be, was to accept the deal and move on.

The psychic cleared her throat. "As for the neurological degradation, it's no longer something you need to concern yourselves with, given that I'm going to have you killed if you ever wear the glasses again. But I'll satisfy your curiosity anyway. Yes, the deterioration is cumulative. It will accelerate if your exposure continues, given that you're already symptomatic."

"Is there a cure?" Scarlett blurted.

"No, of course not. Brain cells don't regenerate," Pixler scoffed. "And since you've begun the downward slide, there's no stopping it. You'll likely be babbling idiots within a decade. But you should know that." The mind-reader suddenly canted her head as a thought struck. "Oh, that's right, you were a guinea pig, not a scientist."

Colton saw fury flash across Scarlett's face, only to be quickly replaced by the fear he was also now feeling. Were they on their way to dementia? Was Jim the lucky one? Would the survivors ever be able to relax again?

Sackler finally broke the stunned silence. "Was Pascal's stroke related?"

The man turned his way and stared for a few seconds before Pixler responded. "Interesting. You think Pascal was also developing the technology, and damaged his brain while experimenting. I know nothing about that, but it seems reasonable to me. Then again, he was facing the fall from atop the world to the bottom of the penal system, so it may well have been natural causes as reported."

Again Pixler paused while her puppet stared. "Oh, he had the same unusual hemorrhagic pattern as Jim Rogers. I see. Well then, yes, I think it's probable that he did as you suspected. Good to know. Thank you."

The messenger pivoted, scanning each of them for a few seconds in silence before Pixler spoke again. "Well, it seems that thanks to your medical issues, I won't need to worry about your resuming legal consultations. But apparently I do need to add that transferring your technology to anyone, including and especially a protégé, will result in Fredo's files being sent to the FBI. Are we clear?"

"Yes," all replied.

"Good. I expect to hear about the firm's closure and your charitable gift on the evening news. After that, I better never hear about you again. If I do, if I get word of a single mind-reading act by *any* of you, I'll have you *all* killed. Are we clear?"

"We're clear."

Pixler's assistant shut the laptop, then addressed them in an icy voice. "I will be watching. For what it's worth, my vote was to keep it simple and kill you. I pray that you'll give me the excuse to avenge Chewie's death."

With that, he stood and left them to their misery.

86
Bad News

CHASE DIDN'T REALLY LEAVE the crooked attorneys to contemplate their fall from health, wealth, and power. With the laptop put away and Vicky offline, he pulled a burn bag from his backpack. He opened it and held it out. "Give me your glasses."

The three lawyers and the engineer looked at one another.

"Give me your glasses, or I'm going straight to the FBI with the phone recordings and the videotapes of your apologies."

Colton Resseque reddened, but managed to ask, "Why?"

"You can't use them, and you agreed to destroy them, but I don't trust you. So I'm going to be destroying them for you. Consider it a kindness. I'm saving you the emotional strain."

Chase waggled the burn bag.

One by one, the four complied.

"Thank you. Now, Colton, kindly retrieve the spare pairs from your office while I wait here with the others."

"I only have one spare."

Chase shook his head, then reached into the bag and withdrew a pair of horn rims. He located the inlaid button near the hinge on the left earpiece and powered them on. Then he donned them and turned back to Resseque. "Kindly retrieve the spare glasses from your office while I wait here with the others. Be quick about it and talk to no one."

The lawyers were quick about it. They enjoyed waiting beneath his gaze about as much as worms on hooks above the water.

With good reason.

He had eleven pairs when all was done, with three additional pairs in different colors coming from Slate, whereas Resseque and

Sackler each contributed two. Trent didn't have an office there, and thus no spare glasses.

"Thank you. Now, we'll go down the street for a repeat performance at your apartments. Then Trent and I will destroy the whole collection in his lab. After that, hopefully I'll be out of your hair—forever."

They moaned and groaned, both verbally and mentally, but all went along, of course.

The already extremely awkward transition was made even more so by the addition of three bodyguards, but they shed two of them after wrapping up on the twelfth floor, and the third after Sackler deposited his entire stash in the burn bag. That left Chase and Trent alone when they entered his apartment-workshop on floor ten.

Under normal conditions, a cleanup operation like this would take days and require pulling a few fingernails. But with the glasses on, Chase found it easy to ensure full and complete compliance— even from slippery New York lawyers and their evil engineer.

"We'll start with your spare pairs," Chase said, locking the door behind them. "Not just the current working models, but the older and broken ones as well."

"We're not really going to destroy them, are we?" Trent asked, as he unlocked the safe that held his stash. "You're going to keep them for yourself. You've got a taste for the power they provide, and now you want more."

"One taste is enough for me," Chase said with a shake of his head. "I'm not about to set myself up for dementia. Good luck with that, by the way."

He glanced around the luxury apartment's main room, looking for instruments of destruction. "I trust you have something in your workshop we can use? If not, we'll make do with the garbage disposal."

The workshop looked like something you'd find at NASA or

Tesla. Not just a wide array of modern tools and electronic equipment, but efficiently organized and practically sterile in appearance. "Let's boot it all up, your computers included, while we get to work with the vises and hammers."

Once they'd pulverized every pair but the ones on Chase's nose, he retrieved a case of Perrier from the kitchen pantry, returned to the lab, and began emptying bottles onto the electronic equipment while Trent looked on in horror. When everything was black, Chase asked, "Where's your external stash?"

Trent reflexively began to lie, but realized the futility and quickly gave up the address of a climate-controlled storage facility on Long Island.

"Get me the keys and write down the entry codes. Everything I need."

Chase found it fascinating, listening to Trent's internal battle as he tried to lie without thinking about it. He had a disciplined mind, but it was impossible to avoid mentally responding to repeated questions delivered when one was under duress.

Once Chase was convinced that he had everything he'd need to access the lawyers' only remaining mind-reading equipment, he changed the topic. "Why didn't you reach out to Vicky? Why did you go straight to assassination?"

The one-word answer flashed faster than Trent's lips, and it told Chase everything he needed to know about the engineer's soul. "Expedience."

"Okay. That concludes our business. Before I go, I have a message for you from Vicky. Or perhaps I should say, from Quinten Bacca's fiancée." That was a lie. Vicky knew nothing of this, and she never would.

Trent froze.

Chase winked at him as he pulled Vicky's headphones from his backpack. "Not that kind of message. A literal message. A secret voice mail. One for your ears only."

As Trent relaxed a bit, Chase pointed toward the bedroom. "I can't say for certain, but I don't think this is going to be good news. I suggest you take it lying down."

The Hug

The Caribbean

VICKY HESITATED with one foot off the dock while a wave of emotion enveloped her. Although she'd been barraged with similar assaults in the past weeks and days, she'd assumed that the storm was over.

In fact, a deep sense of calm had descended on her—after using her Pradas for the last time. After convincing the people who had killed Chewie that they were headed for dementia. After forcing them to relinquish their careers and donate the bulk of their fortunes to charity. And, perhaps most importantly, after learning that Chase had predicted correctly regarding Pascal's bodyguards. They had not incriminated themselves to the police by bringing up the visit of Margaret Gray.

Given all that, Vicky had to ask why she now found herself hesitating to step aboard the *Vitamin Sea*? To sail off in search of a fresh life and new adventures? Was something left hanging over her head? A smaller matter that had been eclipsed by greater concerns?

No threat came to mind.

It wasn't Pascal's plan. In retrospect, she would be forever grateful to Chase for sparing her that temptation. For allowing her to move on from mind-reading with a clean break.

"Is everything okay?" Skylar asked.

"I'm having second thoughts."

"About abandoning Cassandra?"

Now that she no longer needed to fear assassination, Vicky had seriously considered resuming her business in Vegas. The idea of becoming a headline act in the world capital of entertainment was appealing. So was the opportunity to help clients with her unique style of therapy. But in the end, Vicky decided that she did not want a complicated life. Maybe that would change with time, but she doubted it. She doubted she would ever be comfortable returning to a situation where people might want to kill her. Time would tell. "I don't think that's it. I feel comfortable leaving her behind. For now, at least."

"Are you tired of the yachting life?"

Vicky considered the question. "No. In fact I think it's exactly what I need right now."

Skylar smiled. "I understand completely. The freedom is addictive."

"The weather and food aren't bad either."

They laughed.

"Want to come aboard the *Sea La Vie* for a drink?" Skylar asked.

As Vicky shifted her focus from the *Vitamin Sea* to the *Sea La Vie*, she pinpointed the source of her anxiety and hesitation. The breakthrough stimulated a broad smile, but then brought it down. The *Vitamin Sea* wasn't Victoria Pixler's home. It was *Vicky and Chewie's* home. She wasn't ready to face it alone. To sleep in that bed and eat at that table alone. Chewie's death had ripped a hole in her soul and it still needed time to heal. Someday, the boat would bring back fond memories. But at that moment, the sight poured salt on her wound.

"What is it?" Skylar asked.

Vicky found herself craving her Pradas. She had sworn off mind reading. Hung up her glasses forever. But she had not destroyed them. She couldn't go that far. They were her baby. One she'd sweated day and night for a decade to birth. And, emotions aside, a person never knew what emergency might arise. Like right now, when she needed to know what Skylar truly thought.

Was that an emergency? No, Vicky realized. It was just the first of many temptations in disguise. Could she resist their siren song? Vicky resolved to try. Surely, it would get easier with practice. As she exercised her natural intuition rather than relying on a crutch.

Vicky turned to look her friend in the eye. "A drink sounds great, but to be honest, I want more."

"Dinner?" Skylar said with a knowing grin that morphed into a full hug. "Just kidding. I already discussed it with Chase. You're welcome to stay with us and sail with us on the *Sea La Vie* for as long as you like."

Vicky felt the cold waters part and the sun shine down. "Thank you. I can't tell you how much that means."

"Although we do have one favor to ask," Chase said, joining them on the dock.

"Of course. Anything."

"I'm afraid it will require you to wear your Pradas one last time."

"On the island of St. Croix," Skylar added.

"Oh," Vicky said, unsure what else to say as a frosty feeling set in.

"Did we ever tell you the story of how our path crossed Scarlett Slate's?"

Vicky studied her friends while answering. She detected nothing but warmth and compassion. "Scarlett used her glasses to uncover secrets from your past and then used that information to prevent you from testifying against her client."

"That's right," Skylar said. "Now we're thinking that turnabout is fair play."

Vicky immediately understood, and her heart thawed. "To get the client convicted."

"Exactly. Let's pour some rum punch, then we'll tell you about Maria Mead, and the woman who killed her."

Dear Reader,

I hope you enjoyed *Stolen Thoughts*, my tenth novel. You might be surprised to know that it began with what was originally the twenty-fifth chapter. In the early drafts, the story started with Vicky reading a mind for the first time at Caltech, rather than during the assassination attempt in Las Vegas.

The chapters I cut included the joyous adventure of that discovery and Vicky's heartbreak from realizing that she could never let anyone know what she'd done. They cover the engineering of her Pradas, the death of her mother, Vicky's decision to become a psychic, her meeting Chewie in Reno, the opening of Cassandra in Las Vegas, and the launch of her show at the Bellagio.

As "backstory," those chapters rely more on intrigue than action to keep you turning the pages. While most of my beta readers loved them, many considered the pace too slow for a Tim Tigner story. Ultimately, I agreed and restructured the novel.

If you'd like to read the cut chapters (those who do report being very happy that they did) you can get them immediately and free of charge in eBook form simply by sending an email to StolenThoughts@TimTigner.com.

On another topic, this novel opens with an expert quote on the current state of mind reading, taken from the September 6, 2020 episode of 60 Minutes. To watch the in-depth news story, search for "CBS News 60 Minutes mind reading."

Likewise, for expert insight regarding how tech companies are currently reading our minds, search "Everybody Lies" for summaries of Seth Stephens-Davidowitz's bestselling book by that name.

Thanks for your precious attention and kind reviews,

Pushing Brilliance

Chapter 1

The Kremlin

HOW DO YOU PITCH an audacious plan to the most powerful man in the world? Grigori Barsukov was about to find out.

Technically, the President of Russia was an old friend—although the last time they'd met, his old friend had punched him in the face. That was thirty years ago, but the memory remained fresh, and Grigori's nose still skewed to the right.

Back then, he and President Vladimir Korovin wore KGB lieutenant stars. Now both were clothed in the finest Italian suits. But his former roommate also sported the confidence of one who wielded unrivaled power, and the temper of a man ruthless enough to obtain it.

The world had spun on a different axis when they'd worked together, an east-west axis, running from Moscow to Washington. Now everything revolved around the West. America was the sole superpower.

Grigori could change that.

He could lever Russia back into a pole position.

But only if his old rival would risk joining him—way out on a limb.

As Grigori's footfalls fell into cadence with the boots of his escorts, he coughed twice, attempting to relax the lump in his throat. It didn't work. When the hardwood turned to red carpet, he willed his palms to stop sweating. They didn't listen. Then the big double doors rose before him and it was too late to do anything but take a deep breath, and hope for the best.

The presidential guards each took a single step to the side, then opened their doors with crisp efficiency and a click of their heels. Across the office, a gilded double-headed eagle peered down from atop the dark wood paneling, but the lone living occupant of the Kremlin's inner sanctum did not look up.

President Vladimir Korovin was studying photographs.

Grigori stopped three steps in as the doors were closed behind him, unsure of the proper next move. He wondered if everyone felt this way the first time. Should he stand at attention until acknowledged? Take a seat by the wall?

He strolled to the nearest window, leaned his left shoulder up against the frame, and looked out at the Moscow River. Thirty seconds ticked by with nothing but the sound of shifting photos behind him. *Was it possible that Korovin still held a grudge?*

Desperate to break the ice without looking like a complete fool, he said, "This is much nicer than the view from our academy dorm room."

Korovin said nothing.

Grigori felt his forehead tickle. Drops of sweat were forming, getting ready to roll. As the first broke free, he heard the stack of photos being squared, and then at long last, the familiar voice. It posed a very unfamiliar question: "Ever see a crocodile catch a rabbit?"

Grigori whirled about to meet the Russian President's gaze. "What?"

Korovin waved the stack of photos. His eyes were the same cornflower blue Grigori remembered, but their youthful verve had yielded to something darker. "I recently returned from Venezuela. Nicolas took me crocodile hunting. Of course, we didn't have all day to spend on sport, so our guides cheated. They put rabbits on the riverbank, on the wide strip of dried mud between the water and the tall grass. Kind of like teeing up golf balls. Spaced them out so the critters couldn't see each other and gave each its own pile of alfalfa while we watched in silence from an electric boat." Korovin was clearly enjoying the telling of his intriguing tale. He gestured with broad sweeps as he spoke, but kept his eyes locked on Grigori.

"Nicolas told me these rabbits were brought in special from the hill country, where they'd survived a thousand generations amidst foxes and coyotes. When you put them on the riverbank, however, they're completely clueless. It's not their turf, so they stay where they're dropped, noses quivering, ears scanning, eating alfalfa and watching the wall of vegetation in front of them while crocodiles swim up silently from behind.

"The crocodiles were being fooled like the rabbits, of course. Eyes front, focused on food. Oblivious." Korovin shook his head as though bewildered. "Evolution somehow turned a cold-blooded reptile into a warm white furball, but kept both of the creature's brains the same. Hard to fathom. Anyway, the capture was quite a sight.

"Thing about a crocodile is, it's a log one moment and a set of snapping jaws the next, with nothing but a furious blur in between. One second the rabbit is chewing alfalfa, the next second the rabbit *is* alfalfa. Not because it's too slow or too stupid ... but because it's out of its element."

Grigori resisted the urge to swallow.

"When it comes to eating," Korovin continued, "crocs are like storybook monsters. They swallow their food whole. Unlike their legless cousins, however, they want it dead first. So once they've trapped dinner in their maw, they drag it underwater to drown it. This means the rabbit is usually alive and uninjured in the croc's mouth for a while—unsure what the hell just happened, but pretty damn certain it's not good."

The president leaned back in his chair, placing his feet on the desk and his hands behind his head. He was having fun.

Grigori felt like the rabbit.

"That's when Nicolas had us shoot the crocs. After they clamped down around the rabbits, but before they dragged 'em under. That became the goal, to get the rabbit back alive."

Grigori nodded appreciatively. "Gives a new meaning to the phrase, *catch and release.*"

Korovin continued as if Grigori hadn't spoken. "The trick was putting a bullet directly into the croc's tiny brain, preferably the medulla oblongata, right there where the spine meets the skull. Otherwise the croc would thrash around or go under before you could get off the kill shot, and the rabbit was toast.

"It was good sport, and an experience worth replicating. But we don't have crocodiles anywhere near Moscow, so I've been trying to come up with an equally engaging distraction for my honored guests. Any ideas?"

Grigori felt like he'd been brought in from the hills. The story hadn't helped the lump in his throat either. He managed to say, "Let me give it some thought."

Korovin just looked at him expectantly.

Comprehension struck after an uncomfortable silence. "What happened to the rabbits?"

Korovin returned his feet to the floor, and leaned forward in his chair. "Good question. I was curious to see that myself. I put my first survivor back on the riverbank beside a fresh pile of alfalfa. It ran for the tall grass as if I'd lit its tail on fire. That rabbit had learned life's most important lesson."

Grigori bit. "What's that?"

"Doesn't matter where you are. Doesn't matter if you're a crocodile or a rabbit. You best look around, because you're never safe.

"Now, what have you brought me, Grigori?"

Grigori breathed deeply, forcing the reptiles from his mind. He pictured his future atop a corporate tower, an oligarch on a golden throne. Then he spoke with all the gravitas of a wedding vow. "I brought you a plan, Mister President."

Chapter 2

Brillyanc

PRESIDENT KOROVIN REPEATED Grigori's assertion aloud. "You brought me a plan." He paused for a long second, as though tasting the words.

Grigori felt like he was looking up from the Colosseum floor after a gladiator fight. Would the emperor's thumb point up, or down?

Korovin was savoring the power. Finally, the president gestured toward the chess table abutting his desk, and Grigori's heart resumed beating.

The magnificent antique before which Grigori took a seat was handcrafted of the same highly polished hardwood as Korovin's desk, probably by a French craftsman now centuries dead. Korovin took the opposing chair and pulled a chess clock from his drawer. Setting it on the table, he pressed the button that activated Grigori's timer. "Give me the three-minute version."

Grigori wasn't a competitive chess player, but like any Russian who had risen through government ranks, he was familiar with the sport.

Chess clocks have two timers controlled by seesawing buttons. When one's up, the other's down, and vice versa. After each move, a player slaps his button, stopping his timer and setting his opponent's in motion. If a timer runs out, a little red plastic flag drops, and that player loses. Game over. There's the door. Thank you for playing.

Grigori planted his elbows on the table, leaned forward, and made his opening move. "While my business is oil and gas, my hobby is investing in startups. The heads of Russia's major research centers all know I'm a so-called *angel investor*, so they send me their best early-stage projects. I get everything from social media software, to solar power projects, to electric cars.

"A few years ago, I met a couple of brilliant biomedical researchers out of Kazan State Medical University. They had applied modern analytical tools to the data collected during tens of thousands of medical experiments performed on political prisoners during Stalin's reign. They were looking for factors that accelerated the human metabolism—and they found them. Long story short, a hundred million rubles later I've got a drug compound whose strategic potential I think you'll appreciate."

Grigori slapped his button, pausing his timer and setting the president's clock in motion. It was a risky move. If Korovin wasn't intrigued, Grigori wouldn't get to finish his pitch. But Grigori was confident that his old roommate was hooked. Now he would have to admit as much if he wanted to hear the rest.

The right side of the president's mouth contracted back a couple millimeters. A crocodile smile. He slapped the clock. "Go on."

"The human metabolism converts food and drink into the fuel and building blocks our bodies require. It's an exceptionally complex process that varies greatly from individual to individual, and within individuals over time. Metabolic differences mean some people naturally burn more fat, build more muscle, enjoy more energy, and think more clearly than others. This is obvious from the locker room to the boardroom to the battlefield. The doctors in Kazan focused on the mental aspects of metabolism, on factors that improved clarity of thought–"

Korovin interrupted, "Are you implying that my metabolism impacts my IQ?"

"Sounds a little funny at first, I know, but think about your own experience. Don't you think better after coffee than after vodka? After salad than fries? After a jog and a hot shower than an afternoon at a desk? All those actions impact the mental horsepower you enjoy at any given moment. What my doctors did was figure out what the body needs to optimize cognitive function."

"Something other than healthy food and sufficient rest?"

Perceptive question, Grigori thought. "Picture your metabolism like a funnel, with raw materials such as food and rest going in the top, cognitive power coming out the bottom, and dozens of complex metabolic processes in between."

"Okay," Korovin said, eager to engage in a battle of wits.

"Rather than following in the footsteps of others by attempting to modify one of the many metabolic processes, the doctors in Kazan took an entirely different approach, a brilliant approach. They figured out how to widen the narrow end of the funnel."

"So, bottom line, the brain gets more fuel?"

"Generally speaking, yes."

"With what result? Will every day be like my best day?"

"No," Grigori said, relishing the moment. "Every day will be better than your best day."

Korovin cocked his head. "How much better?"

Who's the rabbit now? "Twenty IQ points."

"Twenty points?"

"Tests show that's the average gain, and that it applies across the scale, regardless of base IQ. But it's most interesting at the high end."

Another few millimeters of smile. "Why is the high end the most interesting?"

"Take a person with an IQ of 140. Give him Brillyanc—that's the drug's name—and he'll score 160. May not sound like a big deal, but roughly speaking, those 20 points take his IQ from 1 in 200, to 1 in 20,000. Suddenly, instead of being the smartest guy in the room, he's the smartest guy in his discipline."

Korovin leaned forward and locked on Grigori's eyes. "Every ambitious scientist, executive, lawyer ... and politician would give his left nut for that competitive advantage. Hell, his left and right."

Grigori nodded.

"And it really works?"

"It really works."

Korovin reached out and leveled the buttons, stopping both timers and pausing to think, his left hand still resting on the clock. "So your plan is to give Russians an intelligence edge over foreign competition? Kind of analogous to what you and I used to do, all those years ago."

Grigori shook his head. "No, that's not my plan."

The edges of the cornflower eyes contracted ever so slightly. "Why not?"

"Let's just say, widening the funnel does more than raise IQ."

Korovin frowned and leaned back, taking a moment to digest this twist. "Why have you brought this to me, Grigori?"

"As I said, Mister President, I have a plan I think you're going to like."